SASHA SUMMERS

Honey Be Mine

CANARY STREET PRESS

CANARY
STREET
PRESS™

Recycling programs
for this product may
not exist in your area.

ISBN-13: 978-1-335-45257-3

Honey Be Mine

Canary Street Press
22 Adelaide St. West, 41st Floor
Toronto, Ontario M5H 4E3, Canada
CanaryStPress.com

Printed in U.S.A.

To Auntie Ann and Uncle Jeff—for inspiring me
to follow my dreams and supporting me along the way.

CHAPTER ONE

ROSEMARY HILL LAY on the picnic blanket watching a ladybug crawl up a single blade of grass. The blade tipped, and the little bug reached out a spindly leg, searching. She held one finger out for the bug, smiling as its shiny red back parted long enough for wings to emerge so it could fly from grass to proffered finger. It was a perfect, quiet day, something she hadn't had in a very long time. No deadlines or worries or expectations or responsibilities. After working nonstop for the last few years, she didn't know what to do with herself.

"You've been so quiet." Tansy lay beside her on the blanket. "What's up?"

Her other sister, Astrid, sat with her lap full of tiny wild white and yellow daisies that she was turning into chains. "I mean, you don't have to talk about it, if you don't want to."

Tansy snorted. "Yes, she does. We don't keep secrets, remember?"

Tansy had always taken her role as the big sister seriously, especially after their parents died. She was the no-nonsense sister—eager to get to the bottom of things and make an action plan. Astrid, however, tended to focus on the emotional support first and the details later. As the youngest, Rosemary had been babied by them both her whole life.

She continued watching the ladybug crawl along the side of her hand. "I've only been home for a couple of days." She glanced at Astrid. "Very, very eventful days." She held her hand up, giving the ladybug access to the honeysuckle vine that ran up and around the tree they were picnicking under. Between her aunt's perfect wedding, Astrid's pregnancy announcement, and Tansy's engagement, Rosemary didn't want to dampen her loved ones' spirits.

"And now we have a moment's peace, so…" Tansy rolled onto her side to face her, propping herself onto her elbow. "Spill it—spill *all* the tea."

Rosemary smiled. Tansy wasn't going to let up until she got what she wanted. But she wasn't going to make it easy on her big sister. "I have missed you." She pushed Tansy's elbow out from under her, causing her sister to flop onto the blanket. Rosemary giggled and sat up, scooching out of Tansy's reach. "And you, too." She hugged Astrid.

"She gets a hug. I get a shove. I see how it is. Fine. Don't talk." Tansy sat up, too. "Is there any more food?"

Astrid shoved the picnic basket her way. "Feel free to eat my sausage roll." Her face pinched. "The smell is too much—" She broke off, fanning herself.

"Why did you pack them then?" Tansy pulled a sandwich from the basket.

"It sounded delicious when I was packing up our breakfast picnic." Astrid shrugged. "Now? Not so much. *But* I have gone three whole hours without throwing up, so I'll call that a win."

Rosemary couldn't imagine. "Poor thing."

"Pregnancy sounds like so much fun." Tansy eyed the sausage roll, shrugged, then took a bite. "I think I'll follow Aunt Camellia's lead and stick to dogs and cats and parrots and donkeys and…all that."

"That sounds like a conversation you need to have with Dane. Your future husband might have an opinion on children versus an animal sanctuary." Astrid turned the daisy chain into a ringlet and placed it on top of Rosemary's head. "Perfect."

All three sisters smiled. For a moment, they were little girls again. Astrid was making them all daisy chain crowns, Tansy would lead them off on some grand make-believe adventure, and Rosemary would follow along—content to be with them.

And she was. Content. She'd missed her sisters so much. Her home here in Honey, Texas. Her bees.

"I wonder if *all that* will go to Van's place with Camellia." Astrid started making another daisy chain. "Is it bad to admit I'm having a really hard time picturing that?"

"What? Not seeing Aunt Camellia in the kitchen every morning? It seems…wrong. I mean, it is *her* kitchen. Right here. At Honey Hill Farms." Tansy took a slightly more aggressive bite, the dangly bee earrings she wore shaking. "Her home."

Rosemary had been pondering the same thoughts since she'd arrived three days before. Honey Hill Farms was only as magical as it was because of the people who lived there. Well, and the bees, of course. Her aunts, Camellia and Magnolia, were the heart and soul of the farm and the sisters' rock. They'd stepped up when the girls were young, giving them the unconditional love, guidance, and space to grow up free and strong. Rosemary liked to think the aunts had been successful. She and her sisters were all incredibly capable young women.

At least, she'd thought she was. Now… The last few months proved she still had a lot to learn.

"Life is all about change. And making the best of things." Rosemary nibbled on the inside of her lip. That's what she needed to do now—make the best of things. And letting go of what had happened between her and Dr. James Voigt.

Just thinking about him had her throat constricting and her stomach in knots. She had no one to blame but herself, really. She'd been too dazzled to see the truth. Dr. James Voigt, expert entomologist and melittologist, had been her mentor. She'd trusted him. Why would she have suspected him for the lying thief that he was? There was a very real chance his renowned "genius" had been stolen from some other too-eager and naïve research assistants. Someone like her—focused on making important discoveries and incorporating them into practical applications for beekeepers and others in the apiology field. She blew a long strand of hair from her face and pushed down the mix of anger and frustration she'd been fighting for the last couple of weeks. There was no point in being upset. It was done and over with, and there was nothing she could do about it.

"You're making that face." Astrid reached over and took her hand. "The one you used to make back in high school when Libby or Kate had been extra mean to you." She frowned.

"Why ruin a perfectly lovely day by bringing either of *them* up?" Rosemary no longer woke up dripping sweat when one of her high school tormentors entered her dreams, but she did avoid thinking about them— if possible.

"Sorry. That was below the belt." Astrid sighed. "But

you really *can* tell us what's going on. It might make you feel better."

"We're here for you." Tansy took her other hand and gave it a solid squeeze.

"I'm just…" Rosemary mumbled to a stop. She loved her sisters dearly. Out of the whole world, they'd always been here for her. But it felt wrong to come home and dump her problems—her mistakes—on her sisters. "There's so much good stuff happening, I'm just soaking it all up. The sunshine. Being here. With you." She tilted her face to the sky, the heat of the Texas sun instantly warming her cheeks.

"And?" Tansy pushed. "We're your big sisters, Rose. We know you. I know when you've got a secret—just like I know when Astrid's telling a fib. Like Astrid said, it's all right there." She pointed at Rosemary's face.

"Maybe she's not ready to share." Astrid patted her hand and went back to making daisy chains.

Rosemary was fully aware that they were both watching and waiting. "Telling you will make you upset, because you love me. And I don't want you to be upset, because then I'll get upset, too. And I'm trying really hard to let it all…go."

Astrid and Tansy kept right on staring at her.

"The project lost funding." She let out a slow breath.

"Oh, Rosemary." Astrid let the daisies fall into her lap, her expression pained. "I'm so sorry."

"Which means I'm out of a job." She plucked at a blade of grass. "At loose ends."

"Wait. You mean, you're not leaving? You're *staying*?" Astrid's grip tightened on her hand. "Here? Home? With us?" Her smile was bright and oh so happy.

"For now." Rosemary squeezed her hand back. Astrid had always been the one to see the bright side of things.

"I'm sorry. I shouldn't be smiling." Astrid's attempt not to smile was an utter failure. "I *am* sorry the project is over, but I'm not sorry you're back home. I've missed you. We've missed you." She glanced at Tansy.

Tansy nodded. "I'm sure someone will snap you up for another project soon. You were working with one of the field's experts. Your work won't go unnoticed, Rosemary. Don't worry."

"Well…" She took a deep breath. "The thing is, my research wasn't…exactly…attributed to me."

There was a stretch of silence.

"What?" Tansy murmured. "What are… Wait. Is Dr. Voigt taking credit for your work?"

"But he can't do that." Astrid shook her head, her long strawberry blonde hair shimmying.

"He can, and he is." Rosemary shrugged. "He literally pulled everything off the shared server and deleted all the working copies—right before the rest of us learned the project hadn't received continued funding."

Tandy's face went scarlet. "What a complete and total di—"

"How awful," Astrid said. "There has to be someone, anyone, you can tell about this?"

"Not really. He is *the* Dr. James Voigt—a renowned expert in our industry. I'm a postgrad research assistant with no significant independent credits or discoveries to my name. Why would anyone listen? Or believe me anyway?" She blinked, ignoring the sting in her eyes. "Honestly, I feel like such an idiot for trusting him." She shook her head, refusing to shed any more tears over the situation. "I just need to figure out what to do next."

Tansy was all but fuming. "But, Rose, you need to know—"

"Please, Tansy, let it go." Rosemary added an extra, "Please," for good measure.

"It's just that—"

"No. Really. I'd rather not talk about it or him anymore."

There was another stretch of silence—heavier this time.

"There's a lot I can do here. The bees, of course. I've missed so much." Rosemary smiled at her sisters, eager to change the subject. She looked at Tansy. "I mean, Dane is no longer the villain. That's huge." She turned to Astrid. "And I barely know Charlie and the girls. Your husband, which is so weird to say, and stepdaughters."

Astrid squeezed her hand again. "They're delightful. And easy to love."

"The girls are, yes. But Charlie's a little…" Tansy paused, tapping her pointer finger to her chin. "Quiet? Prickly? Awkward? Um…"

"Shy." Astrid frowned. "Not everyone has a big, loud, and loving family like us. It's a lot to take in—a lot to get used to."

"Whatever." Tansy rolled her eyes. "He thinks Astrid is the sun and the moon and the center of the universe, so he's growing on me."

"Oh, I picked up on that much." Rosemary grinned. "All you have to do is look at him to know that." And she'd been instantly won over by Charlie Driver's obvious adoration for her sister. He was quiet and reserved, yes, but he was entirely in tune with them. And when he smiled, it was entirely because of Astrid and his daughters. "If that's all I knew about him, that would be enough to make me like him."

Astrid's face lit up. "He's…he's… Well, I love him so much."

"Yeah, yeah, we know." Tansy rolled her eyes again.

"Really?" Rosemary pointed at Tansy. "You, who can't keep your hands off Dane Knudson? Or lips." She laughed. "I'm gone a couple of years, and I come back to find one sister canoodling with her nemesis and the other sister married and pregnant. Not to mention Aunt Camellia marrying Van. Is there something in the water? Maybe I need to drink bottled water?"

"Oh, please." But Tansy was laughing, too.

"What's wrong with falling in love and being happy?" Astrid shrugged, pressing one hand to her stomach. "I, for one, am blissfully happy."

"When you're not throwing up." Tansy wrinkled up her nose.

"When I'm not throwing up." Astrid sighed, working quickly on the next daisy chain. "Oh, wait. Total change of topic here, but…" She set the daisy chain aside and pointed at the picnic basket. "I didn't know if you two had seen today's paper? In the basket. I can only imagine how it's going to go over with the gossips."

"Well, *now* I'm curious." Tansy leaned forward, moved a few things around, then pulled out the paper. "What… Ohmygawd. Everett?" She pressed a hand to her mouth. "This is…"

"Everett?" Rosemary perked up. Everett Taggert was her onetime best friend. They'd kept up by video chats for the first couple of years she was in California. Over time, more and more time passed between conversations. But this last year or so, things had been so chaotic, they hadn't spoken. And she'd missed him. She'd expected to see him at her aunt's wedding—but he hadn't come.

"Look." Tansy turned the paper so Rosemary could see.

There, on the front page of the *Hill Country Gazette*, was Everett's picture. He looked handsome. That familiar smile. The thick overlong hair that fell forward onto his forehead. The crinkles at the corners of his dark eyes. He'd always had one of the warmest smiles. He looked good… But the headline of the article was not. "'Honey's Future Looks Bright—Thanks to Lewis County's Most Eligible Bachelor,'" Rosemary read aloud, in shock.

"Poor Everett." Tansy was laughing hard. "He is going to get *so* much grief for this."

"The article does praise him for all his hard work as the county parks and recreation director." Astrid went back to her daisy chain. "How committed he is to honoring all the communities' traditions while finding ways to drum up new tourism opportunities. Mayor Contreras says some really nice things, too. Once you get past the headline, the article is great."

"*If* you get past the headline." Rosemary shook her head.

"Oh no, it's not *just* the headline. They mention he's single in the article, too. Once. Or twice. Honestly, it's equal parts praise for his work ethic and ingenuity and…how handsome and available he is. Along the lines of, whoever catches him will be one lucky lady sort of thing." Astrid frowned.

Rosemary was mortified on Everett's behalf.

"They're really trying to revitalize the paper. They've been doing a monthly highlight on the people that serve the county and towns." Tansy's laughter was dying off. "I guess they thought going more sensational would help boost sales?"

This might boost paper sales, but at what cost? Small towns loved gossip. The juicier, the better. Not to mention that the eligible-bachelor thing undermined any and all of Everett's accolades that might be listed in this article. Poor Everett. She'd reach out to him. Something told her they'd both benefit from a mutual pep talk.

"YOU SAID THE equipment had been *shot* up?" Everett Taggert wasn't sure whether to be amused or really pissed off. It was fair to say he was feeling both.

"Well, isn't it?" Dennis Hobart, mayor of Alpine Springs, gestured to the relatively new exercise stations currently speckled with bright green and pink paint.

"Being shot up and being used as paintball targets are…very different things." Everett crouched, eyeing the splatter marks, and took a deep breath.

"It's still vandalism, isn't it? A crime has been committed here, am I right?" The man put his hands on his hips. "Everything *was* shot up—by a paint gun."

Everett tried not to grit his teeth. Hobart was right, a crime had been committed. But as far as Everett was concerned, a paint marker "gun" versus a legitimate firearm offered two very different levels of threat. "I'm not happy to see the state of the park, Mayor Hobart, but I'm relieved that the damage was done by a paint gun, which is considered sport equipment, not a potentially lethal firearm." Surely the man could understand there was a significant difference?

Hobart just stared at him.

Everett stood and stared back.

"What do you propose to do about it?" Hobart snapped.

"Get a cleanup crew out here." He ran a hand along the back of his neck. After Mayor Hobart's panicked call, Everett had called the local game warden, the county sheriff, and the state highway patrol—determined to pool every resource in the area to prevent things from escalating. Because that's what should be done when folk were driving around shooting at things close to populated areas. Shooting as in guns. *Real* guns. Not paint guns. Now, he'd have to make the same phone calls all over again to apologize. This was vandalism and warranted investigation, but it didn't warrant having the entire county on standby and braced for a serious-threat-level event.

Thank goodness.

"And?" Hobart didn't seem satisfied. "As the county parks and recreation director, isn't there more *you* can *do*?"

"I've already reached out to local law enforcement so we can find out who did this." Today was the start of a new school year, so he was ninety-eight percent certain this was the handiwork of some bored teenagers— probably some last hurrah of summer. But whoever it was, they needed to face consequences. Defacing public property wasn't okay. Paintballs weren't lethal, but they sure stung like a sonofabitch if you got hit by one at close range.

"Good." Hobart nodded. "Good. I won't stand for this sort of desecration. Not on my watch. You understand?"

Everett nodded, his jaw clenched tight. He wasn't the quick-to-temper type, but today was testing that. Rather, Mayor Dennis Hobart was testing that. Still, better to be relieved at the truth than riled up over the way the man had presented things to Everett. He took pictures, made some notes on his phone, and walked Hobart back to his office before climbing into his truck. He hadn't had time to check in with his office this morning, so as he drove back to Honey, he called his office.

"Morning, boss." Libby Owens-Baldwin, his recently hired secretary, answered on the second ring.

"Morning. I'm headed to the office now. Anything I need to know about?"

"Nope. Pretty quiet." She paused. "Everything okay?"

"Yep. Had to make a run to Alpine Springs before I came in."

"I must have missed that on the calendar. Okay, I'll make a fresh pot of coffee."

"I'd appreciate that." He disconnected and let the drive soothe his nerves. Until he reached his office, he wasn't going to think about Mayor Hobart, the paint splatters all over the park, or the phone calls he'd have to make. He turned on the radio and scrolled through the stations. Nothing worth listening to. He flipped off the radio and peered out the window.

The late August sun had turned things mostly brown and brittle. An occasional sunflower stood defiantly amid the dry grasses, swaying in the still-balmy breeze. A few Hereford cattle grazed in a nearby field. There were a couple of handmade signs along the roadside advertising this weekend's farmers market before he drove past the You're Entering Honey Country sign. By the time he parked in front of the county courthouse, he'd relaxed.

Libby looked up from her computer as he stepped into the office. "Hey, boss. I put the paper and your messages on your desk. I'll get you a cup of coffee."

"Thank you." He headed for his office, but his phone pinged so he paused and pulled it from his pocket.

A text from his sister, Jenny.

We missed you this morning, but thanks to one of the Bee Girls for bringing over the onesies for the baby goats, Gramma Dot isn't mad at you.

Damn. He'd forgotten. Once Mayor Hobart called, picking up knitted onesies from the Hill place was the last thing on his mind.

Then an image popped up on his screen. He'd expected to see Astrid or Tansy—not Rosemary. Rosemary Hill. Rosebud to him. He swallowed, staring closer at the picture. She hadn't changed. She was still as beautiful as he remembered. His Rosebud.

Nope. Not mine. She'd never been his.

In the picture, she and Jenny were laughing as they each held up a onesie-clad goat kid. Gramma Dot and his mom grinned alongside them. They all looked so happy, he found himself smiling.

"Aw, how cute." Libby stood at his side, a mug of steaming coffee in her hands but her eyes on his phone screen. "Who is… Is that Rosemary Hill?"

"Looks like it." He closed the image and tucked the phone back into his pocket. He'd expected her to hightail it out of Honey now that her aunt's wedding was over—not drop by to visit his mother, sister, and grandmother. But from the looks on their faces, the visit had been a good thing. *Today's been full of surprises.*

"I guess she came to town for her aunt's wedding." Libby had a thoughtful look on her face. "Probably not staying for long, though."

He shrugged.

"You don't know?" She smiled up at him. "I always thought you two were close."

"We were. I guess. Sure." He frowned. "I mean we are…friends." Friends that had only talked a handful of times the last twelve months or so.

Her brows rose, and her smile grew. "Right. *Friends.*" But the emphasis on the last word was a little too pointed to miss.

"Good morning, Everett." Lorna Franks, his education and outreach facilitator, opened the door. "Libby." There was a hint of frost in her voice.

"Lorna," Libby gushed, her smile bright. "How are you? Did you bring your adorable baby?" She paused, giving Lorna a once-over. "You're getting your figure back. Good for you."

Lorna opened her mouth, then shook her head. "Everett, this will be a quick visit. Do you have a moment?"

"Of course." He opened his office and stood aside, a sinking feeling settling into his stomach. He nodded his thanks as Libby pressed the cup of coffee into his hands, then pulled his office door shut behind him. "What can I do for you?"

"It will never not be weird to walk in here and see *her*. Why did you hire Libby Owens?" This was a whisper. "Wherever that woman goes, she leaves a wake of destruction behind her. And no, I'm not exaggerating. She and her sister love nothing more than to stir up trouble. You don't need that here, in your place of work—or in your life."

He sat on the edge of his desk and crossed his arms over his chest. "She was the only qualified applicant." This wasn't the first time he'd gotten a talking-to about hiring Libby. There was plenty of talk about the Owens sisters, he knew that, but the applicant list had been short. As in Libby and one other person. What choice had he had? All he wanted was someone who'd show up for work, do their job, and be pleasant. So far, Libby had done just that. "I'm thinking you didn't come in just to ask me about my secretary?"

"No." Lorna sat in one of the chairs facing his desk. "Everett, I'm here to give you my two-week notice. I need to be home right now—I hope you understand."

Everett had been expecting as much. Lorna was one of the most efficient and likable people he'd ever known, and he'd miss having her around. But he respected her decision to stay home with her baby girl. Even if it did leave him shorthanded.

"It's not that I don't love my job, Everett. I do. Working remotely, part-time—it's a sweet deal. And you're a dream to work for." She sighed. "But this isn't where my heart is."

He nodded. "I appreciate the notice."

"Of course." She stood. "And you know I'll help with my replacement. Whatever questions they have, I'll only be a phone call away."

"I appreciate that, too." He cleared his throat. "I don't suppose you have anyone in mind?"

"I'd say one of the Hills. They've been pretty much in charge of the Junior Beekeepers for months now anyway. But I think Tansy might be too busy with the agritourism stuff she and Dane are developing. Astrid's a newlywed and pregnant, so her plate is pretty full, too. Any idea if Rosemary is staying in town?"

He shook his head. Everything he'd heard about Rosebud was that she was living the life she'd always wanted. There was no way she'd trade that for this—even if he was a dream to work with. And he was happy for her.

"I'm sure you'll find the right person." She leaned forward to whisper, "A hint, the right person is *not* Kate Owens-Knudson."

He chuckled. While he'd never had any negative firsthand dealings with Libby, he couldn't say the same for her sister, Kate. She'd gone and married his best friend's father—then done her best to tear that family apart. "Thanks. I'll try to remember that."

Lorna chuckled. "I better let you get back to work." She paused. "Did you see the paper yet?"

"No." He walked with her to the door. "Haven't had time yet."

"Oh." She smiled. "Well, you made the front page. And…it's a good article."

"Good." That was something. But, for now, being in the paper was the least of his worries. "Take care." He closed the door behind her, then turned to Libby. "Can you find Lorna's job description for me? I want to review and update it before we post the opening."

"Oh." She glanced at the now-closed door. "Can do, boss. Anything else?"

"Not that I can think of." He stifled a yawn. "I've got a lot of phone calls to make." Phone calls he couldn't put off any longer.

"I'll do my best to keep things quiet out here." She laughed, smoothed her tight sweater over her chest, and smiled at him. She did that sometimes. Smile and look at him like she was expecting something more. There wasn't anything more, so with a nod, he went back into his office.

He pulled the door closed behind him and sat behind his desk. While he waited for his computer to load the day's schedule, he sipped his coffee. It'd been a long day, and it wasn't even ten in the morning. He took a sip of his coffee—scanning his messages and the paper.

"What the hell?" The headline jumped out, mocking and impossible to miss. "On the front page?" He shook his head. *What have I ever done to Daisy Granger?* He'd thought he was friends with the woman who'd interviewed him, but this… This was just mean. And now that it was out there, there was nothing he could do about it. *Great. Just great.*

First things first, those phone calls. He had no doubt everyone was scrambling to come up with a safety plan—active-shooter threats were nightmare-scenario situations that were both time-consuming and high stress. The sooner he could assure them things weren't what they'd been led to believe, the better.

The reactions he got were mixed. Some were amused. Others, not so much. But the overall consensus was relief. That, Everett decided, would be what he'd focus on. Relief. He'd take paint-gun vandalism over potential casualties all day, every day.

Around noon, Libby poked her head in to tell him she was taking lunch. When she asked him if he wanted to come with her, he declined. Hiring her had led folk to speculate, but so far, there hadn't been much talk linking him and Libby Owens-Baldwin outside of the office. He'd like to keep it that way.

He was poring over next year's proposed operating budget when there was a knock on his office door.

Dane Knudson, his best friend, leaned inside. "Earth to Everett?"

He set the papers aside. "What brings you into town?" He held his breath, waiting for Dane to start teasing him over the damn newspaper headline.

"Lunch. You free?" He nodded at the desk. "A man's gotta eat."

Everett stood. "I could eat." Maybe Everett had caught a break and Dane hadn't seen the paper. "Where's Tansy?"

"Spending some time with her sisters." Dane shrugged. "She and Astrid are worried about something being up with Rosemary, so I figured I should make myself scarce. Let them talk."

If he'd thought things through, he wouldn't have asked, "What's going on with Rosebud?" But the question was out, and Dane was grinning at him. No matter how many times he told his best friend his feelings for Rosebud were over and done with, Dane didn't buy it. "Come on, now." Everett sighed. "You set me up for that."

Dane shrugged, then slapped him on the back. "Food."

While they walked from the courthouse to Delaney's, Everett forced himself not to think about what Dane had said. If Rosebud's sisters were worrying, then something was up, but they'd sort it out. The three of them had always been close—in tune with one another. A couple of years and a thousand-plus miles wasn't enough to change that. She had plenty of people to help her; she didn't need him in the mix.

It was a Monday, so Delaney's wasn't too crowded. The fact that it was the first day of school might have played a part, too. Which reminded him. "How are you doing? Your little brother's senior year and all. Is Leif excited?" He glanced at his friend.

Sure enough, Dane's jaw clenched tight. "Oh, he's

excited, all right. That's all that matters. I'd be happy if he spent as much time on his studies as he does courting Kerrielynn, but it is what it is."

Everett laughed. "Young love."

"Can hurt like hell." Dane shot him a long look. "You'd know all about that."

He ran a hand over his face.

Dane grinned.

"It's too early to start drinking, so how about we change the subject and *not* talk about Rosebud anymore?"

"Sure." Dane nodded. "Let's give that a try." But he shook his head.

Once they were seated and their orders were in, Everett told Dane about Lorna resigning and the paintball vandalism in Alpine Springs.

"Damn." Dane sat back, his brows high. "I bet making that second round of phone calls was...fun." He chuckled. "That Dennis Hobart is something else. I don't think that man has ever had a good day—at least, he's never acted like it."

"At least his bad mood is warranted today." Everett took a sip of his iced tea. "I'd be pissed off if my brand-new park equipment had been trashed like that."

"Any idea who'd do this?" Dane leaned forward to rest his elbows on the table.

"The sheriff's going to do some digging—that's his jurisdiction, not mine. But if I were to guess, I'd say it's a bunch of kids pulling some end-of-summer stunt. Like we used to do." He grinned at Dane. Summers got long in small towns with limited things to do.

"Not that we ever destroyed property like that." Dane

frowned. "If we had and we got caught, my dad would have tanned my hide. Then yours."

Everett nodded. It was one thing to pull a harmless prank. It was something else entirely to deface public property at the taxpayers' expense. "Do me a favor, though. If you hear something, let me know?"

Dane nodded. "Now, what are you going to do about Lorna? It's not a surprise, but still, she was good at her job."

"Don't I know it." He shrugged. "Of course Lorna said she'd help train her replacement—that helps. But it's not going to be easy to find someone that's good with people, knows all the festivals and the area, and gets excited about educational programming."

"A needle in a haystack if you ask me." Dane nodded. "Maybe you should offer Lorna more money to stay."

Everett chuckled. Lorna leaving had nothing to do with money and everything to do with her growing family. He respected that. It was time to find a replacement. And the sooner he got the job posted, the sooner that would happen.

"I hate to bring this up, but Tansy's convinced your secretary is after you. Considering we're talking about Libby Owens-Baldwin, I can see where she's coming from." Dane gave him a long assessing look.

"I appreciate the concern and all, but it's not going to happen." He chuckled. "Libby's doing a good job, but I won't date an employee or a coworker. You can pass that along to Tansy. And my mother. And my sister. And Gramma Dot." He paused. "Should I be offended that all the women in my life seem to think I need protecting? Or flattered?"

Dane laughed. "Flattered, I think. It means they care."

"So they're not implying that I'm incapable of making good choices when it comes to my personal life?" He sighed.

"I'd buckle up, because thanks to that article this morning, your personal life is now everyone's business." Dane was laughing harder then.

There it is. Everett sighed. He'd been careful not to date many women from Honey because he didn't want the whole town planning his wedding before there was a second date. That was not the way it worked. He'd grown up watching his parents live their vows every single day—working through the good and the bad times, giving unconditional love, and truly being a partner in all things. That was what he wanted, and he wasn't going to settle. Until then, he needed to be prepared for the hell he was going to catch over that damn newspaper headline.

CHAPTER TWO

THE TAGGERT PLACE was a working goat farm. Meaning herds of red and brown and black and white goats dotted the hillside, and a whole host of baas and bleats filled the air, along with the occasional tinkling of a bell.

Rosemary had learned the difference between milk goats and Angora goats when she was very young. The Taggerts took their goats to a lot of the same festivals her family's Honey Hill Farms would attend. While the Hills sold their honey and beeswax goods, the Taggerts offered goat-milking demonstrations and how to weave Angora hair into thread. Many a time, she had lent a hand at their booth when she was younger.

"Rosemary." Violet Taggert, Everett's mom, poured her another cup of tea. "I'm glad you stopped by. We didn't really get a chance to talk at Camellia's wedding." She pushed the plate of cookies closer to her. "I want to hear all about California and what you've been up to."

"There's not much to tell." Not much she wanted to share anyway. "Work. It's not exactly the way I imagined it would be—but it keeps me busy."

Violet cocked an eyebrow. "That's all? You're too young to spend all your time working, Rosemary. You're in California. Young, single, pretty, and smart. You should get out, live a little, make some memories. I know how dedicated you are to the bees, but I'm pretty sure they'd be okay with you taking some time for yourself every now and then."

"I'm not so sure about that. Bees don't take time off." She smiled at the way Violet sighed and shook her head. "I've always been more of a homebody. But I did go hiking whenever I had any downtime."

"That's not exactly what I had in mind, but I guess that's something." But Violet smiled. "It's so good to have you home. I know I'm not the only one that's missed you." She grabbed her hand and gave it a squeeze.

Since Violet had always been friendly with her aunts, Everett had always been one of Rosemary's friends. Growing up, the Taggert house had been like a second home. Violet and Leland Taggert had, in many ways, served as the parental figures she and her sisters lacked—giving them a special place in Rosemary's heart.

"I can't thank you enough for saving my babies," Gramma Dot spoke up, rocking in her chair with a teacup in one hand. "I didn't want them catching a chill."

"You're a hero, Rosemary," Violet whispered—for her ears only. "Everett was going to get a stern talking-to if those onesies didn't show up. I appreciate you bringing them by."

"I was happy to do it." Partly because Aunt Mags had told her how distressed Gramma Dot was getting over the lack of her new baby goat onesies and partly because she hoped to see Everett. She'd only been here a few days, but still, she'd expected to see him by now.

Jenny, Everett's younger sister, sat on the couch. "Now your babies are safe and warm, Gramma Dot."

"As they should be." Gramma Dot's nod was firm. "Though I imagine they'll be getting hungry soon."

"I'll get the bottles ready." Jenny pushed off the couch. "But you should let me feed them, Gramma Dot. Those little guys get a little eager around feeding time. You might end up with bruises all over you."

"These little darlin's wouldn't do that," Gramma Dot cooed, obviously smitten.

Jenny exchanged a look with Rosemary, then headed into the kitchen.

"That child acts like I haven't been doing this for fifty-plus years." Gramma Dot shook her head. "I was raising goats long before she was a twinkle in Leland's eye."

Violet smiled. "She's worrying over you, Mama Dot. She means well."

Gramma Dot sighed, offended nonetheless.

"Bottles are ready," Jenny called out.

The three women stood and headed into the kitchen. The large playpen Gramma Dot's goat kids called home took up a good portion of the kitchen. Jenny opened the large playpen gate and stepped inside. "Which one do you want to feed? Marilyn or Clark?"

Gramma Dot went into the pen and closed the gate behind her. "I fed Marilyn earlier. I don't want Clark getting jealous."

Jenny smiled. "I don't think they'll notice, Gramma. As long as they're getting fed, they're happy."

"Well, I notice." Gramma Dot sniffed. "And I'm not picking favorites."

Rosemary had always gotten a kick out of Gramma Dot. The old woman was headstrong and opinionated but absolutely adorable. Even more so now. She wore jean coveralls and sat on the kitchen floor, already patting and cuddling the two goats that ran to her. When Aunt Mags shared Gramma Dot was struggling with early stages of Alzheimer's, Rosemary had been devastated for the Taggert family.

"Fine." Jenny took one of the bottles and one of the goats to the far side of the pen, sat on the floor, and offered it to the goat.

"Here you go, Clark, you handsome lad." Gramma Dot giggled as the goat kid attached itself to the bottle, drinking like it'd been on the verge of starvation—a highly unlikely scenario as Gramma Dot tended to spoil "her" kids.

It was a relief to see how little the old woman had changed. Dot was pushing eighty but still full of zip and opinions.

"I sure hope they don't get milk all over their new onesies." Gramma Dot frowned. "Maybe we should have taken them off before we fed them?"

"We just put them on," Jenny pointed out.

It hadn't been an easy process, either. The goat kids had no interest in being clothed. If it wasn't for Gramma Dot's insistence, chances are the onesies would have been tossed aside.

"Rosemary?" Gramma Dot looked at her, her eyes narrowing just the slightest bit. "Is there some special someone out there in California? A surfer, I bet. Doesn't everyone in California surf?"

Rosemary laughed. "Not everyone. And I'm sorry to disappoint you, there's no surfer boyfriend. There's no boyfriend."

"No?" Jenny's grin was a little suspect. "That's too bad."

"Then why are you smiling?" Violet asked Jenny.

"Am I?" Jenny stopped smiling, but there was a twinkle in her eye. "I wasn't."

"Do you surf now, Rosemary?" Gramma Dot tilted the bottle so the kid could drink every last drop.

"No, ma'am."

"That's good. Wouldn't want you eaten up by a shark." Gramma Dot nodded. "You know people die every year from shark attacks? They do. Some even in California. Don't you start surfing."

"I won't." Rosemary nodded.

"How long are you here?" Jenny had to tug to get the empty bottle away from the goat kid. Marilyn was not pleased about this new turn of events. Neither was Clark—now that the bottles were empty, the wailing began.

"Poor little things." Gramma Dot clucked. "I bet you're cold." She shot a look Jenny's way. "And don't you try to tell me otherwise, missy. How many kids have you raised, missy? Human or goat? I'd say I know what I'm talking about."

Jenny held up her hands in surrender and opened the plastic tub along one of the sides of the pen. "Fine. Here are their blankets. Don't want the baby goats inside the house to freeze to death."

"I hear you being all sassy." Gramma Dot crossed her arms over her chest.

Jenny pressed a kiss against her grandmother's temple. "I take after you."

Gramma Dot burst into laughter. "I should say so." Once the kids were tucked into their quilts, she seemed satisfied. "And they're nice and warm." Gramma Dot nodded her head. "See? No more crying."

It was true; both the goat kids' eyes drifted shut, and shortly thereafter, they drifted into sleep. Once Jenny had them on a large stuffed dog bed, she and Gramma Dot closed the gate behind them.

Once they'd tiptoed down the hall to the family room, Gramma Dot turned to her. "I didn't get my hug from you when you got here, so come and give me a hug, Rosemary." Her hug was surprisingly strong—like Gramma Dot.

After they'd all gotten comfortable and had doctored their tea accordingly, conversation resumed. So far, Rosemary had learned what all the Taggert siblings were up to. Grady and his wife were settled and working in Wyoming, Clayton was happy living the navy life aboard a submarine, and Everett was serving as the county parks and recreation director.

"I bet he is spitting nails over that newspaper article." Jenny frowned. "Did you see it?"

Rosemary nodded. "The article was great." She'd had no idea how hard he'd been working for the town—and the county. But that was Everett. When he committed to something, he did so with his whole heart.

"I don't see what the problem is. It's the truth. He's doing all sorts of good things for Honey, and he's single. That article might help him finally find a wife so he can get started on that family he's wanted for so long." Gramma Dot sighed. "I don't know why he's dragging his feet."

"Mama, you can't rush love." Violet smiled at her mother-in-law. "Everett has always been a hopeless romantic. You know that."

Rosemary grinned at that. She remembered Everett telling her that his granddad had told him, being the eldest, it was up to him to carry on the Taggert family name. Everett had taken that to heart. Even young, Everett talked about having a big loving family of his own.

"He is." Jenny grinned, glancing at Rosemary. "True blue, too. Whoever he ends up with, she'll have the sort of husband and partner any gal would be lucky to have."

It was surprising someone like Everett hadn't settled down. Jenny was right, Everett was the real deal. If he couldn't find someone to love him, what chance did she have? It wasn't exactly a cheery thought.

"What about you? Are you heading back to California soon?" Jenny asked, sipping her tea.

"No. I'm staying." Rosemary peered into her teacup. "For a while, I think. I've missed being home."

"Staying?" Gramma Dot's grin was on the sly side. "Well, that's good. Everett will be happy."

She hoped so—assuming she ever caught up with him.

"We're all happy you're staying." Jenny shot her grandmother a look—a look Rosemary wasn't sure what to make of.

Gramma Dot glanced back and forth between them, all wide-eyed innocence. "That's what I said."

Rosemary sipped her tea. "What about you, Jenny? What are you up to?"

"Farming." Jenny tapped her chin. "Goats. And farming." She paused. "Did I mention goats?"

Rosemary laughed.

"A farm doesn't run itself." Violet shrugged. "But don't act like that's all you've been up to. She's met some fellow from Elginston."

Rosemary listened while Jenny blushed and tried to downplay this "outsider" she was clearly smitten with.

Then conversation shifted to town talk—namely the latest ruction between Nicole Svoboda and her gossip-mongering mother, Willadeene Svoboda.

Growing up, Rosemary had wondered what it would be like to have parents. Her parents had died when she was little, and her memories of them were a bit fuzzy. At the same time, she thought it would be easier to have no parents than to have one like Willadeene. Ever since she could remember, the woman's name was synonymous with gossip and heartache and a whole lot of drama. Nicole had grown up surrounded by all the things Rosemary did her best to avoid.

"Nicole's tough, tougher than I am." Violet's tone was pure sympathy. "First Willadeene was going to sell her part of the beauty shop to some private investor, now she's trying to get Nicole to buy her out at way above market value."

"There's something not right about that woman." Gramma Dot added a sugar cube to her tea. "And no one can convince me otherwise." She used the little tongs to add another cube. And then another.

"Willadeene was horrible to Silas Baldwin, too. You know he's an appraiser over at the bank?" Jenny waited for them all to nod. "When he didn't assess the shop at the value she'd wanted, she went back to the beauty shop and started dragging up his divorce and how he was incompetent and a whole slew of nasty insults. I was just *lucky* enough to be getting my hair done that day." There was no missing Jenny's sarcasm.

"That's mean." Rosemary knew firsthand how hard it was to be on the receiving end of that sort of talk. "I didn't know Silas was married."

The women exchanged disapproving looks.

"It didn't last long." Violet shrugged.

"It's sad when a marriage doesn't last." Gramma Dot shook her head. "But you young'uns have it easy. Back in my day, you had to wait until your spouse died to be rid of them."

Rosemary almost choked on her tea.

"Mama." But Violet hooted with laughter.

When Jenny stopped giggling, she said, "I don't think anyone was surprised by the divorce. Libby and Kate have always been inseparable. Kate's divorce was final, so Libby did the same. Silas was the only one that didn't see it coming."

"Libby?" Rosemary set her teacup down, the name instantly making her stomach churn. Now she definitely felt for Silas. "Libby Owens?"

All three Taggert woman nodded.

Other than her family and Nicole, no one knew that Libby Owens had been personally responsible for the torment and anxiety Rosemary had struggled with through her high school years. Her older sister, Kate, had been no better. The sisters had delighted in making Rosemary cry. Somehow, they'd managed to make Rosemary testing up two grades in school into a character flaw. Nothing was off-limits. From her dead parents to her braces, hand-me-down clothes, and painfully shy nature, Rosemary was an easy target. Libby had delighted in finding new ways to tear down everything about her. All she could say now was, "Poor Silas."

"And now poor Everett," Jenny snapped.

That grabbed Rosemary's full attention. "What do you mean, poor Everett?" What did Libby Owens have to do with Everett?

"She's *just* his secretary, Jenny." Violet shot her daughter a look. "That's all."

"So far. She's working him over, Mom. Telling him how she's changed. And trying. And wanting a fresh start. I think she wants to get into his pants. Maybe even make him future ex-husband number two." Jenny snorted. "If she keeps throwing her boobs at him, who knows what might happen."

Rosemary didn't like the picture Jenny was painting. Everett was a good guy—through and through. He'd always believed the best in people. While that was admirable, in this case, it could be a detriment.

"Jenny." Violet's eyes widened. "Give your brother some credit."

"Mom." Jenny shrugged. "He's a man. Some men are helpless against the power of boobs—a power that can be used for good or evil."

"Isn't that the truth?" Gramma Dot nodded, sounding very grave. "I've used mine for both—a time or two."

They were all laughing then. Hard. But long after tea was over and she was headed home, an all-too-familiar hollowness settled into Rosemary's stomach. It had taken years to get over the self-doubt and loathing Libby's torment had caused. She didn't want to project her stuff onto Everett, but…she didn't want to see him toyed with or hurt, either. Everett didn't need that.

No, no. Everett would be okay. He had a good head on his shoulders. Boobs or not, Rosemary had to believe Everett was smart enough to take make the right choices for himself.

EVERETT GLANCED AT the clock. It was almost six. He'd hoped Monday was a fluke. But today, Tuesday, proved otherwise. First, the newspaper article had flooded his inbox with interested single ladies within Lewis County and beyond. Second, his brothers had sent him a bouquet of flowers with a big Cupid balloon and a bachelorette pageant-type sash. Lastly, after sifting through a dozen messages, he'd had to tell Libby to throw any nonbusiness phone messages directly in the trash. But all of that was nothing compared to the news of a second case of vandalism.

"Here are the fliers for the emergency town meeting. I can't believe this is happening. Here." Libby placed a stack of fliers on the corner of his desk.

It was hard to get his head wrapped around it.

She scanned the bright yellow paper. "We've never had this sort of thing happen. Paintballing public spaces? What a mess. Do you think it will happen here?"

He shrugged. First, Alpine Springs. Now, Elginston. "I hope not."

When he'd seen Christina Rivas's name pop up on his phone this morning, he'd felt an instant pang of unease. Unlike Dennis Hobart, Christina Rivas was a levelheaded and community-focused mayor that served Elginston well. That was why she was so upset that one of the detailed historical murals lining Main Street had been peppered with bright orange and green paintballs.

"All we can do is get the word out and have folk on alert. With everyone on the lookout, we might figure out who's doing it and stop it." At least, that's what law enforcement was hoping for. Since this was their area of expertise, he wasn't going to question their advice. He stood. "I appreciate you staying late."

"Not a problem." She leaned against his desk. "Are you sure I can't help distribute these?"

"I'm good. Thank you." He glanced her way. She had a nice smile—but there was something about the look in her eyes that triggered warning bells. "I'll see you in the morning."

"Whatever you say, boss." She pushed off his desk and sauntered slowly to his door. With a flutter of a wave, she left, pulling the door closed behind her.

He ran a hand over his face, finished typing the email he was sending to the Honey Chamber of Commerce members, and hit Send. Once that was done, he grabbed the fliers and headed out to canvass Main Street.

It was a surprisingly cool evening. There was a gentle breeze whispering through the trees that lined the lawn surrounding the courthouse. He glanced up, marveling at the shades of pink and purple feathering the wide sky. Evenings like this reminded him to take time to appreciate the town he called home. While he'd enjoyed his college years, he'd been eager to get back home. This was where he belonged—where he was happiest.

Honey had always embraced its name and the resource that put the little town on the map. Wherever you looked, bees and flowers and honey were found. But somehow each shop still had its own unique character. Bee Friendly Blooms had painted their window with a pastel rainbow of flowers, fat, buzzing honeybees, and butterflies of all sorts. The red brick face of the Greater Hill Country Bank was on the austere side, but the two oversize planters on either side of the chocolate-brown door were full of whimsical metal flower sculptures and beehive-shaped solar-powered lanterns. He was so caught up in exploring that he failed to see someone rounding the corner—until he slammed into them.

Instinct had him grabbing the person by the shoulders and releasing the stack of yellow fliers to rain down around them.

"Sorry. I should have looked where I—"

"Everett?" It was Rosebud, those green eyes staring up at him. "It's you." And she sounded so damn happy about it. "I thought I'd run into a brick wall. Have you gotten taller? You seem taller. All around bigger." She smiled up at him, all welcome and enthusiasm.

"Just me. I'm sorry." He held her shoulders—which didn't send his heart into overdrive. There were no butterflies or nervous sweats. This was good. This was normal.

"Since it's you, I'll forgive you." She held up her pointer finger. "This time."

"I appreciate that." Her smiles were contagious. And after today, it felt good to smile. "Hey, Rosebud."

"Hey, yourself." She stepped close and wrapped her arms around his waist to hug him. "It's so good to see you. You weren't at Aunt Camellia's wedding."

His arms went around her. "You were looking for me?" It shouldn't matter, but it did. And he'd be lying if he said she didn't feel good in his arms. She always had. *Dammit.*

"Of course." The look of disbelief she shot him was adorable. "I've missed you. Just like you've missed me. Don't try to deny it."

He shook his head. There was no denying it. He couldn't stop himself from giving her a once-over. Still beautiful. Still Rosebud. With those flashing eyes and that slow sweet smile of hers.

"It's so good to see you. Finally." She was studying him, too. "If I didn't know better, I'd think you were avoiding me."

Which was exactly what he'd been doing. His chuckle was uncomfortable. "Me? No."

"That's a relief." Her arms slid from his waist, and she stepped back, her gaze zeroing in on the fliers now littering the sidewalk. "What's all this?"

He stooped, picking up fliers. "Just work."

"Let me help." She knelt beside him and collected more of the papers. "A town meeting, huh?" She scanned one of the fliers. "Oh. Well. This isn't good."

"Yeah. My thoughts exactly." He sighed, collecting the last pages.

"Paintball." Rosemary stood, reading the information. "They targeted the park in Alpine Springs? And Elginston's murals? That's awful." Her brow furrowed. "Those towns rely on tourism as much as Honey does. How long has this been going on, Everett?"

"Not long." But he didn't want her worrying over it, so he teased, "About as long as you've been back in town… Hmm."

"Ha ha. You've got me." She laughed. "Any idea who's doing this?"

"Not so far." Her laugh made him smile. "Trying to get the word out. Have folk on alert. The more eyes and ears on this, the better. Libby emailed the Main Street Business Association, and I reached out to chamber of commerce members about the meeting. Hopefully, everyone will show."

"Libby?" Rosemary's swallowed, her voice unsteady as she said, "Right. Libby Owens."

"She's my secretary. Libby Owens-Baldwin, actually." He gave her a long look. Was she going to give him grief for hiring Libby, too? Nah. It wasn't Rosebud's style to gossip or tear a person down—something he'd always respected. "But she and Silas divorced."

"Right. How nice. I mean… Not that she's divorced… That she is your secretary." She tucked a long strand of her thick red hair behind her ear. "Your mother might have mentioned that."

"I'm sure she did." He could only imagine what else his mother might have mentioned. "Mom said you had a nice visit. I appreciate you bringing over those onesies for Gramma Dot." He shook his head. "She's convinced those onesies are essential to keeping those babies warm."

"I don't know how essential they are, but the goat kids do look adorable." She glanced up at him. "You know I love your family. They've always made me welcome and treated me like one of their own."

"Yeah, I guess they're all right."

"You guess?" She laughed, then shook her head. "You're hilarious."

He grinned, glad he could still make her laugh. "I try."

"So, what are you doing with these?" She held up the flier she'd read.

"I'm putting one in each of the mailboxes of the businesses along Main Street. Hopefully, the shop owners will hang them in their windows tomorrow. There's a good portion of Honey that hates technology—especially emails and texts. Unless I want to go door-to-door, I'm hoping these old-fashioned fliers will do the trick."

"I finished closing up the boutique, so I can help." Rosemary held out her hands. "Tansy and Dane are my ride home, and they won't be along for a bit."

"Even after I almost knocked you down?" He wasn't flirting with her. Or was he?

"Even after that." Her gaze met his, searching. "I can see why you'd be a bit distracted. This sort of thing doesn't happen around here." She glanced at the fliers, then her extended hands again. "Let me help."

He handed her some fliers. "I appreciate it, Rosebud."

"You know…" she walked with him to the next business, folding a flier and tucking it into the mailbox "…you're the only one that's ever called me that."

"I can call you Rosemary, if you'd rather." He couldn't remember when or why he'd started calling her that, only that it stuck.

She shook her head. "It'd be weird if you did."

"Good. You'll always be Rosebud to me." Okay, that was probably—definitely—flirting. He kept walking, sliding a flier through the mail slot in one shop door. "How long are you staying in town?"

She paused, holding open one of the mailboxes. "I'm staying."

"Staying? Here?" He was so shocked, he stopped and stared at her.

"For now, yes. Sorry to disappoint you." She seemed almost defensive about it.

"No, no. It's just I heard… Word is you were real happy." He broke off, noting the stiffening of her posture. Was he wrong? Had something happened? He tucked a flier into the next mailbox, and she closed it. Even though it was none of his business, he asked, "You okay?"

"I'm great." She moved on to the next door and held

open the mail slot in the green door of Bee Friendly Blooms. "Really great."

"Uh-huh." Everett slid a flier through, noting the edge to her voice. "I'm glad to hear it."

"And you?" She took a deep breath and turned to him. "What's new in your world, Everett?"

"Work, mostly." Try as he might, his gaze kept returning to her. He'd missed her. That was all.

"So I see." She glanced at the stack of fliers. "County parks and recreation director? That sounds super important."

He chuckled. "Does it?"

"I think so." She opened the next mailbox. "What, exactly, does that mean?"

"It means I wear a lot of different hats. My office is here, since Honey is the county seat. But I'm all over working with Texas Parks and Wildlife and every town in the county, planning events and festivals, programming for kids and seniors, summer camps and sporting events…that sort of thing. That's all."

"That's *all*?" She looked impressed. "I'd think managing festivals alone would be a full-time job. All those personalities and expectations. It sounds like a whole lot of pressure. Do you like it?"

"I do." He grinned.

"You always were a people person." She shrugged. "I guess someone has to be."

He laughed then. "Just like I couldn't spend all day in a lab."

"Not every day. Some days I was out in one of the university apiaries. Those were the best days. A handful of people, working with the bees and studying their behavior. But it wasn't the same as being here. Our bees. Our apiaries. Like Dorothy says, there's no place like home."

They kept delivering fliers as they talked.

"I'm sure your family is thrilled you're sticking around." He was. He could only imagine how happy her sisters would be.

"I think so." Her smile was genuine once more. "But I have to find something to do. I like to stay busy, you know? Tansy and Astrid have been doing a fantastic job running the farm since I left. I don't want to, I don't know, cramp their style."

"Did they say that?" He had a hard time picturing that.

"No." She tucked a strand of red hair behind her ear. "It's me. I guess, with so many changes, I don't know exactly where I fit anymore. Does that make sense?"

"Kinda." But the Hill sisters, the Bee Girls, were inseparable. "A few things haven't and won't change. This is your home, Rosebud. And they're your family. You want to do something, they'll support you. You'll always fit here."

Her green eyes locked with his. "And you'll always be the best friend a girl could have?"

That's me. The friend. "Yep." And he was content with that. It hadn't been easy for his heart to let go of Rosebud, but he had, and thankfully, she was none the wiser. He'd never risk losing her friendship—one of the most important friendships of his life.

They talked about Jenny, Gramma Dot, and the baby goat kids while they finished that side of Main Street. They'd just crossed to the other side when Dane's truck appeared.

"Looks like your ride is here." Everett took the fliers from her.

But Dane pulled in and parked. "Well, if it isn't Honey's most eligible bachelor?" He climbed out of his truck, Tansy sliding out behind him. "And Rosemary."

Really? Everett shot Dane a warning look. He wasn't in the mood for Dane's teasing.

"I'm helping Everett pass out these fliers." If Rosebud knew or heard Dane, she didn't act like it. Instead, she handed a flier to Tansy. "We should all probably plan on attending the meeting."

Tansy read over the flier, nodding. "Definitely. Wow." She glanced at Everett. "Need an extra hand?"

He held his hand up. "That's nice of you but—"

"But we'll get it done in half the time." Rosebud took a stack of the fliers off the top. "Come on, Tansy, we'll start at the other end and work our way down."

The two sisters were halfway down the street before he could stop them.

"Hill women." Dane clapped him on the shoulder. "There's no stopping them, so you might as well get out of the way and let them do what they want."

"I'm not complaining. Today has been…*something.*" He glanced at Dane. "I'd appreciate it if you'd drop the whole bachelor thing." He waited for Dane to nod. "Great." He glanced at the sisters making their way back to them. "You know, I've still got some phone calls to make. Think they'd help with that?"

"Probably." Dane followed him, reading one of the fliers. "Now Elginston, huh?"

Everett nodded. "I don't want this getting out of hand."

"I hear you. I bet folk are real upset over the mural. That's not going to be an easy fix." Dane glanced his way.

"You could say that again. You can't exactly take a sandblaster to a work of art. But Mayor Rivas is already planning some sort of fundraiser to get the artist to repaint it."

"That's good." He lowered his voice "You hear Rosemary's planning to stay around for a while?"

"Yep." But he suspected there was more to it. He didn't believe her when she said she was great. Something had happened to make her give up the work she'd wanted more than anything. Dane had said Tansy and Astrid were worried about Rosebud—something was definitely up. Not that he was upset she was staying. It'd be nice to have Rosebud around.

"I was thinking." He was watching Everett a little too closely as he said, "Rosemary would be perfect for Lorna's job."

He swallowed his initial *hell no* and managed, "Offer Rosebu—Rosemary the job?"

"It makes perfect sense to me." Dane's eyes narrowed just a bit. "I don't see why not. Do you?"

Everett thought a moment. "She's overqualified." Which was true.

"Maybe." Dane shrugged. "But it can't hurt to ask."

Everett glanced down the street at the sisters. They were talking and laughing, doling out the fliers as they went. Dane had a point. It could be good for both of them. Hadn't she just said she was looking for something to do with her time? He needed someone familiar with the festivals, who could take on the outreach classes, and who knew the area. He needed someone he could rely on. Rosebud more than fit the bill. And—contrary to Dane's belief—he was no longer in love with her. There was no reason not to ask her. "Maybe I will."

"ALBIE, I TOLD you she'd be back." Dot Taggert smiled at the framed photo of her husband that sat on her vanity. "I told you and I was right." With her brush, she pointed at her reflection in the mirror. "*I* was right. Wasn't I, Pigeon?" Her gaze darted to the fluffy white cat sprawled across her comforter.

Pigeon responded with a slow flick of her tail.

"You're no help, Pigeon." She chuckled and went back to brushing her long white hair. Ever since she was little, it was one hundred brush strokes every night, then braiding it for bed. "I can't help but wonder if Everett will finally put his heart out there." She sighed. "I hope so, Albie. I know he's lonely. He's too young to be lonely." She ran her fingers along the seahorse-covered glass frame. "I wish you were here to guide him."

When Albie died, a part of her died, too. There wasn't a day that went by where she didn't turn to ask him a question or hope to see one of his quick, mischievous smiles. Every time she realized he wasn't there, it was like she'd lost him all over. The hurt was enough to make her wonder if a person could grieve to death.

Albie wouldn't like her thinking that way. He said every morning you opened your eyes was a blessing, and you owed it to live it to the fullest.

"I'm trying." She swallowed against the jagged lump in her throat. She kissed her fingertips and pressed them to the smiling photo of the love of her life. "I promise I am. I can't go anywhere until that boy is happy now, can I?"

She stood, crossed to the bed, and pulled back the covers.

Pigeon mewed.

"I'm sorry to disturb you, Pigeon." She slid between the cool cotton sheets and leaned back against the pile of pillows. "Come on."

Pigeon sat up, stretched leisurely, then sauntered across the quilt to lay along Dot's legs—where she'd stay all night.

"That's my girl." She rested a hand on the cat. "What would our Albie say to Everett now, Pigeon? Hmm? I wonder." She stroked Pigeon's back absentmindedly. "I'm afraid he's wasting time, Albie."

She'd never forget the day Albie had come home from one of his special fishing trips with Everett. While Albie never said as much, Dot had always known her late husband was closest to Everett. The two of them clicked—likely because they were so alike.

"Dottie, our boy has found his seahorse." Albie had grabbed her around the waist and spun them around the kitchen.

Everett had been twelve years old, but neither of them had doubted the seriousness of their grandson's devotion. He'd always been a thoughtful boy. Careful and considerate with others—especially little Rosemary Hill. She'd seen it the very first time he sat quietly beside the girl, using a goat kid to try to lift her spirits. When she laughed, the look on his face had been priceless.

The question was, did her laugh still make her grandson look that way? And if it did, how could she help her grandson win the love of his life? She glanced at Albie's photo and sighed. "Don't you worry, I'll figure something out. But I wish you were here."

CHAPTER THREE

"YOU REALLY SAID THAT?" Rosemary's stomach hurt from laughing, and it was wonderful. Closing up their family's Main Street shop, the Hill Honey Boutique, was a chore—but with Nicole there to help, it was almost fun. Nicole, one of her oldest and dearest friends, had the unique ability to make any story amusing—even if the topic wasn't all that funny. Like now: Nicole's latest run-in with her mother, Willadeene Svoboda.

"I did. Am I thrilled that I'll be little Ginger's guardian until her mother is deemed fit by the state? No. But would I be able to live with myself if such a sweet and shy little girl was handed over to CPS?" Nicole's lavender-streaked locks shimmied as she shuddered.

Rosemary was just learning about how Nicole had suddenly become guardian to her cousin's five-year-old daughter. Nicole had shared what little Ginger had been through before arriving on her doorstep, and it was heartbreaking.

"Or worse, Willadeene? Absolutely not. Not that Willadeene would take a kindergartner in—she's not fond of young children. I guess there's not enough real drama at that age?" She paused. "Oh, and Benji told her to stop trying to manipulate me." She puffed up with pride. "I hate that he feels the need to champion me, but...he had a point. Should I worry that my son has no filter?"

"Kind of like his mother?" Rosemary sprayed cleaner on the glass countertop. "What did Willadeene say to that?"

Nicole made the face she always made when they were talking about her mother—simultaneously tense and puckered up like she was sucking on something sour. "Oh you know, the typical stuff about Benji not being grateful or respecting his elders and how she won't be around forever." She shot Rosemary a narrow-eyed look. "You don't want to know what I was thinking when she said that." She shrugged, straightening the selection of bee-centric aprons. "Anyway, she stormed off after that. She has to have the final word, or she will literally come back in a room just to ensure she gets it—and then make a grand exit." Nicole twisted up her hair and shoved a long golden hairpin through the unruly knot. "I told Benji respect should be earned, and as far as I'm concerned, his grandmother needs to earn his respect back."

"You're a good mom, Nicole. Don't let her make you doubt that." Some things hadn't changed at all in Honey. Like triple-digit heat in the summer, Astrid being able to predict when a beehive needed to be split or requeened, and Willadeene Svoboda sowing dissension and getting into other people's business wherever she went.

"Thanks for having my back." Nicole blew her a kiss.

"Always." Rosemary finished wiping off the glass counter. "There is no one else I can rely on to make sure I know *everything* that's happening with who and where."

"It's true." Nicole nodded. "I know *all* the things." As a lifelong Honey resident and part-owner of the local

Busy Bee Beauty Salon, Nicole had the inside scoop on pretty much anyone and anything worth knowing. But unlike her mother, Nicole only shared with the Hill women, affectionately referred to as the Bee Girls—and never with malicious intent.

"I keep thinking Willadeene is going to mellow with age." Nicole plugged in the vacuum. "But how much older does she have to get?" She turned it on and ran it over the small honeycomb-print rug that covered the boutique floor, singing the latest Taylor Swift song loudly and off-key.

Rosemary was laughing again. She stared around her family's boutique with a full heart. She might not have planned to come home this way, but it was just what she needed. Familiar smiles and spaces and names. A slower pace. It was nice to have time to truly appreciate the world around her—not just the slides on her microscope and the work in her lab.

"Is it clean enough? Think Aunt Camellia would approve?" Nicole asked, peering around the shop.

The Hill Honey Boutique was their aunts' pet project—and their pride and joy. The tiny little Main Street shop featured all sorts of beekeeping tools and novelties, fresh honey, coloring and recipe books, and more. Everything they carried was hand-selected and, preferably, made by local artisans and crafters. Aunt Camellia had exacting standards on what they sold *and* how welcoming and tidy the shop was kept.

Rosemary took a long assessing look around the space. "I think so." She smiled. "We can call it a day and lock up."

"Oh good." Nicole stowed the vacuum in the back stockroom. "Are you sure you don't need a ride?"

"I'm certain. We're going to eat at Delaney's before the meeting tonight." She glanced at the honey-hive cuckoo clock on the wall. "I'm supposed to meet them in ten minutes or so. With Aunt Camellia on her honeymoon, mealtime has been more fend-for-yourself than usual."

"Really?" Nicole shot her a surprised look.

"Well, Aunt Mags is dealing with Shelby and baby Bea and Roman—"

"Ooh, right, the hot widower guy." Nicole grinned. "I'm not normally into silver foxes, but wowza, he is easy on the eyes."

"I'm not sure Aunt Mags has noticed." Rosemary *had* noticed the tension between the two of them.

Of all the surprises she'd come home to, learning her beloved Aunt Mags's secret was the biggest. As in, a secret baby she'd given up when she was a teenager. If Shelby hadn't shown up on the front porch—with her own baby on her hip—looking for her birth mother, Rosemary wondered if they'd ever have known about Shelby. Aunt Mags had always valued her privacy.

But now Shelby and her baby, Bea, were a fixture at Honey Hill Farms.

How Shelby's adoptive father, Roman Dunholm, was going to fit into the mix was still a bit of a mystery. As a widower, he'd missed his daughter and granddaughter and had stopped off in Honey to surprise them. It had been a surprise, all right. Even more surprising? Aunt Mags inviting the man to stay for a while.

"Mags has totally noticed. Are you kidding?" Nicole wiggled her eyebrows. "It won't be long before the two of them are doing the horizontal mambo—if you know what I mean?"

"Ick." Rosemary grimaced, collecting the stack of mail from the counter. "I know what you mean."

"Whatever. Someone should be getting some." Nicole sighed. "Speaking of… What do you make of this whole Everett bachelor thing?"

"That was a leap." Rosemary frowned.

"Was it?" She shrugged. "I bet he's getting all sorts of attention from that article. From ladies, I mean. Didn't that picture make him look dreamy?" She waited for Rosemary to nod. "Too bad Everett's always been like a brother to me." She sighed. "I mean, he's the real thing, you know? A decent guy. You know, a unicorn."

"He is." She wished she'd had more time to catch up with him, but she understood. He had a whole lot on his plate right now—she'd seen the strain on his face.

"Anyway, I'll be at the meeting, but first I've got the whole bedtime routine with Ginger. I can't ask Benji to do that. He's still a kid, you know?" Nicole stood aside while Rosemary locked the bright yellow front door of the boutique. "It's sure to be an interesting evening." She waved as she climbed into her little truck parked right out front. She started the engine, triggering a series of not-so-comforting rattles and thumps. "It's fine."

Rosemary winced when Nicole shifted from Reverse into Drive. "I hate to tell you this, but that metal-on-metal grinding that's happening—" she pointed at the truck "—isn't normal."

"I know." Nicole sighed. "But it's only when I change gears. It's fine now." She winked at her. "See you later."

"Night." Rosemary waved, cringing at the metal scraping that echoed as Nicole drove away, then walked down Main Street toward Delaney's.

From the number of cars and trucks lining the street,

Delaney's was busy. She sat on the bench out front and flipped through the mail. One envelope in particular caught her eye. The Annual Texas Beekeeper's Convention. It *was* that time of year, and oh, the timing was perfect. She needed something to help her shake off her funk, and this was just the thing. A long weekend of bee-loving, bee-focused lectures and hands-on classes from the country's leading experts to motivate and excite her. She opened the program, scanning over this year's offerings.

Best practices of queen-rearing. Organic treatments for mite prevention. New revenue streams through agritourism and beekeeping classes. Honeybee removals. And more. She was familiar with several of the presenters and knew they'd have useful information. It would be good to reconnect with other professionals—to feel valued and exchange ideas and knowledge for the good of the industry. But then she saw the keynote speaker, and she crumpled the brochure in her hands.

Dr. James Voigt discusses his genome-mapping project. With plans to assemble the most high-quality maps of the genomes of at least 125 bee species, Dr. Voigt seeks to identify and target the specific genetic differences between bee species, highlight strengths and weaknesses, and eventually, link functions to specific genes.

It went on, but she stopped reading. She knew what it said; it was her summation. Almost word-for-word. The man really had no conscience. None. It turned her stomach.

"Rosebud?" She hadn't realized Everett was standing in front of her. "You look white as a sheet. Are you feeling okay?"

No. I'm not. I'm upset. I'm...furious. But her throat was too tight to speak, so she nodded.

He sat beside her on the bench. "What's that?" He nodded at the brochure she held with clenched fists.

She shook her head, her grip tightening on the paper. "Nothing." *Everything.*

"Is that why you're white-knuckling it?" He held his hand out for the brochure.

She gave it to him, pushed off the bench, and shook out her hands. It didn't matter. It didn't... But it *did*. He was coming to *her* home state to present *her* research as his—as the keynote speaker.

She pressed her eyes shut and took a deep breath.

Chances were he didn't even know where she was from. And if he did, it wouldn't matter. This was all about the man's ego. He had the chance to flex his academic muscle in front of a room full of his peers, and he would never pass that up.

"Annual Texas Beekeeper's Convention. That's next weekend. Nice that it's taking place right down the road this year. Tansy and Dane were trying hard to get Honey to host it, but we're just not big enough." Everett smoothed the glossy brochure on his lap. "You planning on going?"

She nodded, shifting from foot to foot.

"You should submit a workshop, share your research and all that." He smiled up at her. "I won't pretend to act like I know what you were researching—other than bees. And that it was important."

"It was important." She swallowed. And if the information was out there, wasn't that enough? Even though the project still had some work to do, they'd made progress. With any luck, Dr. Voigt's new project and crew would complete the study and compile a registry that all beekeepers would benefit from.

"You thinking of trying to find another project?" One of his dark brows rose.

"No." She sighed. "Not now anyway. I promised Aunt Mags I'd touch up the bees and flowers painted throughout the house and... I have a picture book idea for Bea." She'd been doodling for days, but saying it out loud made it something real—something hers. "Maybe?" She glanced at him, watching his reaction as she sat beside him.

"That would be something special." He rested his elbows on his knees and leaned forward, nodding. "You should do it. You always loved drawing and painting. You're good at it, too. You have lots of talents, Rosebud."

"That's nice of you to say." She bumped his shoulder with her own. Everett had always been supportive. She'd missed that. She'd missed him. "I can't believe you remember my art."

"Mom still has that painting you did. The one with the bee and the sunflower?" He shrugged. "It was in a place of honor, too, right over the mantel. I think it's in Gramma Dot's room now."

"Really?" That was a surprise—a sweet surprise. The sort of thing that eased some of the knots from her stomach. She tucked her hair behind her ear. "Well, Everett Taggert, you made my day." She smiled at him, a real smile full of thanks.

"Glad to hear it." He cleared his throat. "I was wondering... That is, I want to ask you something. But you don't have to answer right now. You can think about it. And, if it's not something you'd be interested in, I'll understand." He ran a hand along the back of his neck, his gaze locking with hers.

Rosemary rarely saw Everett nervous, but he was. And for some reason, she was, too. His dark brown eyes searched hers, flooding her stomach with anticipation. What was he going to ask her?

"You know Lorna Franks?"

Lorna? "I do." She wasn't sure where this was going.

"Now that she's got a baby, she wants to stay home—and I respect that. But it's left me in a pickle of a spot. She handles all the classes and booths, scheduling volunteers and that sort of thing." His brown eyes swept over her face. "I was wondering if you'd be interested in the job? It's part-time. You can work from home—we'd meet once a week or so, just to touch base." He hesitated. "Even temporarily?"

She was stunned. That wasn't at all what she'd hoped...thought he'd ask. A job. A job she'd be good at. Why was she...disappointed?

"Like I said, you don't have to answer right away. I was thinking, since you're here, it might be something you'd enjoy. You know every festival in Lewis County—every festival in the surrounding counties, too, I bet. There's not much in the way of classes right now. A senior gardening class and one for kids. You can make it bee-friendly gardens, if you want. It'd be your program." He broke off and shook his head. "That's my sales pitch. I'll let you think it over. But, please, think it over."

After that earnest plea, she couldn't immediately dismiss his offer. "I'm not exactly a people person, Everett. You know I get awkward and… Well, I'm more of a…behind-the-scenes sort."

He shook his head. "I wouldn't ask you if I didn't think you could handle it." He stood. "I should probably head over to the city hall, make sure things are set up for the meeting in a bit." He handed her back the brochure. "I'll see you there?" He waited for her nod, then headed across the street to the county courthouse.

She sat, watching him, thinking over what he'd said about her painting, her book idea, and the job. He'd never know how much his words meant to her. Things had been tough recently—but they wouldn't stay that way. Like Everett said, she had lots of talents. Instead of holding on to what she'd lost in the past, it was time to focus on the good to come. Whether she went to the annual beekeeper's convention or took Everett's job offer, she had options. And she had the time to figure out which option was best for her.

EVERETT HAD COME into this evening's meeting anticipating certain things—like Willadeene Svoboda's overreaction. She didn't disappoint. This sort of performance was what she lived for, and since she had a business on Main Street, she had plenty to say.

"I'm assuming the reason you've called this meeting is because you feel our Main Street and businesses are in danger?" She glanced back and forth between him and Mayor Contreras.

"Danger is a strong word." Everett knew to tread carefully. "And we're *hosting* this event at the request of Sheriff Myers—who will be here presently." He scanned the growing crowd for the man.

"All we can do is our due diligence. Keep our eyes

and ears open. Make sure our security systems are up-to-date—add security cameras, if you're able," Mayor Contreras said.

"Some of us don't have the budget for fancy security systems, Mr. Taggert." Willadeene leveled a narrow-eyed glare his way. Willadeene's friends sat around her, nodding—each of them puffed up with pride and self-importance. "Perhaps we could set up an anonymous tipline with the *Hill Country Gazette* instead of using it to find dates, Mr. Taggert? Or should I say, Honey's Most Eligible Bachelor?" She paused, appreciating the chuckles scattered throughout the room.

Leave it to Willadeene to make sure his humiliation was as far-reaching as possible.

Willadeene kept going. "It seems to me that we, the townspeople of Honey, should be able to rely on our mayor, city staff, and law enforcement to take care of this sort of thing. If we can't, perhaps the townspeople need to consider finding leadership that can."

There it was. The dramatic ultimatum. It'd happened faster than Everett had expected, but it still caused a ripple through the audience.

Mayor Contreras nodded. "And when elections roll around in six months, I encourage you to vote and let your voice be heard."

There were a few laughs in answer to that, easing some of the mounting tension in the room.

"But now isn't the time to divide the town, now is the time to pull together—to work together," Everett said, glad to see such a big turnout.

He knew most of the people gathered. Other than his college years, he'd lived his whole life in Honey. While there were a few that insisted on speaking out for the sake of being heard, most of the townsfolk were good, reasonable people. Like his parents. Well, they were a little on the defensive side at the moment. His mother and father sat, whispering to one another and shooting daggers at the back of Willadeene's head. They were protective of him—and it made him smile.

It was a relief to see Tansy Hill's long-suffering eye roll and Dane struggling to hold back a chuckle. Rosemary was looking at the woman with a mix of alarm and amusement. Magnolia Hill, however, did not look the least bit amused.

"Until you tell us what's being done, I think we have the right to speak up. So what is being done? Other than all of us just waiting to see who's vandalized next?" Willadeene resembled a red-faced bulldog. "Mayor Contreras, I'd expect a more progressive plan from you."

Everett stepped aside, all too happy for Honey's mayor to take center stage. Robbie Contreras had served as mayor of Honey for two terms, and from what he'd told Everett, those two terms had given him a mild heart attack and an ulcer. That was why Everett had taken on more responsibilities—to help Robbie out. Few knew that Robbie wasn't going to run for reelection. As far as Everett was concerned, that was a real shame. Robbie was a good man, and he'd been an excellent mayor.

"We're coordinating with officials in Alpine Springs, Elginston, Rose Prairie, and Glendale, Miss Svoboda." Mayor Contreras scanned the sheet of paper on the podium before him. "Local and state police are on alert. They suggest we implement a city watch—which they will provide the training for."

"Security systems? City watch? So you're expecting us to invest our time and money on something that may or may not happen?" Jed Dwyer managed Coffey Motors, right on the edge of Main Street. If the man wasn't the best mechanic in three counties, no one would put up with him. He was a big man, known for being impatient, hotheaded—and raising three sons who seemed to be following in their father's footsteps. "This has happened, what, two times? And it didn't happen here, so I don't see what the big deal is. This is a lot of fuss over nothing." Jed crossed his beefy arms over his chest and leveled a hard stare Mayor Contreras's way.

Everett had gone to school with Jed. And for a while they'd been friends. There'd been plenty of gossip surrounding Jed's family. His philandering mother. His alcoholic and abusive father. Later, his mother dying and leaving the kids with their father. Jed had started picking fights in elementary school and kept picking them until high school graduation. Over the years, CPS had been involved a time or two, but Jed and his sister had never been taken away from their father. If Jed was a hard man, he had plenty of reason to be.

"I'm sorry you feel that way, Mr. Dwyer." Mayor Contreras's smile was tight. "After talking with law enforcement, we felt it was prudent to share what was happening. The city watch program will be strictly volunteer. The more volunteers, the better. Miss Owens-Baldwin has a sign-up sheet for those willing to take the training." He pointed across the room at the table where Libby sat, her ruby-red smile shiny under the fluorescent lights. "As I said, this is strictly volunteer. I know how supportive our community can be. I hope that sign-up list reflects that."

Everett was relieved when the meeting finally wrapped. But even after the meeting had officially adjourned, people lingered. The tones ranged from concern to anger, but Everett did his best to offer hope and redirect the energy into something proactive—like signing up for the city watch. He was happy to see there was a line to sign up for the training. It was all the confirmation he needed that Jed and Willadeene were in the minority.

"Everett?" Leif Knudson, Dane's younger brother, nodded a greeting. "I know you're really busy and all, but do you have a second? I… We wanted to show you something." His voice was low. "Kerrielynn found it."

Kerrielynn nodded. "It was on Instagram. And Tik-Tok."

"Okay." Everett followed the teens to a less-crowded corner of the room. "What's up?"

Leif held up his phone. "It's Alpine Springs."

Everett watched the video. It was barely a minute long—long enough to show a couple of people in ski masks firing their paintball guns at what appeared to be one of Alpine Springs's exercise installations. "Do we know whose account this is?" The last shot had part of the Alpine Springs's City Park sign visible.

Kerrielynn shrugged. "No idea. It's like a dummy account."

The account, @paint.ballers, had been formed a week ago. He read aloud, "'#PaintBallChallenge. Join me for #tagurit #paintballtag #tagthecountry.' Well, this sucks." This wasn't the sort of news he was hoping for. "Can anyone find this online?" There were three other videos, too. He'd bet money one of them would show Elginston's mural being defaced.

"Yeah. It's a public account. And they're getting a lot of followers, too. People posting their own #Paint-BallChallenge videos." Kerrielynn tucked her phone into her pocket. "It's not viral, though."

"Yet," Leif added, too grave for Everett's liking.

"You didn't recognize anyone?" It was a long shot. The two in the video were wearing masks and the one shooting the video wasn't visible—plus, no one had said a word.

Kerrielynn and Leif both shook their heads.

"I appreciate it. I'll let Mayor Contreras know and share the info with law enforcement." Would they be able to track down the culprits with such little information?

"Also, my mom wanted me to tell you that you should run for mayor." Kerrielynn smiled. "She said she was really proud of how you handled yourself."

"Thanks, Kerrielynn. That's nice to hear." And once he'd figured out who these @paint.ballers were, maybe he'd consider it.

"I've been saying the same thing." Robbie Contreras clapped a hand on his shoulder. "I'd say we did okay. The line looks good—plenty of volunteers means a better chance of preventing this mischief from happening here."

"You need to see this." Everett pulled out his phone, opened Instagram, and found the @paint.ballers account.

"What does that mean? All the hashtags or pound signs? I'm old, kids. That's a whole other language that I have no interest in learning." Robbie scowled.

"They're trying to make it into an online challenge. That's a thing. They get other people to do the same thing and post it, and it can get really popular. It's how people go viral," Kerrielynn explained.

"Might not hurt to watch the other videos they've posted. See if we can get a feel for who and where they might be?" Everett could only hope they weren't as careful in all the videos.

"Yeah, yeah, I guess so. I'm definitely too old for this." Robbie shook his head. "Thanks, Kerrielynn, Leif. I appreciate this. If you hear anything—"

"We will let you know." Kerrielynn nodded. "Right away."

"See you." Leif took Kerrielynn's hand and led her across the room and out the door.

"Good kids." Robbie sighed, scratching his chin. "Think this will help us? Or hurt us?"

"Honestly?" Everett waited for his nod. "If this thing catches on… Well, I've got a bad feeling about it."

"Yeah, that's what I figured. Stop by my office in the morning? We can watch these…challenge videos." Robbie shook his hand. "I'm leaving before I get cornered by Willadeene or one of her cronies. I need a beer."

"You've earned it." Everett chuckled and shook the man's hand. "I'll see you in the morning."

As the crowd started to disperse, he headed to the sign-up table Libby was manning. The line was almost gone. The local veterinarian, Dr. Abraham, gave him a nod. The mayor's two sisters and Main Street business owners, Angela and Martina Contreras, thanked him for having their brother's back. And once he'd finished signing up, Dane turned and greeted him with a clap on the back.

"You good?" Dane asked. "That was something. Leif talk to you?"

"He did." Everett ran a hand along the back of his neck. "I wasn't expecting that."

"Well, we're all signed up." Tansy hooked her arm through Dane's. "City watch reporting for duty. Will we get matching shirts and night vision goggles? Kerrielynn is all excited—she's gone full Nancy Drew detective mode."

"Is that a good thing?" Everett laughed. "And as far as I know, no night goggles."

"That's disappointing." Tansy sighed.

"What's disappointing?" Libby asked.

Everett hadn't heard her approach—the woman was downright stealthy. "The lack of spy gear for the city watch."

"We've got quite a long list for the training, boss. Good news, right?" Libby held up the clipboard. "Even Jed signed up. He's all bark and no bite."

Everett didn't know about that, but he was glad the man had had a change of heart.

"Oh, Tansy." Libby's red smile seemed tight. "I noticed Rosemary was here. But she didn't sign up. Does that mean she won't be staying around, or is she…too busy to help out?"

Everett glanced at Libby. It seemed like an awfully pointed way to ask a question.

"I mean, I'm sure she's super busy and all." Libby blinked rapidly, hugging the clipboard to her chest.

"I signed up for her. I appreciate your concern for Rosemary's well-being." The hint of sarcasm in Tansy's words was impossible to miss. "It's…unexpected."

"I think it's time to go." Dane slipped an arm around his fiancée's shoulder. "Everett, whatever you need, let me know."

"Same here, Everett." Tansy patted his arm. "Good night."

"Those Bee Girls, always ready and willing to help." Libby watched as Tansy and Dane left. "Growing up, I always wanted to be one of them. They have such a loving family—so close. Kate and I... Well, you know all about our family." She sighed and pulled her long blond hair over one shoulder. "But Rosemary has never liked me. Back in school, no matter what I tried to do to draw her out of her shell or put a smile on her mouth, she went out of her way to avoid me. Kind of like tonight."

He was surprised to hear this. Rosebud had been super shy and on the awkward side in high school. And he couldn't remember Rosebud having a negative word to say about anyone. Ever. And tonight, she'd been upset over something to do with the annual beekeeper's convention. *If* she'd avoided Libby, that was probably why. "Maybe now things can be different."

"How's that?" Libby asked, plucking an invisible something from her sweater—her very tight, curve-hugging sweater.

"I offered Rosebud... Rosemary the job. Lorna's job." He shrugged. "If she takes it, it means you'll be working with her every once in a while. Might give you two a chance at friendship."

Libby's face lit up. "She's staying? Oh, how *fun*. I bet she'll take the job. She just adores you."

He frowned. "We've always been friends."

"Exactly. You've always been special friends." She put her hand on his arm and squeezed. "Oh, I hope she takes the job. You know how hard I've been trying to get away from all that negative talk and gossip. I've made mistakes, but I've learned from them. I'd love to try again with Rosemary. I'm sure we'll be the best of friends in no time."

Everett was heartened by Libby's enthusiasm, but felt the need to caution her. "She hasn't said yes."

"Oh, fingers crossed. I guess we'll have to wait and see." She patted his chest. "I'm going to call it a night, boss. You should get some rest, too. You'll doubtless be heading off more phone calls and emails from the rest of the single ladies in the Hill Country."

He frowned. "Right." Some of the emails he'd received were *not* okay. He'd quickly learned not to open any email attachments, too. "Night. And thanks for the hard work." He took the clipboard she offered before she left.

As tired as he was, a quick inventory of the sign-up sheet was rewarding. His instincts were right—most of Honey would do what it took to keep their small town safe.

And if he was right about that, then maybe he'd be right about Rosebud. She'd said she needed something to do—a way to connect with her hometown and feel useful again. This job would do that, and then some. Libby being excited about working with Rosebud was the icing on the cake. After all, having a team that worked well together would make it feel less like work. As far as Everett was concerned, it was a win-win.

CHAPTER FOUR

"I ALMOST FORGOT how pretty our hives are." Rosemary sat on the edge of the Lavender-Blue bee yard, her sketch pad on her lap. Every hive box in the apiary was painted a different shade of lavender or blue with hand-painted whimsical accents like a shower of stars, blowing dandelion wisps, or snowflakes falling.

"Really?" Astrid put her hands on her hips. "That's sad."

It was sad. But she'd learned early on that thinking about home made her homesick—which was counterproductive. Her whole life, she'd been told she was meant to do big things. Poppa Tom, her grandfather, said it was her mission to use every bit of her smarts to make the world a more bee-friendly, bee-focused place. Her grandmother and the aunts had agreed.

Her sisters were her biggest cheerleaders. If she applied for an accelerated summer program, they'd help her pack. If she took extra college hours, they'd help her study. She was always going and doing—always. If there was an hour of unscheduled time in her day, she'd find a use for it. She was single-minded in her pursuit to achieve more and more. She never thought to slow down or consider her choices or how she wanted her future to look. It was no wonder she had her doctorate in entomology by the age of twenty-four.

Getting in to the UC Davis program had been an honor. That was it—the start of her mission. She'd hit the ground running, working hard and contributing as much as she could toward the research study—until it was gone.

She glanced down at the bees she'd sketched out. Four little bees climbing up the side of the star-speckled hive box, wearing daisy crowns—like Astrid liked to make—and sweet smiles. Technically, bees didn't smile or wear daisy crowns, but she wanted her story for Bea to have equal parts whimsy and facts.

"Can I see?" Astrid asked, sitting on the ground beside her. "Oh, Rosemary." She rested her head on her shoulder. "They are precious."

"You think so?" She ran her finger along the edge of the beehive, smearing the thick line and softening the whole image. "That's better."

It helped that Honey Hill bees were gentle enough for her to work without protective gear. Being up close to the creatures she'd dedicated her life to was giving her all sorts of inspiration for her storybook. The tickle of tiny bee feet as a worker bee crawled along her arm. The whisper of fluttering wings when one flew by her ear. The up-close view of a bee—unobscured by mesh or net.

She could see every tiny hair that covered a bee's body. And the way they moved. So busy. Always going. The way they used their front legs to push the collected pollen to their hind legs and stored it all in the dense hair structure that acted as the pollen baskets.

The variation in pollen was just as dramatic as each bee. Some bee pollen baskets were vibrant yellow. Others looked like tiny tangerines. The color of the pollen showed where the bee had gone foraging—and would impact the flavor of the honey they'd eventually harvest. Since their hives were placed by the lavender fields, the pollen was muted and dark and perfect for the earthy lavender-flavored honey it would produce.

"I didn't forget about our hives." Rosemary stared out over the bee yard. "It was a self-defense mechanism. If I thought about being here, it was hard to remember why I was there."

"I can imagine." Astrid lifted her head and looked at her. "Actually, I can't imagine leaving. Everything I love is here. Now that you're back, everyone I love is here." She rested her head on her shoulder again. "I know it's selfish and you've been through a lot, but… I'm so happy you're home."

Astrid was a gentle soul with a huge heart. She had the ability to be both wise and empathetic—and not just with the bees. And she was so easy to love. Maybe that's why the bees talked to her. Not talking as in human words, but communicating nonetheless. Poppa Tom said Astrid was a bee whisperer. And since there was no proof to the contrary and plenty of proof to support his claim, no one questioned it.

"Have you made up your mind about going to the convention?" Astrid stood and wiped her hands on the apron she wore. "Part of me thinks you should go just to sock the guy in the nose." She mimicked the action, her expression determined. "Heck, I want to. Maybe I should go."

"While I appreciate the support—" Rosemary laughed "—you're a mother now, you can't go around socking people in the nose, Astrid."

"Um, the whole mama bear thing is real. And Nova

and Halley would totally support my decision. Charlie would… Well, he might prefer it if I handle things a bit more diplomatically, but he'd still support me." She smiled. "He does that. Always."

Rosemary closed her sketch pad and stood. "I thought the mama bear thing was about protecting your kids?"

"You're my little sister, Rose. Close enough." Astrid smiled at her.

"You've got a point." Her sisters had always been protective of her. If it hadn't been for Poppa Tom, Willadeene Svoboda would still be talking about the ruckus that would have unfolded between her sisters and Kate and Libby Owens. Thankfully, his cooler head and wise counsel had reminded them that the Owens girls didn't have the loving and supportive family she and her sisters had. Even though the knowledge didn't make the bullying bearable, it had helped her endure it silently. The one time Poppa Tom had gone to the school to try to intervene hadn't made a difference, so Rosemary had only shared with her sisters.

"Do you think that's enough?" Astrid pointed at the new pea gravel they'd spread beneath the hives earlier.

Honey Hill Farms used a variety of anti-varroa-mite and anti-hive-beetle tactics. Their hives were all elevated off the ground and mounted on platforms. The ground below the hives was covered with river rock or pea gravel. Sprigs of thyme—a natural deterrent to hive invaders—grew in several places among the bee yards. And then there were the chickens and guinea fowl that roamed the property, happily making a meal of any would-be hive invaders.

Rosemary walked around the hive stands and nodded. "I think we're good."

"Good." Astrid blew a strand of hair from her face. "I'm feeling nauseous. I could use some water and shade."

"Oh, Astrid. I'm sorry. I got caught up in my drawing." She hurried to clean up, loaded their spades into the wagon, then grabbed the handle to pull it along behind them. "Are you sure you should be out and about like this?"

Astrid snorted. "I'm pregnant. Not an invalid."

"Right. Got it. Okay." She shrugged. "I've never been pregnant, you know. In fact, I think you're the first pregnant person I've known. Is that weird?"

"You tend to hang out with bee addicts whose only real relationships are with bees, so no, not really." She glanced at her sister. "Circling back to the annual convention. Tansy and Dane are presenting on their agritourism venture. She'd never admit it, but she's nervous."

Tansy was nervous? Her big sister was always confident and purposeful. At least, that's how she acted. But if she was nervous… It made Rosemary's decision easy. Tansy had always been Rosemary's cheerleader, and now it was Rosemary's turn. "Then I'll go. It will help her to see a few goofy faces in the audience."

"That's what I was thinking. Maybe I'll go, just for the day?" Astrid grabbed her free hand. "Maybe me being there will help you, too? I know it won't be easy for you."

"It will only be hard if I let it be." She was done letting Dr. James too-big-for-his-britches Voigt get in her head. It was hard to align the charming man who'd bolstered her confidence and inspired her to work harder and get more results with the man who'd stolen her work. Though nothing had happened between them, he'd been fully aware of how enamored she was with his experience, knowledge, and respected reputation—and he'd taken full advantage of that and her. She'd never suspected he was setting her up, why would she? But he had, and she was devastated. Betrayed. Angry. *Enough of that.*

They followed the trail around the lavender fields and along the fence. While the temperatures weren't unbearably hot, the air was balmy and heavy with fragrance. "It's one of the scents I can still tolerate. Thankfully." Astrid took a deep breath. "I can't say the same for mint or laundry detergent or corn chips." She stuck her tongue out. "Gag."

Along the way to the house, Rosemary found herself caught up in all things familiar and precious. The large Spanish oak that stood alone by the fence. The windmill on the old Wallace place—barely visible when they reached the top of the hill. The gray and rotting bits of wood that once served as their tree house and spy fort for keeping tabs on the evil Knudsons. The tree house was gone, but the memories she and her sisters had made were things she'd always treasure.

"Oh, lookee there." Astrid nodded at one of the flower beds along the front of the house. More specifically, the two people working in the flower bed. "Aunt Mags and Mr. Dunholm."

Rosemary wasn't sure what was going on between the two of them, but for Shelby's sake, she hoped they'd called a truce. "Mags loves to garden. Maybe he does, too?"

The closer they got, the louder the conversation between Aunt Mags and Roman Dunholm became.

"I'm sure your fertilizer is adequate, but we compost

for a reason." Aunt Mags knelt on a folded towel, her wide-brimmed hat shielding her face.

"I'm not suggesting you replace the compost. Only mixing the two." Roman stood with his hands in his pockets, his gaze traveling over the overflowing flower beds.

"I'll take that into consideration." She went back to spreading the compost mixture around her beloved rosebushes, asters, and chrysanthemums.

Roman chuckled. "Something tells me you won't."

Rosemary grinned. He was right about that. Aunt Mags did things the way her parents had—and her grandparents before that. It would take a miracle for that to change.

"Did we miss lunch?" Astrid asked, glancing back and forth between the two of them. "Not that I'm all that hungry."

"I had a bite not too long ago." Aunt Mags sat back, her green eyes fixing on Astrid. "But you should eat, Astrid. For the baby."

"I will." Astrid sighed. "Assuming I can keep anything down."

"Try, at least." Aunt Mags nodded. "You should join them, Roman. Since you're something of a chef, I'm sure you could...whip something up for them?"

Roman had a rather nice smile. "Fine. I'll leave you alone."

As hard as she tried, Rosemary couldn't stop her smile. At least he had a sense of humor.

He turned to them. "I do make a mean grilled cheese."

"That sounds good." Astrid climbed the stairs to the wide wraparound porch and the screen door leading into the kitchen.

Inside, Shelby and Bea were playing with blocks on the kitchen floor. When Rosemary walked in, Bea pushed herself up and trotted forward with outstretched arms. It delighted her that, even after so few days, Bea had decided to love Rosemary.

"Hey, little bee." Rosemary picked up the toddler. "How are you?"

"Bla ma ma si." Bea nodded as if she'd said something of the utmost importance.

"You don't say?" Rosemary nodded back. "You've been busy."

"Da da ma pa wee." This time the toddler smiled and clapped her hands.

"I wish I knew what you were saying so I could be that excited." Rosemary carried Bea across the kitchen, pulled a pitcher of lemonade from the fridge, and poured Astrid a tall glass. "Have a seat, sis, please." She carried the glass to the table and set it before Astrid, and since Bea was now reaching for Astrid, handed off Bea as well. "I know you're *only* pregnant, but you should rest now and then."

"You have no idea how right she is." Shelby pushed off the kitchen floor. "My pregnancy was a piece of cake. I ate whatever I wanted and never got sick—which is probably why I gained thirty pounds." She shrugged and went on, "*But* if I could go back, I'd nap more. Like, whenever I had a chance. I don't think I've slept, really slept, since Bea was born."

Astrid looked horrified.

"Unless I left Bea with my mom or dad," Shelby was quick to add. "Dad has a way with babies. Maybe it's his soothing voice? Bea never cried with him."

"It's true." Roman started cutting slices from a fresh

loaf of crusty bread. "My résumé should include being good with babies. I make amazing pancakes and grilled cheese. And I know a thing or two about gardening." He glanced out the kitchen window.

"She wasn't interested in your input on the garden, huh?" Shelby asked.

He shook his head.

"She takes a while to warm up to people," Rosemary offered. "And she's...very territorial, too. The kitchen is Camellia's domain. The gardens—all of them—are Mags's."

"She might be a teensy-weensy bit set in her ways." Astrid sat back, smiling at Bea. "But we love her, don't we, Bea? We love our Mimi *so* much."

"Mimi." Bea clapped her hands and turned, searching the room.

"She'll be along in a minute, love." Shelby smiled. "She needed a break from Grampa."

"What did I do?" Roman looked genuinely perplexed as he dropped a pat of butter into the skillet he was heating over the gas stovetop.

Shelby looked at Astrid, who shrugged, before they both looked at her.

"You're here." Rosemary paused, thinking before she went on, "She's only just got Shelby and Bea in her life. I'm sure, deep down, she feels threatened. Maybe scared you'll whisk them away."

Roman expression grew thoughtful. "I suppose I should set the record straight." He nodded, his mind made up. "Now, who wants one of my world-famous grilled cheese sandwiches?"

Rosemary wasn't sure whether to admire the man's confidence or be scared for him. Mags could be a fearsome opponent. Not that they were opponents. She was certain both he and Mags wanted Shelby and Bea to be happy and loved—putting them on the same team. They just needed to realize that.

By the time they were munching on their delicious grilled cheese sandwiches, Rosemary had a fully formed story. Her little bee book could teach Bea about bees and facing one's fears. Bees didn't let bad weather or drought or fire scare them away from taking care of their hive. Families were the same. Thats why, for Shelby and Bea, Mags and Roman *would* work through this.

If she was going to put that out there, she should probably do it, too. Face her fears and stop letting other people have control over her emotions. Like James Voigt making her feel like an idiot. Or panicking every time she saw Libby. Enough was enough. She'd talk to Libby, see that her dread was unfounded, and consider Everett's job offer. He needed help, and after all the times he'd been there for her, it was her turn. She had a plan. Now all she had to do was—do it.

"Lunch was good, Mom, thank you." Everett dropped a kiss on his mother's cheek.

"Of course." She smiled up at him. "I know how you like chicken spaghetti. And you know how I like it when you stop by." She patted his cheek. "Now, you take this out to your dad while I clean up."

"Yes, ma'am." He took two fresh glasses of iced tea and headed out the front door and onto his parents' front porch. "Here." He handed one tea to his father. "From Mom." He turned, watching his grandmother walk across the front yard with her goat kids trailing after her. "She's something else." He took a sip of his iced tea.

"You can say that again." His father leaned against the porch railing. "Any word on the whole paintball fiasco?"

"Fiasco. That's a good word for it." He shook his head. "Social media. I don't speak high tech, but there are a couple of ways to create an anonymous account on this TikTok platform, so…" He shrugged. "There's no way to track down who's posting."

"I don't understand how any of that works." His father was frowning. "You're telling me a person can post this stuff online without having to sign up or join up or register somehow?"

"Yep." Everett finished off his tea and set the glass on the railing. "It's a mite frustrating."

"I bet it is." His father's sigh was long and frustrated. "It seems to me that whoever is doing this has some real issues, son. You're not worried about that?"

"I'm worried about plenty." He glanced at his father. "Speaking of—how are things going with Gramma Dot?"

"Fine." But the furrow between his brows said otherwise.

He suspected his parents kept a lot of his grandmother's struggles quiet. Out of respect or pride, he wasn't sure. But he understood. It was hard for him to see Gramma Dot on one of her off days, he could only imagine how hard it was for his father. To see his mother in a temper? Yelling things and not making sense or recognizing him? It hurt his heart, and his father's heart was likely breaking. "She wasn't all that fine the day of Camellia and Van's wedding. I've never seen her like that—not herself and ready to fight."

His father's gaze locked on his mother—who was happily feeding the chickens with her goat kids following her every step. "It's going to get worse. I know that. But I can't put her in some home. Not yet. Not while most days are fine—"

"Whoa, Dad." Everett placed a hand on his father's arm. "I didn't mean that. I meant how are *you* doing with Gramma Dot? What can I do to help?"

"Son, you already do so much. Too much." He gave Everett a long look. "It seems to me that Mayor Contreras is expecting a lot for someone employed by the county. You should be getting a raise."

He glanced at his father. "He's trying to get me to run this next election."

His father's brows rose. "For mayor? You want to do that?"

Everett chuckled. "I don't not want to."

"My boy. Mayor of Honey." His father grinned. "I'll be."

"I don't know. It's only a couple of months away... There's a lot that would need to be done if I decide to do this."

"Good thing you've got an army of friends and family to get things done then." His father winked at him.

"What are you two handsome boys talking about?" Gramma Dot held the porch railing as she took the porch steps, one at a time, and joined them.

"Oh, you know, Gramma Dot. Being handsome and solving the world's problems. That sort of thing." He draped an arm around her shoulders. "What have you been up to?"

"Feeding goats." She smiled down at the two babies circling her. "And cleaning up after goats. The sweet little things." The goats bleated in unison, as if they knew she was talking about them. "You two are getting spoiled, aren't you? But they helped me feed the chickens. Oh, and earlier we made some cornbread to go with the stew for supper tonight." She paused, her smile mischievous. "We as in me and your mother, not me and the goats."

"Well, that's a relief." Everett laughed.

"I do love your cornbread, Momma." His father rubbed his hands together.

"Don't I know it? But don't you go trying to sneak any, Leland Taggert." She wagged her finger at him. "You'll just have to hold your horses."

"Yes, ma'am." He chuckled.

"There's plenty for you, Everett, if you want to stay. Plenty for a date, too. Though I notice you're here without one. Again. You ever heard the expression, getting a little long in the tooth? I can't account for it. Didn't that article stir up any new prospects? Or light a fire under Rosemary?" She pressed a finger in the middle of his chest. "What's going on with you two anyway?" Gramma Dot peered up at Everett, her brown eyes alert and focused. "She's the one that should be having dinner here by now."

Where had that come from? "Rosebud and I are just friends, Gramma Dot. You know that." Maybe she wasn't as clearheaded as he thought.

Gramma Dot's brows rose high, and she clucked her tongue in disapproval. "Leland, you have a brilliant son. You know that. I know that. But sometimes, he's downright dumb." With a muttered *humph*, Gramma Dot walked to the door, held it wide so her baby goats could go in, then pulled it shut behind them.

His father was laughing.

Everett scratched the back of his head. "That was out of nowhere. That doesn't concern you?"

"Not really." His father clapped him on the shoulder. "Your mother and grandmother have been set on you marrying Rosemary Hill since you were knee-high to a grasshopper. When she left, it was hard seeing how you pined after her. Now that she's home, the two of them are hoping the two of you will finally get together."

Everett stared at his father. Dane was the only one he'd ever confided in, and over the years, he'd learned to regret it. Otherwise, he thought he'd kept his feelings for Rosebud under wraps. Apparently, not. But... "*Pined* after her?" He blinked. "I've never *pined* after anyone." At least, he'd never admitted to it.

His father stared back.

"Never happened," he murmured, hoping that would be the end of it.

"Uh-huh." His father crossed his arms over his chest. "Okay, fine. I'm not siding with my mom, but she does have a point. If you're still wanting a big family, you need to find someone to settle down with—and make me some grandbabies while you're at it."

Subtlety wasn't a thing in the Taggert household.

Everett chuckled. "Yeah, well, I'm pretty sure I've dated most of the single ladies hereabouts."

"You still seeing Daisy Granger? She's a nice one."

"No. She is very nice." He and Daisy got along fine, but there was no spark between them. "We just don't... We're meant to be friends. At least, I thought we were. Then she wrote that damn article."

"She did, didn't she?" His father chuckled. "And the principal? Katrina Lopez? You two had a handful of dates."

"We did." And he'd laughed a lot. Katrina had a great sense of humor. "We didn't click." He sighed. "I do want a family, and I have been dating, Dad. You think I'm happy I haven't found someone I want to bring home yet? I'm not. But I'm not going to settle, either."

His father studied him for a long time. "Is there any truth to what Jenny's been saying about the Owens girl?" He cleared his throat. "I know you're an adult, and you've got a good head on your shoulders but… Well, I know she's something to look at, but what else? What's inside, Everett? You need to know that, son. Because what's on the inside won't change. I guarantee the outside will."

Everett squeezed his father's arm. "I love you. And I hear everything you're saying. I have no interest in Libby Owens. None. She is my secretary, and she's been a good one so far. That's the only interest I have in her—doing a good job. I've told Jenny that—Mom and Gramma Dot, too. But for some reason, they don't seem to believe what I'm saying. I've got eyes, I know she's a fine-looking woman, but I am *not* interested. And I won't date someone I work with. Ever. That's a headache in the making."

His father chuckled. "All right, I believe you. And I'm relieved to hear it. If you had brought home one of those Owens girls, family dinners and holidays would have been all kinds of heartburn."

"Not going to happen." He shot his father a look. "And I'd appreciate it if you'd tell Jenny, Mom, and Gramma Dot it's not going to happen whenever it comes up?"

"Done." His father shook his head. "Now, back to

the whole mayor thing. You should think long and hard about this."

He told his father about the most recent conversation he'd had with Robbie Contreras. After the two of them had watched the TikTok videos @paint.ballers had posted, they'd had an open and frank discussion about Everett's future. Robbie was set on endorsing Everett as the next mayoral candidate. He'd taken the time to list some of Everett's most recent accomplishments—things that would help voters see him as a strong and capable candidate.

"By the time it was over, he'd almost convinced me," Everett finished. "But running for office can get mean and stressful." With Gramma Dot's mood swings and the ongoing struggle that came with a family farm, he wasn't sure he wanted to put a public spotlight on his family. "Maybe now isn't the time."

"In all my sixty-seven years, I've learned things rarely happen at the right time." He used air quotes around *at the right time*. "Ever since you were little, you've been a hard worker. You made up your mind you were going to do something, and you did it. If you make up your mind about this, I expect I'll have a mayor for a son in three months." He grinned. "You know we'll paint signs and campaign and do whatever you do in an election."

Everett gave his father a one-armed hug. "I appreciate that, Dad. And the talk."

"Nice to feel like I've got something to contribute." His father pointed at the front door. "Living with three women—all of whom know better than me—I might as well be talking to myself."

But he knew his father wouldn't have it any other

way. Jenny had talked about getting her own place a time or two, and each time, his father had pointed out all the reasons she should stay put. If his father had it his way, they'd all still live under one roof together.

The only reason his parents hadn't put up a fight when he'd bought his little fixer-upper was because they'd thought he'd be filling it up with his own family. While he hoped that would happen eventually, he'd snapped up the thirty-acre property and his one-hundred-plus-year pier-and-beam home because it'd been a steal—and one hell of a good investment. After three years, he was almost done making improvements.

"Everett," Gramma Dot called from inside. "Your phone is singing. Is that normal?"

Everett grinned. "It's ringing."

Gramma Dot held the door open. "That's singing, not ringing." She handed over the phone. "But it's been singing for a while, so you might want to answer it."

Everett took the phone and frowned. "Thanks, Gramma Dot."

"Leland, come help me with the step stool, will you?" She waved his father inside.

"What are you needing the step stool for, Momma? You know you're not supposed to be climbing on things." He pulled the front door shut behind him.

Everett answered the phone. "Everett Taggert."

"Everett? Joe Kerr. How's your Thursday going?" There was a smile in the man's voice.

"Well, so far so good. Been a while since I've heard from you, so I'm wondering if that's going to change?" He paused, waiting for the mayor of Rose Prairie to confirm his fears.

"'Fraid so, Everett. Last night. Main Street shops—

one window's going to need to be replaced. And some damage over at the high school." He sighed. "I hear you're the man coordinating efforts on this whole paint-ball mess?"

Everett stared out over the fields and barn and goats, processing this update. *Two* separate locations had been vandalized? So far, they'd targeted one place. "I'm working with the sheriff's office and the state troopers to get a city watch training set up."

"Hmm. Might be too little too late for us, but I'm expecting Sheriff Myers soon, so I'll see what he has to say about it. Didn't know if you wanted to come see the damage for yourself?"

Want wasn't exactly the right word. He'd gone to Elginston and Alpine Springs—now he felt obligated to investigate in Rose Prairie. "I'll head that way." He blew out a slow breath. "Until I get there, you might want to have a look at @paint.ballers online. Whoever's doing this likes having an audience. So far, they've been careful about what they post, but I'm hoping they'll get sloppy, and we'll find something to catch them."

"Kids." The man groaned. "I swear, if my daughter doesn't post pictures wherever she goes, it's like it didn't happen. I don't get it."

"Neither do I, Joe. I'll see you in twenty." He disconnected and tucked his phone into his pocket.

While there was no concrete proof that it was kids at the root of what was happening, it was the only thing that made sense. Who else? As far as he knew, there wasn't anyone with a major ax to grind with the county. The idea of a group of disgruntled Main Street busi-ness owners masking up, causing damage, *and* figur-ing out all the bells and whistles of posting online was laughable. Right now, he could use a laugh—so he did. What else could he do?

He used the time it took to drive to Rose Prairie to come up with a plan. He'd follow up with the sheriff about the paintballs themselves. There weren't a lot of retailers selling supplies, so that might give them some sort of lead. It was flimsy, but it was a place to start—which was more than they had at the moment.

DOT CROSSED HER arms over her chest, giving Leland her tried and true mom-face. "You watch your tone, son."

Leland ran a hand over his face. "Momma, Everett's got a lot on his mind—he's real busy."

"Too busy to be happy?" She clicked her tongue in disapproval. "I'm surprised at you, Leland. Your boy is all work, no play. That's not healthy. You know that, too."

Violet stopped washing dishes to face them. "What are you two carrying on about?"

Dot waved her hands. "Just me sticking my nose in where it's not wanted, is all."

"Momma, I didn't say that." Leland pinched the bridge of his nose.

There it was. That look. The one that made her realize she was a burden to her son, his lovely wife, and the entire family. They didn't want her here, but out of a sense of deep obligation, they wouldn't send her away. She didn't want to live someplace that smelled like institutional gravy, bleach, and mold, but she didn't want to be a drain on her son and his family. "I think I'll go lie down."

"Are you okay, Momma Dot?" Violet wiped her hands

on a kitchen towel, her gaze bouncing between her and Leland.

"Yes, yes." She forced a smile. "Just old and tired, is all."

Before she reached her room, she heard Violet say, "Leland, what happened? She was upset."

Dot paused, straining to hear. It was past time to change the battery in her hearing aid.

"I came down too hard on her," Leland mumbled. "I… I know she meant well by bringing up Rosemary to Everett. She and Dad always thought they were made for each other."

"So did I. Would it be so bad?" Violet's voice carried.

"Of course not, Violet." Leland's sigh was all impatience. "But what happens between them is none of our business. Our boy's got more than enough pressure on his shoulders without pushing our wants on him. I get the sense he's about reached his limit."

But it isn't just what I want. Frustration pressed in on her. It happened now and then. She didn't like it— losing her temper. Half the time, she didn't even know why she got so upset, she just did. The best she could do was go to her room and hope it'd pass without her taking it out on anyone else.

Poor Everett. The day of Camellia Hill's wedding, he'd come to get her but she couldn't find her pearl necklace. She always wore her pearl necklace on special occasions—it was a gift from Albie. But it was lost, and Everett's efforts to help her had been halfhearted at best… Still, there'd been no cause to call him selfish or a disappointment. And there was no way to take those horrible words back.

No, it was best to be alone until she'd sorted herself.

Then she could figure out what to do about Everett. After the way she'd treated him, she had to make it up to him somehow. *And I will. Somehow, someway, I'll help my boy be happy.*

CHAPTER FIVE

WITH A DAB more yellow and a tiny dollop of orange, Rosemary had the perfect color. She swirled her fine-tipped brush in the paint and leaned forward to touch up the honeybee "flying" along the hallway of the house.

She didn't know who had originally painted the bee. Her great-grandmother Sybil Hill, perhaps? Apparently, she'd been quite the eccentric when she arrived on the farm. All Rosemary knew for certain was that this little bee had always been here—adding to the magic of her home. It was up to her—her sisters and aunts—to keep that magic alive for all the Hills to come.

With a few careful dabs and featherlight brushstrokes, the faded bee came to life. She sat back, making certain it was just right. Once the gold, yellow, and yellow-orange colored hairs met with her satisfaction, she turned to white, black, and a few hints of brown.

"Wow."

She thought she was alone, so the voice almost had her dropping the paper plate she was using for her paint palette. "Leif."

"Didn't mean to scare you. I was trying to keep it quiet—so I wouldn't interrupt you, but man, that bee looks like it's about to fly off the wall and out to one of y'all's bee yards." He leaned forward, his blue eyes inspecting her work. "That's awesome, Rosemary."

"Thanks, Leif." She smiled, wiping off the tip of her paintbrush. "I'm finished with all the bees upstairs. And the flowers and vines, too." She stretched. "I didn't realize how late it was getting. How was school?"

"It was…school." Leif shrugged.

"I don't know if that's a good thing or not?"

The expression on the teen's face made him look exactly like his big brother had looked back in high school—back when Tansy and Dane hated each other. "I mean, I'm glad it's Thursday." He yawned. "Plus, there's a Junior Beekeepers meeting tonight. Tansy said you might be coming?"

"That's the plan." If Rosemary was going to consider Everett's job offer, it wouldn't hurt to get familiar with some of the clubs and classes that would fall under her oversight. According to Tansy, the Junior Beekeepers were pretty self-sufficient and wouldn't need a lot of hands-on supervision. Mostly, they required an adult present to track hours, keep up with club requirements, and be at the meetings in case of an emergency. Since the club was a joint venture between the school district and the parks and rec office, the club was well funded and had plenty of community support. "I should probably start getting myself together." She headed for the kitchen. "First, I need some tea. Want a snack?" From what she'd witnessed, Leif was always hungry.

"Sure." He grinned and followed her into the kitchen. "Dane's not around? I wanted to talk to him."

"Sorry, no. I think he and Tansy are over at Viking— working in the new honey house y'all are building over there." That Tansy and Dane were working together on the Knudson family's neighboring honey farm still made her smile. She paused, noting the concern on the teen's face. "Can I do anything?"

"I don't know if there's anything to be done. I just…" He shrugged. "I overheard some kids talking at school today about the stuff @paint.ballers—"

"Who?" Rosemary turned on the electric kettle.

"Oh, whoever is paintballing everything is posting it all online. That's their account name. @paint.ballers."

She blinked. "You're kidding. That doesn't sound very smart." She pondered this information as she pulled a plate from a cabinet, opened the cookie jar, and pulled out several cookies. "Why post for the world to see? They were breaking the law, weren't they? What good could come from making their antics public?" She put the plate of brown sugar honey cookies and honey raisin oatmeal cookies on the counter beside him. "If they're posting everything, who is it, and why haven't they been stopped?"

"Thanks." He took a cookie. "They're wearing masks. And they don't talk." He shrugged. "They're not smart, but they're not completely stupid." He ate another cookie. "Kerrielynn's been watching all their stuff—I think she's hoping to figure out who they are." There was pure adoration all over his face. "She's eavesdropping on everyone, hoping to hear something."

She smiled and put a tea bag into her teacup. The electric kettle pinged, so she poured the boiling water into her cup. "You want some tea?"

He shook his head. "No, thank you."

"You've got my full attention, now, Leif. What did you overhear?" She was more than a little curious.

He finished his brown sugar honey cookie before saying, "Donny Dwyer was talking to someone—I didn't see who—about how it's supposed to rain tonight, so

Clay, Donny's older brother, said they were going to hold off on going to Glendale. He was probably talking to his little brother, Eddie, but I'm not certain. The brothers don't have a lot of friends." He took another cookie. "Anyway, Glendale and Honey are the two towns that haven't been paintballed yet. And the Dwyers are always doin' stupid things so—" He broke off and shrugged. "Believe me, the brothers are bad news. I know."

Rosemary didn't want to disappoint Leif, but there wasn't a lot to go on there. Leif was right that Glendale and Honey hadn't been vandalized—yet—but automatically linking the Dwyer boys' visit to Glendale to this @paint.ballers seemed like a stretch.

"I figure I should tell Dane so he can tell Everett. Just in case." He ate another cookie.

It can't hurt. She knew how heavily this was weighing on Everett. It was weighing on everyone. "Just in case." She nodded, sipping her tea.

"Sorry." He stared at the now-empty plate.

"It's okay. I just wanted tea." She smiled. "I was planning on going by Everett's office before the Junior Beekeepers meeting. I can tell him, if you want."

"That'd be great. Thanks." Leif nodded. "I should probably head out. I'm supposed to pick up Kerrielynn. We're doing snacks for the meeting and have to set up." He nodded and headed out of the kitchen.

"See you later." She took a deep breath. All she had to do now was get cleaned up and go to Everett's office. "Time to grow a backbone," she murmured. It would help if her stomach wasn't roiling, there wasn't sweat beading her upper lip, and her hands would stop shaking. *Ugh.*

She didn't normally put a lot of time into her appearance—the bees didn't care. But she wasn't going to spend time with the bees, she was going to see Libby Owens. And she was going to go looking like a woman, not the awkward teen girl she'd been. Once she saw that her high school bullying was over, all the sweating and shaking and nausea would go away.

She showered, dried, and made an attempt at styling her long hair straight, and even put on a little lipstick. *Nope.* She wiped the red off and turned to her closet. Something she felt comfortable in, yet confident. Her favorite green button-down shirt, a denim pencil skirt, and her calf-high leather boots. Perfect.

"Rosemary?" Tansy's voice carried up the stairs, followed by footsteps. "Rosemary? Are you—" She peered into Rosemary's bedroom. "You look nice. What's happening? Where are you going?"

"I figured I'd go into town and talk to Everett." She rubbed her hands against her thighs. Her palms were sweaty.

"Oh?" Tansy's brows shot up. "You got dressed up to see Everett?"

If Tansy knew what she was planning to do, she'd probably try to stop her. Or worse, she'd want to go with Rosemary and be overprotective and make things even weirder than it was going to be. Thats why she said, "Yep."

Tansy blinked. Then again. "Okay."

"Can I take your truck? I'll meet you at the meeting later on?" She tucked a strand of her hair behind her ear, beyond antsy.

"S-sure." She pulled the keys from her pocket and held them out.

Rosemary took the keys, the shaking of her hands causing them to jingle.

"Are you okay?" Tansy glanced from Rosemary's face to her hands and back again.

"Fine." She pressed her hands against her hips. "Eager to get going."

"Don't let me stop you." Tansy's smile was brilliant. "You look gorgeous, Rosemary."

Which was nice, but not what she was going for. "Thanks." She swallowed. "Okay. Do I need to bring anything to the meeting?"

"Just yourself." Tansy hugged her.

Rosemary wound up clinging and hugging her back, hard. "Will do." She let go, forced a smile, then ran down the stairs and out the front door.

The drive into town wasn't too long—but it felt interminable. She went through various scenarios in her head, then gave up. This didn't need to be such a big deal. She took deep, calming breaths all the way from Tansy's truck to the door leading into the courthouse. A quick scan of the directory sent her down the hall and to the left.

Then she was there. Standing in front of the Lewis County Offices for the County Parks and Recreation Director and the County Clerk.

Okay.

She rubbed her hands on her skirt and opened the door. Four green leather chairs sat along the wall to the right. A magazine rack sat in that corner. A water cooler in the opposite. The room was empty—except for Libby. She sat behind the desk, humming along to the music coming from her computer and filing her nails. Rosemary stepped inside, then stopped when she heard Libby talking.

"No, no, she's not pregnant. She's only saying she's pregnant to keep him." Libby snorted then. "I mean, how often does that work?"

Rosemary paused, her dread returning. Who was Libby talking about?

"I know." Libby laughed. "It's too predictable. Some people never learn." She turned, her eyes widening when she saw Rosemary. "I'll have to call you back." And she hit the button on the phone.

They stared at each other for a moment.

Rosemary was trying not to dissolve into a puddle of sweat and anxiety. She had no idea what was going through Libby's head. Only that one minute, the woman's face was completely blank, and the next, Libby was wearing a brilliant smile.

"Rosemary." Libby stood and came around the desk. "You're here. And look at you." She stopped, leaning against her desk and crossing her arms over her chest. "You don't look a thing like the little girl you were in high school. My goodness." That smile was doing nothing to relieve the tension clamping down on Rosemary's intestines.

"Hi, Libby," she managed, her tongue oddly heavy. "How are you?" She drew in a slow, deep breath and resisted the urge to wipe her hands on her skirt again.

"I'm wonderful." Her blue eyes blinked. "Really."

Rosemary glanced at Everett's office.

"Oh, Everett's not here—if that's why you're here." Her smile warmed. "Poor thing. He's running all over the place dealing with this whole paintball nightmare."

Rosemary swallowed. "I can imagine." There was

something familiar about Libby's gaze. Something predatory. *No.* It was only her insecurities playing with her.

"Everett's just the best. I've never known anyone like him. He's just…" Libby leaned against her desk and sighed. "Well, you *know* Everett. Always caring too much and helping other people."

The way Libby said it, caring too much sounded like a character flaw.

"He's so busy trying to fix everything, he's not sleeping well at all…" She broke off, her eyes going wide. "I mean…"

What did she mean? Rosemary waited, the silence growing strained.

"I've never met anyone who does so much for everyone else. He's…amazing. A real inspiration." Her eyes fluttered. "I'm trying not to worry about him but—" She pressed her hand to her chest—resting it over her heart. "That's what you do when you…care about someone, isn't it?" She sighed.

What? Her stomach felt icy cold and hollow. Libby *cared* about Everett?

"Anyway, enough about that. Are you here about the job?" Libby waved her hand, that blue gaze and too-bright smile never wavering. "I'm glad he listened to me and offered you the job. I told him you'd be perfect for it and that you'd want to help him. That's what friends do, isn't it? You two have been friends forever. You are staying, aren't you?"

Rosemary nodded, numb. "For now."

"Of course. Between the two of us, we can take care of him. For now." She winked at her. "With the election coming up, he can use all the friends he can get."

"Oh." Rosemary was having a hard time processing everything. "Why is that?"

Libby's laugh sounded like she looked—pretty and alluring and feminine. "I keep forgetting you've been gone, Rosemary. So much has changed, hasn't it?" She smoothed her golden hair from her shoulder. "Where to start? You wouldn't believe all the plans he has. *So* many. He has big dreams. Just like you've always had. Anyway, it will mean so much to us if you support his mayoral run." She paused. "I mean him, of course." She winked again. "*He* would appreciate it."

Us. Because they were…involved? Everett and Libby? Was that what Libby was implying? It didn't sound right. Or feel right. He was listening to *Libby's* recommendation to hire Rosemary. And Everett was going to run for mayor? Her head was spinning.

The office phone started to ring.

"Oops, give me a sec." Libby went around the desk and pressed a button. "You've reached the County Parks and Recreation Director's office. This is Libby Owens-Baldwin. How can I help you?" She tucked her hair behind her ear, showing the earpiece she wore. "Hey, Everett." Her voice softened. "Were your ears burning? I was just talking about you." There was a pause. "Can do. Okay." Another pause—followed by Libby's husky giggle. "Oh, you. Hush. I'm at work, boss. What do you want for dinner tonight?"

Rosemary had to leave, or there was a very real possibility she'd throw up right here in Libby's office. "I have to go," she whispered.

"Oh. Hold on." She clicked a button. "I'm really glad we're going to work together—for Everett. He deserves only good things. I know you agree." She paused, her expression almost...vulnerable as she murmured, "I'll tell Everett you stopped by, and don't worry, I'll make sure he calls you."

"Oh, of course." She gripped the doorknob.

"Wonderful. Bye, Rosemary." She waved and hit the button on the phone. "Just text me if you want something special. You know you can have *whatever* you want."

Rosemary headed straight for the bathroom and splashed ice-cold water onto her face and the back of her neck. Was Libby implying—in a subtle yet not-so-subtle way—that she and Everett were a couple? That couldn't be right. And yet there was no shaking it. The idea was there. Stuck in her head.

But...was it *true*? Libby had made a career out of getting in her head—just because.

She stared at her reflection, willing her stomach to stop somersaulting and twisting about.

Libby was right, she had been gone awhile, and there had been some big changes. Did that mean Everett had changed? Or Libby? No. Everett was a rock. He had a good head on his shoulders, he always had. She swallowed against the lump in her throat. *If* he was involved with Libby, that meant Libby *had* changed. That was the only thing that made sense.

There was also the chance that Libby did care about Everett, but Everett didn't reciprocate... A preferable and more likely scenario. *That* made sense.

That was probably the case. Probably. So why wasn't she relieved?

EVERETT SCRATCHED AT the stubble lining his jaw. He was tired of being tired and frustrated, but after spending a couple of hours in Rose Prairie, he was both. If Dane hadn't reminded him to stop by the Junior Beekeepers meeting and put in a good word, he'd be on his way home and to bed. As it was, he was walking along the path that led around the high school to the large metal building that housed a lot of the school's agricultural programs.

There was the slightest drop in temperature which was a nice break from the constant triple digits of the summer months. He paused long enough to enjoy the deep red and purple edging the horizon—the lingering clouds thin and feathery. Fall was coming.

There was a surge of laughter from inside the building, pulling Everett along. His time in Rose Prairie had taken longer than he'd anticipated, so he was glad he hadn't missed the entire meeting. When he stepped inside, the chatter and laughter and upbeat energy of the group helped ease some of the tension from his shoulders.

A huge Welcome New Junior Beekeepers banner hung along the far wall of the building—explaining why the parking lot was so full. He'd been so busy, he'd forgotten that this was the first meeting of the year. Tonight was all about getting students, and their parents, excited about the club and what they'd be doing in the year ahead. To say the room was packed was an understatement.

"Everett!" Tansy waved from the table beneath the banner, all smiles.

He smiled and worked his way through the crowd until he reached the table she was standing beside. "This is quite a turnout."

"It's cool to be a beekeeper, didn't you know?" She shrugged, in her element.

"I'm sure all the PR the Bee Girls and Honey Hill Farms has been getting has a little something to do with that." He glanced around the room, astonished at the number of new faces.

"What can I say? Winning that competition has done good in more ways than we could ever have imagined." Tansy was beaming.

Less than six months before, Honey Hill Farms had entered their Blue Ribbon Honey in a big honey competition. Not only had it won them the distribution deal with Wholesome Foods, it had put the all-female beekeeping family in the limelight. They'd been on local and national talk shows, in the newspapers, podcasts, and every other outlet with any sort of following. Tansy and Dane had used all the furor to begin building a very solid online following—streaming their time with the bees, making honey, or gushing about one another and their bees.

"I'm glad you made it." Tansy gave him a long assessing look. "How are you doing, Everett?"

He shrugged. "It's been one of those days." It had been one of those days all week. "I'm fine." He eyed the table covered in food, and his stomach growled.

"As official snack table hostess, go on and help yourself. We've got plenty of snacks. So eat something."

"Don't mind if I do." It was a good thing he'd had such a hearty lunch at his folks' because he hadn't had time to eat since. "You always have this much food?"

"We weren't sure what the turnout would be like, so everyone brought something." She nodded at one towering stack of brownies. "Astrid sent those with Halley.

My sister cracks me up. Half the time she's so nauseous she can barely move, the other half she's trying to win stepmother-of-the-year."

"Brownies are always a hit." He reached for one and took a bite. "Mmm."

"Aunt Camellia's recipe." Tansy grinned. "If it's her recipe, it's delicious."

"That's the truth. Those are dangerous." He reached for a cupcake. "I'll see what kind of dent I can make."

Tansy chuckled. "How did it go with Rosemary?"

He licked a glob of sprinkle-covered frosting off his thumb. "Rosebud? I haven't seen her today." He took a huge bite of cupcake.

Tansy's smile gave way to a frown. "Really?" Her gaze wandered. "I'm confused. She said she was going to see you."

She had? Maybe, hopefully, that meant she was going to accept his job offer? His gaze followed Tansy's to Rosebud. She sat among a large group of teens, nodding and talking with them, making notes on the tablet in front of her. She was entirely focused on whatever they were doing. The sleeves of her green blouse were rolled up, and she'd twisted her thick red hair up and stuck three pencils through the messy bun hanging low on the back of her head. She looked so relaxed and happy. Her smile was quick and…beautiful.

The observation didn't sit well with him, so he shoved the rest of the cupcake in his mouth.

"Thanks for coming." Dane clapped him on the shoulder. "You want to say a word before we officially adjourn and the snack table gets rushed?"

He nodded, his mouth too full of cupcake to answer. He took the water bottle Tansy offered him and chugged half of it as Dane led him to the podium strategically placed beneath the welcome banner.

"Remind them to sign up for projects, will you?" Dane murmured to him before stepping behind the podium. "If I can have your attention?" Dane tapped on the mic, causing the rumble of conversation to die down. "Everett Taggert, the county parks and rec director, is here to say a few words about the program. After that, snacks."

There was a lot of clapping at that.

"I know the applause is for the snacks, so I'll get to it." Everett grinned. "I'm impressed by the turnout." From where he stood, he could see everyone. Familiar faces and not so familiar. "I might be a bit biased when I say this program has become one of the best in the state. It's true. We have educated leaders like Dane Knudson of Texas Viking Honey." There was a smattering of applause. "And the Hill sisters from Honey Hill Farms, who've put our little town on the map." Lots of applause now.

His gaze landed on Rosebud. She had the sweetest smile, proud and enthusiastic. Those green eyes of hers were vibrant beneath the fluorescent lights—downright mesmerizing. *She* was mesmerizing. He took a deep breath, fighting against the pressure in his chest. *No. No. No.* No being mesmerized by Rosebud. Especially not when he was standing in front of a roomful of people.

"And we have the support of the school system and the county." He gripped the podium and forced himself to stop looking at her. "Why?" He cleared his throat. *Why, what?* What was he saying? He waited until his focus cleared.

"Not just because this region relies on honey for a

substantial part of its income—though that's important." He paused while the adults chuckled. "This group goes above and beyond learning about bees and honey. They're devoted to helping the next generation care about the environment, their community, and the world as a whole." He shrugged. "I have every confidence that our Junior Beekeepers will be the ones making big changes in the future. Welcome to the Junior Beekeepers. It's going to be a great year. Now, remember to sign up for projects and then, help yourself to the snacks."

There was a surge toward the snack table—which had Astrid and Nicole running to Tansy to help.

He found himself wandering in the direction of Rosebud's table, where a group of kids were still clustered.

"It doesn't take up a lot of room. Or resources. There's definitely a right way to do this. Let me do some research before we get too excited." Rosebud scanned her list again.

"Too late." Kerrielynn was all smiles. "I can't believe you'd be willing to do this, Rosemary. It's just… This is so cool."

Rosebud sat back, her smile so bright Everett's throat went tight. "That's me. The cool Hill sister." She was giggling then.

"I'm still learning, so I'm lost, but if y'all are excited, I'm excited." Halley was staring at the list, a dubious expression on her face.

"Then get excited." Benji Svoboda nudged her.

"Uncle Van will help sponsor this, I bet." Oren Diaz pointed at the list. "Heck, he'll probably sponsor the whole thing."

"What *are* you working on?" Everett asked, peering over her shoulder to look at her notes.

"Nothing." Rosebud covered the paper. "Yet. Thinking out loud, is all." But when she looked up at him, her expression shifted. "Good... Nice speech. Everett." Her smile wavered. Her gaze fell from his. She was *definitely* less enthusiastic. "I'll go help Tansy with snacks." She stood, shoved her folded-up notes into her pocket, and headed over to her sister—a good portion of the kids she'd been talking to trailing after her.

Dane shot him a questioning look.

Everett shrugged. "I didn't do anything."

"Uh-huh." Dane glanced after Rosemary. "That's why she hightailed it out of here as soon as she saw you?"

That was sort of how it looked, but that wasn't how it was. He glanced after her. Last time he talked to Rosebud, things were good. Weren't they? She seemed fine now. Laughing at something Tansy had said. Maybe he had done something? But what?

He turned back to see Dane, Kerrielynn, Leif, Benji Svoboda, Halley Driver, and Oren Diaz all staring at him.

Great.

"Leif." Kerrielynn nudged him. "Leif heard something that might help with... You know."

Everett didn't know. He frowned.

"Right." Leif nodded, then leaned forward. "I don't know if it has anything to do with the paintball stuff, but I figured I'd tell you."

Which caught his full attention. Considering there were zero leads, he'd take what he could get.

Everett listened as the boy recounted the conversation he'd overhead between one of the Dwyer boys and some unknown participant. Under normal circumstances, he wouldn't think anything of it. But there was nothing normal about what had been happening. And, as much as it pained him to admit it, where there was smoke, the Dwyer boys were often fanning the fire causing it.

"Also…" Kerrielynn held out her phone. "I was watching the Alpine Springs video again, and I saw this." It was a screenshot. "One of them has braces."

Everett narrowed his eyes, enlarging the image. "Well, I'll be. You've got good eyes, Kerrielynn."

"I might have watched it a few times." Kerrielynn glanced at Leif. "Okay, a lot of times. But, see, it paid off."

Maybe. He was pretty sure rounding up every braces-wearing Lewis County resident wasn't feasible. Heck, a third of the teens in this building had braces. Still, it was something. "Can you text that to me?"

She nodded, clicking away on her phone. "The Dwyer boys don't have braces, though." Kerrielynn looked almost apologetic when her gaze met Leif's.

"That's okay. We shouldn't assume anything—about anyone." Everett didn't want this to turn into a thing. Those boys had it hard enough without being accused of this. If Jed ever got wind of it? Those boys would get a whooping whether or not they had a thing to do with it. "I'm asking you to keep this between yourselves. People talk. A lot. We don't want things getting out of hand."

"I won't say a word. Having a grandma like Willadeene has taught me…" Benji grimaced "…that words can hurt, and people can get mean. Even nice people."

"Aw, Benji." Halley hugged him. "You'd never do anything like that."

"He's laying it on thick so you'll hug him." Oren Diaz laughed. "And it worked."

There was a lot about these kids that reminded Everett of himself, Nicole, and the Hill sisters at this age. Or him and Dane. Things had been simpler. The biggest stress back then was turning in homework, making sure the pasture gates were latched behind him, and whether or not he'd get to borrow his dad's truck for the football game that weekend.

"We won't say anything, Everett," Kerrielynn assured him.

"Nope." Halley pretended to lock her lips and throw the key over her shoulder.

"Anyway, it's innocent until proven guilty." Oren shrugged.

Technically, that was true. But the court of public opinion wasn't always too keen on the facts if the story was too juicy to pass up. Since everyone in the county wanted to find out who was responsible, this was probably one of those stories. And now that Rose Prairie had been hit in *two* places, people were going to be more on edge than ever.

"Anything else?" Dane asked Leif.

"Nope." Leif glanced at Kerrielynn, Benji, Halley, then Oren. "Anything?"

"I'm not Miss Sherlock over there." Oren pointed at Kerrielynn.

Benji shrugged. "Nope."

"And there's no new posts." Halley glanced at Kerrielynn.

"Not yet." Kerrielynn was looking at her phone. "It

looks like they post the day after. If something were to happen today, it'd be up tomorrow."

"You're really on this, aren't you?" Everett smiled at the girl. The sheriff and Everett had only recently picked up on that. As long as these yahoos stayed on schedule, there'd be a new post showing the damage done to Rose Prairie.

"That's why we're calling her Miss Sherlock now." Benji chuckled.

"Without the hat." Oren cocked his head to one side. "Or the pipe. He smoked a pipe, didn't he?"

Benji shrugged. "I like the way a pipe smells."

"Yuck." Halley wrinkled up her nose. "No way."

"Anyway." Leif hugged Kerrielynn. "If something comes up, Kerrielynn will probably be the first to know."

"Yeah." Kerrielynn blushed. "It's just… These guys—girls—people are destroying stuff. *And* they're trying to get, like, famous by doing something bad. It…it makes me *so* mad."

Leif smiled at her. "You're cute when you're mad."

Her cheeks went a darker red as she leaned into the hand he pressed against her cheek.

"Ugh," Benji groaned.

"Right? I'm getting food." Oren stood. "Come on." Benji followed him to the snacks.

"Try the brownies." Halley trailed behind them. "They're Aunt Camellia's recipe."

"They're mine." Benji cut around Oren and sprinted for the table.

"Isn't there anything else we can do?" Kerrielynn asked, taking Leif's hand in hers.

Everett shook his head. "With any luck, they'll get

cocky and make mistakes." His hands were tied, and he hated it. He had absolutely no control here—no way to get a handle on it. His frustration returned with a vengeance.

"Okay." Kerrielynn didn't look any happier about it than he was. "We'll keep our ears and eyes open."

Leif lightly tugged at her hand. "We need to check the sign-up sheets before everyone starts leaving."

"Right." She nodded and dragged him along behind her.

Dane sighed, giving him a hard look. "This whole thing sucks."

"Yep." Everett couldn't have said it better himself.

"Anything new?" His voice was low. "You look a little…"

"Tense? Yeah, well, I am." His gaze locked with Dane's. "Rose Prairie got…paintballed last night."

"Damn," Dane hissed, studying him. "You eat yet?"

"A brownie. A cupcake. They were pretty good." He'd planned on grabbing a couple more for his dinner before he headed home.

"Let's go. Lemme just tell Tans real quick." He headed to the snack table.

Everett found himself watching Rosebud. Like it or not, he liked that she was home. He liked seeing her. He smiled—right about the time she looked his way. She held his gaze, but her smile seemed…strained.

What the hell? Something was going on. But what?

"Let's go." Dane grabbed his arm. "Before you pass out."

He was bone-tired, but he'd like to find out what was

going on with Rosebud first. When he looked back, she was nowhere to be found. *Great. Just great.* Another mystery he'd have to figure out.

CHAPTER SIX

HONEY HIGH SCHOOL's cafeteria had changed since Rosemary graduated. Which was a good thing—she didn't have to worry about flashbacks or panic attacks. Her high school years were equal parts academic and intellectual successes and abject humiliation and torment. The mural of the large honey badger—Honey High School's mascot—scowled at her from its place on the wall. Rosemary resisted the urge to scowl back.

She was here because this was the only place big enough to host today's city watch training. After Dane shared what had happened in Rose Prairie, she hoped everyone in Lewis County would be attending the training.

She and her sisters sat in folding chairs around one of the two dozen round tables that had been set up. She had a notebook in her lap for notes, but since the meeting hadn't started, she'd doodled a climbing vine along the edge of the page. Her notebooks from school and university were covered in little birds, bees, flowers, or snippets of home. Now that she was almost done creating *ABC's with Baby Bee* for little Bea, she had more ideas than ever.

She was just finishing a flying bee and a butterfly when Kerrielynn Baldwin stopped beside her chair.

"Hi, Miss Hill—Rosemary." The teen girl waved.

"Morning, Kerrielynn." She put her pen and notebook on the table. "How are you?"

"I… Can I tell you something?" The girl shifted from one foot to the next.

Rosemary wasn't sure what was coming. She wasn't the talker—that was Tansy. And she was nowhere near as empathic as Astrid. But if Kerrielynn wanted to tell her something, she'd listen. "Of course."

"I, you know… I…" She paused and shook her head. "Ohmygosh. I think you're awesome… Well, I want to be just like you. You're so smart and calm, and…you have it all together. You know? You're so young, and you're, like, a doctor and doing all this research and stuff. Really *doing* it." She glanced at Tansy, then Astrid. "I mean, you all are awesome. Of course."

Rosemary was in shock. Awesome? Her? This bright, outgoing, bee-adoring young woman wanted to be like her? It was mind-boggling. And so precious. The only thing Kerrielynn had gotten right was the smart part. She wasn't calm or together—she was freaking out over sitting in her old high school cafeteria. Hardly worthy behavior for anyone's role model. Still, it touched her heart that Kerrielynn felt this way. Very much.

"She is pretty awesome, Kerrielynn. I totally agree." Astrid nodded. "She's the smartest person I know."

"Same," Tansy agreed. "Neither of us graduated from high school at, what, ten?"

Kerrielynn's mouth dropped open. "Really?"

"No." Rosemary laughed. "I was *not* ten."

"Have a seat, Kerrielynn." Astrid nodded at one of the chairs.

Rosemary pulled out the seat beside her.

"Okay." Kerrielynn hung her backpack, with little

bees embroidered all over, on the back of the chair. "My brother Silas is here, too. Is there room?" She nodded at the back of the room where a handful of groups had gathered to chat, get coffee, or refreshments.

"There should be." Rosemary scanned the chairs. Even if Charlie, Leif, and Dane all sat with them, there was room for a few more.

Leif arrived seconds later, a paper plate stacked high with pastries and donuts. "Hey." He sat, pushing the plate toward Kerrielynn. "I brought enough to share."

Kerrielynn eyed the plate and laughed. "With the whole table?"

Leif frowned, glancing from the overflowing plate to each of them. "I guess."

Rosemary grinned and shook her head. "We ate."

"You go ahead, Leif." Tansy nodded. "You're a growing boy, after all."

Leif sighed, scooting his chair close to Kerrielynn's. "I don't think I've stopped being hungry since Camellia left." He sounded so forlorn.

"When we get back from the beekeeper's convention next weekend, she will be home." Tansy sighed. "Thank goodness."

Rosemary wasn't the only one missing her aunt. When she'd been in California, she'd pored over every one of Aunt Camellia's weekly letters and care packages. The woman was a human rainbow—full of praise and support, eager smiles, warm hugs, and a never-ending banquet of lovingly prepared food. Her time away had taught Rosemary how to survive without her aunt's cooking, but nothing ever tasted as good.

"Astrid, your hubby is here." Tansy waved over her shoulder. "And he's looking for you."

"Is he?" Astrid turned.

Charlie Driver's well-crafted mask of indifference dissolved into an adoring smile the moment he saw Astrid. It was one of the dreamiest things Rosemary had ever seen in real life. That was love. It rolled off the man. Warm. And tangible.

The only thing she'd ever felt that passionate about was bees. With the exception of two fellow bee enthusiasts who wound up preferring the bees to her, her dating life was mostly first dates. There'd never been a time when she'd had to worry about hard feelings or broken hearts. She'd been too busy looking for that "big thing" Poppa Tom was so certain she was destined for. The big thing she'd been expected to chase down since she was a little girl.

What is it, Poppa Tom? What am I meant to be doing? Why can't I settle for a littler thing and just...be happy?

And she was happy. At least, she was getting there. She was happier being home. She was happier because she wasn't alone. But as she peered around the table of blissful couples, she realized she did want more. Maybe? After she figured her life out.

Eventually, Silas Baldwin and Nicole took the other seats at the table. While Nicole's brand-new rainbow highlights caught everyone's attention, conversation soon turned to the known details of the latest vandalism in Rose Prairie.

"They targeted the gym and the field house at the high school. Every window was covered in paint. Doors, too," Silas Baldwin said. "And it was the oldest shop on Main Street. The window already had a crack in it, so that plus age is probably why there was such damage."

Dane's brow creased with concern. "Still, they'd have

to shoot from pretty close range to get the whole window to shatter like that."

"And there wasn't any video surveillance?" Charlie frowned.

"I got some installed as soon as we had the town meeting." Nicole shook her head. "I figure it might not deter these paintball idiots, but it might stop Willadeene from getting into the petty cash again."

Silas chuckled. "She's something."

"If by something you mean manipulative, guilt-mongering, gossip-spreading, pot-stirring, or anything along those lines?" Nicole's brows rose, waiting for his answer.

"Well." Silas pulled at the collar of his shirt as he flushed a mild red. "Yes?"

That caused everyone at the table to laugh.

"What is she wearing?" Tansy's eyes went round, her focus on the back of the room.

All heads pivoted in the direction she was looking.

Libby Owens-Baldwin was replenishing the coffee station. How she managed to do anything with such long red nails was a marvel to Rosemary. But Libby didn't seem to have any problems stacking the paper cups or putting more creamer and sweetener packets in their respective baskets.

But Tansy wasn't referring to Libby's nails—she was referring to Libby's barely-there black skirt. It was terrifyingly short. So short, Rosemary held her breath when Libby stretched across the table for more napkins. She wasn't the only one that noticed, either. At least half the room had stopped what they were doing to watch Libby work.

"Are you okay, Silas?" Kerrielynn's tone was hostile. "I can tell her to leave."

"I'm fine, little sis." Silas's voice was calm and gentle. "It's been four months."

Oh, right. There were at least ten years between Kerrielynn and her brother, but it was clear they were devoted siblings. Rosemary glanced at the man that had once been married to Libby. He seemed, on the outside, relatively unscathed. She couldn't help but wonder if he was a little more scarred on the inside.

"You deserve better, Silas." Nicole's smile was gentle. "You're one of the good ones."

"See, I'm not the only one who thinks so." Kerrielynn nudged him. "But I can still tell her to leave. Leif will totally back me up." She glanced at Leif who, with a mouth full of food, nodded.

"Warning, Willadeene has entered the building." Nicole sighed, all sarcasm as she added, "Let the fun begin."

Willadeene *and* Everett. From the looks of it, she was giving him an earful. *Poor Everett.* There was an air of impatience about him, she could feel it. When he paused, his gaze swept the room—and collided with hers. Willadeene was still going at him, so Rosemary mouthed, "Hi," and lifted a thumbs-up in encouragement.

He grinned, the corners of his brown eyes crinkling. As far as smiles went, Everett had one of the best.

Willadeene said something that had him sighing, rolling his eyes, and facing the older woman—but not before Rosemary realized how frazzled he was. There were dark smudges under his eyes and a light stubble along his angled jaw—a jaw that was now clenched tight. Finally, Willadeene stopped ranting and leveled him with a narrow-eyed glare. Everett nodded, but didn't say a word.

Poor Everett.

That was when Libby stepped forward, inserting herself between Willadeene and Everett, and the entire room went silent.

"Miss Owens." Willadeene's head-to-toe inspection was blistering. "It seems you've forgotten your pants."

Rosemary wasn't the only one who gasped.

"Why wear pants when you've got legs like mine?" Libby shrugged. "I'm always a bear when I haven't had my morning coffee. I can make you a cup, if that will help?"

In that moment, Rosemary felt grudging respect for Libby Owens. It took a lot of nerve to stand up to Willadeene Svoboda, even more to send the woman off in a huff—which was exactly what she'd done. As Willadeene brushed past their table, Rosemary caught sight of the fury on the older woman's face. Chances were, Libby would regret publicly ruffling Willadeene's feathers.

The excitement was over, and the low-level hum of conversation resumed.

"Okay, indecent skirt or not, she's sort of a badass right now," Nicole whispered.

Silas's snort suggested otherwise. "She and Everett a thing now?" he asked.

From the way Libby was currently pressing a coffee cup into Everett's hand—and standing ridiculously close—it would be easy to draw that conclusion. That Libby had offhandedly said Everett wasn't sleeping well didn't help, either. Rosemary nibbled on her lower lip.

"No. Everett's got his eyes wide open." Dane was quick to defend his best friend.

She wanted to agree with Dane, but…what if he was wrong? *Not that Everett's personal life is any of my business.* If he was happy, that's what mattered—even if the idea of Libby and Everett together did trigger every one of her internal warning alarms. And make her nauseous. And sad.

At the moment, Everett appeared confused. He glanced at the coffee cup in his hands, then Libby. He said something, set the coffee cup on the table, and took a big step away from Libby. And another. Libby seemed amused, her laugh light and airy as she shook her head and went back to cleaning up the refreshments table.

When Everett turned, his gaze scanned the crowd—a furrow on his brow. Next thing she knew, those brown eyes locked with hers, and he was heading directly toward her.

Seconds later, he was squatting by her chair. "Hey, Rosebud. I was hoping I'd see you."

That's nice. "Hey, yourself." She resisted the urge to smooth his thick, too-long brown hair from his forehead. Up close, his exhaustion was evident. And concerning. "You survived Willadeene. Impressive." She paused, attempting to tease. "Any internal bleeding? Bruises or breaks?"

He chuckled. "I don't think so."

He had a nice face. A handsome face. *Really* handsome. Had he always been so…looked so…like this? How had she not noticed that? She swallowed. "Happy with the turnout?"

"I am." He yawned. "I'd be happier if all this wasn't necessary. And if whoever is doing this would stop."

"I think we all would." She nodded, lowering her voice. "Are you okay? I know you've got a lot on your shoulders. Is there anything I can do?"

He stared at her for a long time—so long she found herself noticing all sorts of new and fascinating things about him. She'd never get long dark eyelashes like his, even with mascara. One of his eyes had a speck of gold in it. Brown and gold and tawny. His eyes were beautiful and warm. That was a good word for Everett. He was warm. And he smelled good. Astonishingly so.

She took a deep breath.

"I wanted to make sure we... Are we okay?" he whispered.

Were they okay? Yes. Was what she was currently feeling okay? She didn't know. But, right now, he was tired and stressed and needed her reassurance. "We are great."

"Good." He took a slow breath, his posture easing.

"Not to interrupt you two, but you want me to find you a chair, Everett?" Dane asked. "Or are you going to sit on the floor?"

There were a few muffled snickers from around the table.

"No." Everett stood. "As much as I'd like to stay at the cool kids table, I told Mayor Contreras I'd sit up front in case I needed to lend a hand."

"You've been doing that a lot, Everett. Good practice for when you're Mayor Taggert." Nicole gave him a saucy grin. "A little birdie came by my shop and told me they heard you're being prepped to run?"

Which was what Libby had told Rosemary. But was it true? It wasn't that Rosemary didn't want Everett to run for mayor—he'd be an amazing mayor—but if that was true, then the rest might be true, too. And she really wanted to know the truth.

Everett ran a hand over his face. "Let me figure out what day it is before I commit to doing something that important, how about?"

Which meant no? Didn't it? Or was that just a dodge? It wasn't an answer at all.

"Boo." Nicole sighed. "I was going to make shirts with my Cricut machine."

"I'll let you know." Everett shook his head. "But if I do run, Rosebud gets to design the shirts." He pointed at her doodles. "She's the artist." He gave her shoulder a brief squeeze and headed to the front of the room.

Rosemary stared after him, oddly conflicted. Everett had always been her friend. He still was. But…he'd always been Everett. Not an incredibly handsome man with beautiful eyes who smelled so incredibly good. Now he was Everett, plus all those things—and she didn't know what to do or think about it.

EVERETT TOOK A deep breath and sat at the mostly empty table reserved for local government. He glanced back at the table where Rosebud was sitting, glad he'd taken the time to set things right between them. Theirs was a lifelong friendship—but he didn't want to take that or her for granted. When her gaze met his, her smile was as warm as ever. Things were fine. They were fine. And that mattered.

When she turned toward Kerrilynn, he pulled out his phone. No alerts. No videos. Nothing had happened last night? On the one hand, these vandals were likely teens. Last night, Friday night, meant football games and bonfires and hanging out with friends. If they'd been paintballing, they'd miss out on the fun. Maybe he'd caught a break, and this damn headache was over as quickly as it had begun.

"You're that bachelor guy from the newspaper, aren't you?" There was a teen boy sitting opposite him—someone Everett didn't recognize.

"Everett Taggert." He nodded.

"Yeah. I thought so. And that's your secretary?" The boy was openly staring at the refreshment table and, likely, Libby.

Libby. That was a whole other headache. "Yes." He felt bad for snapping at her, but she'd caught him off guard. She hadn't needed to stand that close to him or hold on to his hands while she handed over the cup of coffee she'd made him. That sort of thing got people talking—which was the last thing he needed.

"Yeah, well, that makes sense." The boy blew out a low whistle. "I'd stay single. She is *hot.*"

Who the hell did this kid think he was? His sleep-deprived brain came up with a whole slew of inappropriate things to say to put this kid in his place, but he knew better than that. "She's a good secretary." He bit out the words, not bothering to hide his temper. *If this kid is smart, he'll shut up.*

"I bet." The boy's smile was oblivious. "Like it matters. I mean, *look* at her."

Everett stared at the boy. Growing up, this sort of disrespect would have had him shoveling up each and every bit of goat poop on their family's property. It had taken him a while to realize not all parents took such a hard line when it came to how to treat, talk to, and talk about a woman. Namely, not to objectify them or make disparaging remarks, especially in public—like this dumbass kid.

Since he couldn't pack this kid off to his folks' place and hand him a shovel, he'd have to swallow his anger and try talking. "It does matter." He took a steadying breath. "It's not how she looks or dresses that matters—"

"It's what's inside?" The kid glanced at him then. "Come on, man. Really? No one else can hear you, so you can save the whole women-equality crap."

Everett saw red. He didn't have the bandwidth for this.

"Everett." Dennis Hobart chose that moment to sit at the table next to the kid. "I hope this isn't a waste of my Saturday."

Things keep getting better and better. He glanced back at Rosebud's table, seriously regretting his decision to make himself available to Sheriff Myers and Mayor Contreras. They knew just as much as he did.

Dane saw him and waved. Then the whole table waved at him.

Everett grinned.

"Wes," Hobart barked at the boy. "Where's your homework?"

"At home." The boy glared at Dennis Hobart.

"I told you to bring it. Your mother told you to bring it." Dennis ran a hand over his increasingly red face.

"Guess I didn't hear you. Or her." Wes shrugged. "Or I didn't care."

Everett was stunned silent. This kid was Dennis Hobart's son? He wasn't sure who to empathize with, the father or the son. Either way, it wasn't pretty.

Thankfully, Mayor Contreras walked up with his wife, Lisa—ending any further exchanges from the Hobarts. Mayor Alex Jimenez and a city council member joined them, representing Glendale. Willow Creek's mayor, Midge Ludwig, Elginston's Christina Rivas, and Rose Prairie's Joe Kerr filled up the rest of the seats. When Everett tried to offer up his chair to Sheriff Myers, the sheriff said he preferred to stand. Everett was stuck in the middle of it when the ranting started.

"I don't understand why these little sonsabitches haven't been caught yet." The vein running across the middle of Dennis's forehead seemed to swell with every word he said. "Why's the rest of Lewis been left alone? Honey, Glendale, and Willow Creek haven't been targeted by these…chicken-sh—"

Christina Rivas held up her hand. "Language, Dennis, please. I understand you're upset, but let's keep this professional." She shot a pointed look at Wes Hobart—who was still staring at the back of the room.

Midge Ludwig sneered at Dennis—the long-standing feud between the two mayors was no secret. Dennis Hobart was a pill, but Midge Ludwig was almost as grating and outspoken as Willadeene Svoboda. "Christina, remember who you're talking to."

"Fine." Dennis practically spit the word. "Criminals. What's the reason some of us have been vandalized? And you all have not?" He pointed at Mayor Contreras, Mayor Jimenez, and Mayor Ludwig.

"It's nice to hear you're so concerned." Midge rolled her eyes.

"We don't know what's going to happen next, do we, Dennis? I'm sure we all hope Honey and Glendale are left alone." Sheriff Myers shook his head. "But since there's no guarantee, here we all are. We're going to have to stay vigilant. All of us."

"You're not up for reelection any time soon, Myers." Dennis sighed. "I don't need fancy speeches, I need results. *And* a way to pay for the damage those little shi—um, vandals caused to our new park equipment." He turned to Everett then. "Any luck finding funding?"

"I'm thinking he might be too busy fending off all the single ladies that read his article." One of Midge's drawn-on eyebrows rose.

"Not my article." Everett held up his hands.

"It was a good article." Christina's smile was sympathetic.

"There was an article? All I saw was something about you being a bachelor." Joe chuckled.

Everett sat back and took a deep breath. On the one hand, no one was arguing anymore. On the other hand, he hadn't had near enough coffee for this. If he was going to make it through the first hour of training, let alone a whole morning of it, he'd need caffeine. Since Libby was nowhere to be seen, it should be safe.

"If you'll excuse me a sec." He stood and headed to the back of the room, eager for the breathing room. If dealing with that sort of negativity was part of the job, was he seriously considering running for mayor?

"Everett." Jed Dwyer was refilling his coffee cup. His two older sons stood along the back wall—looking about as fed up as Everett was feeling.

"Jed." He took a cup, added a packet of sugar and creamer, then filled it from the stainless steel commercial coffeepot. "How's your morning going?"

"Better than yours." Jed nodded at the table. "Looks like a lot of bitching and whining going on from back here."

Everett's laugh slipped out before he could stop it. "Yeah, well." He sighed. "Everyone's on edge."

"Hmm." Jed sipped his coffee. "The whole damn county is here." His gaze swept the crowd. "Perfect time for troublemakers to cause all sorts of trouble."

"Fair point. We'll have to hope they're not smart enough to figure that out." Everett frowned. "Lucky for us, they seem to wait until it's dark, and this will be long over by then."

"I'm going to hold you to that." Jed finished his coffee and threw his cup away before joining his sons.

Everett refilled his cup, in no hurry to go back to his seat. His gaze swept over the crowd, watching the good people of Lewis County watching Sheriff Myers take his place at the podium.

"Good morning." Sheriff Myers was a big barrel-chested man with a big presence. He was, for the most part, a likable man. "I know each and every one of you would rather be out enjoying your Saturday than sitting in here, am I right?"

There was a murmur of agreement.

"But you being here—well, that means something to our community. The mayors and I were just saying this means we've got each other's backs."

The room was silent as Sheriff Myers delivered an account of what had happened in the neighboring towns and the estimated cost of the damages so far. As expected, there was a fair amount of outrage. But a couple of reactions stood out.

At one point, the Dwyer brothers exchanged a look. The middle brother, Donny, mouthed what looked like *I told you*, but Everett couldn't be sure. Eddie, the youngest, looked nervous. But Clay just scowled at both of his brothers, and the three went back to staring straight ahead. Unfortunately, Jed Dwyer caught Everett watching his boys—and the warning packed into the man's hard-eyed stare was unnerving as hell.

Great.

The other was Wes Hobart. Everett thought the kid had dozed off. The boy had rested his head on the table, but as soon as Sheriff Myers detailed the damage in Rose Prairie, the boy sat up and grinned. It didn't mean the boy had anything to do with the vandalism, but it did mean the kid was on his way to surpassing his father when it came to being a Grade A ass.

He'd almost resigned himself to going back to his chair when his phone started vibrating. He glanced down at the screen. His sister, Jenny.

Sheriff Myers was beginning the slideshow for the training—no one would notice if he stepped out for a minute.

He answered as soon as he was standing in the hall outside the packed cafeteria. "What's up?"

"Well… I know you're super busy, but I'm sorry, I really need help." Her voice was strained and anxious.

"What's going on?" He frowned, peering into the cafeteria.

"Gramma Dot. She sort of… Well, she's stuck in a tree."

Everett ran a hand over his face. "Literally?"

"Yeah…" Jenny sighed, the unmistakable bleating of goats in the background. "And Hoyt, Mom, and Dad went to that goat auction this morning—they're probably still on the road. They won't be back until late."

"I'll be there as quick as I can."

"I'll try to convince her to stay put. But hurry, okay?"

"Yep." He disconnected and sent Dane a quick text explaining there was an emergency at the farm and asked him to inform Mayor Contreras and Sheriff Myers. His patience was gone and being diplomatic wasn't at the top of his list.

He'd almost reached the doors to the parking lot when he heard his name called out. He turned, braced for resistance, to find Rosebud running his way.

She was breathless when she reached him. "I thought you could use an extra hand? Maybe?"

"Thanks, Rosebud."

She nodded, pushing through the heavy metal doors ahead of him without saying a word. That was the thing about Rosebud—she seemed to know what he needed before he did. Like now. Having someone along to keep his mind from worst-casing things would help. And he could tell her just about anything, and she'd never tease or pick at him or ply him with questions. It made being with her easy.

Once they were driving to the farm, she asked, "What's happened?"

"I'm not sure." He shook his head. "Jenny said Gramma Dot's stuck up a tree?" He glanced her way.

She blinked, her green eyes wide. "Right. Well, that happens... I suppose."

He laughed, surprising himself.

She smiled, then laughed, too.

And things felt a little better.

"Everett, I'm worried about you." Her gaze traveled over his face, her own expression grave. "You look tired. Like you're running on fumes."

Is it that obvious? He nodded. "Maybe."

"I... Well, you've always been someone everyone

could count on." She turned in her seat, facing him. "And while it's a good thing to be nice, obviously, people can take advantage of that. Of you. Because you are you." She paused, shrugging. "The thing is, you can be nice and still say no. It might be hard for you at first, but laying down some boundaries might be a good thing. Or you'll wear yourself out."

She was right. And damn, she was pretty. It was a good thing he had to keep his eyes on the road, or he'd likely wind up staring at her. "Are you saying I'm a nice guy?"

"Yes. But that wasn't my point—"

"I know, Rosebud. I'm teasing you." He sighed. "About six months ago, Robbie—Mayor Contreras—had a minor heart attack. He's kept it quiet, not wanting people grabbing on to it and making it into a thing… When he asked me to help out, I couldn't say no. Somehow, what started out as a temporary arrangement seems to have become an expectation." He glanced her way. "He's done. He has no intention of running for office again. In fact, he's trying to convince me to run for mayor."

"Oh wow." She was quiet for a minute. "That's amazing—if you want to run for mayor?"

"I haven't had the time to really think about it. I like the idea of being mayor—and I do love working with people—and the community." At the same time, his life had become all about what needed doing, without any downtime. "But not if it's going to be like this. Relentless." He glanced at her. "And that article didn't help. Kinda hard to be taken seriously when that's hanging over me."

"You've got a lot of stress in your life, Everett." She

sighed, wholly sympathetic. "Maybe you need to come work with the bees."

He looked at her then, confused.

"You used to say it helped clear your mind." She tucked a strand of deep red hair behind her ear.

"Right." He smiled, a twinge of guilt forcing him to admit, "I might not have been entirely truthful about that."

"Oh?" She frowned.

"Growing up in Honey, it's almost a crime not to be a fan of them—bees." He shrugged, turning off the main road. "I'm...well, I'm not. A fan. Bees make me nervous."

"What?" She shook her head. "Why didn't you say something? You helped me so many times."

He milled over how to answer this, driving along the one-way frontage road until he reached the long gravel drive leading to his parents' farm. There was no reason not to be honest with her. Honestly, it was kind of funny. "I only said that because I was so in love with you, Rosebud. Back then, I'd have swum with sharks if it meant I'd get your undivided attention."

She was staring at him, her mouth hanging open.

"But that was a long time ago... I got over you." He forced a chuckle, waiting for her to laugh and wishing he'd kept his mouth shut.

But she didn't laugh or smile—she stared at him.

Yep, big mistake. He flexed his hands and took a deep breath. *Dammit all.*

He turned his attention out the window, scanning the fence line for any sign of his sister or grandmother. The silence seemed to grow and grow until he was gripping the steering wheel with both hands.

"There she is." There was panic in Rosebud's voice.

Because his Gramma Dot was sitting in the lower branches of the large Spanish oak in the pasture closest to the house.

How did she get up there? He stopped, put the truck into Park, and jumped down. Things had gone from bad to worse. Hopefully, he'd get Gramma Dot down safe and sound, and this entire morning wouldn't be a complete disaster.

CHAPTER SEVEN

ROSEMARY COULD HEAR her pulse in her ears. Thumping. Loud and fast and strong.

I was so in love with you.

Everett? Everett had been in love with her? When? How?

Now that her chest had collapsed in on itself, she was having a hard time catching her breath. Not that the sensation was unpleasant. More like the opposite. She was warm and tingly and surprisingly giddy. Until what else he said played through her mind.

I got over you.

If Gramma Dot hadn't started yelling, Rosemary would probably have remained frozen in place. But Gramma Dot was yelling, and Everett was jogging to the tree where the old woman was perched. High. Too high—especially for someone pushing eighty years old. Beneath the tree, Jenny Taggert was white-faced and pacing.

Rosemary was out of the truck and running after Everett.

"Albie." Gramma Dot leaned forward, peering down at Everett. "Albie, is that you?"

"No, Gramma Dot, it's Everett." Everett stopped beneath the tree.

"Albie…" Gramma Dot let go of one of the branches she was holding on to and tipped forward.

"Gramma, hold on to those branches." Jenny gripped the tree trunk and stared up at Gramma Dot. "Hold on."

There was no sign that the old woman heard her granddaughter. "There you are. I've been looking for you, Albie. Where have you been?"

Rosemary's heart hurt then. Albie Taggert was Dot's husband. The two had been inseparable since they'd met in grade school. His death had been hard on Gramma Dot—and Everett. Albie Taggert hadn't just been Everett's granddad, he'd been Everett's hero and idol.

"She's really confused, Everett." Jenny glanced from him to her grandmother. "And she's starting to get tired."

Seeing Gramma Dot so out of sorts tore Rosemary's heart out. Not just for poor Dot, but for Everett and Jenny, too.

"It's going to be okay." Everett nodded. "I'm going to get the ladder."

"I was trying to get you some apples, Albie. You love my apple pie." Gramma Dot glanced up into the branches of the tree. "But this isn't an apple tree." Her forehead creased. "Albie? Albie, where are you going?"

Rosemary saw the muscle working in Everett's jaw and put a hand on his back.

Everett glanced her way, then back at his grandmother. "I'm going to get the ladder. I'll be right back."

"No." Gramma Dot shook her head. "Don't leave me, Albie. Please stay. Just stay."

The last thing they needed was for Gramma Dot to get agitated and fall. "You stay put, Everett. We'll get the ladder." Rosemary grabbed Jenny's hand, and together, they ran to the barn.

"It's inside." Jenny pulled open the door and ran in with Rosemary on her heels. "There."

They tilted the wooden ladder forward, each took an end, and hurried from the barn back to the tree. Everett propped it against the tree, made sure it was steady, and climbed up.

"Rosemary?" Gramma Dot blinked, confused. "What are you doing here?"

"I wanted to come check on you and your baby goats." She smiled up at the old woman. "I hope that's okay."

"Of course it is." But Gramma Dot was looking at Everett, who'd climbed the ladder and was standing in front of her. Her forehead furrowed, then cleared. "Everett. Sweet boy... I'm so sorry." She covered her mouth with one hand and started to sob.

Jenny grabbed Rosemary's hand, quietly crying at her side.

Rosemary gave her hand an encouraging squeeze. "She'll be okay, Jenny."

"What are you apologizing for?" Everett cradled Gramma Dot's cheek. "You saved me from that boring meeting."

Gramma Dot sniffed, then giggled.

"You trying to show your baby goats how to be a goat? Tree climbing?" he asked, taking her hand.

"They know how to climb. It was Clark..." She glanced down at the two baby goats curled together beneath the tree. "I thought he was stuck."

"Ah. This was a rescue mission?" He nodded. "Well, let's show them how it's done, okay?" He stepped down onto the ladder, still holding her hand. "I'm going to go first. You hold on to the top rung, okay?"

"I know how a ladder works." Gramma Dot nodded. "I'll try not to fall on you."

Rosemary squeezed Jenny's hand again, smiling at her. "Sass is always a good sign."

Jenny sniffed, but she was smiling as she nodded.

It was slow going, and though she did her best not to react, Rosemary held her breath as Everett and Gramma Dot made their way down the ladder. Everett kept talking to her, telling her where to step next or where to put her hands—and Gramma Dot argued the whole time.

"I don't know what all the fuss is about," Gramma Dot said as soon as she was standing on the ground, her hands on her hips.

Everett chuckled. "I wanna know how you got up there in the first place." He peered up into the tree.

Rosemary had been wondering the same thing.

"I climbed. I've climbed quite a few trees in my time." Gramma Dot's smile was a mix of defiance and pride. The baby goats were up now, hopping and jumping around her and bleating happily. "Hello, babies. Come on. It's almost time to eat." She headed for the porch, the goats trailing after her, as if nothing out of the ordinary had just happened.

"Well…" Jenny drew in an unsteady breath. "That was…something."

Everett drew his sister in for a hug. "It's all fine now."

Jenny clung to him and nodded. "Thank you."

He pressed a kiss to her temple. "You don't need to thank me, Jen. I'm just glad it turned out okay." He eased his hold, rubbing her upper arms.

"And thank you, too, Rosemary." Jenny hugged her then. "I should probably go in and make sure she doesn't leave the stove on again." She sighed and ran after her grandmother.

"I didn't do anything." Rosemary started walking

to the house, but Everett's hand clasped her arm long enough to stop her.

"You did, Rosebud. You were here for me. And Jenny." Everett's gaze locked with hers. "I think seeing you helped jog her memory. Helped her realize where she was and who was with her." His jaw clenched tight again.

Rosemary couldn't bear it. Everett was hurting something fierce. She wrapped her arms around his waist and hugged him. "I'm so sorry, Everett. That must have been hard. Seeing her confused." Her hold tightened. "And... I know how much you miss Granddad, too."

His arms were strong about her. "I do."

For a minute, they stood—the only sound the distant bleating of sheep. It was okay to simply be quiet with Everett. But now, that didn't feel right. This morning, she'd seen him badgered and dumped on, scowled at and humiliated, and struggle with grief. Grief over the loss of Granddad and of the woman his Gramma Dot once was. It wasn't fair. "What can I do, Everett?" she asked, glancing up at him.

His smile was slow and gentle. "This...works." His hand pressed against the middle of her back.

It was the slightest pressure—but she felt it, in the pit of her stomach. "Okay," she whispered. She was all too content to stay wrapped up in his arms and soak up the warmth in those brown eyes. "You...you give the best hugs."

"I do?" He smoothed the hair from her forehead.

It was getting hard to breathe again. Now that it was just the two of them, she was increasingly aware of Everett. Everything about him. His scent. His touch. His arms heavy around her. And how devastatingly handsome he was. And when his gaze shifted to her mouth, a jolt of anticipation raced down her spine and shook her to her core. *What is happening?*

"Rosebud," he murmured.

She couldn't say a word. She should. But what? Something was *definitely* happening. For her anyway. She was tingly and flushed, a hollow ache centered in the pit of her stomach, and her heart was close to beating its way out of her chest. Most concerning of all was how much she hoped Everett would kiss her.

His voice echoed in her head. *I got over you.*

Right. It was enough to snap her out of it.

She rested her head against his chest and pressed her eyes shut. Any minute, he'd let her go, the world would keep on spinning, and all the Everett-inspired-weirdness putting her insides in knots would vanish.

Instead, one big hand splayed against her back, anchoring her against him.

It was too much. Not just the touching and warmth and how incredible he smelled, but how terrifyingly right it felt to be like this—held in Everett's arms.

My best friend.

She gently but firmly let him go and stepped back.

"Thanks." Everett ran a hand along the back of his neck, his gaze sweeping over her face.

She cleared her throat and managed to say, "Anytime." She could still feel the weight of his hand against her back—still hear the thud of his heart in her ear.

"Guess we should give Jenny some backup." He nodded at the house. "And then I need to figure out how to keep Gramma Dot from getting back up that tree." He glanced at the tree, scratched his chin, then shook his head.

Rosemary was grateful for the distraction. She took

a steadying breath and turned all of her attention on the tree. The tree. Not on Everett or how the breeze lifted his overlong hair and swept it onto his forehead. "I think cutting off those two limbs would take care of it... But even with those limbs, I'm impressed she managed to get all the way up there."

"Well, that's Gramma Dot for you. Expect the unexpected." He glanced her way and smiled. "It helps that she's *real* stubborn." He shrugged. "I think you're right. I'll go get to work and take those off."

"I'll go help Jenny." She tucked her hair behind her ear and headed for the porch stairs, eager to put some space between them. Even though she felt his gaze on her, she didn't slow or look back. Instead, she hurried inside, closed the back door, and leaned against it until she'd caught her breath. *This is bad. This is wrong. This is* Everett.

"That looked pretty intense." Jenny stood at the sink. Over the farm sink was a window. A window that would have provided a clear view of the yard—and the unnervingly intimate exchange between her and Everett.

"Oh." She did some weird flutter thing with her hands, then shoved them into the pockets of her jeans. "No. Just... Well, you know."

Jenny's eyes went round, but there was the ghost of a smile on her lips. "I really don't."

"Where...where's Gramma Dot?" She glanced around the room.

Jenny glanced at the clock on the far wall. "This is naptime. She and the goat kids are piled up in quilts on the couch. They'll snooze for a couple of hours."

"She's probably exhausted." The whistle of the tea kettle made Rosemary jump.

"Are you okay, Rosemary?" Jenny asked, pulling teacups from the cabinet.

"I'm fine." Which might have been believable if her voice hadn't cracked.

Jenny didn't bother hiding her smile. "Tea?"

Rosemary nodded. "Can I help?"

"There are some cookies in the cookie jar. I know Everett likes cookies with his tea." Jenny nodded at the two-tone brown ceramic jar at the end of the counter. "Gramma Dot does, too—if she wakes up early."

Rosemary had spent enough time in the Taggert kitchen to know where everything was. She pulled a plate from one cabinet, stacked it high with store-bought cookies, and carried it to the kitchen table. When Jenny brought the teapot to the table, they sat.

"You know, I've always loved these cookies." Rosemary reached for one of the cream-filled chocolate sandwich cookies.

"Really? I wish my mom baked the way your aunts do." Jenny took a crunchy chocolate chip cookie from the plate. "Gramma Dot will bake now and then—but only when there's someone to supervise." She put her cookie on her saucer and sat back in her chair. "I feel so terrible about today. This is the first time I've been left alone with her, and I go to the bathroom for two minutes, and this happens." She glanced at the kitchen window.

"Jenny, this wasn't anyone's fault." She reached across the table to pat Jenny's hand.

"Still…" Jenny shrugged, staring out the window. "Everett has enough to worry about without racing home to play superhero."

Outside, Everett was sawing away on the lowest limb.

Each motion was packed with force—the grating sound echoing loudly. Even though it made perfect sense for him to have removed his long-sleeved button-down shirt to do physical labor, Rosemary wasn't prepared for the view. The tight white undershirt hugged and shifted with his every move, revealing how fit and strong he was. And he was. The cuffs of his undershirt stretched around his biceps, and with his shirt tucked into his jeans, there was no missing the muscles in his broad back.

Oh goodness.

The tingles were back—stronger now. She pressed her eyes closed, but it didn't help. Instead of blocking Everett out, she could feel his arms around her and see the tender expression on his handsome face when he'd swept her hair aside.

He'd *loved* her—over and over, his words replayed. Learning that had somehow pulled aside the veil she'd always seen him through. Everett had been and always would be wonderful and special to her. Yet everything was different now. What she was feeling was so much... more.

Her chest deflated in on itself again, but her heart kept thundering along. She didn't want to believe it, but...did this mean... Was she... Now that he was over her, could she be falling for him?

I COULDN'T HAVE planned it better myself. Dot smiled down at the two goat kids sleeping on her lap, giving them each a pat. She was bone-tired but too worked up to sleep. She was pleased as punch over the day's events. Well, not getting confused or getting stuck in that tree—but the rest of it.

Everett and Rosemary. Just as she suspected.

She's still his seahorse, Albie.

And it tickled her pink.

But she was struggling with another question. How had she ended up in that tree? She couldn't remember that part. One minute, she'd been with Jenny in the kitchen. The next, she was in that tree, picking apples to make an apple pie for Albie. And then Albie was there…

Her heart twisted sharply.

No. Not Albie. Everett.

She pressed a hand to her head, willing the fog to lift so she could make sense of what had happened. Try as she might, she couldn't piece together the rest of it.

"It doesn't matter so much, does it?" she whispered, stroking one baby goat, then the next. "Thanks to Everett, Rosemary, and Jenny, I didn't break a hip or fall out of that tree. Everett and Rosemary are meant to be together. And neither of you have tried to eat your onesies. I'd say, overall, it was a good day."

For now, what else could she want? She smiled, rested her head on the back of the sofa, and closed her eyes.

EVERETT CHANNELED ALL of his pent-up frustration and anger into the grating back-and-forth pull of the saw. The paintball. The mayors and politicking. The stupid newspaper headline. Gossip. Willadeene. Libby. Gramma Dot. His exhaustion. *And* Rosebud.

He pulled with all his might, cleaving the lower branch from the trunk of the tree. It fell to the ground. One down. He wiped the sweat from his forehead with the back of his arm.

Normally, he didn't let things get to him. What the hell was wrong with him?

Instead of answering that, he started in on the second branch. He needed time. A whole lot of it. If he didn't keep a firm grip on his emotions, he'd make a fool of himself all over again. Not just with Rosebud, but everything.

Rosebud.

She'd offered him comfort—that was all. Instead, he'd gotten lost in the way she fit against him. He couldn't shake how good it had felt to have her arms around him and her head resting against his chest. He shouldn't have buried his nose in the soft hair atop her head or breathed her in. But there was no stopping him. She still smelled sweet, like strawberries. She still used the same shampoo. Maybe that's what kicked him in the chest and flooded him with memories and feelings he thought he'd put behind him. One minute he was fine, the next his restraint was gone and he was holding on to her for dear life.

Stupid. So damn stupid.

It would be easy to fall for Rosebud again—as easy as breathing.

Not gonna happen.

He was a grown-ass man, not some naïve kid. Loving her now was no different than loving her then. Her whole life, she'd had one goal: to make Poppa Tom and her family proud, to go off into the world to do big important things. That hadn't changed. Rosebud was still all about the bees. She was here now, but she wouldn't stay. She'd said as much.

He kept on sawing, the thickness of the wood resisting his efforts and jarring his shoulder.

Fine. He could use a fight. He kept on working, harder and faster until he was winded and dripping sweat. Over and over. Finally, the limb began to sag, giving him the push to finish strong. When the branch hit the ground, he propped his arm against the tree trunk and rested his forehead against it.

"Everett?" It was Dane.

Dammit. Everett turned, stunned to see Dane's truck parked along the fence. "When did you get here?"

"Long enough to see you attacking that tree." Dane nodded at the scarred trunk. "Everything all right?"

He nodded. *No. Not a damn thing.*

"What the hell happened?" Dane hopped over the fence and made his way to the tree.

"Gramma Dot." He pointed at the tree. "Maybe she's spending so much time with the goats, she thought she was one of them?" His attempt to laugh failed.

Dane gave the tree a once-over, then turned to him. His gaze was long and assessing.

Everett didn't say a word. Dane could give him looks, ask him questions, or tease him mercilessly, but he wasn't going to respond. If he did, he didn't know what he'd wind up unloading onto his friend. And that wasn't right.

"Did the meeting already wrap up?" Everett asked, tugging his undershirt free from the waist of his pants and wiping off his face.

"Hell no. Are you kidding? Lunch break." Dane sighed. "You weren't answering your phone, so I figured we'd head out and make sure everything was okay."

"We?" He glanced at Dane's empty truck.

"Tansy is inside. We brought burgers." Dane eyed the tree limbs on the ground. "Need help with those?"

He'd been hoping that chopping the branches into logs for the woodstove would wear out the rest of his irritation. That would have to wait—for now. "I can manage. I'm just gonna drag them behind the barn."

Dane gave him another questioning look, but Everett avoided making eye contact this time. "Okay."

"Thanks, though." He nodded and picked up the saw. "I'll be in soon."

"Yep." Dane headed for the house.

It didn't take long for Everett to put the wood behind the barn and the saw away. If he lingered too long, he'd have to come up with an excuse. He was too tired for that. Hell, he was too tired to deal with people. But there was no getting out of it. First, he'd sit through lunch and do his damnedest not to be aware of every little adorable thing about Rosebud, then he'd have to put on his poker face and return to the city watch training to get questioned and berated by the good people of Lewis County. He'd rather take down the whole damn tree than do either.

He took a deep breath and stared up at the blue sky overhead.

Rosebud was right about something else. He did miss Granddad. If Everett needed an ear, Granddad listened. If Everett needed advice, Granddad had it. He missed the man's unfailing can-do attitude, his ability to put a positive spin on even the most dire of situations, and his contagious full-body laugh. If Granddad was here right now, what would he tell Everett? Hell, he'd be happy just to hear his laugh.

He trudged back across the yard to the house, physically drained. Unfortunately, he couldn't say the same for his emotions. Not that it mattered. He had people counting on him. Period. That was all he could focus on. He opened the back door and stepped inside, all eyes on him.

Jenny. Tansy. Dane. Gramma Dot. And Rosebud— no, Rosebud was the only one not looking at him.

"Everett Michael Taggert." Gramma Dot stared at him in shock. "Land sakes, what happened to you? You look like you lost a battle, boy."

Everett chuckled. "The tree did put up a fight."

"Well you'd best go wash up before you sit down at your mother's table." Gramma Dot clicked her tongue.

"Yes, ma'am." He walked toward her, his arms wide. "You don't want a big hug first?"

That got the entire kitchen laughing. Good. Laughter would do him some good.

"Everett," Gramma Dot squeaked, edging away from him. "You behave."

"That's no fun." But he dropped his arms. "Don't eat all my fries." He hurried from the kitchen and down the hall into his old room. He'd been out of the house for years, but he still kept clean clothes there—in case he spent a day helping out here on the farm.

Which he hadn't done all that much of recently. One more thing to add to his to-do list.

He took a hot shower, willing the heat to ease the knots of tension from his muscles. One thing Granddad had told him over and over was to break a problem down into manageable pieces. Normally, he was good at that. Bit by bit, figuring things out until the whole was no longer problematic. He'd just let too many things get too big.

It's up to me to prioritize what's worth my time and energy.

He ran a comb through his hair, dressed, and returned to the kitchen.

"Fries are gone." Dane held out an empty bag.

"They're not." Rosemary held out a different bag. "There's plenty. And extra ketchup."

Because she knew he liked extra ketchup on his fries. Why did she remember that? *No, dammit, it doesn't matter.*

"Oh, come on, Rosemary. Just trying to have a little fun here." Dane sighed and sat back in his chair.

"Rosemary's looking out for you, Everett." Gramma Dot patted Rosemary's hand. "As always."

Leave it to Gramma Dot to make things real awkward, real fast.

He sat, determined not to get in his head about Rosebud. Not anymore anyway. "So catch me up on the training." He pulled the burger from the brown paper bag, unwrapped it, and took a big bite.

Tansy and Dane exchanged a look.

He swallowed. "What?" He didn't miss the way Tansy elbowed Dane in the ribs.

"Nothing." Tansy smiled. "The training's going really well so far."

Dane nodded, his lips pinched and his eyes tight.

"Lots of questions. People interacting." Tansy glanced at Rosemary.

"Great." He picked up a fry. "What else? And don't tell me there's nothing else, because you two are about as subtle as a flying brick."

Tansy glared at Dane—who shrugged. "What? I didn't do anything."

"Eat something, Everett." Jenny pushed his burger forward.

He took a bite of his burger. "Go on," he mumbled around the bite.

"Willadeene." Dane shrugged. "Being Willadeene."

Everett nodded and swallowed. "And?" He took another bite.

"Well, first there was the thing with Libby." Tansy shifted in her chair. "Then you left, and Rosemary followed you out. Then that whole most eligible bachelor thing came up." She paused. "Did you date Daisy Granger? The reporter who wrote the article?"

"Dates. As in two." He frowned. "But that was a while back. Nothing serious." He risked a glance at Rosebud. "Why?"

Rosemary tossed the French fry she'd been nibbling onto the table.

"Is that what that old hag is saying?" Jenny sat back. "That Everett got the good press because they dated?"

"Seriously?" He set his food down and ran his fingers through his hair. "That article was good press? I'd hate to get bad press."

Dane chuckled.

"That Willadeene Svoboda needs a swift kick in the butt." Gramma Dot shook her head. "She's always been a bully. Always. I remember when she was younger, she had her cap set for your father."

Everett turned. "She did?" This was news to him.

"Yes, sir. She couldn't stand how smitten he was with Violet. She was madder than a wet hen when they started going steady." Gramma Dot's eyes narrowed. "She grew up spoiled, don't you know. Got everything she ever wanted—until her daddy up and died. After that, things weren't so easy. I don't think she's ever come to terms with not getting whatever she wanted."

Everett had never thought about why Willadeene was the way Willadeene was. He didn't spend much time thinking about the woman at all, except doing his best to avoid her. "There's nothing I can do to stop Willadeene from being Willadeene. No need to get upset over it."

Dane glanced at him, trying not to grin. "So that article hasn't given you so much female attention that it's given you a big head and distracted you from doing your job?"

Everett laughed. "Right." He shook his head and kept on laughing.

"I told you." Dane nudged Tansy back. "He's not upset."

"I'm glad." But Tansy looked relieved.

"I don't understand why she's taking aim at you. You're trying to help everyone." Rosemary crossed her arms over her chest, clearly upset. "What can she possibly gain by spreading negative rumors about you?"

"Entertainment?" Everett shrugged. "Don't let her get you worked up, Rosebud. She's not worth your time." He picked up his burger again. "She's upset because she wants me, or someone, to find out who's responsible for this whole paintball mess. As much as I'd like to be the one to figure that out, the county parks and recreation director has no jurisdiction in any of this. None. Zip. For some reason, I'm just the guy everyone calls."

"Because everyone knows you're the reliable one." There was a V between Rosebud's brows and starch to her voice as she added, "They take you for granted—that you'll fix it."

And she was upset. *Well, hell.* Everett covered his grin by taking another bite of burger.

"Like you always do." Jenny nodded.

"And there's all the mayor talk," Tansy pointed out.

"Fine. Y'all have convinced me. I'll stop being so reliable." He tried to tease, wanting to lighten the mood. "And I'm not doing anything for anyone anymore."

"Right. You're not wired that way, Everett." But at least Rosebud was smiling now. "If someone asked you for help, you'd help. Even when you're exhausted—like now. And we all know it."

One minute she was defending him. The next she was worrying over him. Everett took a big bite of his burger so he didn't have to answer.

It was Gramma Dot's snore that broke the silence.

"Naptime," Jenny whispered. "She was almost asleep when Dane brought in those burgers. She loves a good burger."

Gramma Dot was out cold. Her head nodding back and her mouth hanging open.

"I could go for a nap." Dane patted his stomach. "That was a filling lunch."

"Tough." Tansy started picking up the trash. "We have to go back into town. You want to ride with us, Rose?"

"Sure." She helped Tansy finish cleaning up their lunch mess, glancing his way as she said, "And you can do whatever you need to before heading back."

"No. I need to go, too." Everett devoured the rest of his burger in three bites, then stood. "You going to be okay?" he asked Jenny, nodding at their sleeping grandmother.

"The tree isn't an issue anymore." She patted his arm. "Something tells me today's adventure has worn her out. Besides, you have to go, so hold your head high and don't give Willadeene the upper hand."

"Willadeene Svoboda is the last of my concerns." He gave her a quick hug. "But I appreciate you wanting to stand up for me."

By the time he reached his truck, Dane, Tansy, and Rosebud were already pulling out of the driveway.

It was probably for the best. He could use the drive to sort through all the crap he was struggling with and decide which was his to hold on to. Did he want to be mayor? Was it his responsibility to be point man on the county's vandalism issue? And what the hell was he doing about Rosebud?

Nothing. He was doing nothing. Starting now, he'd make sure to keep all his Rosemary-centered thoughts and feelings firmly in the friend zone. Because that's what she was. His friend. Hoping for anything else would only end in heartbreak when she left. His. Not hers.

CHAPTER EIGHT

ROSEMARY'S EYES POPPED open before the sun was up. But really, she hadn't slept much. Yesterday had… Well, yesterday had been a revelation. Everett's disconcerting and heartbreaking confession. The overwhelming want and awareness being held in his arms had caused. And the fact that every second of the rest of the day she'd been distracted because of *him*.

From the ghost of his touch on her back to the way he'd looked at her mouth when she'd thought—hoped—he was going to kiss her to how completely unfazed and professional he'd remained for the rest of the city watch training. He'd been fine while her mind had been all over the place.

She tiptoed around the house, made herself a cup of coffee, and enjoyed it on the porch. There was something about watching the world come alive. The long fingers of sunlight reaching up along the horizon to spread and blur into a canvas of cornflower blue and drifting fluffy white clouds. The crickets' nighttime serenade replaced by a variety of birdsong. She smiled as she sipped her coffee, appreciating the gusto with which the birds greeted this new day.

That's how I'm going to embrace the morning. Happy and upbeat and full of hope. Honestly, in the week since she'd been home, so much good had happened. Had it only been a week? She counted back through the days. Okay, nine days, but still.

She'd written an entire children's book and delighted as each illustration came to life on the page. Her first meeting with the Junior Beekeepers club had inspired her to look into adding queen-rearing here on the farm, and Everett had offered her a job. Not so shabby for nine days. She took another sip of her coffee.

And just like that, she was caught up in Everett again. Not only what he'd said—which was still mind-boggling— but all the new and fascinating and unsettling things she'd begun to notice about her longtime friend. Like how… manly he was. Sweet, always, but most definitely manlier than she'd thought of him anyway.

Not that him being unbelievably handsome suddenly changed their friendship. It didn't. Nothing could. But the whole wanting him to kiss her and, possibly, con- sider her more than a friend certainly did.

Everett had been a fixture in her life since she and her sisters had moved to Honey Hill Farms years ago. He'd become her best friend the day he'd found her cry- ing behind his barn. The aunts had thought it would be good for the girls to make new friends and brought them to the Taggerts' for lunch. While Tansy and Astrid ran off with Jenny, she'd been missing her father and gone to find a quiet place alone.

She'd been crying so she hadn't realized Everett was sitting beside her until the baby goat in his arms bleated— scaring her half to death.

"This is Samson," Everett had said, his too-big cow- boy hat sitting low on his ears. "I'm bottle-feeding him. You want to help?"

She'd sniffed, eyeing the black-and-white baby resting his chin on the boy's arm. "Will he bite?"

Everett shook his head. Even then, there'd been something soothing about his warm brown eyes. "Did you know a goat has a four-chambered stomach? They can also tell when you're happy or sad. Oh, and watch this." He put Samson on the ground. Seconds later, Samson was jumping and hopping. His front half didn't always line up with his back half, making his movements awkward and silly enough to have Rosemary laughing.

That was the start of it. Since then, Everett had always been able to make her laugh. He'd been a constant. Supportive and funny and there whenever she wanted or needed him. And in all that time, she'd never once picked up on or wanted anything other than his unwavering friendship.

Until now. *When it's too late.*

It wasn't too late to help him. He'd offered her a job because he needed help. If taking this job took some of the stress off his big broad shoulders, she was happy to do it. If she were being completely honest with herself, she didn't mind the idea of spending more time with Everett.

Maybe she was being ridiculous. She'd have to deal with Libby. *That won't be fun.* And if Libby was telling the truth about being involved with Everett, she might be setting herself up for a whole lot of hurt.

But if Libby wasn't being entirely truthful, then who knew… Maybe it wasn't too late. Maybe there was a chance for them. She swallowed. Her and Everett?

"You look serious," Shelby whispered, carrying her own cup of coffee as she sat in one of the overstuffed wicker chairs along the wide wooden porch that circled the entire house. "Am I intruding?"

"Please." She welcomed the intrusion. "Just waking up with the sun."

"It's my favorite way to start the day." Shelby tucked her legs up and under her, her puffy eyes peering out over the softly pink sky. "When Bea sleeps in, I get a little me time."

"Me time is important." Rosemary glanced at her cousin. She looked so much like Aunt Mags there was no denying who her mother was. "I don't feel like we've had a lot of time to get to know one another."

Shelby looked at her, smiling. "I've got the inside scoop on you—from Mags and Camellia and your sisters. Basically, you're a genius who's going to save the world someday. Or do something of equal importance."

"That's a lot of pressure." Rosemary winced. "I was just sitting here thinking about how nice it was to be home—no world-saving included."

"I'm sure they'd be just as happy with that." Shelby grinned. "But it's nice to know how much they believe in you."

"It is. It's just... I don't want to disappoint them, either." Yes, they were happy she was here now—they'd missed her. But in the long run, would they be saddened if she stayed—content to live the life of a beekeeper on her family farm? *Would that make me happy?*

"First, I don't think that's possible." Shelby's look was considering. "Second, and more important, this is your life, Rosemary. You're the only one that really knows what's best for you."

Rosemary nodded, heartened by Shelby's advice. "Now, tell me something about you."

"Like what?" Shelby stifled a yawn. "I've lived a rather uneventful life."

"You have your own graphic design business. You tracked down your birth mother. And you're raising your daughter on your own." She paused. "May I ask what happened to Bea's father?"

Shelby stared into her coffee. "I don't know. One minute, we're in love, and I know he's the one. The next, I'm telling him we're going to have a baby, and poof, he's gone. Disappeared without a trace." She blinked, her smile teasing as she said, "The ultimate ghosting."

"Oh. Oh, I'm sorry, Shelby." She'd no idea. And now… Her heart hurt for her cousin.

"Me, too." Shelby shrugged. "His loss. He has no idea what a treasure Bea is. And he never will." She smiled at her. "It was hard in the beginning, but I got over it. Bea helped with that. And thanks to my dad, I was never alone. He's always been my number one fan."

"It's clear he adores you." Rosemary had very few memories of her parents, but those she had were like a warm bear hug. They might be gone, but their love was always with her.

The steady chant of "Ma ma ma" on the baby monitor cut their conversation short, and Shelby went in to get Bea up. Rosemary headed upstairs to get dressed, deciding now was a good time to clear her head and inventory the honey house.

A text from Astrid pinged her phone.

Need to check Hive 47 or 46 in Fairy-Tale Village. Queen trouble.

Only Astrid would send this sort of text before eight

on a Sunday morning. Still, if Astrid had a feeling—there was a reason. She typed back, Heading out now, and hit Send.

There was a knock on the wall between her bedroom and Tansy's, followed by a muffled, "Hold on. I need five minutes."

Ten minutes later, Tansy and Rosemary found Astrid waiting for them at the Fairy-Tale Village bee yard.

"Good morning." Astrid singsonged the greeting, looking fresh and awake and beautiful as ever.

"Ugh. Not yet, it's not." Tansy yawned. "It is Sunday, you know? I bet your husband is going to wake up and wonder where his wife is."

"Charlie got up with me. He doesn't sleep much—and not at all without me." Astrid's smile was dreamy. "He and the girls are going to make cinnamon rolls and bring them over to the house."

"That's very sweet." Rosemary parked their wagon full of supplies under a nearby cedar tree. She dug out the worse-for-wear smoker and opened the cannister. After she was satisfied with the burlap packing, she lit the fabric on fire and closed the lid, giving the bellows a few good pumps to feed the small flame.

"Are the bees talking to you in your dreams now?" Tansy reached up to straighten her ponytail.

Rosemary took the lid off the hive box and gave the bellows pump on the smoker several solid squeezes, puffing clean white smoke into the box. The bees retreated farther inside.

"I forgot to say anything yesterday." Astrid shrugged. "Pregnancy brain, I guess. Yesterday was just…weird."

"It was." Rosemary nodded. More than weird. For now, she'd set all that aside and focus. Bees first.

She pulled the J hook hive tool from her back pocket and took a deep breath, letting the buzz and hum calm her. All around her, bees flew about their business. One bee hovered close, then perched on the edge of her J tool. It explored the surface—oblivious as she held the tool up for a closer inspection. With the sun shining down, the little bee's vibrant gold coloration and translucent wings were nothing short of a work of art. Growing up the way she had, it was no wonder that beekeeping was second nature to her. Like breathing. Or painting. It was an extension of who she was—fundamental to who she was—while losing none of its magic. It was her duty to take care of these beautiful winged ladies so they could take care of Rosemary and her family. A seamless partnership.

Everett doesn't like bees.

She slid the J tool between two frames in the hive and gently separated them. Working with care, she scanned each frame in the hive box—front to back, top to bottom. "I don't see a queen."

Astrid's smile was victorious.

"Yeah, yeah, the bees told you." Tansy glanced at Rosemary. "Are you sure?"

"Queen cups." Rosemary pointed at two knobby structures. "No queen cells, though."

The difference between a queen cup and a queen cell was substantial. A queen cup looked like a tiny upside-down teacup while a queen cell resembled a protruding inch-long peanut. A queen cup was empty and didn't necessarily mean a thing. A queen cell meant a new queen was inside and soon to be hatched.

While the queen was, for the most part, the ruler of the hive, it fell to the worker bees to make sure the queen was still fit to rule. If the worker bees felt the queen was getting too old, not laying enough eggs, or slacking off in her other duties, the worker bees would replace her. For the worker bees, the health of the hive was their top priority.

"Not yet." Astrid peered into the hive box. "Is Dane getting a new queen?"

"He will tomorrow." Tansy tugged a weed free from beneath the hive stand.

"Have you thought about queen-rearing here, on the farm?" Rosemary slid the last frame back into place.

"Not really." Tansy shrugged, then gave her a long look. "Why?"

Rosemary put the lid back on the hive box. "I was thinking about it. I know Astrid's been keeping up with the bee log—tracking traits for each apiary and colony." She glanced at Astrid, who nodded. "Knowing which will produce the best queens is the hardest part. I mean, there's no point in pursuing queen-rearing if we would have to settle on less-than premium genetics. We'd regret that in the long run." She brushed her hands off. "The rest is easy—mostly supplies. It'll be an investment in the beginning, but it would pay itself off. After a while, we could look into selling queens, too. I mean, you and Dane are looking into ways to continue to diversify income streams, Tansy. Why not this?"

Astrid and Tansy were both watching her, smiling broadly.

"What?" She crossed her arms over her chest. "Why are you two looking…like that?" She pointed at them.

"You keep saying *we*." Tansy pointed at her.

"And you're excited." Astrid hugged herself.

Rosemary grinned. "When I mentioned it to Kerrielynn and some of the other Junior Beekeepers, they got excited. Which got me excited." She picked up the smoker. "It's been a while since I had that sort of enthusiasm—without all the pressure."

"Oh, you'll get plenty of enthusiasm from them. Even when it's triple digits and they're in a full bee suit, they're enthusiastic. Really, those kids are awesome." Tansy glanced around the bee yard. "Any other bees requesting our attention before we head back to the house, Astrid?"

Rosemary and Tansy exchanged a quick grin as Astrid stepped into the middle of the bee yard and paused—listening. Neither one of them could explain their sister's uncanny connection with the bees, but neither one of them doubted it.

"I think we're good. No. Wait." Astrid grinned. "The bees are happy you're staying, Rose."

"They told you that?" Tansy rolled her eyes. "Now you're just making stuff up."

"How do you know they didn't?" Astrid asked, her hands on her hips.

Rosemary started laughing. "Who knew you could get so feisty? That's normally Tansy."

"Hey." Tansy's brows rose, then she shrugged and nodded. "Okay, fine. That's true."

The three of them were almost back to the house when Rosemary asked, "Did you know Everett had a crush on me?"

Astrid's eyes were round as saucers, and Tansy giggled.

"You *knew*? Of course, you knew." Rosemary blew at the hair falling into her face, stunned that she'd been so clueless. How could she have been so close to Everett and not known? "Why… How… You never said anything." Why hadn't they said anything? "I feel…"

"What do you feel?" Astrid asked.

"I don't know." Rosemary shrugged. "Bad. Clueless. Sad."

"That's a lot." Tansy tucked her arm through hers. "Would it have made a difference if you'd known?"

"No." She shook her head. "I had blinders on—single-mindedly pursuing my dreams. Back then, I wouldn't have seen Everett as…as an option." And now that option was gone.

Astrid hooked her arm with Rosemary's free arm. "Do you want Everett to be an…option?"

Maybe. Yes. She shook her head, her throat going tight. "Everett is…"

Why had it taken her so long to *see* him? Not just as her Everett but as Everett, the man. The kind, distractingly handsome, hardworking, funny, bighearted man who'd be an amazing partner—the forever kind. She swallowed but her throat only got tighter. *Everett.*

"I think…so," she whispered.

It was the truth. And it was terrifying.

As ALWAYS, the Hill family kitchen was buzzing with activity. Roman Dunholm might be Shelby's adoptive father but, as a relative stranger to Everett, it was odd for the man to be in the Hill kitchen making piles of bacon. Not that anyone else seemed bothered by it. Shelby had scrambled eggs going, Magnolia was stacking fresh-baked biscuits on a plate, and Leif was setting the table. But even with all the commotion, he noticed three were missing… Most notably, Rosebud.

Not that he'd come here looking for her. He hadn't. At least, that's what he was telling himself.

"Blah daw gi." Bea's voice was full of enthusiasm.

"Okay." He nodded, not sure what to make of her gibberish. Somehow, Everett had wound up holding Bea. The sweet-tempered baby girl had never met a stranger. Every time he visited, she acted like he was a long-lost friend she was delighted to be reunited with. "You're going to have your momma's hair, you know that?"

"Ma ma ma da." Bea grinned and patted his chest. "Ya?"

"Uh-huh, sure." He glanced at Shelby for translation.

"Sometimes it makes sense." Shelby shrugged. "Sometimes not so much."

Everett chuckled. "That's fine. You tell me all about it, Bea. I just didn't want to miss anything important."

"Gee na wasi ga." Bea nodded, chattering on, pointing at the dogs or Lord Byron, the parrot, and nodding some more. Her little face was just as animated, from broad smiles to eyebrows rising in question.

"Whatever story she's telling, she's got a lot to say." Dane poured himself a cup of coffee. "Want some?"

Everett shook his head. "My hands are kinda full at the moment." He smiled at Bea.

Bea clasped her hands together and beamed back at him.

Cutest tiny human ever.

"I can take her," Roman and Magnolia spoke at the same time.

The two gave each other a long look—then smiled.

"I don't mind." Everett stepped back. "We're having a deep and meaningful conversation, aren't we, Bea?"

Bea nodded. "Gi ma hi."

The back door opened, and Tansy walked in. "Good morning. Looks like the gang's all here." She glanced around the kitchen, her eyes widening when she saw him. "Everett. Were your ears burning? Is that what brings you by this morning?"

"I brought him." Dane leaned against the counter. "I figured he could use some friendly faces after yesterday."

That was true. But now Everett was more than a little curious to know what had been said about him—and by whom.

"Not that he needs a reason to stop by." Magnolia reached for her teacup. "I take it yesterday was challenging?"

He really didn't want to dwell on yesterday. "Challenging is about right." But he was feeling a little better today. He had a plan. He'd laid it all out there, chosen what mattered to *him*, and was going to keep his eye on the prize.

Astrid walked through the back door, took one look at the bacon Roman was frying, and covered her mouth. She backed outside again—turning an alarming shade of green. "I think I'll sit on the porch."

He couldn't see Rosebud, but he heard her say, "Go sit, Astrid. I'll get you some water. Crackers?"

"No. No. Don't worry about me. I just need…fresh air." Astrid groaned, moving out of view.

"Poor thing." Magnolia shook her head.

"We're not having kids for a long time." Tansy leaned against Dane and looked up at him. "Just wanted to give you a heads-up on that."

"Fine by me." Dane's arms slid around her waist and

pulled her against him. "I'm not ready to share you yet anyway."

"Gag." Leif waved his hands. "Seriously. No one wants to hear that stuff this early."

Roman laughed, turning the bacon over.

Rosebud came in—not acknowledging anyone as she headed straight for the cabinet, pulled out a glass, and turned on the faucet. She tucked her hair behind her ear, her expression concerned. Worried about her sister, no doubt. Even when she was worried, he couldn't help but notice how pretty she was. It'd be nice if he'd stop noticing.

"Tay." Bea pointed at Tansy. "Tay and D and Ma and Ro Ro."

"Ro Ro is here. Morning, Bea. How are you?" Rosebud finished filling a glass with water and turned, a sweet smile on her face. "Oh. Hi. Everett."

"Morning, Ro Ro." He grinned, loving Rosebud's laugh. There was a rosy glow to her cheeks. He liked it.

"Ro Ro, yeah." Bea smiled at him in approval.

"Back up. To yesterday? You said it was challenging?" Shelby asked.

Everett hadn't realized he was still watching Rosebud until Dane nudged him in the ribs, making Everett jump and give Bea a squeeze. "Sorry, Bea. That was Dane's fault." He apologized to the toddler, then glared at Dane. "I'm holding a baby, man."

Bea imitated Everett's glare to perfection.

"Okay, okay." Dane held up his hands. "I'm sorry. I'm sorry, okay, Bea? And I'm sorry Everett is a clueless jack—"

Tansy covered Dane's mouth with hers. It didn't take a second for Dane to melt into her kiss.

"Ugh. That's one way to shut him up." Leif slouched into one of the kitchen chairs.

Dane had done him a favor. Admiring or staring at Rosemary wasn't in line with the whole friend-zone-only decision he'd made yesterday. A decision he was going to stick to, dammit, no matter what. Besides, Shelby had asked him a question—a question he still hadn't answered.

"From what I heard, lots of folk felt more in control by the time the day was over. I think it helped to learn that most of the paint used in paintballs is washable. A little peroxide, some soap, a whole lot of patience. It's a pain, but for the most part, the paint will come off." Everett ran a hand along the back of his neck. "Sheriff Myers had state troopers and game wardens on hand to help out so it wasn't just him up there, a talking head."

"Hold on a second." Rosebud took the glass of water to the back door. "I don't want to miss anything, but I want to take this to Astrid." She hurried out the back door.

"The training was great." With a sigh, Tansy slipped out of Dane's hold. "It looks like there were plenty of people signing up to take shifts, too. We did."

Dane nodded.

Everett could only hope this whole city watch thing would be warning enough to put an end to the paint-ballers' reign of terror. "So far, so good."

Rosebud came back. "Okay, I'm back." Her gaze darted his way.

He smiled. *Dammit.*

"It wasn't the training. It was other stuff—typical stuff mostly." Dane shrugged, taking the cup of coffee Tansy poured for him. "Thank you." He winked at her.

"Dennis Hobart acting like Everett was supposed to come up with funding to fix the damages. Man, does he need an attitude adjustment."

"So does his son, Wes. Guy's a...tool." Leif frowned. "He almost got into a fight with Clay Dwyer over something. Then he tried hitting on Kerrielynn. And Grace. And Halley. And he was all kinds of rude about Libby."

Everett didn't know anything about all that, but he wasn't surprised.

"He sounds like a charming boy." Magnolia's disdain was almost comical.

Dane chuckled and went on, "And once Hobart was done making noise, Willadeene couldn't wait to join in, too."

"That woman." Magnolia's voice was brittle. "She's not happy until everyone else is miserable."

Roman finished putting all the bacon onto a platter. "Remind me to avoid her."

"Don't worry. As long as you're with Aunt Mags, you're safe." Rosemary smiled at her aunt. "Even Willadeene knows better than to cross verbal swords with Magnolia Hill." But when she glanced back at Everett, her brow furrowed deeply. "What did she want from you, Everett?"

It wasn't so much what she wanted done as what she wanted known—whether she was reminding one and all that, since they had no way of knowing where or what the bastards would do next, this whole training was a sham to benefit his career, or her not-so-subtle implication that he'd accomplished as much as he had in his position because he'd been *involved* with the right women to advance his career. Either way, Willadeene Svoboda had made sure everyone in the cafeteria heard her *ob-*

servations. While he'd like to think most folk would laugh off her accusations, there'd been a fair amount of looks, whispers, and uncertainty directed his way.

"To hear herself talk." Everett made a silly face at Bea. Willadeene might be a pain in his rear, but he could handle it. "You tell Rosebud there's nothing to worry about, Bea."

"Ro Ro no wee?" Bea waited, her hands waving back and forth.

"Right. No worries." Everett grinned at Bea, then Rosebud—who was smiling again. And what a smile.

"Come here, little Bea." Shelby held her hands out. "Breakfast yums are ready."

"Yum-yums." Bea leaned out, reaching for her mother. "Yum."

"Yums for everyone." Magnolia waved everyone to the table. "Charlie and the girls should be here any minute."

"Should we set up outside on the porch?" Everett asked, glancing at Rosebud.

"For Astrid? You're a genius." Rosebud smiled up at him.

Dammit all. He shouldn't like that she looked so pleased with him. This was going to be a hell of a lot harder than he thought.

"Excellent idea." Magnolia crossed the kitchen, opened one of the cabinets lining the wall, and pointed at the top shelf. "There are trays up there."

Tansy located some folding tables, Shelby and Roman set them up, and everyone else helped move the food, plates, and utensils onto the wide porch that wrapped around the Hill family home. They were just getting settled when Charlie, Nova, and Halley came walking across the yard.

"Are we having a picnic?" Nova was skipping. "I like picnics."

"Yes." Astrid held her arms open for her stepdaughter. "A porch picnic."

"We brought bunches of cimmanon rolls." Nova ran up the porch stairs and climbed into Astrid's lap. "Since you and the baby like cimmanon."

"The baby likes cinnamon?" Everett glanced at Astrid. He knew Astrid was able to commune with the bees, but this was news to him.

"Nova means Astrid hasn't thrown up anything that's cinnamon," Halley explained. "Since she's throwing up everything else, Nova thinks the baby must like cinnamon."

"Deductive reasoning." Charlie ruffled his youngest daughter's hair. "It makes sense."

Nova beamed up at her father, then leaned forward to speak to Astrid's still-flat stomach. "Hi, baby, it's me. Your big sister Nova. Hope you're having a good morning in there." She patted Astrid's stomach.

He hadn't realized Rosebud was beside him until she said, "Nova's very excited about being a big sister."

"I can see that." Everett was impressed. Charlie and Astrid hadn't been married all that long, but it was clear the four of them were already a strong family unit. Nova was a character—full of energy—and she clearly adored Astrid. Halley might be a teen, but she didn't shy away from giving Astrid a hug or helping unpack the cinnamon rolls onto a platter.

Charlie, quiet as ever, stood beside Astrid's chair. He brushed hair from Astrid's shoulder, letting a strand run between his thumb and fingertips. It was an oddly intimate gesture from such a reserved man.

"He does that," Rosebud whispered, leaning closer to him. "Little things. Touches and smiles and stuff. There's something extra romantic about the way he is with my sister."

Everett understood what she meant. Charlie Driver cherished his wife openly—the way a husband should. He'd grown up seeing his father treat his mother the same, Granddad with Gramma Dot, too. He used to wince and groan whenever either couple would kiss or hug or give each other compliments. Now, he appreciated they'd given him a road map for what to do— someday.

"You're saying that's not romantic?" Everett nodded at Dane and Tansy.

Tansy was currently sitting in Dane's lap, her arms around his neck, while Dane was looking at Tansy's mouth with very definite intentions.

He turned, curious to see Rosebud's take on the couple.

She looked at the couple long enough for her cheeks to turn red. "They're... Well... There's no denying they're in love with each other." She paused then, looking up at him.

What did that look mean? She was looking for something... Hard.

"I'm so hungry." Nova held up one finger. "I only ate one cimmanon roll."

"Only one?" Astrid shook her head. "You must be starving. Let's eat."

With a group this size, sitting down to a meal together was quite a production. And Everett enjoyed every minute of it. It reminded him of being young. Growing up as one of five kids, there'd always been this sort of chaos. He, Hoyt, and Jenny were still in Honey—but they were all too busy to get together very often. And now, with Gramma Dot's bouts of forgetfulness and temper, meals didn't always end well. Not that it could be helped, of course.

The first order of business was for the kids to share their first week of school. It was a big year all around. Nova was in kindergarten, Halley was a high school freshman, and Leif was a senior. While they each had their own stories to share, the overall consensus was good. Nova, especially, couldn't wait for tomorrow.

"Being excited for a Monday." Everett grinned at the little girl. "That's a first. You must like school."

Nova nodded. "I do. I have friends, and my teacher is nice, and we get to play games at PE, and my lunch box and backpack have stars that glow in the dark."

"That would make me excited about school, too." Rosebud paused. "Do you think they make lunch boxes and backpacks with glow-in-the-dark bees?"

Nova shrugged.

"Lots of kids are talking about the paintball thing." Halley's forehead creased. "Benji is really worried about it. He says his mom is stressed out over where they'd get the money to fix stuff if their beauty shop gets paint-balled."

"A lot of people are worried about that." Dane glanced his way. "And expecting Everett to help out."

"That's what insurance is for." Magnolia shot him a look. "*Not* our county parks and recreation director."

"Agreed." Rosebud nodded.

"That's assuming you have good insurance." But Everett understood the frustration. Some insurance companies made filing a claim an ordeal, and even if it was approved, getting that claim paid could take time. It was one more thing on top of an already highly stressful situation.

"Are things okay with Jed?" Tansy murmured.

"What happened with Jed?" Rosebud paused, a bite of cinnamon roll halfway to her mouth.

Tansy shrugged. "Dane said they had some sort of run-in after we left."

Everett shot a look at Dane. He got that he shared stuff with Tansy but why this? "That might have been partly my fault." If he hadn't turned a suspicious eye on the Dwyer boys, Jed wouldn't have gone at him that way. Once the meeting had adjourned, Jed had made sure Everett knew how displeased he was by the rumors that his boys were involved with the vandalism. He also warned Everett to be careful of what he said and did when it came to his boys. If Everett made it hard on his boys, Jed would make sure it was doubly so for Everett. "But everything will be fine."

"Astrid, can you bring the baby up to school for show-and-tell?" Nova asked. "Show them where the baby is growing in your tummy."

That caused a ripple of laughter from everyone at the table.

Everett chuckled, too, reaching for his cup of coffee—when Rosebud's hand rested on his forearm. He didn't like seeing the concern on her face. And yet, he liked knowing she cared about him. A lot. Maybe too much. "It's all good, Rosebud," he whispered. He took a deep breath, unable to ignore the sudden pressure in his chest at the way she smiled up at him.

"I've been thinking." She took a deep breath, her voice so low he had to lean closer to hear her. "If the offer still stands, I'd like to accept the job."

This was good news. But he was panicking. Working with Rosebud on an almost daily basis shouldn't test his friend-zone plan. At all. So why was he already worrying about it?

"Unless you've found someone else?" She nibbled on her lower lip as she studied his face.

Don't even think about her lips. Or stare at her mouth. Breathe and say something. "No...the position is open." He might not be looking at her mouth, but it was taking a lot of effort not to. "I don't want you to feel pressured. Or do this because you're worried about me." As much as he needed help, was this wise?

"I'd be lying if I said I wasn't worried about you, Everett. I do want to help." Her smile was tentative. "But I think, maybe, this could be a fun job. Even if it is temporary. Chances are you'll find someone who is better with people than I am." She shrugged. "Until then, I think I could be good at it—even being as people-phobic as I am."

He chuckled. "People-phobic?" She might think she wasn't good with people, but he didn't know a single person that didn't like her. "Is that a term?"

"I don't know. If it's not, it should be." She blew a strand of hair from her face. "What do you think? Do you still want me?"

Well, damn. That was the problem. He did want her. "Yes." For the job, too.

"I was hoping you'd say that." She lit up, tapping her spoon against her glass of orange juice until all eyes turned her way. "I have an announcement." She looked so damn happy. "Until Everett can find a permanent re-placement, I'm taking Lorna's old job—with Everett."

Astrid clapped, Tansy cheered, and the whole table erupted into congratulations and excitement.

It was a good thing. He *did* need the help. Rosebud was reliable and smart and would move heaven and earth to be the best at whatever she did. That was just who she was.

He didn't miss that she'd said it was temporary but… well, there was a chance she'd fall so in love with the job that she'd have no reason to leave. And if she stayed? Well, that changed things. Or did it?

He ran a hand along the back of his neck, feeling a fool. It hadn't even been one day into this new, stream-lined, hyperfocused plan of his, and he was already failing. Epically.

DOT TAGGERT SAT shelling peas at the kitchen table. She listened as her granddaughter, Jenny, carried on about the fella she was seeing. Until the boy put a ring on Jenny's finger, Dot wasn't too keen on getting attached to the young man. Besides, he hadn't even bothered to come by the place and meet Leland. It might be an old-fashioned notion, but Dot felt strongly about a young man showing enough respect to meet a girl's father—especially if he was interested in serious courting.

Not that anyone asked me.

"Is Everett coming for dinner?" Leland asked, peer-ing over the top of his newspaper at Violet. "It'd be nice to have us all around the table."

"Why don't you give him a call? If you asked him, I bet he'd come." Violet's smile was sweet.

Dot was mighty pleased with the way her Leland and

Violet talked to one another. She liked to think she and Albie had set a good example, but there was no way of knowing. All that mattered was her son was happy, her grandchildren had been brought up to be good hard-working people, and they were a loyal and supportive family. That was enough to make any mother proud. And she was.

"All right, I'll do that." Leland set aside his paper and took the phone Jenny handed him.

Thankfully, Leland hadn't turned in the old landline phone for one of those fancy calculator-size phones all the young people were carrying around in their pockets. They made an awful racket—and never stopped. If Everett tossed his singing phone, she suspected it'd make his life less complicated.

"Son," Leland said into the phone. "Where are you?" There was a long pause. "Ah, well, that explains the noise. Sounds like a good reason to celebrate." He chuckled. "Your ma and I were hoping you'd make it to dinner?" He nodded. "Good. That's good. I love you, too." He stood and returned the phone to its cradle. "He'll be here."

"What and where is he celebrating?" Jenny asked the question before Dot could.

Her son's smile was delighted. "He's with the Hills. It seems Rosemary's agreed to take Lorna's job." He hooked his thumbs into his belt loops and rocked up onto his heels.

Dot couldn't help but grin. A look at Violet, then Jenny assured her they were all feeling the same thing. "That is good news."

"Now, it's a job." Leland nodded. "It's not a marriage

proposal, so let's not get too excited." But he was still grinning.

Dot didn't say a word. She was too busy coming up with a plan. If Rosemary was taking Lorna's job, then she'd be in charge of the senior gardening club. And even though Dot didn't like gardening all that much, she knew what had to be done. If her memory served, the next meeting was coming up soon. She'd be there. And she'd make certain Everett was the one to chauffeur her there and back.

The more time the two of them spent together, the more likely it was the two of them would figure out what she already knew—those two were meant to be together.

CHAPTER NINE

IT HAD BEEN a busy Monday morning. After Rosemary had done a varroa-mite check on all the hives in Alice's Wonderland bee yard, she and Astrid had added the information to their bee ledger and compared numbers for the last few months. By then, Tansy showed up with the new queen for the queenless hive. After confirming the hive was still queenless, Rosemary put the cage-like queen clip in the hive and watched as the small wooden-and-mesh box was surrounded by the hive's bees. It'd take a few days for the bees to chew through the sugar stopper holding the new queen inside the small cage. By then, the hive would have become accustomed to the queen's scent and welcomed her home.

"We'll go back on Thursday to check on them," Tansy said once they reached the house, holding the kitchen door open.

Rosemary stepped into the kitchen. "Unless you hear something before then, Astrid. A distress call—that sort of thing."

"I'll keep my ears open." Astrid nodded.

"This is amazing, Rosemary." Shelby looked up from the thick sketch pages covered in Rosemary's illustrations and lettering: the completed draft of *ABC's with Baby Bee*. "And you painted all these?"

Rosemary nodded, relieved to see Shelby's reaction.

She'd been nervous since she'd left the book on the table for Shelby before heading out that morning. "I did."

Bea clapped her hands and reached for her. "Ro Ro."

Rosemary scooped her up. "Yes, little Bea." She leaned forward and gave Bea a bunny-nose rub—earning a gleeful giggle from the toddler. She sat, holding Bea on her lap.

"This is…amazing. I already said that, didn't I? And how you made the ABC's bee-focused." Shelby laughed. "I had no idea you were so talented. I mean…wow."

"That's our Rose." Astrid sat across from her.

"Astrid, would you like some peppermint tea?" Aunt Mags asked. "It's supposed to soothe upset stomachs."

"Yes, please." Astrid smiled at her aunt, then turned to Shelby. "Rosemary's an artist. She was always getting in trouble in school for her art."

"She did." Tansy reached for a slice of honey spice bread. "I'd forgotten about that. Because she'd doodle on all her homework."

"Not trouble so much as…a talking-to." Aunt Mags handed out napkins. "I think it was frustrating for her teachers. Here she was, this little thing, creating works of art along the edges of her schoolwork, getting her work done in a third of the time of the rest of the class, *and* making high-enough grades to test out of several grade levels."

"She's also a genius." Astrid said this to Roman.

Roman stood, feeding oyster crackers to Lord Byron. "So I hear."

"So I hear. So I hear." Lord Byron bobbed on his perch.

"Don't talk with your mouth full," Aunt Mags muttered to the parrot. "You might choke, and wouldn't Camellia be sad to come home and find you stuffed and mounted on your perch?"

Lord Byron squawked loudly at Magnolia.

"He knows what you're saying." Roman chuckled at Aunt Mags's dismissive snort.

"If he did, he'd be scared of me enough to stop stealing my jewelry or leaving birdie droppings in my shoes." Aunt Mags scowled at the bird.

Roman snorted with laughter before saying, "You could publish that book, Rosemary. It's a lovely story, and the pictures are rich and vivid."

"Thank you." Rosemary was touched by his kind words. "But honestly, it was meant for the Hill babies. Little Bea." She glanced at Astrid. "And the baby-on-the-way."

"Nova has started calling the baby Nuc." Astrid laughed.

"She's so clever." Tansy laughed, too.

"Before long, she'll be just as in love with the bees as she is with the stars." Rosemary took the plate of honey spice cake from Aunt Mags and put it on the table close to Astrid. "It has cinnamon in it."

Astrid eyed the plate, then took a slice. "I want her to love bees, certainly, but I hope the stars will always be special to Nova and Halley—it connects them to their mom."

Rosemary looked at Astrid, then Tansy. She appreciated how much the two of them had done to help her hold on to the memories she had of their parents. From going through photo albums, sharing stories, or watching one of the few VHS tapes of holidays or special events. Astrid would make sure her stepdaughters knew and loved their mother. "They're lucky to have you." She winked at Astrid. "So is little Nuc."

"Nuc, eh?" Aunt Mags shook her head.

"What's a nuc? Is this a bee thing?" Roman fed the last cracker to Lord Byron and sat in a nearby chair. "Pretend I don't know a thing about beekeeping."

"Dad, you don't know anything about beekeeping," Shelby whispered loudly.

"Shh, they don't know that." He pretend-whispered back, grinning. "So what's a nuc?"

That had everyone laughing.

"Nuc is short for nucleus colony." Rosemary helped Bea stand on her lap. "It's a small bee colony or hive. It's also slang for the hive box you can buy with a queen and some brood already inside."

"Okay." But the confusion on the man's face only increased.

Shelby was flipping through the thick cotton pages again. "I have a friend that could scan this and turn it into a board book." She glanced at her daughter, happily bouncing on Rosemary's lap. "That way, I wouldn't be scared to read it to her. This is too beautiful and fragile to be handled by excitable toddler hands."

"She has a point." Aunt Mags sipped her tea.

Astrid and Tansy nodded.

"Then Nuc and Bea would have their own copies," Roman pointed out.

"That would be terrific." Rosemary made a funny face at Bea. "Wouldn't it, Bea? Your Momma is so smart. Your grampa is, too."

"Even if I am sadly incompetent when it comes to bees." Roman took a slice of cake. "This is delicious, Mags. I've already sneaked two pieces."

"It's an easy enough recipe. My culinary skills are limited compared to my sister." Mags peered at the man over the rim of her teacup.

"Aunt Mags, everyone's culinary skills are limited next to Aunt Camellia." Tansy pointed at the plate. "That is fabulous. Period."

"Agreed." Astrid devoured her piece in a few bites, then sat back, her eyes fixed longingly on the plate. "But I'd better take a minute before I eat some more."

"Solid plan." Shelby nodded. "Make sure Nuc is a fan."

"Mamama." Bea reached for Shelby. "Ro Ro Mamama."

"You got it." Rosemary stood and handed Bea to Shelby. "I have to go get ready for work anyway. How weird is that?" She shrugged. "I'm meeting Lorna and Everett over at city hall to go over the job. Lorna has a notebook or something."

"Are you excited?" Tansy propped herself on the table.

"Nervous?" Astrid's gaze bounced between her and the plate of cake.

"Yes. To both." Rosemary took a deep breath.

"It's Everett." Aunt Mags smiled at her. "You can do no wrong in that boy's eyes."

Am I the only one that didn't know Everett had feelings for me?

While that once might have been true, he'd said that was no longer the case. *I got over you* left no room for misunderstanding.

"If Lorna's job notebook is anything like her Junior Beekeepers binder, everything will be laid out—and I mean everything." Tansy shrugged. "Oh wait, I guess I should officially hand it over to you now." But her sister sounded disappointed.

"I'd *really* appreciate it if you and Dane kept doing what you're doing. At least until I get a handle on all my duties." Rosemary waited, hoping she'd read her sister's reaction correctly.

"Oh good. Yeah, Dane and I really love working with those kids." Tansy laughed. "Of course we'll keep working with the Junior Beekeepers—so you can't have the binder."

That caused another round of laughter.

A half hour later, Rosemary was sitting in one of the meeting rooms used for the city council. If it wasn't for the tall windows, the room would have been too dark and confining. As it was, the curtains were drawn wide, and the warm fall sun flooded the wood-paneled room.

"I think it's all here…" Lorna sat beside her, the largest binder Rosemary had ever seen open between them. While they pored over the pages, Lorna kept gently rocking the infant car seat where baby Fiona slept. "I double-checked everything. I want this to be as easy a transition as possible."

Fiona squeaked, drawing both Lorna and Rosemary's attention.

"She's the tiniest human I have ever seen." Rosemary studied the sleeping infant. "She's so pretty, Lorna. Like a perfect baby doll."

"She's sweet, too," Lorna gushed proudly. "Bud and I are lucky, that's for sure." When it was clear the baby wasn't stirring, Lorna tapped the binder. "Any questions?"

Rosemary was in awe—and slightly overwhelmed. Tansy hadn't been kidding about Lorna's organizational skills. The binder was color coded and tabbed for every holiday, event, festival, or farmers market in the county. "Not at the moment. I mean, Lorna, this is about as thorough a road map as I've ever seen. You're amazing."

"Nobody knows this but…" Lorna lowered her voice and leaned closer. "I replaced Nell Ogden, Corliss's sister—remember her? She still works over at the high school and she still has that tall white hair—and she's still one of Willadeene's cronies. Anyway, she left after twenty-five-years. As you see, she was very particular about everything. I've just kept it up."

"Your secret is safe with me." Rosemary smiled.

She slid a second leather-bound binder to her. "This binder holds all the county contacts. Names, addresses, emails, phone numbers, and their preferred form of communication—they're all up-to-date." She went over every detail, piece by piece. "Of course, there's a digital copy of all this, too. But I don't like sitting hunched over a computer."

"You've made it so easy." With this information, the job was pretty turnkey.

"Knock, knock." Libby poked her head in. "Would either of you ladies like a cup of coffee?"

"No, thank you." Lorna's tone was icy.

"I'm fine, thank you." Rosemary managed a smile.

"Okay. Everett told me to make sure you two were taken care of." She flashed her glossy red smile. "He was so sorry he couldn't be here, but you know, he had to go to Willow Creek. Apparently, there's paint all over the bronze statue of the town's founder and the big willow tree it's under." She sighed. "Oh well, I'll let you get back to it." And she pulled the door closed behind her.

"I can't stomach that woman." Lorna glared at the

door. "Bud is best friends with Silas Baldwin. The hell she put Silas through? It was unconscionable."

Rosemary didn't know what to say to that.

"I'm trying not to be mad at Everett for hiring her. It's not like there were a lot of alternatives." She shrugged. "He said it was just Libby and someone who wasn't qualified."

Don't ask. Don't ask. But the words came out anyway. "You don't think, maybe, she and Everett…" She couldn't finish the question.

"No, no. Oh, Rosemary. No." She was adamant. "Nothing's happened yet, but before too long, she will be throwing herself at Everett. Especially now that he's been in the paper and all. Leopards never change their spots, Rosemary. She loves attention. I only hope he doesn't get sucked in by those baby blues or that body she likes to show off in all her skintight clothing." Her head shake was vehement. "I feel bad lumping a poor leopard in with the likes of her."

The door opened again, and they jumped apart, but it was Everett who stepped inside. Unfortunately, seeing him sent a thrill along Rosemary's spine and left her grinning like a fool.

He took one look at the two of them and asked, "Do I want to know what the two of you are talking about?"

"Training." Lorna pointed at the binder.

Rosemary nodded, but she felt the heat in her cheeks. He'd know she was lying.

"Uh-huh." He smiled and peered down at Fiona. "How's the angel? Sweet as ever?"

In answer, baby Fiona wriggled—a soft cry emerging.

"Way to go, Everett." But Lorna was smiling. "It's okay, Fi." She scooped up the baby.

"You know you can give her to me." Everett held his hands out, gently taking the baby from Lorna and cradling her against his chest. "All she wants is some time with her Uncle Everett."

It wasn't surprising that Everett was gentle, of course, but Rosemary was transfixed all the same. Watching this big strong man hold this tiny precious bundle with such tenderness had her heart tripping over itself and her stomach achy and warm.

"I'm sure that's what she wanted." Lorna rolled her eyes, but she was smiling.

"I know it was." Everett grinned down at the baby. "You tell your momma how it is, Fi." He carried the baby around the table and sat facing them. Once he had Fiona settled comfortably against his chest, he looked up at Rosemary. "How's it going? Are you all ready for the Bar-Bee-Q and Beverages Fest? It's weekend after next."

Rosemary was still processing how incredibly handsome he looked with a baby in his arms. It took her a minute to realize both he and Lorna were looking at her expectantly. "What?" She froze, his words finally sinking in. "Oh, well…"

"Everett Taggert. Stop being mean." Lorna giggled. "Don't fret, Rosemary. We're ready to go. Sign-ups are done. Everyone's paid. And the map has already been sent out." She flipped through the binder and pointed. "All here. It'll be easy. Everyone who's coming this year has participated before. And anyway, Everett has promised he will be on hand to help you out."

Everett sat back in his chair, gently patting baby Fiona on the back, a crooked grin on his face. "I'm not worried. Rosebud and I will be just fine."

Everett might not be worried, but she definitely was. That crooked grin knocked the air from her lungs and erased any and all doubt she'd had about how she felt for this gorgeous, kindhearted man. Falling for Everett was no longer a hypothetical.

It was real.

It had happened.

She was in love with her best friend. Wholly. Unconditionally.

And even though it hurt, terribly, to know he no longer returned the sentiment, she'd do her best to give him the help he needed—without letting her heart get in the way.

IT WAS MONDAY. In every sense of the word. He'd barely stepped foot inside his office when he'd gotten the call from Mayor Ludwig in Willow Creek. It'd been stupid to hope this whole paintball thing was over, but after an uneventful weekend, he'd hoped anyway.

Willow Creek was the worst so far. From the looks of it, the perpetrators had stood in one spot and unloaded a barrage of paintballs on the bronze statue of the town founder, Lyman Adams, and the massive old willow tree behind it. The paint was so thick, no bronze was visible. He was no expert, but he was pretty sure safely cleaning the bronze was going to be no easy feat. Mayor Ludwig and the city council had all been on hand—understandably sad and angry.

He'd been pissed off and out of sorts the whole drive home. Hell, he'd probably still be upset. But Libby had told him Rosebud was here, and for reasons he wasn't going to dig into, his temper steadied some.

Now he was holding sweet little Fiona, sitting across

from Rosebud, and things were starting to look up. But, man, he did wish he could read Rosebud's thoughts. She was wearing the strangest expression. Surprised, sort of. Resigned? Disappointed? There was a whole bunch going on inside that beautiful head of hers.

Fiona wriggled and squirmed against him, grunted once, then let out a big burp.

Everett laughed. "Dainty little thing, isn't she?"

"Her daddy would be proud." Lorna laughed. "She'll settle down now, you'll see."

"One burp, and all's right with the world?" Everett sighed. "Wouldn't that be nice."

"Libby mentioned Willow Creek." Rosebud's brow furrowed. "Was it bad?"

"Folk aren't happy." He kept patting Fiona's back. "I'm hoping they'll post again soon, and maybe there'll be something useful."

"All this social media stuff." Lorna closed the binders, stacked them together, and slid them to Rosemary. "The kids seem to think it's a fast way to get famous—no matter what they do."

"It's amazing the power it can wield." Rosemary's gaze flitted from his face to baby Fi. "Dane and Tansy seem to have it figured out. They've started getting stuff from companies and fans to test in their videos or live feeds. Sort of like a sponsorship." Rosebud tucked a long strand of her dark red hair behind her ear. "It's really helped with online sales, too. I can't see these @paint.ballers hoping for the same results."

"Who knows, maybe they're hoping to get endorsed by a paintball company." Everett chuckled.

"Can you imagine?" Rosebud's green, green eyes went round. "That would be horrible."

"Knock, knock." Libby opened the door. "There's a delivery for you, Everett." She paused. "Oh, look at you with that baby? Isn't that a picture? How sweet is that?" She fluttered her eyes—it was a newer habit he'd noticed.

Everett stood, continuing to pat little Fiona's back. "What sort of delivery?"

"Oh, you should come and see." Libby waved him forward. "It's a...surprise."

He wasn't in the mood for any more surprises. "Good or bad?" He frowned at the odd smile on the woman's face.

"I guess that's up to you." She shrugged and left the room.

"Great." He bent to hand Fiona back to her mother.

"Let Rosemary hold her for a while." Lorna nodded at Rosebud. "I have one more thing I need to show her, and then we're done for the day."

"Rosebud?" He knelt, carefully shifting Fiona into Rosebud's arms. "She's a tiny thing, isn't she?"

The reverence on her face was a kick to the chest. She was guileless—truly enraptured by the baby in her arms. And that look, that honest-to-goodness awestruck reaction, took his breath away.

"She's so precious." It was the softest whisper. "So... small. Her fingers. Her nose." Her gaze bounced his way. "Isn't she perfect?"

His throat felt tight, but he managed to say, "Yep." He took a deep, unsteady breath and wished they could stay this way a moment longer.

"Boss—" Libby stopped short inside the door.

He stood and forced his attention to...anything other than Rosebud. Lorna was watching them with wide, curious eyes. So Libby was the safe choice. "I'm coming."

Libby didn't look happy. In fact, the way she was looking at Rosebud was downright…hostile. "I'm so sorry to interrupt." Her tone was clipped.

Since Rosebud hadn't done anything to earn that look, something else must be going on. But what? If it had anything to do with the damn @paint.ballers, he was going to lose it. "Is everything okay?" he asked.

"Yes." Libby's expression shifted, her smile timid. "I just need a few minutes of your time, is all."

Everett frowned, a sense of dread building. "Okay." He gave Lorna a thumbs-up. "You keep up the good work. I'll check in later, Rosebud."

Libby didn't say a word until they'd entered the lobby of the Parks and Recreation office. When she opened the door, she stepped aside so he could go first.

"What the hell?" He paused inside the door, eyeing six large flower arrangements. Had he missed something? Was it Libby's birthday? "Are those for you?"

"No." Libby laughed. "They're for you." She closed the door. "Everett, you've got a fan club." She held out one of the cards. "The delivery driver said some of these came in over the weekend, but since we were closed, they had to wait to deliver them all today."

Everett read the card. "To Lewis County's Most Eligible Bachelor, I'm the woman you've been waiting for." He handed her back the card, confused.

"Want to read the others?" She had three more in her hand. "One of them even included their phone number."

"I don't understand." What was happening?

"This." She waved him toward her computer. There he was—that damn article—on the computer. "Someone shared the article online—then a whole bunch of other people did, too." Libby stepped around beside him.

He was so surprised he laughed. At this point, what else could he do?

Libby's hand rested on his arm. "You've had so much thrown at you, I thought this might put a smile on your face."

"Well, it did." He laughed again. "I don't get it, but whatever."

"That you're handsome? It's sweet that you're humble, but come on, boss, you're quite a catch." She stepped closer to him—too close. At least, too close for him.

"Anything else?" he asked, putting the desk between them.

"Your mother called." She handed him the message slips. "So did Mayor Contreras. Oh, and Daisy Granger called, too."

He took the slips and headed for his office. "Thanks." His mother never called him at work, the others could wait.

"What do you want me to do with the flowers? And the cards?" she called after him.

That could wait, too. "I'll take care of them later. Thanks." He pushed the door shut behind him, dug his cell phone out of his pocket, and called his mother.

"Morning, Everett." He didn't detect any distress in her voice. "I hope you're having a good Monday morning?"

"It's kept me busy." He sat at his desk and turned on his computer. "What's up?"

"Gramma Dot had a doctor appointment this morning. I wanted to let you know that she's finally agreed to go on that medicine. Doc says it should make a big difference."

"That is great news, Mom." It felt like a weight had been lifted off his shoulders—well, one of them anyway.

"I think the whole episode in the tree really shook her up." His mother sighed. "And I wanted to thank you for Saturday. It's hard to see Gramma Dot in…a state."

"She was an angel compared to the day of Camellia and Van's wedding." He definitely didn't want to think about that. Gramma Dot was feisty but not mean—until that day. He didn't know who that woman had been, but she sure as hell hadn't been his Gramma Dot. Hopefully, this medicine would stop that from happening again. "I was more worried about her falling and hurting herself."

"Thanks to you, she's fine." There was a pause. "I appreciate you and Rosemary coming to the rescue. So does your dad."

"I wasn't looking for thanks, you know that." He stared blindly at the computer screen.

"But you're okay?"

He took a deep breath. "Gramma Dot thought I was Granddad… Other than that, fine." That had hurt. Having her plead with him to stay—as her beloved Albie—had damn near torn his heart out.

His mother's indrawn breath wavered. "Oh, Everett. I'm so sorry."

He hurried on, "Something about seeing Rosebud snapped Gramma Dot out of it." And he was grateful. He glanced toward his office door, remembering Rosebud cradling little Fi close. His damn heart grew too big for his chest—his ribs and lungs going tight.

"Rosemary has always held a special place in Gramma Dot's heart, you know that." There was a smile in her voice. "Mine, too."

He smiled and sat back in his chair. "Yeah, Dad told me."

"Told you what? Leland, what did you say to Everett?" A pause. "About me and your mother and Rose-mary?"

"He said you and Gramma Dot were hoping Rose-bud and I would get together." He chuckled. "I guess I should be glad the two of you never tried your hand at matchmaking. That would have been disastrous."

"Everett Michael Taggert." Her outrage was clear. "That's a horrible thing to say. For all you know, we might have had you two happily married by now."

Everett shook his head, still smiling. "We'll never know."

"That sounds like a challenge," his mother snapped back.

"No. No way, no how." He sat forward. The last thing he needed was his mother and grandmother getting in-volved in his personal life—especially when it came to Rosebud. Thanks to that article, it was as big a mess as his professional life. "I love you both, and while I ap-preciate the concern, I can take care—"

"Oh, Everett. Sometimes you're just like your father. Stubborn. Too stubborn for your own good." She was upset now. "I've held my tongue for years, but—well, enough is enough. No, Leland, let me be. You love that girl. We all know it. Now she's home, and you two have a real chance at happiness. What are you waiting for?"

"Who are we talking about?" he tried to tease.

"Everett Michael Taggert." Her sigh was pure indig-nation.

"Mom, I've got a call coming in," he lied. "Willow Creek."

"I'm sorry, son." She sighed. "You're working, and here I am, sticking my nose into your business."

"It's okay, Mom."

"I hope it's nothing serious. I love you."

Everett disconnected. The last time he'd lied to his mother, he'd been in high school, and it was to cover his butt over something stupid he'd done. Today he'd lied because he wasn't sure how to answer her. He spun around in his leather office chair and stared out the window at the courthouse lawn. If he couldn't have an outdoor office, at least he had a peaceful view. He needed more peace in his life.

His mother was right. He'd always loved Rosebud. He probably always would. But that didn't mean they had a future together. Considering how she'd reacted when he told her how he'd felt, he had no reason to be encouraged. Not that he wanted to be encouraged. He was no more willing to risk their friendship today than he had been years ago. He needed to remember that, to hold on to that, and not do anything he'd regret.

Dammit.

In the span of forty-eight hours, he'd gone from guarding his heart to fighting to hold on to it. For now, he'd have to keep up the fight.

CHAPTER TEN

ROSEMARY'S WEEK HAD been eventful: emailing a self-introduction to the entire festival-and-event contact list; inventorying the supplies and confirming volunteers for her first senior gardening club next week; meeting with Lorna again to firm up the next few months' calendar; hosting two study sessions for the Junior Beekeepers club and Benji's upcoming apprenticeship beekeeper's exam; the surprise arrival of a box of board-book copies of *ABC's with Baby Bee* that Shelby's friend had expedited production on; cheering on Bea's first steps—then laughing over the toddler's launch into a full-fledged run; and trying to mentally prepare for this weekend's Annual Texas Beekeeper's Convention.

Not to mention how gooey and soft her insides went every single time Everett was around. Which, thankfully, hadn't been all that often.

The one good thing about this weekend's Annual Texas Beekeeper's Convention? She got a break from Everett. When he was around, she found it hard to think—let alone function. Since she knew a run-in with Dr. James Voigt was imminent, she wanted all her wits about her.

Every time she looked around the bustling convention center, she braced herself for seeing the man. So far, she'd seen dozens of familiar faces eager to welcome her home.

"Have you missed it?" Astrid asked, taking a jar of Honey Hill Farms' Blue Ribbon Honey from Rosemary.

Rosemary nodded, unpacking boxes of Honey Hill Farms honey for Astrid to arrange on the honeycomb display rack Tansy had designed and built. She had missed conferences. She'd missed working the Honey Hill Farms booth at festivals and here at the convention. The lectures were useful and inspiring, the networking was invaluable, and the open-to-the-public Honey Expo was always a lucrative endeavor for Honey Hill Farms.

"I know I've said it before, but… I'm so glad you're here." Astrid grabbed her hand and gave it a squeeze. "It's like a piece of me was missing."

The words resonated deeply with Rosemary. Her work had been engrossing and satisfying—to a point. But every day she'd missed the presence and company of the other Bee Girls. Aunt Mags and Aunt Camellia. Tansy and Astrid.

"Aww." Nicole Svoboda carried another box to the booth. "You guys make me wish I had a sibling." She set the box down and sighed.

"You do." Astrid tugged her in for a group hug. "Maybe not by blood, but by choice."

"It's true." Rosemary hugged their friend—who they all agreed was an honorary Bee Girl. "It wouldn't be the same without you."

"It wouldn't." Nicole hugged them, laughed, then let them go. "Oh, hold on." She turned to dig through her oversize purse. "What do you think?" Nicole hadn't changed her rainbow-hued streaks for the convention, but she had created an impressive fascinator. A mini hive sat jauntily on her head with several wired felt bees in midflight about the hive. "Now, watch…" The bees and hive blinked. First white, then yellow lights.

"I want one." Astrid was mesmerized.

"Right?" Nicole put her hands on her hips. "I'll make you one to wear to all the fall and spring festivals, I promise." She turned to Rosemary. "You want one?"

"As an official employee of the county, I'm not sure it's appropriate business attire." Plus, she wasn't keen on the idea of drawing any more attention her way than necessary.

"Boo." Nicole waved her hand. "Where's the fun in being professional anyway?"

"Mom." Benji stopped dead in his tracks. "What's on your head?"

"Do you like it? I made it." Her wide smile was almost as bright as the blinking lights on her head.

"No." Benji took a step back. "Can you take it off?"

"Benji." Nicole's smile drooped. "Really?"

The boy took a deep breath and said, "Nah, it's cool. Just messin' with ya."

But Rosemary saw how hard he had to work at his smile—and it was precious. Nicole had become a mom as an early teen, but she'd never been anything other than an awesome mom. As a result, the bond between the mother and son was unshakable. If his mother was excited about her eye-catching fascinator, he'd get excited, too.

"Hey." Leif walked up to the booth, his gaze locking on the fascinator. "Hey, Nicole, you know your head's blinking, right?"

"Yup. Don't be too jealous." She turned, opened a folding chair, and pointed at it. "I love you, Astrid. Now sit."

Astrid pulled the chair closer to the honeycomb display shelf and sat. "But I'm still setting up the booth."

"Fine." Nicole handed her some jars of honey. "Do it sitting down. You know the next couple of days will be long ones."

"Welcome to the Annual Texas Beekeeper's Convention." Kerrielynn came walking up, her phone held out in front of her. "This is the end-all, be-all for Texas beekeepers. Did you see what I did there? End-all, *bee*-all?"

"What's she doing?" Rosemary asked Leif.

"She's taking some marketing class, and one of the units is social media marketing." Leif's voice was low. "She's been filming everything for the last two days."

"Everyone say hi." Kerrielynn turned her phone toward the booth. "Nicole...your hat. Wow."

Rosemary wasn't sure the wow was a bad wow or a good wow, but Nicole took it as the latter and smiled proudly. "This is for a class?" she asked Kerrielynn.

"Yes. Hi, Rosemary. Everyone say hi to Rosemary Hill. She's one of the Honey Hill Farms Bee Girls *and* a bee genius. She's my inspiration." Kerrielynn stood beside Rosemary and put her phone into selfie mode. "And she has the most gorgeous hair, don't you think?"

Rosemary had a hard time seeing herself on camera, but she tried to smile. If this was for a grade, she knew how important it was. Being a devoted A student all her life, she'd make sure not to do anything that might damage Kerrielynn's vision.

"I'll take you on a tour of the whole expo once everybody's set up. You'll be amazed. I did it again. *Bee* amazed." Kerrielynn waved at the camera. "*Bee* back soon." She turned off the phone and rubbed her cheeks. "Smiling all the time is work."

"It's a pretty smile." Leif draped an arm around her shoulders.

"You're only saying that because I'm your girlfriend." She smiled up at him.

"It's true you have a pretty smile. But I'm also saying it because you're my girlfriend." He dropped a kiss on her cheek.

"You two are adorable," Nicole called out. "Just be *careful*—you know what I mean—because being teen parents is hard work."

Rosemary was so surprised, she burst into laughter. She wasn't the only one. Astrid looked to be on the verge of hyperventilating.

Leif rolled his eyes but didn't seem too bothered. Poor Kerrielynn, however, was beet red.

"Mom." Benji was horrified. "Kerrielynn could have been live streaming."

"What?" Nicole shrugged. "I'm telling it like it is, is all. Why would that message going out into the world be a bad thing?"

"Really?" Benji shook his head, his face dark red.

"What happened?" Dane arrived, an oversize box under each arm. "Whatever it was, I need in on it." He glanced at Astrid. "You going to make it?"

Astrid was hugging herself, tears streaming down her cheeks.

Tansy followed Dane into the booth, little Nova and Halley in tow. Halley was pulling their worse-for-wear wagon behind her with more supplies.

"That's everything— Whoa." Tansy took in the mixed reactions. "What did we miss?"

Nicole adjusted her fascinator. "I just said—"

But Benji cut his mother off. *"Nothing."* He waved

both his hands. "Seriously. I have to be here to test, Mom. Don't make it suck."

Rosemary managed to stop laughing. Maybe now wasn't the best time to tease. The kids were all taking an important exam later that afternoon. Benji was testing to become an apprentice beekeeper, and Kerrielynn and Leif were taking their advanced beekeeper tests. Technically, Leif could test for his master's level, but he didn't think he was ready yet. Each level of certification had different qualifications that included hours as a practicing beekeeper, hive ownership and management, and a written exam. Without completing all the qualifications, there was no certification.

"You're going to do great," she said. "You knew everything we reviewed. Plus, Dane and Tansy wouldn't have signed off on your hours if they didn't think you were ready."

Benji shrugged. "Yeah, well...tests stress me out."

"I'm sorry." Nicole took off her hat and came out of the booth to her son. "Forgive me? Please."

Benji sighed. "Yeah."

Nicole hugged him. "And you're going to kick that exam's ass. Don't you worry."

"Does an exam have an ass?" Dane deposited the boxes he was carrying in the booth.

"Halley, isn't *ass* a bad word?" Nova asked.

"Yes." Astrid held out her arms. "It is. And no one will say it again."

Nova ran to Astrid and climbed into her lap. "Okay."

Tansy nudged Dane. "You're not helping." Her whisper was loud enough for everyone to hear.

"I am." He nodded at the boxes. "I carried those inside, didn't I?"

"You're infuriating." Tansy rolled her eyes.

"It's a good thing I'm hot." He grinned. "And you like me."

"A little." Tansy stood on tiptoe and wrapped her arms around his neck. The kiss, for *them*, was short and restrained. With a wink, Dane started sorting and stacking boxes.

"Why aren't you warning them about... Well, you know?" Leif asked Nicole. "Look at 'em."

"You have a point, Leif." Nicole shook her head.

"No, please, no. Pregnancy bladder is a real thing, and I don't think I can take it if I start laughing like that again." Astrid held up her hands.

"Fine. I'm going to walk the room. Check out the competition." Nicole adjusted her fascinator and headed off.

"Are you sure you're okay?" Halley glanced at Benji, who shrugged, then nodded.

"Kerrielynn, what's this social media project about?" Rosemary attempted to change the topic.

"It's a lot." She made a face. "I need to create a YouTube channel, post daily, and track my views and followers. Live stream teasers or interviews—things to boost interest. And develop a consistent brand, too." She ticked off each item on her fingers. "Obviously, I'm doing the life-of-a-beekeeper sort of thing." She paused. "I'm hoping I can film at the senior gardening club meeting next week, Rosemary? Since we'll be helping out. If that's okay, of course?"

"Remind me before the meeting starts, okay?" The senior gardening club would be Rosemary's first public interaction as the education and outreach facilitator. She was surprisingly nervous—even with Lorna's meticulous notes. But she was excited, too. It was never too late to share the importance of bees. She hoped the senior gardening club would eagerly embrace her bee-friendly gardening plans.

"Can do." Kerrielynn sighed. "I figure it can't hurt to have extra footage."

"Yeah, she's got to create a ten-to-fifteen-minute film as her final." Leif took her hand.

"That sounds like a lot of work." Astrid's brows went high.

"I'm basically recording *everything*." Kerrielynn shrugged.

"That's smart. Easier to have something to edit than be short of content." Halley helped Benji open boxes.

"Ooh, make sure you tag Wholesome Foods in your posts, Kerrielynn. They'd love it, and it would help me with our social media posting, too. If you don't mind?" Tansy winked.

"Um, seriously? I totally will." Kerrielynn was thrilled.

Rosemary listened, overwhelmed. "I know it's an important way to market nowadays, but I'm so glad you're into all that stuff, Tansy. As far as the farm goes, I wouldn't know where to start." The idea of having to be on all the time was too daunting for her.

"Agreed." Astrid nodded. "Rosemary and I are happy to stay behind the scenes on that side of things."

"It's not really that hard. You just sort of pretend the camera is someone you're talking to, someone that's interested in what you're saying. But honestly, I don't know if I'd enjoy it as much without Dane." She glanced at her brawny fiancé.

Rosemary nodded, but her gaze snagged on the very handsome man heading for the booth. Instantly, her insides were doing that gooey melty thing. "Everett?" she murmured. It was him. And when he smiled at her, her knees turned to jelly. "I mean, Everett's here."

"I brought him. I damn near had to force him, but I figured after the week he's had, he could use a break from all the people-pleasing and politicking." Dane pulled the tie from his hair, smoothed it back, and pulled his long blond hair back into a man bun. "That okay?"

"Oh…yes. Of—of course," she stammered, feeling the heat creep into her cheeks. *Stop blushing. Act normal.*

"You sure?" Dane asked, his blue eyes a little too intent on her face.

She swallowed and nodded. It was fine. It was good. Dane had a point. Everett did deserve a break.

"Rosemary, these are gorgeous." Astrid was staring into one of the boxes. "You wrote a book. That's amazing. It looks like something you'd find in a bookstore or a library." She sat, the books in her hands. *"ABC's with Baby Bee."*

"Ooh, the bees are so pretty." Nova's eyes went round as she stared at the page.

"*You* wrote that, Rosemary?" Kerrielynn hurried to Astrid's side. "Ohmygosh. Leif, look."

"Those weren't supposed to come with us. I guess the boxes got mixed up?" Rosemary frowned. "Hopefully nothing important was left behind." She turned, scanning the boxes—only to find Everett, standing right there, beside the booth.

"Hey, Rosebud. What's the trouble? Do I need to go back and get something?"

"Hey, yourself." She smiled. He'd just arrived, and he was already offering to drive an hour and a half back to Honey. "You will not be going anywhere. Except that chair—to relax."

"Yes, ma'am." He sat and grinned up at her. "What's going on?" He nodded at the group clustered around Astrid.

There was no reason for her to be shy about her book—this was Everett and her family and friends. And yet she was. "There was a mix-up, and the book I wrote for Bea and Nuc is here."

He was up out of his chair and joining the others.

She stood, flooded with insecurity. She wished the box of books wasn't here, that everyone who mattered wasn't reading it, and most important, that they liked her little book. Not that it was for them. It wasn't. And yet, she was proud that her idea had turned into a real live book that her nieces and nephews might enjoy.

"We're live at the Annual Texas Beekeepers Convention and it's story time." Kerrielynn had her phone out again. "Look at this beautiful little story about the bees by Rosemary Hill."

Oh no. Rosemary was frozen. The books were for family—not this...

"Come on, Nova, let's read." Everett sat, looking bigger than usual with little Nova perched on his lap. "'A is for Astrid, that gives bees sweet pollen.'" He held up the book, pointing at Rosemary's detailed illustration of the flower and buzzing bees. He turned the book back and continued reading, "'B is for bees and baking, things full of rich honey.'" He turned the book again, showing the bees circling a plate of cookies and a jar of honey.

While Everett kept reading to Nova—and anyone who happened to be watching Kerrielynn's live stream—Rosemary's discomfort gave way to something else.

Every single one of her friends and family were reading a copy of her little book and smiling at her pictures. Sure, it could be that they loved her and would support her no matter what. But what if the book was actually good? What if her little bee book could do big things? The sort of things Poppa Tom would be proud of. Not just for her nieces and nephews but a whole new generation of beekeepers?

"This is beautiful, Rosebud." There it was again—the Everett smile that turned her into a puddle. "I'm proud of you."

Rosemary let those words roll over her before soaking them in. He was proud of her. And for the first time in a long time, she was proud of herself, too.

WHEN DANE HAD suggested Everett come with him to this weekend's beekeeper's convention, his yes came out without a second's hesitation. He needed a break from Honey and the paintball nightmare, Mayor Contreras putting too much on him, trying to appease damn near everyone, and the fiasco with the flowers, cards, and emails from what must be every single woman in the county. He'd more than earned a break.

But the primary reason for coming was this right here. Seeing Rosebud. And that smile, that bashful pride over her creation and the praise she was getting, made him oh so glad he was here to see it.

"Can I read it, Everett?" Nova took the book out of his hands and flipped it back to the beginning. "I can try to read it to you."

"Why don't you read it to me?" Astrid patted her lap. "And the baby."

"Okay. Next time, okay, Everett?" Nova smiled as

she climbed down from his lap and hurried to Astrid's side, the book clutched to her chest. "Nuc, Nuc, Aunt Rosemary wrote a book for us."

Rosemary's laugh was soft, an expression of wonderment settling on her beautiful face. Until it was gone. In a span of five seconds, she'd gone from glowing and proud to white as a ghost and agitated. Whoever or whatever had caught her attention wasn't good.

He turned, looking behind him to see a group gathered around a man. The man looked familiar. It took a minute for Everett to place him. He was the guy on the beekeeper's convention brochure. *The brochure that upset Rosebud so much.*

It hadn't been the brochure. It had been this guy.

He stood and came to stand at Rosebud's side—not that she seemed to notice. Her jaw was tight, her hands were clasped in front of her, and her gaze was glued on the man. So this guy was *definitely* the problem. Whoever he was, Everett didn't like him.

"Rosemary, this is precious," Tansy gushed. "Not enough to make me want to have kids anytime soon, but eventually, this will be their favorite book." She did a double take. "Rose?"

"Yes?" The word erupted from Rosebud. "I'm sorry?"

Tansy frowned, staring in the direction Rosemary was looking. "You know, Dane could totally take him. And probably make it look like an accident."

"Who am I taking?" Dane asked, cracking his knuckles.

Everett knew who, he just didn't know why. He wanted to know. Badly.

"No one." Rosemary's whisper was vehement. "Let's forget it." She took an unsteady breath.

Damn, he didn't like this. She was upset. Really upset.

Rosebud hurried on to say, "We should finish getting the booth set up—"

"We've got it." Kerrielynn was armed with a clipboard and pen. "The deal was we help out if we come to the convention, so we're helping out. I've got a list." She tapped the clipboard with a pen.

"And we know better than to argue with her." But Benji was smiling. "She can get real bossy, real quick."

"You wouldn't know what to do if she didn't tell you," Leif jumped in, ever quick to defend Kerrielynn.

"I sure wouldn't know what to do." Halley shrugged. "All this bee stuff is still new to me."

"How are you liking the whole beekeeping thing?" Everett knew this was a topic near and dear to Rosebud's heart. With any luck, it would be just the thing to distract Rosebud from the man smiling too big and talking too loudly.

"It's a lot." Halley sighed. "I don't want to mess up."

"That's the great thing about being in a family of beekeepers, Halley. You've got tons of resources close by." Rosebud's smile was encouraging. "I'm happy to help out whenever I can."

"Really? Thanks, Aunt Rosemary. I mean, I know you're super busy, though. Kerrielynn told me you're like, a big deal in the bee industry—I mean, in apiculture. Now you've got your job and your book and the bees and all."

"I'll never be too busy for you. You're my niece, Halley. I've never had a niece before. I'd love to spend more time with you. Whether we're talking bees or not."

Rosemary's surprised expression gave way to pleasure when Halley hugged her.

"Cool," Halley said, giving her a solid squeeze before letting her go. "I'd like that, too."

Kerrielynn and Halley took Rosemary up on her offer, instantly bombarding her with beekeeping questions. Everett was grateful. She was most at ease when she was talking bees.

"Seriously, who are you offering me up to pummel?" Dane whispered to Tansy.

"Dr. Voigt over there." Tansy practically spit out the words.

"Got it." Dane shrugged. "Yeah, he looks like an asshole."

"That's a bad word." Everett pointed at Nova, who was reading one of Rosemary's books to Astrid's stomach.

"Right." Dane winced. "I don't think she heard me this time."

But Everett was more concerned about the man in question. "What, exactly, did this Dr. Voigt guy do?" He studied the man. "Were he and Rosemary…a thing?" Had the bastard hurt her? If he had… He didn't want to think about that.

"You're not going to need me." Dane chuckled. "Everett's got this."

Everett turned to find both Dane and Tansy watching him.

"Oh, Everett." Tansy sighed, her gaze darting to her sister, then Dr. Voigt. "He was her project mentor in California. That lost funding?" She shrugged. "He's also a real…"

"Asshole," Dane whispered. "No doubt."

Nothing Tansy shared explained a thing or eased his

worries. If anything, he was feeling more protective than ever.

Nicole came over to the booth with a satisfied smile on her face. "I'm happy to report that our booth is the best." She gave two thumbs-up. "And we've got about ten minutes before the opening keynote. Anyone free to hold seats? There are a lot of us."

"I'll go." Astrid stood and took Nova's hand. "I can sit anywhere. Anyone else?"

"Everett, you and Rosemary can go." Tansy smiled. "We'll make sure the kids get everything done here and meet you inside, Rosemary?"

"Fine by me." Everett nodded and looked to Rosebud. The more space he could put between her and this Dr. Voigt character, the better. "Come on, Rosebud. You can catch me up on your first week of work."

"Okay." Her smile wasn't fully charged, but there was color in her cheeks—that was a start.

Walking through the convention center hall was educational. Other than acknowledging the importance of the honeybee, Everett had never fully understood the beekeeping industry. There was honey, of course. Honey as far as the eye could see. Flavored honey straws, creamed honey, sweet or savory honey, and more. But there was more to it than that. Walking by booth after booth, he paused to look at the products, equipment, and keeper suits on display.

"You looking for anything while you're here?" Everett asked, holding out the sleeve of a camouflage beekeeping suit.

"Not that." Rosebud's brows rose and she shook her head. "I am looking for queen-rearing equipment."

"Right. Sure. Okay." He nodded. "And that would be what, exactly?"

She grinned. "Grafting tools. Queen cell holder frames. If I'm going to do this with the Junior Beekeepers, I want them to have hands-on experience trying both methods."

"Yeah, that didn't clear anything up for me, Rose-bud."

She laughed. "Right, sorry. Queen-rearing is all about breeding the best bees for the strongest colonies. The short version is you're getting your best bees to create strong, hardy queens so those queens can go on to create strong, hardy hives. Or whatever traits you're looking for in your bees."

"I think I get it." He was pretty sure he didn't, but she was on a roll, and he didn't want to interrupt her.

"The life cycle of any living creature fascinates me. But bees? They just have it down. There's no messing around—no time wasted. They get in, get it done, and keep after it. Queen-rearing is the perfect example of that. Every step of a bee's life is purposeful and impor-tant. I got pretty good at it in California." She broke off, everything about her tensing.

California. The guy. Now wasn't the time to ask questions. "And you're wanting to do queen-rearing here? With the Junior Beekeepers?"

She nodded, looking up at him.

"Sounds like a pretty ambitious undertaking." He waited, knowing she loved a good challenge.

"No." She frowned, shaking her head. "Not at all. From what I've seen, these kids are eager and deter-mined. It's my job to find ways to keep them that way."

"Something tells me you will." He nudged her.

She nudged him back. "And as far as queen-rearing

goes, I tend to lean toward the Doolittle method. Why reinvent the wheel, you know?"

No, he had no idea. But he nodded and said, "I was going to say the same thing."

Rosebud laughed, long and loud.

By the time they reached the ballroom, she'd told him more than he ever wanted to know about queen-rearing. Apparently, larvae were only suitable for grafting the first few days after hatching. After that, it was too late. It was also important to separate the sealed queen cells before the first queen hatched or the new queen would kill the rest. Only one queen was needed for a whole hive—she wasn't going to tolerate any threat to her rule.

"Sounds kinda cutthroat." Everett followed her down the aisle to the row of seats they were holding for the group.

"What does?" Nicole asked, her hat blinking.

"Queen bees." Everett sat and eyed Nicole's head. "Where did you get that hat?" It was an eyesore. The blinking only made it worse.

"I made it." And she was obviously proud of it. "I even put a queen on it." She pointed at one of the felt bees wired to the blinking hive. Sure enough, it was wearing a tiny tiara. "Queen bees are the ultimate girl boss. They get sh—" She paused, smiling at Nova and Astrid. "They get stuff done."

Astrid mouthed *thank you.*

"But they don't wear crowns, Everett." Nova sighed, crestfallen. "And bees dance, too. But they don't wear dance shoes or tutus."

Everett managed not to laugh. "That is a shame."

Astrid and Rosemary kept up a steady back-and-forth of bee facts, with Nicole and Nova jumping in every so often. Everett had nothing, but he was content to sit back, listen, and enjoy the fun.

In time, people started trickling in. Every time one of the large doors opened, a nail-grating screech echoed throughout the room. He made a face—so did Nova. From then on, every time the door opened, they made a silly face at each other. The more people that came in, the more squeaking—until it was impossible to keep up. Nova wound up dissolving into a fit of giggles.

The hall was almost full when Tansy, Dane, Charlie, and the teens showed up.

"We're a chair short." Tansy counted off.

"Nope." Rosemary stood. "I'm going to go check the booth."

"I'll go." Everett stood, grabbing her hand. "This is your thing, Rosebud."

She seemed to be considering his offer. "I'm okay missing this part." She squeezed his hand. "But you can keep me company, if you want?"

Getting out of the room was easier said than done. The aisles were crowded with backpacks and oversize purses or groups of people standing, talking, or blocking the path. By the time they reached the back of the room, the lights dimmed and there was a tapping on the microphone. The room went silent.

"Good morning! I'm so excited to see so many friendly faces—and so many new ones. I'm the president of the Travis County Beekeepers Chapter, Sherry Vasquez, and I want to officially welcome you to this year's Annual Texas Beekeeper's Convention." She paused for the smattering of applause to die down. "Now, we're already running behind, and as we have exams lined up and a lunch, I'm going to cut my speech short and hand it off to our renowned speaker, Dr. James Voigt."

The applause was thunderous, but Rosemary kept edging toward the doors.

"Thank you. Thank you," Dr. Voigt said as the applause faded. "This is quite a crowd."

The doors at the back of the room opened, the deafening squeak reverberating through the room and drawing all eyes.

"I hope that's someone coming in, not someone trying to sneak out." Dr. James Voigt chuckled, and so did the crowd.

But Rosemary wasn't chuckling. She looked defeated. Here they were, close enough to make their escape but aware that doing so would draw attention her way. And knowing Rosebud, that's the last thing she wanted. Instead, she stood against the back wall and crossed her arms over her chest.

"You don't want to make a run for it?" he whispered. "I can cause a distraction? Push someone over? Trip someone?"

She covered her mouth to stifle her laughter. "Everett," she whispered, shaking her head.

He stood beside her—probably closer than was necessary. But she didn't move away.

"Tomorrow, I'll get academic on those of you who dare to come hear my lecture. Today, I want to focus on the incredible work all of us, as beekeepers, do for the world." He smiled out over the crowd. "We are the keepers of the future because, let's face it, without bees, there is no future. It's up to us to make sure that doesn't happen. That our children, our children's children, grow up respecting and caring for the planet in our charge."

A muffled grunt came from Rosebud.

"What's wrong?" He leaned closer.

"He... I wrote that for the funding gala last year." She shook her head. "I'm beginning to wonder if all of his work and research—heck, every word that comes out of his mouth—belongs to someone else. It makes me sick that years of my research and my speeches are being attributed to his big, arrogant talking head." He'd never seen or heard Rosebud this angry before.

Someone shushed them, instantly shutting Rosebud down.

Everett was reeling. Tansy and Dane were right. Dr. James Voigt was an asshole. Of course she didn't want to stand here and listen to the man—he was tempted to lead her out, squeaking doors and all. But she was staying put, so he'd stay with her.

He reached for her hand and gave it a squeeze. He heard her take a deep breath and let it out slowly and gave her hand another squeeze. She was something else, his Rosebud. When her fingers threaded with his, he held on tight.

Because she was *his* Rosebud. Fool that he was, he loved her. Always and forever.

CHAPTER ELEVEN

FOR ROSEMARY, James Voigt's speech lasted for days. At least, that's how it felt. Since she was familiar with most of what he said, she tuned him out. She'd wasted enough energy on this whole situation, and honestly, she'd much rather concentrate on the man at her side.

The man whose hand she was holding.

The man I love.

She glanced up at him in the dimly lit room. He stared, stone-faced, at James—but the tick of his jaw muscle implied he wasn't as calm and cool as he acted. He was angry on her behalf. Her heart thumped along happily, even though she knew he was holding her hand in a very typical Everett show of solidarity. Him being outraged on her behalf wasn't a romantic thing; it was a decent human thing.

She hadn't meant to unload on him or cling to his hand through James's entire speech, but she had. And instead of getting uncomfortable or trying to change the subject or making an excuse to flee, he stayed at her side and kept holding her hand.

She smiled, giving herself a moment to pretend that this was the norm. Her and Everett, holding hands, together. It was a nice idea. And as long as she was studying him, James ceased to exist. So did pretty much everyone else... What other reason did she need to continue ogling—discreetly, of course—this beautiful man? He was beautiful, inside and out. While every inch of him was manly and strong, his smile—his eyes—were kind. Warm. Everett was both those things. *And so much more.*

She blinked, her eyes adjusting as the houselights came up and the reality of their surroundings returned.

"Now that that's over, what happens?" Everett asked, still holding her hand.

What indeed? *Snap out of it.* "I'm not sure."

His gaze locked with hers, his brown eyes sweeping over her face. "You good, Rosebud?" The husky timbre of his voice rolled over her, curling her toes and leaving her a tad breathless. He gave her hand a squeeze, a slow smile spreading across his face.

Oh goodness. She smiled and squeezed back.

"Rosemary." Dr. James Voigt stood right in front of them, smiling and unbothered—like he hadn't taken her work and her dreams away from her not two weeks before.

She was so surprised to see him, she sort of sputtered, "J-James." She blinked, trying to process what was happening. Why would he search her out? Smile at her? Act so…so normal?

James looked back and forth between her and Everett.

"I'm Everett Taggert." But Everett didn't offer his hand—and one was still firmly holding on to hers.

"Dr. James Voigt." He didn't seem bothered by the lack of warmth. In fact, he smiled and turned to her. "Fancy seeing you here." His chuckle was flat.

Was he really surprised? Right. Of course. He hadn't cared about her, only what she was capable of. Which she would have been fine with if he hadn't done the whole stealing-her-work thing. "I live here. In Texas."

James's brow furrowed, his surprise genuine. "Really? For some reason, I thought you were from California?"

"She's from Honey. The town. Honey Hill Farms? You haven't heard of them? They're well respected in these parts—and the beekeeping world." Everett's chuckle was equally forced.

"No." James shook his head. "I can't say that I have. There's a town called Honey? That's a first."

"Where do you hail from, Dr. Voigt?" Everett released her hand, sliding it up her back, and draping it across her shoulders.

Rosemary was oh so grateful for the support.

"I like to think of myself as a citizen of the world." James's expression was smug.

Had he always been so pompous? Once upon a time she'd thought that look was charming. Why? And why was he trying to engage in small talk?

"It's good that I ran into you. Would you be free for a coffee this weekend?" He turned his light blue eyes her way, his grin crooked and his tone warm.

"Coffee?" She needed to get beyond the what-is-happening stage and into the functional-and-articulate stage.

"If you have time?" James continued to stare at her. "I promise it won't take too long."

"Dr. Voigt. Dr. Hill. What are the odds of finding you two together like this?" A woman stood in front of them. "I'm Jane Wilson, I was on the panel selection committee, and I'm moderating your panel tomorrow, Dr. Voigt." She shook his hand, then Rosemary's.

"Nice to put a face with the name." There it was—the Dr. Voigt that oozed charm.

"I was hoping to talk to you both, so this is perfect. I was thinking, since the two of you worked together on the UC Davis project, and there's been that technical glitch with the presentation, and your current research assistant had to unexpectedly cancel, Dr. Voigt, we should ask Dr. Hill to be on the panel, too. I'm sure she could add some insight. Help fill in any holes?"

"Excuse me?" She couldn't be hearing correctly. Technical glitch? What exactly did that mean? Had he lost the information they'd been working on? Or was he reticent to share it?

Everett's hand slid to the middle of her back, his thumb rubbing back and forth between her shoulder blades.

"Oh." James looked just as shocked as she was. And maybe a little mortified, too.

"If you're free, of course." Jane looked back and forth between her and James, her smile faltering. "That way you won't have to 'wing' the presentation." She used air quotes around *wing*.

He was going to wing the last five years of data? No wonder the woman was panicking. As much as she'd love to talk about their work, she wasn't sure it was the best idea. Besides, James clearly didn't want her speaking on *his* panel about *his* research. He didn't like sharing the spotlight. Likely he was also concerned that she might expose him for the lying, thieving fraud he was.

"I'm sure Rosemary has other things to do. I wouldn't want to inconvenience her." James's attempt to sound magnanimous only increased her irritation.

Everett's thumb stopped moving. Tension rolled off

of him. A quick glance revealed his locked jaw and tight mouth—like he was holding back whatever he had to say.

She was grateful for his restraint. "I was planning on attending the panel." Well, she'd been on the fence about attending. But now, there was no way she was going to miss sitting in on this train wreck… She might even enjoy it. Until he started misquoting facts and data and making all the work she'd done less than valid. Then she'd get upset.

"It can't hurt, can it? It sounds like Dr. Voigt here could use the backup," Everett murmured. "You've basically got a photographic memory."

Rosemary shot him a look of disbelief.

"Okay, maybe not photographic memory. More like incredible recall. I guess it's a genius thing." He grinned, his thumb moving in a slow lazy circle against her back.

Whether or not she was involved with it, the program should be getting attention. The more attention it got, the more validity and support—and funding—ongoing research would get. "I'd be happy to present with James." She didn't look at her onetime mentor. "Thank you. And thank you for all the work you've put into the convention. I can only imagine the hours and headaches it's been."

"Thank you. Really. That means a lot." Jane paused. "I have to make sure everything is ready for testing. Here's my card, in case anything comes up." And with that, she hurried off into the crowd.

"You know firsthand what it's like to have your work go unrecognized, don't you, Rosebud?" Everett's words were soft—but not so soft that James could miss them.

From the flare of the man's nostrils, he didn't like what he'd heard. "Can you excuse us for a minute?" James asked Everett.

"Rosebud?" Everett asked. "Your call."

Which prompted an irritated huff from James.

She didn't give a fig about the man's irritation. Goodness knows he'd caused her plenty of irritation, plus frustration, sadness, anger, and more. And now he wanted to talk to her. "What exactly are we going to discuss?" she asked.

James glanced at Everett.

"Everett knows everything." She'd rather hear what James had to say with Everett at her side. That way, if she totally lost it and launched herself at the backstabbing snake, Everett could hold her back.

James wasn't happy about this. There was no trace of his usual smile or upbeat persona. "What does that mean?"

Rosemary swallowed, fully aware of the people milling around and how easily things could be overheard. She knew the truth, but she didn't want to wind up in the middle of some he-said, she-said situation. "I think you know."

James's eyes narrowed. "I think there's been a misunderstanding."

Everett's snort had James's nostrils flaring wider.

"Rosemary, I know you. We spent four years together—working closely together, passionate about the same things and chasing down the same goals. We were a team. You've never been interested in accolades, not really." He sighed. "Does it matter who is credited? As long as accurate, usable information is accessible to beekeepers, isn't that what matters?"

She took a moment to absorb his words. First, he was either being willfully ignorant or the man was really truly stupid when it came to his breech of professional ethics. Second, he had a point about getting the information out there. Both factors helped her make a decision. "That's why, as a member of the team, I'm happy to present with you tomorrow. Everett's right, I could probably recite most of those data tables verbatim, without the PowerPoint I created, so we should be covered regardless of any technical glitches."

James's shoulders slumped, and he shook his head. "That's not necessary."

"It is. Getting accurate, useful information out there is in the best interest of this ongoing project. The more beekeepers contributing data, the better." She paused, waiting for his next argument.

"Your sisters are flagging us down, Rosebud." Everett applied the lightest pressure to her back.

"Right." She scanned the crowd, smiling when she saw every one of her Honey family and friends watching the exchange. Luckily, Kerrielynn didn't have her phone up and recording. "I'll see you tomorrow, Dr. Voigt. Your speech today was very well written." *Because I wrote it.*

Everett steered her around and away from the man. "I've never seen such a civilized ass-kicking, Rosebud. But I'm pretty sure that's what just happened."

She laughed, releasing some of the nervous energy the standoff had triggered. "I wouldn't say that." Her voice wobbled.

Everett's hands clasped her shoulders and turned her to face him. "I would. You were far more generous with that bastard than he deserved, but you still managed to put him in his place. I'm amazed by you. And proud of you." He tilted her chin up, forcing her to meet his gaze.

There was a spark in his brown eyes—something bright and heady and breathtaking. He was proud of her. Amazed by her. But could he love her again?

When his gaze drifted to her mouth, she stopped breathing altogether. Was it possible he felt the crackling hum between them? That this magnetic pull that demanded she stand too close and stare at him too long wasn't one-sided? He might not love her, but was there a chance that Everett Taggert wanted her?

The way his smoldering brown eyes were fixed solely on her mouth suggested it was a possibility. That might be worth exploring. She'd very much like to do some exploring. With Everett.

EVERETT WAS GOING to kiss Rosebud. Right here and now. In front of her family, friends, and from the looks of it, every beekeeper in the state of Texas—and he didn't give one damn.

He'd never wanted to kiss anyone the way he wanted to kiss her. Long and slow. Tasting her. Savoring her. Branding her with his mouth. He wanted her something fierce.

"Everett," she whispered.

He nodded, unable to tear his gaze from her full lips.

"Everett." There was a tremor in her voice.

When their gazes locked, he fought to swallow the groan that threatened to slip out. The look on her face was unexpected. It turned him upside down, shook him around, and pulled the ground out from under him. Even after years of dreaming of this very thing, he wasn't prepared. *She wants it, too.* Rosebud. She wanted him to kiss her. *Damn it all.*

"Have dinner with me tonight." His tongue felt thick, so his words were gruffer than he'd anticipated.

She nodded. "Okay. Yes."

He had the strongest urge to drag her out of the ball-room and find a quiet, *private* place to be alone with her, but he knew they were already going to get a lot of grief for this public...whatever this was. Not that he cared, but she might. "Okay," he murmured.

"Okay." She swallowed and blinked and took a deep, unsteady breath.

Somehow he managed to guide them to the others. Somehow he managed to ignore the awkward, loaded silence that greeted their arrival. Beyond that, he was on uneven ground.

"What did Dr. Voigt want?" Astrid asked, effectively breaking the silence and steering the conversation into a safer direction.

"Nothing." Rosebud's voice was high and tight.

He knew better than to look at her—but did it anyway. The pink flush on her cheeks and dazed look on her face had nothing to do with her run-in with James Voigt. And damn, but it felt good.

"Nothing? That was an awful long nothing." Tansy's not-so-subtle glare was still fixed on the back of the room. "I can't believe he dared to talk to you. I mean, what could he possibly have to say?"

"He's panicking she'll rat him out, is all." Everett glanced at the man in question. "Rosebud handled it like a real champ. Kept her cool. Told it like it was. And she'll be on the panel with him tomorrow—to keep his facts straight." And he was proud of her for agreeing to do it. She'd worked too hard to let some self-inflated wannabe bee guru misrepresent her efforts.

"You are?" Astrid was all smiles. "Oh, Rose, that's amazing."

Everett wholeheartedly agreed.

"Can we come and throw things at him?" Tansy asked. "You know like those old-fashioned movies and plays? Where they boo and throw stuff at the villain?"

Everett also wholeheartedly agreed with this.

Dane pretended to be outraged. "What are you talking about? How old are you?" He laughed at Tansy's livid expression. "Fine. I'll buy some fruit. Stale bread. Whatever. Something hard."

"Excellent." Tansy smiled up at him. "My hero."

"Where are the kids?" Rosebud glanced around, seemingly distracted. "I should get them checked in for their exams."

"No worries, Nicole's on it." Astrid patted her arm. "Benji could barely sit still, fidgeting and stuff."

"Poor Benji. Test-taking anxiety can be crippling." Rosebud shrugged. "It almost got me a handful of times. There's nothing worse than feeling confident one minute then second-guessing yourself when it matters." She glanced his way. "I think I'll go wait with them and catch up with you all later?" She didn't wait for an answer.

Everett watched her leave, replaying the last five minutes. He wasn't suffering from test-taking anxiety, but he was second-guessing everything that had just taken place.

"So." Dane pushed him in the shoulder. "What the hell was that?"

He had no idea. Something good, he hoped. Something he wasn't ready to get teased over, that's for sure. "Don't." Everett held up a hand. "What's the plan now?" Standing around enduring teasing and long questioning looks from the four adults watching him wasn't high on his list of things to do.

"I want to go check on the booth." Astrid wrinkled her nose. "Make sure it's...right."

"I know, I know. You're very particular about the way the booth is set up and need to make sure it meets your standards. I'll come with you—in case you need an extra hand." Tansy winked at her sister. "I wouldn't have expected anything else. I was proud of you for letting Nicole do so much."

"She was very dictatorial about it. I didn't feel like I had a choice." Astrid shrugged. "I think Charlie and Nova are planning on walking around the expo hall before lunch?"

"You're welcome to join us," Charlie offered.

With Charlie, Everett wouldn't have to worry about being plied with questions or teased about Rosebud.

"Come with us, Everett. Later, I can read you the ABC's book." Nova bounced on the balls of her feet, all enthusiasm. "I can read it to Daddy, too."

"I'd like that," Charlie agreed, smiling down at his daughter.

"Or you can come with me, check us into the hotel, and scope out the lunch situation?" Dane held up his hands. "I'll behave."

Everett didn't bother to hide his skepticism.

"Scout's honor." Dane held up his hand.

"You were never a scout." Everett rolled his eyes.

"What's that hand thing supposed to mean anyway? Are you Spock or Spiderman?"

Dane shrugged. "I could use help with the luggage. You'd think we were staying here for a month, not a weekend."

"Fine." Everett preferred staying busy anyway—especially when his brain was on overdrive.

Dane hadn't been kidding about the luggage. Tansy, Rosebud, Nicole, and Kerrielynn were sharing one room. Astrid, Charlie, Nova, and Halley were in another. Dane, Everett, Leif, and Benji were in the last. Among them, there were enough suitcases and bags to fill a luggage store.

The rest of the afternoon was pretty uneventful. The expo hall wouldn't be open to the public until tomorrow, but the Hill sisters made sure everything was stocked and ready. Kerrielynn, Leif, and Benji came out of their exams relieved and exhausted. At lunch, Tansy suggested they all throw on their swimsuits, hit the hotel pool, and relax for the rest of the day.

Relaxation sounded good.

The pool was massive. But the moment Rosebud walked out in her modest green one-piece, there wasn't enough room for him to breathe. Somehow he made it through the whole ordeal without drawing attention his way. It took effort, though, and there was nothing relaxing about it.

While the teens were splashing and playing games and Charlie was helping Nova swim, he was aware of Rosebud every second he was in the water. From how dark her wet hair was to the pale cream of her skin—he had to fight against reaching for her or staring at her.

After two hours, he had enough. He headed up to his hotel room, took a long shower, and cleaned up for dinner.

Dinner with Rosebud.

The knock on the hotel room door was a surprise, but finding Rosebud outside was even more so. She wore her swimsuit, a towel wrapped around her, with her hair dripping onto the carpet. She was beautiful—even with the furrow between her brows and the tightness of her mouth.

"Rosebud." Was she upset? She didn't look happy. "You're going to catch a chill."

"I wanted to make sure dinner was still a go?" She gripped the towel with one hand.

His gaze followed a water droplet trailing along the side of her neck and over her shoulder. He pressed his eyes shut. *Get it together.* He nodded. "If you're up for it?"

"You seemed upset—like you were avoiding me in the pool, so..." Her gaze fell, and she pulled the towel tighter around her, shuddering once.

Out of self-preservation. He didn't want her to think he didn't want to spend time with her—that was the last thing he wanted. But spilling his heart while she was shivering and soaking wet outside his hotel room wasn't a good idea, either.

She frowned then. "Everett—"

"Rosebud, please go get warm. You're so cold your lips are turning blue." And pulling her close and warming her up sounded way too good. The images that came to mind had him gripping the edge of the door. "As soon as you're ready, we'll go eat."

"But it's only four thirty." Her teeth were chattering.

"And I'm ready." He gripped the door harder, his throat going tight.

Her gaze swept over him, pink staining her cheeks. "You look handsome."

"You look beautiful." He cleared his throat, but it didn't help.

"I do?" she whispered, shivering now.

Always. "Rosebud." He drew in a deep breath, the words spilling out of him. "If you catch a chill, you'll get sick, and you won't be able to show up that good-for-nothing bastard tomorrow—I couldn't live with that. So please, go on and get warm and dressed."

With a blinding smile, she said, "I'll be back." And she hurried down two doors to her room and disappeared inside.

Everett spent the next few minutes looking at places for them to eat. He'd rather drive a short distance and be free and clear of anyone and everyone that might interrupt them. Other than having some one-on-one time with Rosebud, he didn't have an agenda.

The door opened, and Dane, Benji, and Leif came into the hotel room.

"Where's the fire?" Dane ran a towel over his head.

Everett shrugged. "What?"

"You're dressed? Going out?" A look of understanding settled on Dane's face. "Oh."

"Oh, what?" Leif asked. "Are we going to dinner already?"

"It's too early." Benji flopped onto one of the beds, wet swimsuit and all.

"I don't think we're invited." Dane smiled. "Is this a date?"

Everett sighed. "Is it any of your business?"

"It's a date." Dane chuckled.

"With Rosemary?" Benji sat up. "Mom said you've been in love with Rosemary since you were little kids. She said you always wanted a big family like you grew up in, and you've been waiting for Rosemary so you could have that together."

All this time, he thought he'd kept his business his business. As it turned out, he was a bigger fool than he realized. Everett shook his head. "She say anything else?"

"You've been waiting for her *all this time*?" Leif's brows rose. "That's some serious dedication."

"I haven't been waiting." He sighed. He'd never waited for Rosebud. It just so happened that he'd never found another woman he could see a real future with. Hell, even if he could see a future with Rosebud, there was no guarantee that would happen.

"Mom did say you've dated everyone in three counties but you didn't pick one because none of them compare to Rosemary." Benji shrugged. "She tells me everything."

Everett glared at Dane—who was laughing.

"You nervous?" Leif asked. "I'd be nervous."

"You were—when you and Kerrielynn started dating you were all, 'I hope she likes me,' and 'what if she doesn't like me,' and 'what if I go in to kiss her and my breath stinks?'" Benji was laughing then.

"Whatever." But Leif was grinning. "So, are you?"

All three of them were staring at him.

"I wasn't," he admitted, taking a deep breath and heading for the bathroom.

"Where are you going?" Dane asked.

"To brush my teeth. Again." And he kicked the bathroom door behind him. It didn't make a difference. Even after he finished brushing his teeth, they were still hooting with laughter.

CHAPTER TWELVE

"ARE YOU OKAY?" Rosemary ran a cool washcloth over Astrid's forehead. "What can I do?"

"Nothing." Astrid sat on the bathroom floor—a telltale green cast to her skin. "I'll be fine. I'm sorry to invade your bathroom, but Nova gets stressed out when I get sick."

"That's understandable." Rosemary sat on the floor beside her. "She's worried about you and Nuc, that's all."

Astrid smiled weakly, resting her head against the bathroom wall.

"Here." Tansy came into the bathroom, a plastic cup in her hand. "Charlie said ginger ale helps." She set the cup on the floor between Astrid and Rosemary and propped herself against the opposite wall.

"I love that man." Astrid sighed. "Even if he did get me pregnant."

Rosemary and Tansy both laughed at that.

"Not that I mind." Astrid laughed, too, then groaned. She closed her eyes and took slow, deep breaths. "My doctor's given me a breathing technique to help with the nausea. Inhale through the mouth, hold it for three, then breathe out through the mouth." She demonstrated.

"Is it helping?" Tansy asked, frowning.

"Sure is. Can't you tell?" Astrid took another breath. Rosemary and Tansy exchanged a concerned look.

"You don't have to be strong or tease or fake it for us, you know." Tansy's voice was gentle.

"Fine. I feel wretched." Astrid groaned, resting her head on Rosemary's shoulder. "I want to go home and sleep in my big bed in the dark with the air turned down." She sighed. "But it'll pass in about thirty minutes, and I'll be fine."

Rosemary rested her head against Astrid's.

"Distract me," Astrid murmured.

"I can do that." Tansy perked up. "Rosemary is going on a date with Everett."

Astrid sat up. "What?" She turned to face Rosemary. "Why on earth didn't you say something?"

"Well…you were throwing up. It seemed like bad timing." Rosemary shrugged. "I don't think it's a date date. I think it's more like two friends catching up." She hoped it was a date.

Tansy rolled her eyes. "What exactly was the conversation?"

Rosemary told them.

"From the way he was looking at you, I'd say it's a date…" Astrid glanced at Rosemary. "If I wasn't so nauseated, I'd fan myself. You get the picture."

Rosemary did. The way he'd looked at her had been electrifying. She'd felt it—to the marrow of her bones. But she didn't want to get her hopes up. "He said he was over me."

Tansy snorted. Astrid's noise was half grunt, half moan.

"Of course he's going to say that." Tansy tightened her ponytail, then pulled her knees to her chest. "I'm assuming this means you're hoping Everett is now an option?"

Even though they were her sisters, Rosemary struggled to answer that. If she admitted her feelings, it would change everything. Wouldn't it? And saying yes, out loud, made it real. But what she felt for Everett was real. "I think I love him." No, that wasn't true. "I know I love him."

"Oh." Tansy's eyes were round as saucers, then her face melted into a huge grin. "That's wonderful news."

"I'm so happy for you, Rose." Astrid smiled at her. "Now, get off the floor and go on your date."

"I can't just leave you here." Rosemary shook her head.

"Yes, you can." Astrid pointed at Tansy. "I've got Tansy. She can go on a hot date with Dane anytime."

"This is your first date. The first of many, I'm sure." Tansy stood and held out her hands. "Come on. Up we go."

Rosemary let Tansy help pull her up. "Are you sure?" She hesitated, glancing at Astrid. "I feel guilty."

"I'd feel guiltier if you stayed here with me when you've got Everett waiting." Astrid blew her a kiss.

"Just remember, with the sleeping arrangements the way they are, things can't get too out of hand tonight." Tansy smoothed Rosemary's hair from her shoulder. "It's too early for that anyway. Better to let the anticipation build—"

Rosemary covered her mouth. "Stop. Ohmygosh. Please stop. You're getting way way *way* ahead of things…" She broke off, shaking her head.

"Maybe, but if things do get out of hand, you'll have to get your own room." Tansy grinned.

"Ignore her, Rose. Have fun." But Astrid was chuckling.

"Just not *too* much fun." This time, Tansy winked.

"I'm leaving. Now." Rosemary hurried from the bathroom, closing the door firmly behind her.

"The walls in this place are really thin." Nicole was sitting on one of the beds, the TV remote in one hand.

Rosemary peered around the wall separating the bathroom and closet from the bedroom. There, sitting on one of the beds were Nicole, Kerrielynn, and Halley.

Kerrielynn's smile was apologetic.

"Hi." Halley waved, seemingly unbothered. "I'm here to watch that reality dating show, but Nova's too young." It was bad enough that Kerrielynn had heard all of that. But Halley, too?

Rosemary was mortified. Everything Tansy had said… *Oh no.* "Tansy was teasing."

"She does that." Nicole nodded.

"Nova teases *all* the time. Sisters can be a pain, Aunt Rosemary." Halley shrugged.

"Have fun." Kerrielynn grinned, but there was definitely pink in her cheeks.

They meant well, but Rosemary wished the floor would open and swallow her. "Did you hear everything?"

"You mean the part where you're in love with him?" Nicole asked.

Halley and Kerrielynn nodded.

"We won't say a thing," Kerrielynn added. "Don't worry."

"My lips are sealed, Aunt Rosemary," Halley followed up. "It's cool. Everett is super sweet and cute. We think y'all would be a cute couple."

"It's true." Nicole grinned. "They've been talking about it since you two had your standoff in the ballroom—in front of basically *everyone.*"

She'd been so caught up in Everett she hadn't stopped

to think about who else might have seen them or what they'd think about it. Before things got even more awkward, she said, "I... I should go."

"You look great." Kerrielynn smiled.

Halley gave her a thumbs-up.

"Don't do anything I wouldn't do." Nicole fluttered her fingers at her.

By the time she pulled the hotel room door shut behind her, her face was flaming. She leaned against the door and took a deep breath. She wasn't exactly nauseous, but her nerves were on high alert, so she took another deep breath, then another.

"Rosebud?" Everett was sitting in a grouping of chairs at the end of the hall by the elevators, the convention program open on his lap.

She pushed off the door. "Hey." With another deep breath, she headed down the hall. "I'm sorry if I kept you waiting. Astrid was sick."

"She okay?" He stood, his dark hair falling onto his forehead when he looked down at her.

"Yes. She's pregnant." Try as she might, her reaction to him was instantaneous. Breathless. Weightless. The molten shift in the base of her stomach. The uptick in her pulse. The urge to reach out and touch him. She clasped her hands behind her back. "Tansy is with her. And so are Nicole and Halley and Kerrielynn."

"Sounds like she's covered." His gaze swept over her face. "You want to go? I tried to find us someplace cool to go but there's highway construction. So traffic is real bad, and there's some sort of festival going on in town. The only place I could get a reservation was downstairs." He held out his hand.

"Sounds good to me." She took it, her every nerve

ending acutely aware of the way his fingers slid between hers.

He glanced down at their hands, the muscles in his throat working as he swallowed.

She and Everett had never had a hard time with conversation. Even the last few years, they'd pick up right where they left off and share snippets of their everyday life. But she waited until they were being taken to their table to start. He held the chair out for her, then sat opposite her—but didn't take her hand again.

Her nerves had her diving into conversation. "Tell me what's been going on with you. Not the stuff I know about—the other stuff."

"What other stuff?"

"I don't know." She paused, thinking. "When was the last time you went fishing?"

He glanced at her, his crooked grin putting crinkles at the corners of his eyes. "Fishing?" He shook his head. "Too long."

"That's your recharge time." She frowned. "Considering everything you're dealing with, I think you should schedule a fishing trip."

His brown eyes flashed. "You think?"

"Yep. The sooner, the better." She nodded and tucked a strand of hair behind her ear.

"Yes, ma'am." He was smiling. "What about you?"

"Fishing?" She knew that wasn't what he meant, but his chuckle was reward enough.

"What are you doing to recharge?" His eyes lingered on her mouth before he reached for his glass of ice water.

Her heart sped up, thumping around inside her chest. "I'm doing it." The words were noticeably unsteady, so she cleared her throat. "Painting."

"I'm glad." His gaze was warm on her face. "And writing books."

"It wasn't planned. Bea inspired me. She's a little sponge, you know? Soaking up everything with a sense of wonder. I wanted to do something for her—to give her something worth soaking up." She shrugged. "That might sound silly."

"Not at all, Rosebud." His smile was encouraging. "You light up when you talk about bees and beekeeping, so I know it's important to you. It's a shame you're not planning on selling the books."

"It's all happening so fast. Who knows what the future will bring." She straightened her silverware, her eyes shifting his way over and over.

"Bee books or not, I am a fan of you and your art." His warm brown eyes were steady on her face. "Who knows? With time and reading your bee books, bees could grow on me."

"That's sweet of you to say, Everett." But then, he was sweet. And handsome. Oh so handsome. *Stop staring.* She glanced down at the menu, picked it up, and blindly scanned the offerings. It took a few tries before she was able to focus on the meal choices versus the man sitting opposite her. By the time the waiter appeared to take their order, Rosemary gave up and ordered a salad and a glass of wine. With any luck, the wine would help her relax.

"Not hungry?" he asked once the waiter was gone.

She shrugged. She wasn't hungry. She was nervous. And since this was Everett and she'd always been honest with him, she admitted, "I'm nervous."

Everett almost choked on the sip of the tea he'd taken.

"Sorry." She tucked her hair behind her ear, wishing

she'd kept her mouth shut. "We've always been honest with each other." Except for the bombshell he'd dropped on her about being in love with her—and being over her, that is. If he was still over her, what was this all about?

"We have. Mostly." His gaze met hers and held. "I'm nervous, too."

Which didn't clear up what was happening between them but was a comfort all the same. All she knew was that, right now, she was drowning in those deep brown eyes and she liked it. He had no idea how flustered she was—how flustered he made her. Or how much she hoped he'd kiss her before the night was over.

LEAVE IT TO Rosebud to cut to the chase. But he was glad. He wanted her to know this was a date. He wanted her to know how happy he was they were here, together—wanted her to know he was nervous, too.

Her cheeks were flushed when her gaze fell from his. "Are you going to run for mayor?"

"That's not what I was expecting." He chuckled.

"No?" Her brows rose. "Hmm… Want me to ask you about your dating history next?"

"No, that's okay." He grinned and sat back. "I don't think I am going to run for mayor. I love my job. I don't love doing Mayor Contreras's job."

She nodded. "You don't think it would be different if you were actually the mayor?"

"I think it would be worse. As it is, I can defer back to him. I might be covering for him, but at the end of the day, it's his responsibility—not mine." He ran his fingers through his hair. "I want to go fishing, have a weekend off now and then, take a beautiful woman out for a meal, and not have to worry about a hundred texts rolling in wanting immediate answers and action." He shrugged. "That's not for me."

She nodded. "Knowing what you want is a good thing."

"Didn't pick up on the compliment I slipped in there?" He watched her cheeks go pink. "What about you, Rosebud? I know coming back to Honey wasn't part of your plan. What's your plan look like now?" He held his breath, hoping like hell her plan included staying here.

"I'm not entirely sure yet." She straightened her napkin and silverware. "But I'm happy."

"Happy is good." He tried not to be too disappointed. If Rosebud was happy, he was happy. That's the way it worked. Would he be happier if she said she was staying? One hundred percent, but he wasn't going to pressure her. Whatever she decided, he wanted it to be what was right for her—uncolored by anyone else's opinions or preferences.

Dinner was served, and conversation went well. They started by reminiscing over childhood memories and ended with Rosemary telling him all about her team in California and filling him in more thoroughly on the James Voigt situation. It only confirmed what he'd already pieced together: the man was a jackass. Worse, the man had hurt Rosebud.

"He wasn't wrong. I've never needed praise or recognition. I wanted to be part of the team." She poked at her salad but hadn't eaten much. "It doesn't make sense for me to be so upset over this."

"Hold up, Rosebud." He pushed away his now-empty plate. "If he'd finished the project with your team, it would have been one thing. But he didn't. He worked behind the scenes to use the team's work to get a better situation—for himself, not the team. He left—taking the team's work and data with him. Is that about right?"

She nodded.

"That's deceitful and dishonorable. I'd say that's enough to make anyone upset." If this James Voigt character ever tried to talk to him, Everett would be hard-pressed to stay civil.

"Enough about all that. What's new with the paint-ball situation?" She was genuinely concerned.

"I'm not sure. After Willow Creek, there's been nothing. And nothing new posted on their account, either—except what they did at Willow Creek. It'd be nice to think it's over, but it's too soon to make that assumption."

"You do deserve a break." She pushed her salad away.

"You done?" He eyed the mostly untouched salad. "You feeling okay?"

She nodded and drained her glass of wine.

"Worrying about tomorrow?" He frowned, itching to put James Voigt in his place. "Don't let that bastard get in your head, Rosebud. Knowing you, you'll give a better and more thorough account of your project. He's the one who should be nervous."

She was smiling when those green eyes found his. "I didn't mean to get you so worked up over this. But I appreciate the support. A lot."

"You'll always have it, Rosebud. In case you didn't know that." His heart, too. Though, for now, he'd keep that to himself.

When the bill was settled, they headed out of the restaurant.

"Want to take a walk?" he asked, in no hurry to end this.

"A walk will do me some good. I probably shouldn't

have had that second glass of wine." She smiled up at him. "Thank you for dinner."

"Thank you for keeping me company while I ate." He nudged her. "Since you didn't eat."

"I ate some." She nudged him back.

They walked side by side, close enough that their hands brushed. It was the most natural thing in the world for him to take her hand in his. The little sigh she made when their fingers twined together made him hope she was feeling the same.

Outside the hotel, the city was loud and crowded. If he hadn't done an online search before their meal, he'd have steered them back inside and out of the noise and chaos. Instead, he forged ahead, leading her down a couple of blocks, past an old church, and another block over—to a pretty green park.

"I could never live in the city." Rosebud sank onto one of the wooden benches along the path. "As nice as this is, I can still hear the cars. There's no peace."

"I don't think I could be truly happy outside of Honey." Unless she wanted him to go with her. If that was the case, he'd have some serious thinking to do. He sat beside her, draping his arm along the back of the bench. "Is that what you want, Rosebud? Peace?"

"Isn't that what everyone wants?" The second she looked up at him, the change in the air was palpable. Electrified. Taut. The current between them alive and magnetic.

His brain stalled out, leaving him adrift in those green eyes of hers. If he leaned forward, he'd be close enough to kiss her. And damn, but he wanted to kiss her.

She leaned into him but didn't say a word—instead she hiccupped. Once, then again.

"Rosebud." He chuckled. "You okay?"

She pressed a hand to her head. "I'm feeling a little woozy." She glanced up at him. "I'm sorry."

"There's nothing to be sorry about." He pulled her against his side. "Rest a bit. Until your head clears." He liked the way her head felt against his chest. He loved the way she sighed as she slid her arm around his waist and tucked against him.

They stayed that way long enough for the shadows to grow long and the color of the sky to go dark blue. He'd have been content to stay here all night but knew that wasn't an option.

"We should probably head back," he murmured against her temple.

She burrowed closer.

He smiled, his arm tightening around her. This was good. No, better than good. This was...right. "We're not in Honey. I don't know how safe Austin is after dark." He wasn't willing to put her at risk, no matter how small that risk was.

"Fine." She sighed, easing out of his hold and standing. She held her hand out to him.

He stood, took her hand, and ever so slowly led them back to the hotel. In the elevator up to their floor, her hand tightened around his. He glanced down at her and instantly regretted it. The way she was studying his face... He swallowed. How many times had he dreamed of Rosebud looking at him with hunger in her eyes? The way she was looking at him now.

The elevator doors opened and they stepped out, the walk to her hotel room door far too short.

"Thanks again for tonight." She stood on tiptoe and kissed his cheek.

He hugged her, aware of how soft and warm she was against him. He dropped a kiss on her cheek. "Sleep tight, Rosebud."

"You, too." Her voice was husky, and her gaze fell to his mouth. "Everett…" She twined her arms around his neck and pressed the soft fullness of her mouth against his.

He should stop this and hold her away from him—

Her lips parted beneath his, and he was lost. Her fingers slid into the hair at the nape of his neck and tugged him closer. He couldn't stifle the moan that slipped out when her tongue touched his. There was no hesitancy in the way her hands slid up and over his chest, only want. She wanted him.

He pressed her tightly against him, anchoring her against the wall at her back. He could feel the rapid beat of her heart against his and hear the rasp of her breathing as he deepened the kiss. Her want for him only fueled his need for her.

And he did need her. Because he loved her. He loved her smile and her laugh, the way she cared about her family—and him. He loved the way she lit up when she talked about her bees or her books or painting, and he loved the fire in her eyes when she'd looked at him in the elevator. There was nothing restrained about the way he was kissing her or the way she clung to him. And even though he wanted her, like this, now and forever, he knew things were moving too fast.

"Rosebud," he murmured, lifting his mouth from hers.

She shook her head, her lips finding his once more.

He groaned, pressing a last kiss to her forehead. "You're going to make this difficult."

She opened her eyes and frowned up at him. "Make what difficult?"

Her voice was husky and all kinds of sexy. With her blazing eyes and flushed cheeks, Rosebud was sexy. And even though he wasn't going to let anything else happen, he did want her. "This." If he wasn't careful, he'd be kissing her again in no time. "Taking things slowly." He eased his hold on her and stepped back. "Being careful. I don't want there to be regrets between us, Rosebud."

"Oh…" She blinked, dazed. "Right." She blinked a few times, her lips swollen from his kisses. "You're right."

Was he? The way she was gripping his shirt—her unsteady breathing made him second-guess himself. It took everything he had not to throw caution to the wind and pull her back into his arms. But this was Rosebud. "I just…"

She stared up at him, her eyes so bright and green he tripped over his words.

"You're you. My best friend. Special." He swallowed, knowing he wasn't saying what he needed to say. "I care about you too much to rush things, Rosebud. You're not sure what you want, and I respect that. And this… Well, I sure as hell don't want to stand in the way of what you do want…or ruin anything." Now he'd gone and said too much.

Her smile was soft and gentle. "You could never do that, Everett."

His heart turned over at the faith on her face.

"Good night." She pressed a kiss to his cheek. "I'll see you in the morning." She used the key card to let herself into her room, waved at him, and closed the door behind her.

The moment she was gone, pure panic sank into his bones.

What was he doing? What was he thinking? By opening up and kissing her and letting his heart get the best of him, he'd done the very thing he'd spent years trying not to do. He'd put their friendship at risk in a big way. He knew she had decisions and plans to make, and he'd inserted himself into the mix. Her choices were hers alone to make. She'd worked too hard to be weighing his wants or feelings when she made any decisions. As much as he'd like to think she wouldn't, he knew better. Rosebud's heart was too big. What he'd done wasn't fair to her. *Dammit all.*

What was he supposed to do now? He had to do something because the thought of losing Rosebud altogether was too much. It kicked up the one thing he didn't want to feel about her: regret.

Somehow, he had to fix this—even if he had to break his heart in the process.

CHAPTER THIRTEEN

IT HAD BEEN a long night, one Rosemary pretended to sleep through. If she hadn't, she'd have been bombarded with questions about what happened between her and Everett. She wasn't ready to share. Not yet. It was all too... magical. She'd kissed him—okay, more like thrown herself at him. He hadn't minded. Not one bit.

I care too much about you to rush things.

She smiled up at the ceiling. All night, she'd replayed their date. The looks. The touches. The way he'd held her tight. And the way he'd responded. The power of his kiss... There'd been no missing the rapid thunder of his heart against hers.

Every time she closed her eyes, she saw Everett's face when he'd held her away from him. Warm. Fighting with restraint. Breathing hard and oh so gorgeous. She pulled the covers over her head and curled into a ball.

"You need to get up, Rose." Tansy grabbed her foot and gave it a wiggle. "Your panel is in an hour."

Right. The panel. But she was too happy to let facing down James Voigt get to her. "I'm up," she murmured, pushed the comforter off, and sat up.

"Wow. You're *glowing*." Nicole sat on the foot of the bed. "But what's with the bags under your eyes?"

Rosemary smiled at her. "Good morning to you,

too." She hadn't gotten much sleep last night. "It can't be that bad."

"Rose, honey, I'm sorry but…" Nicole slipped off the bed, dug through her overnight bag, and returned with a mirror. "The bags under your eyes have bags."

Rosemary peered at her reflection and grimaced. "Perfect." Not that she was going to let it get her down. Nope. No way. Not today.

"I'm assuming things went well last night?" Tansy sat on the other corner of the bed. "Are you going to share the highlights with us?"

She shook her head. "Not yet. Not now…" She broke off, unable to stop herself from smiling.

"Kerrielynn's gone to breakfast with Astrid and family." Tansy leaned on one arm, cocking her head to one side. "If that makes a difference."

She shook her head again.

"Okay." Tansy held up both hands. "Our sister gave me a long lecture about giving you space and respecting your boundaries, so I'm going to try."

"I'm doing your makeup." Nicole carried her overnight bag to the bed. "You need some cover-up. Maybe a little blush."

Rosemary took another look at her reflection and decided not to argue with Nicole. "But don't go overboard, please." She wanted to look her best today. Not just for Everett, but for herself. Yes, she'd be presenting something she knew backward and forward, but a presentation was only as good as its presenter. This was important to her. This mattered. She wanted to knock their socks off and leave an impression.

"What are you wearing?" Tansy asked, opening the closet door but glancing her way.

She shrugged. "I wasn't sure, so I brought a few options. I'll let you pick."

"Excellent." Tansy stood, her hands on her hips and her face determined. "I'm so excited. You've got a chance to put the asshat in his place. Justice for you and who knows how many others. You said you suspected he's done this sort of thing before, so it's up to you to make sure he'll think twice before acting like such a tool on other projects." She adjusted her ponytail, her dangly bee earrings shaking. "Don't forget, we're all going to be there rooting for you."

Her big sister was right. She needed to focus. Last night had been...wonderful but she needed to set all thoughts of Everett, the weight of his arms around her waist, and the delectable taste of his lips aside. For now at least. She'd been given the opportunity to make sure James Voigt accurately presented their data to a group of her peers. She took a deep breath. "All as in who?"

"All." Tansy shrugged. "Like, everyone."

"Except me and Benji. We're manning the booth. But I've a feeling all the science stuff would go over my head anyway." Nicole came forward, eyeshadow palette in hand. "Now, close your eyes."

"I don't wear eyeshadow." Rosemary shook her head.

"You do today." Nicole pointed at Rosemary's eyes with the makeup brush. "Close 'em."

While Tansy pieced together what she deemed a professional outfit, Nicole kept working on Rosemary's makeup until they were all happy.

They went downstairs with a few minutes to spare. Nicole set off for the expo hall while she and her sisters made their way to the meeting room. She gratefully accepted a cup of coffee from Astrid before heading to the front of the room that had been booked for today's lecture. A dais had been set up with a table and three chairs—one of the chairs was occupied by James Voigt.

"Rosemary." His smile was too big and too bright.

"James." She sat, putting her to-go cup full of coffee on the table.

Jane helped them clip on their microphones before introducing each of them. She rattled off accolades that made Rosemary sound far more impressive than she was.

When Jane said, "I've also been informed that she's just finished her first children's book, *ABC's with Baby Bee*," Rosemary sighed and stared out over the crowd. Her sisters were pointing at one another, but Rosemary suspected they were both to blame for this information being made public. Not that she was mad. If anything, it made her proud that her family was so eager to share her pet project. There was an entire row waving and smiling her way.

Everett wasn't there. That was fine. That was good. No distractions. But his absence stung all the same.

"Both of our presenters have spent the last several years working on the bee genome directory. Let's jump right in. Dr. Voigt, why don't you start?"

"Good morning." James turned a charming smile on the full room. "The goal of the project was quite simple. By collecting a sample of at least one hundred and twenty-five bee species—"

Rosemary glanced at him. Did he realize he was quoting the blurb in the program? The blurb she'd written.

"Eventually, linking functions to specific genes."

He paused. "So far we've collected and begun mapping seventy-six distinct species."

Eighty-nine species.

"We've chosen six priority categories. Mite resistance, productivity, climate susceptibility, pesticide susceptibility, evolution and specialization, and nonnative bee impact." He turned to her. "Would you like to add anything?"

Rosemary nodded. "Mapping will help breed heartier bees, but there's more to it than that. For example, if we're able to map an endangered species' DNA, researchers can go into the field to that specific bee's known habitat and swab flowers for matching bee DNA. This will prevent unnecessary damage to a specimen or taking it from its natural habitat."

A murmur of surprise rolled through the audience, encouraging her to go on. She hadn't meant to get carried away, but she couldn't stop. This project had been her world for four long years. It had been thrilling to see them discover the slight physiological changes of one species due to the reduction in access to a primary pollen source.

While she talked, she kept her focus on Tansy or Astrid. When they both started to look a little glazed over, she realized she'd carried on too long.

"Thank you for that interesting insight, Dr. Hill." Jane smiled at her, then turned to James. "What have you found to be the most significant discovery you've made during this project, Dr. Voigt?"

Rosemary almost tuned him out when he started talking. He talked in circles, repeating things without expanding on their processes, data, or the implications. She glanced at James, only to find him studying her.

"But as you just heard, having the best of the best on my team is the real reason we've accomplished as much as we have." James nodded at her. "Without Dr. Hill's tireless determination, attention to detail, and her ability to assess and dissect complicated patterns, I don't think we'd have made the progress we made over the last three years."

She blinked, stunned. It was nice that he was publicly acknowledging her efforts, but it didn't undo how he'd handled things or put her back on the project she'd loved. Maybe that was why she corrected him. "Four years."

There were a few chuckles in the audience.

"See? Detail oriented." James grinned at her. "Crossing every *T* and dotting every *I*."

Her smile was grudging before she glanced out—searching for her sisters and finding Everett instead.

He *was* here. He was smiling at her and mouthing, *good job*, while giving her two thumbs-up. That was all it took to have her smiling back at him.

"The bee genome project has been picked up by the National Science Institute—along with some private funding. Are the two of you continuing your work there?" Jane asked.

James nodded. "At least, I'm hoping Dr. Hill will consider joining me for the next phase of research. The project has been fully funded for another five years, and there's no one I'd rather work with than Dr. Hill. As you can all see, she gets results and those results will benefit us all."

Rosemary was dumbfounded. First, he was giving her praise, now he was asking her to come work with him again? Or was he trying to come across as magnanimous and powerful? Either way, she felt every eye in the room on her. All she could say was, "I don't know what to say."

"After listening to what you've had to say here today, I think we can all understand why Dr. Voigt would want you back." Jane smiled. "Have you been on hiatus while the project was undergoing restructuring?"

She wasn't flattered, she was suspicious. What was James up to? And while she knew she wasn't on hiatus and restructuring was an awfully kind way to describe what had happened, she decided nodding was the easiest answer.

"And you've written a children's book?" Jane asked.

"For my nieces and nephews, yes." She glanced at her family and the smiles on their faces. "It's an ABC book all about bees."

"How delightful." Jane smiled. "Do you have a copy with you?"

"Yes." Nova's little voice echoed. Seconds later, she came skipping up the aisle, one of the board books in her hand, causing a chorus of laughter from the audience. Nova held the book up until Rosemary took it. "Aunt Rosemary did all the pictures and words, too." She grinned, turned, and skipped back to Astrid and Charlie.

"That's my niece Nova." Rosemary's cheeks were burning as she handed over the book.

"You did the illustration?" Jane studied the cover of the book.

"I did." She shot her two very guilty-looking sisters a narrow-eyed look. Were they enjoying this? Seeing her squirm?

"I'll open the floor to questions. If you have a question, please use the mic so everyone can hear it." Jane pointed at the mic in the middle of the aisle.

Rosemary did her best to ignore Jane flipping through her book and resisted snatching the book back when James reached for it. It wasn't like he could steal her book from her or take credit for the idea.

Once again, she looked Everett's way. He was glaring at James—who was reading her book. It was oddly comforting—and had her grinning like a fool.

By the time the Q&A finished, Rosemary had reached her peopling quota for the day. She accepted Jane's thanks for participating and her praise for the book and practically jumped off the dais to avoid any further interaction with James.

Tansy was waving her toward them, Astrid was clapping, and Kerrielynn seemed to be filming. Before she reached her cheering section, a woman stepped in her path.

"Dr. Hill? I'm Amanda Sifuentes, from Texas A&M University." The woman held out her card.

"My alma mater. It's nice to meet you." Texas A&M had the best apiculture programs in the state. It's where she, Astrid, and Tansy had all gotten their undergraduate degrees—like Poppa Tom before them.

"I was really blown away by your lecture, your thorough knowledge of genome sequencing, and your enthusiasm. It was contagious."

Rosemary nodded, her attention fixing on the very tall, very handsome, very sweet man walking her way. Everett, smiling at her, like he was proud of her. Her poor heart didn't stand a chance.

"I'd love to sit down with you and discuss an associate professorship opening we have—something I think you'd be a perfect fit for."

Rosemary blinked, the woman's words slowly registering. An associate professorship? At Texas A&M? But before she could respond, Everett was beside her, and she was struggling to concentrate. "I'm flattered," she murmured before nodding Everett's way. "Hey."

"You did great, Rosebud." He smiled down at her. "My mind is still trying to figure out exactly what you said, but I know it was impressive."

Amanda Sifuentes laughed. "She is quite the font of bee-centric information, isn't she?" She held out her hand. "Amanda Sifuentes. Dean for Texas A&M's entomology department."

"Sorry for interrupting. Everett Taggert. Lewis County parks and recreation director and Rosemary Hill's best friend." He shook her hand. "Nice to meet you."

"You, too." Amanda turned back to her. "I know we all have places to be, so I'll keep my sales pitch short. As you know, Texas A&M is the best apiculture program in the state. Our research objectives differ slightly from the genome-mapping project, but I think you'll find we have a lot of exciting opportunities in the coming years. I'll be doing a presentation on some of our latest programs at two. If you're free, it might give you a more in-depth look at what we're working on."

Rosemary nodded, beyond flattered. "I'll be there."

"Wonderful. Maybe we can get coffee afterward? Depending on what you think of the presentation, of course." The woman laughed. "I'll see you later this afternoon."

Rosemary stared after the woman, taking time to steady herself before she faced Everett. For some reason, she felt close to tears. The last twenty-four hours had been a lot. James. Everett. Her book being outed. Now Amanda Sifuentes. A lot, a lot. The last thing she needed to do, especially here, was cry. She took a deep breath. "Did you hear that?"

Everett nodded. "After your presentation, I'm not surprised." His brown eyes swept over her face. "Texas A&M is where you went to school. It sounds like a good fit. I'd think working there would be kind of like coming home, wouldn't it?"

Except he wouldn't be there. Neither would her sisters or aunts or Honey Hill Farms. And while she was flattered Amanda Sifuentes thought she was up for the job, Rosemary wasn't so sure she wanted it.

EVERETT WAS TRANSFIXED by Rosebud. She was on in a way he'd never seen her before. This was what fed her and thrilled her—this was who she was. Bee expert, advocate, educator, and artist. She was all those things and so much more. And he loved who she was. She grew animated when she talked, her features fluid and absolutely captivating. Somehow she'd managed to turn thirty minutes of scientific mumbo jumbo into something relatable and inspiring.

After seeing her in action, he realized she was wrong about herself. She wasn't just a people person, she was an inspiring leader. He didn't know a thing about beekeeping—he wasn't all that fond of bees—but she'd managed to impart their importance to the world, not just the audience in the room. Why was she working under someone like James Voigt when she could be guiding and encouraging her own team?

If there'd been a neon sign flashing overhead, it

couldn't have been more obvious: Rosebud had to do this—right here. Research and educate her peers. Be a leader in her industry. Follow her passion—even though that would likely take her from Honey. And him.

He'd lain awake most of the night, knowing what he had to do—this morning only confirmed his decision. Everett was her best friend, he needed to support her. He'd encourage her to consider this job with Texas A&M. If she decided to go back to the genome project, he'd find a way to muster enthusiasm—even if he wanted her as far from that leech James Voigt as possible. Whatever she wanted, whatever filled her with the joy he'd seen on her face, he'd help her find it.

He couldn't ask her to give this up for the life *he* wanted. So, he wouldn't. He'd tell he valued her friendship too much to jeopardize it by pursuing anything romantically, even if it tore his heart in two. Considering he'd never outright lied to Rosebud before, he hoped he could pull it off.

"Are you all right?" Rosebud asked.

He would be, in time. "Yep."

"Ohmygosh." Kerrielynn rushed up. "That was amazing."

"You were totally in charge up there." Halley nodded, looking at Rosebud with a budding case of hero worship.

"As far as I'm concerned, you were the only presenter on that stage." Astrid hugged her. "I'm so proud of you."

Me, too, Rosebud. So damn proud.

Tansy joined in the hug, and the three of them squished together with their eyes closed and their arms holding tight. There was such love on the sisters' faces. He knew how much Tansy and Astrid had missed having their baby sister around—and how much they'd hate to see her go. But like him, they'd smile and wave and send her off without blinking an eye. Because, like him, Rosebud's happiness was what mattered most.

"Who was that lady you were talking to?" Kerrie-lynn asked once the hugging was over. "She was one of the exam proctors."

The woman who might help make Rosebud's dreams come true. He swallowed. At least she'd be here in Texas.

"She has a serious RBF." Halley shook her head.

"RBF?" Astrid asked.

Halley covered Nova's ears. "Resting bitch face." She lifted her hands.

Everett managed to cover his laugh with a cough once he saw the disapproval on Charlie's face.

"Halley." There was a gentle warning in Charlie's voice.

"What? I didn't *use* the B word. I was only explaining what RBF meant." Halley shrugged.

Charlie sighed, but smiled. "And now we all know."

"What is that?" Nova asked, young and innocent.

Everett waited to see how this was going to play out.

"Nothing." Charlie sighed, no longer smiling. "Teenager stuff."

"Oh." Nova nodded. "Teenagers are weird."

That got everyone laughing.

"That's Amanda Sifuentes, isn't it?" Dane asked. "I think we've talked to her a few times, Tansy. The apiary program at Texas A&M?"

"Yes, that's her." Rosebud nodded. "She's the dean of entomology there." Rosebud glanced at the business card in her hand. "She was impressed with the lecture."

Everett studied Rosebud's face. Amanda Sifuentes had all but offered Rosebud a job. A big, important job from the sounds of it. That was the sort of thing he would expect Rosebud to share with her sisters. But she wasn't. Did that mean she was leaning toward working with Voigt again? He hoped not but... *Whatever she wants.*

"The way you were throwing those fancy scientific words around *was* pretty impressive," Dane teased.

Rosebud rolled her eyes and laughed. "That was the goal."

"How about we move this outside before Dr. Voigt gets to you?" Tansy glared across the room.

Sure enough, James Voigt was edging his way toward them.

"I am sort of curious if he was serious about the job," Rosebud murmured as they headed out of the meeting room.

"You are?" Astrid's eyes went round. "But...why?"

"Even after the sh..." Tansy glanced at Nova and shook her head, a V forming between her brows. "After what he did? Rose, why?"

"I believe in the goal of the project." That was Rosebud, able to see the big picture. "We'll all benefit from it."

She nibbled on the inside of her lower lip—making it hard for Everett not to remember how her mouth felt beneath his. He sucked in a deep breath and stared at the geometric pattern in the hotel carpet at his feet.

"I'm not saying I could work with him again. I don't know if I could." Rosebud's voice lowered. "I know that's selfish—"

"Selfish?" Everett blurted out, his eyes finding hers. "Rosebud, that's the last word anyone could ever use to describe you."

The smile she gave him wobbled, and then her gaze fell from his.

His chest collapsed in on itself. What was going on inside that head of hers? He needed to know—soon.

"Well, you did rock it, Rosemary." Kerrielynn held up her phone. "We're going to go film some stuff. But we'll be in room C for Tansy and Dane's agritourism talk, if that's okay?"

"Sounds good. Y'all stay together." Tansy pointed at Kerrielynn's phone. "And remember to tag the farm and Wholesome Foods if you post, please."

"Will do." Kerrielynn nodded.

"Stay together," Charlie said, smiling at Halley's overdramatic eye roll and her mumbled "okay, geez."

"She'll be fine. They're good kids, they look out for one another." Astrid took Charlie's hand, watching Halley, Leif, and Kerrielynn disappear into the crowd.

"Everett has a point, Rose. Not that you asked me, but I don't want you working for that tool." Tansy took Rosemary's hand. "If you do go back to academia, dig around and find out all you can before taking a position."

"That's good advice no matter what field you are in," Charlie said. "Coworkers can make or break a productive working environment."

Everett was pretty sure that was the most he'd ever heard the man say. "Isn't that the truth?"

"Interesting, considering who you work with every day." Dane's grin was all mischief.

Was he talking about Rosebud? Or Libby? Either way, he wasn't going to touch it. Instead he turned to Rosebud. "You shouldn't work with someone who doesn't value or acknowledge the contributions you make. That's not selfish, that's smart."

"I know this *is* selfish, but it would be nice to have you stay in Honey for a while, Rosemary." Astrid took Rosebud's other hand. "You have to be here when Nuc is born so you can read him or her your book."

As sweet a picture as that painted, he wouldn't say as much.

"I'll be here for Nuc's birth, whether I'm living in Honey or not. I promise." Rosebud's words all but confirmed she was thinking about leaving.

"Can we go to the art room now?" Nova tugged on Astrid's arm.

"Oh, there's an art room?" Rosebud smiled down at the eager little girl. "I want to go, too."

Charlie, the sisters, and Nova all headed one way while he and Dane went to check in on Nicole in the booth.

Dane glanced his way. "You going to tell me what happened last night?"

Hell no. "Nothing."

"Really?" Dane nodded at someone they passed. "Here I thought we were friends."

"I realized we're better off as friends." He shrugged, hoping Dane would believe him.

"I'm sorry, what?" Dane blew out a low whistle. "When did that happen? Because I'm pretty sure you were like a kid on Christmas morning last night before your date."

He shook his head. "It's what makes sense. What's best for us both."

Dane came to a stop. "I know what you're doing, Everett. Don't. It's okay to go after something you want, you know? Or someone."

"I can't lose her friendship, Dane. That's real and reliable and...enough." He took a deep breath. "Besides, you saw how she was up there, Dane. Voigt wasn't the only one wanting her on staff. That woman from Texas A&M wants her, too. She deserves a job that'll give her that fire every day." He wanted that for her.

Dane stared at him.

He leveled his best friend with a hard glare. "If you go and tell Tansy any of this, I will kick your ass."

"I won't." Dane crossed his arms over his chest, emphasizing his muscles. "But I'd like to see you try."

"Whatever." Everett started walking again, hoping that was the end of it.

"You're a real jackass, you know that?" Dane shook his head, then started walking again.

"Yeah, I do." He was grateful when they reached the booth. As much as he wanted to believe Dane wouldn't repeat this entire conversation to Tansy, he was worried. "I mean it about Tansy."

"Oh, believe me, I'm not getting in the middle of this." Dane held up his hands. "And in case you didn't hear me the first time, you're a jackass."

Everett spent the next hour at the booth. While Nicole gabbed with customers and sold honey, he and Benji unloaded the last of the boxes and restocked the shelves. Dane had gone out to the truck to see if they'd overlooked a box of honey. At the rate things were going, they'd sell out before the day was over.

As he was rearranging the display, an older woman pointed at him. "You're the guy."

"The guy?" Everett frowned. What now?

"The one reading that book to the little girl?" The woman smiled. "My daughter sent me the video on Instagram and asked me to find you." The woman pulled out her wallet. "Please tell me you still have copies because I want to get one for my other grandbabies, too."

Everett and Benji exchanged a look.

"Kerrielynn." Benji grinned. "She *is* recording *everything*."

At least this was about Rosebud's book and not something to do with that bachelor article.

"We don't have any copies available at the moment." Nicole's smile was sympathetic. "But if you want to leave your email address, I'll let you know when we get more in."

Had Nicole sold Rosebud's books? If she had, he knew Rosebud wasn't going to be happy.

"That's a shame." The woman gazed over the display. "My daughter got me watching the videos Tansy and Dane post when they're beekeeping. They are the cutest couple. And the other two sisters are so pretty, aren't they? I hadn't seen the other one until that video this morning. I didn't know what she was talking about, but it's clear she's smart as a whip."

Everett chuckled at that.

Nicole held out a tablet and pen. "Jot your email address down, and I'll let you know about the books."

The woman wrote her email address and handed back the tablet. "I can't wait." She looked around. "I was hoping I'd see one of the Hill sisters or Dane."

"There's Dane." Nicole pointed. "Looks like he found another box of honey."

"My goodness, he *is* handsome. My daughter was showing me the picture of that actor, the one who plays Thor? A lot of fans online think they could be twins, but I don't think they look all that much alike. Dane is far handsomer." The woman said this in all sincerity.

Everett was chuckling again. If Dane had heard that, he'd be grinning from ear to ear. He hated being called Thor or being compared to the actor that played him.

"Dane, you have a fan," Nicole said, taking the box from Dane and handing it to Benji.

"Thanks to you and the Bee Girls, I've been planting bee-friendly flowers and making sure they have water, too." The woman smiled up at Dane.

"That's nice to hear. The bees and Tansy and I appreciate your efforts."

"And then the video of that hot guy—that's what my daughter said, not me—over there reading that book popped up on your feed, and I had to come get a couple of them." The woman's face fell. "Too bad you're out of books."

"I've got your email. I'll be sure to let you know." Nicole scanned the paper. "Gladys."

"Alrighty, dear." Gladys paused. "Dane, can I get a picture with you? My daughter will be so jealous."

Dane chuckled. "No problem."

Everett took a picture of Dane and Gladys, then helped her pick out two Texas Viking Honey T-shirts, several jars of honey, and a box of Honey Hill Farms Milk & Honey soap. "You all keep on posting the good work," she said as she moved on.

"She's like the thirtieth person that's stopped by here hoping to buy a book or see you or Tansy or Astrid or Rosemary or the hot reading guy." Nicole pointed at Everett. "I feel like y'all should post appearance times and charge for pictures. You'd make loads of money."

"Where are Rosebud's books?" Everett didn't see the box anywhere.

Nicole lifted up one of the table coverings. "I hid

them. I mean, I was tempted to sell them, but I wasn't sure Rosemary would ever forgive me."

"Now Everett's the hot reading guy? Because most eligible bachelor isn't enough?" Dane found this a little too amusing.

"I'm happy not being either." Everett shot a glare Dane's way.

"I saw the video." Nicole shrugged and turned to Everett. "If I didn't know you so well, I'd have to agree."

Everett was laughing now. "Fair enough."

When Rosebud and the others showed up, Nicole got a kick out of sharing everything all over again.

Everett didn't hear the rest of the conversation. Rosebud had walked to the edge of the booth and was digging through a box. He took a deep breath and headed her way, flexing his hands at his sides. The sooner he got this over with, the sooner things could get back to normal. At least he hoped that would be the case.

"Hey, Rosebud." His voice was low, for her ears only.

She glanced up at him, a smile instantly on her lips. "Hi." A blush stained her cheeks. "How did you sleep last night?"

Her smile had him swallowing against the tightness of his throat. "Fine. Fine." He cleared his throat. "I wanted to talk to you about that."

"Okay." She took an unsteady breath, biting on her lower lip.

He shoved his hands into his pockets so he wouldn't smooth the hair from her shoulder. "You're my best friend, Rosebud, and nothing will change that." He hoped like hell she'd believe what he was saying. He wasn't. "The thing is, I don't want to change that. You and me, best friends. That's the way it should be, you know? Last night was…" Wonderful. Everything he always wanted. "A wake-up call. It made me realize what I want, and well, I'm hoping you'll be okay if we stick with the status quo. Maybe, I don't know, pretend that last night didn't happen?" He tried to chuckle.

She stared at him for a long time, her smile fading away until her expression was unreadable. And it hurt. Something fierce. "Oh… Right…" She swallowed.

"But hey, today has been a good day." He forced a smile. "You knocked Voigt down a peg and got two job offers doing what you love to do." He did his best to sound upbeat. "Whether you take the job with Voigt…" he paused and frowned "…or Texas A&M…" he paused and smiled "…I'll back your decision." *Stop talking. Stop talking, now.*

The silence stretched on so long, his stomach had tied itself into a hundred tiny knots.

Finally, she said, "Thanks, Everett. I can always count on you to support me." Her smile was small but warm. "And last night…forgotten." She blinked rapidly. "I agree. I… I value our friendship too much to do something…we'd regret."

Too late. But he did his best to keep on smiling as he asked, "We're good?" He couldn't do this. He couldn't stay. He'd already told one lie. It wasn't hard to tell another. "I've got to head back to Honey, but I wanted to make sure we were okay before I took off."

She nodded. "We are. Like you said, nothing can change our friendship." Her gaze wouldn't meet his, and she was blinking rapidly. "You've always been honest with me, Everett. I appreciate that." She took a deep breath. "I guess I'll catch part of Amanda's talk." She walked across the expo hall and out the door.

Everett watched her go, the crippling pain in his chest familiar. He'd been here before and survived. He'd do it again.

CHAPTER FOURTEEN

FOR ROSEMARY, the rest of the convention was a whirlwind.

She caught a few minutes of Amanda Sifuentes's lecture and met to have coffee with her later that afternoon. The Texas A&M program was as impressive as she'd known it would be. Their research department had a state-of-the-art facility, extensive resources, and multiyear funding for their current projects. The application process was lengthy, but Amanda unofficially assured her multiple times that the team would be ecstatic to have her onboard.

But as grateful as she was about Amanda's offer, she found it hard to get excited about the position.

Tansy and Dane's presentation was a success. Over the course of the weekend, she'd been surprised by how many people said hello to her—people she didn't know. But after the presentation, she realized the extent of the couple's online presence.

The room was packed wall to wall. While there were beekeepers looking for information about agritourism ventures and how it would impact their current business, a large number of the audience was here for the Hill family and the "Viking" Dane Knudson. They wanted to hear about Honey Hill Farms' Blue Ribbon Honey contest win, the Hills' deal with Wholesome Foods, as well as silly bits of information like what Dane and Tansy did on dates, had the sisters all wanted to be bee-keepers, what sex Astrid's baby was, and a whole slew of too-personal questions that Tansy and Dane somehow managed to dodge while remaining charming and engaging. Once their presentation wrapped up, she posed with pictures along with her sisters and Dane.

"I told you. You could totally charge for pics and media appearances." Nicole nodded at the line of people waiting.

Through it all, Rosemary managed to shove down the hurt and sadness that threatened to swallow her. It wasn't the end of the world. Everett would always be in her life and her best friend. That had to be enough. She had to convince her heart that was enough. There was no other alternative.

Sunday afternoon was a relief. They returned to Honey Hill Farms to find Aunt Camellia and Van at home. Amid the feast Aunt Camellia prepared, the new-lyweds announced their intent to live there, on Honey Hill Farms. Poppa Tom and Granna Hazel's suite of rooms were only ever used when all the other bed-rooms were full, which was a rarity in the sprawling old house. Why not renovate the space and give it to the newlyweds?

Everyone was thrilled, of course. They'd all been struggling with the idea of life on the farm without Ca-mellia's warmth making it complete. And though she remained as subdued as ever, Rosemary suspected Aunt Mags was the happiest about this new arrangement.

That evening, they gathered around the television for the video Kerrielynn had made so the aunts and Van could see some of their convention adventures.

Watching Everett read to Nova was especially difficult, but she did her best not to let it show. The problem was, the more she tried not to think about Everett, the more he seemed to pop up. In conversation, stories, or videos. Each and every time she heard his name, she was reliving that evening and her heart twisted itself into knots.

Painful or not, she appreciated Everett's honesty.

For him, nothing had changed. But for her... It was going to take time for the hole in her heart to heal. Eventually, she'd stop thinking about how big and tall and gorgeous and completely out of reach Everett was. Eventually, their friendship would be all she needed.

Early Monday before the rest of the house was stirring, Aunt Camellia made her a cup of coffee and said, "Rosemary, I'm worried about you." She slid a plate of honey oat muffins and honey butter biscuits onto the table. "I know you're a grown woman and fully capable of taking care of yourself, but I've been known to have good solid shoulders to lean on and ears that work just fine, if you need someone to listen."

Rosemary turned her coffee cup in her hands. "I'm sure Tansy and Astrid have filled you in on...things?" She glanced at her aunt. Her sisters had been shocked over Everett's change of heart, but so far, they'd respected her wishes to leave it alone.

"They've mentioned a few things. But you're the only one that knows what's really weighing you down. That's what I'd like to hear about." She sipped her coffee, put the cup on the table, and reached into her apron pocket. "If you're inclined to share, that is." She held up an oyster cracker. "How's my boy?" she crooned to Lord Byron. "How's my handsome boy?"

Lord Byron cooed and fawned over Aunt Camellia. She was his person; the bird tolerated everyone else. "Handsome boy," he echoed.

"Yes, you are." She fed him another cracker and ran her fingers over his head. "So handsome."

Lord Byron clucked and whistled, closing his eyes and leaning into her touch.

Rosemary watched the familiar exchange. Lord Byron had been here when she and her sisters had come to live on Honey Hill Farms years ago. Even then, he'd adored Aunt Camellia more than anyone or anything—except maybe oyster crackers.

Aunt Camellia nodded at the plate. "Eat something and settle your stomach."

How did her aunt know her stomach was upset? Because she always knew, just like she always gave good advice. *I do* need *advice.* "I'm not sure what to do about Everett." Rosebud leaned forward to rest her forehead on the kitchen table. The second she closed her eyes, she could see him. Those warm brown eyes staring at her like kissing her was the only thing that mattered. No, that's what she'd wanted to see. That wasn't how he felt. She swallowed against the lump in her throat.

"Does something need to be done?" Aunt Camellia asked.

She shrugged, her forehead still on the table. "I don't know. I hope so. I need to…to be happy with our friendship." Her words were muffled.

"When did you stop being happy with your friendship?"

"When I fell in love with him." She raised her head, meeting her aunt's gaze.

"Oh." Aunt Camellia blinked. "I see."

"I don't know how to make that go away. But I need to because *this* hurts." She ran her hands over her hair. "I can't stop seeing him as…" She shrugged, words failing her. "Manly Everett." She winced.

"He's always been a man, dear." Aunt Camellia fed another cracker to Lord Byron and sat across from her. "But I think I understand what you mean. I'd known Van for years before I realized what dreamboat of a man he was." Her expression softened. "I hate that I wasted so many years being so blind."

Rosemary nodded. "At least Van loves you back."

Aunt Camellia's smile was sympathetic. "And Everett doesn't?"

She shook her head. "He said he wants to stay friends. Always. He doesn't want anything to happen that might ruin that." Like kisses that had turned her world upside down and made her realize what a kiss could be. Kisses he wasn't going to waste time thinking about. Her chest grew hollow and achy.

Aunt Camellia frowned, pushing the plate across the table. "I'm sorry you're hurting. Heartache is no slight thing."

Rosemary nodded.

"This likely won't offer much consolation now, but you're young and strong, and things have a way of working out like they should. It might not feel that way now, but give it time." She patted her hand. "And eat."

She sat up and put a biscuit and muffin on one of the plates Aunt Camellia had put on the table. "Seeing you and Van together makes things better. I'm so glad you're so happy, Aunt Camellia."

Her aunt's face was wreathed in smiles. "I am, too. He's the sweetest man on the planet. It was his idea to make this our home. I think he understood how important it was for me to stay here." She peered around the kitchen—her kitchen. "I can't imagine living anyplace else."

Rosemary looked around the room, too. While she loved the big old house where she'd spent her childhood, it wasn't these walls that made it her home. It was the people who lived within them. Still, she could understand why her aunts might feel differently. They had lived their whole lives here.

"You've freshened up all the bees and flowers throughout the house—better than ever, I'd say." Aunt Camellia took a muffin for herself. "You've taken a very important job with Everett, you've written your first children's book, and I hear you're going to start queen-rearing here on the farm?" She peeled the wrapper off the muffin. "It sounds to me like you're been keeping yourself busy."

Rosemary nodded.

"But are you happy?" She broke off a piece of her muffin. "You can stay busy from dawn till dusk, but it won't matter if you're not happy."

She didn't have to think about her answer. She *was* happy. Being home, with her family, finding new ways to fuel her passion. Even with the hole in her heart, she was happy.

Could she stay that way, wanting Everett and not being able to have him? Worse, wanting Everett and seeing him happy when he found the woman he did want? Just thinking about it was a knife to the heart.

"I was offered a job at Texas A&M. A good job." She shrugged, nibbling on the inside of her lip. And while she knew she'd throw herself into work and savor the challenges she'd likely face, that wasn't the same thing as being happy.

Before her aunt had a chance to respond, Van walked into the kitchen. "Good morning." He made a beeline for Camellia.

Aunt Camellia was up before he reached her side, welcoming him with open arms. "Good morning." She tilted her head back and accepted his quick kiss. "You sleep all right?"

"Like a log." He dropped another kiss against her temple. "Morning, Rosemary." He grinned. "Anyone need a refill?" He nodded at their coffee mugs.

"You sit and chat with Rosemary." Aunt Camellia guided him to a chair and patted his shoulder when he sat. "I'll get you a cup of coffee."

"How's life, Rosemary?" he asked, totally serious.

She smiled at the older man. "It's good." Other than this thing with Everett, it was really good. That was what she needed to focus on. All the good in her life. There was so much good. "Almost as good as this biscuit." Rosemary picked up the biscuit from her plate, and she took a big bite of Aunt Camellia's light and flaky and perfectly buttery biscuit. "And you? How's life, Van?"

"I don't think it could get any better." The man's light blue eyes were trained on Camellia, watching her with a gentle smile on his face.

It wasn't long before the kitchen started filling up. Magnolia arrived with Bea on her hip and Roman trailing after them. Tansy came in yawning and bleary-eyed but perked up at the sight of Aunt Camellia's baked goods. When Dane and Leif trailed in the back door, Camellia pulled another tray of muffins and biscuits from the oven and made Leif sit and eat before sending him off. Astrid and Charlie wandered in a bit later after dropping the girls at school.

There was something wholly satisfying about being surrounded by all the people she loved most. Well, almost all of them.

"Did Leif mention all the DMs about your book?" Dane piled several biscuits onto his plate.

Rosemary shook her head. "I don't think he said one word. Aunt Camellia was too busy feeding him." Not that Leif seemed to mind. The boy had grabbed another two muffins on his way out the door.

"A growing boy needs to eat." Aunt Camellia shrugged. "A bowl of cereal doesn't stick to the ribs. No offense, Dane."

"None taken. Dad and I have gotten better at bacon and eggs, but it can't compare to your cooking, Camellia. Why do you think the two of us show up for breakfast every morning?" Dane eyed the biscuit he was holding with a sort of reverence. "For the company, of course."

They all laughed.

Having Dane around no longer felt odd. He fit, Rosemary realized. He was family.

"I suspected as much." Aunt Camellia sat beside Van, smiling at her husband as he draped his arm along the back of her chair.

Shelby was the last one to join them. "You let me sleep." She glanced at the clock. "I don't think I've slept this late in…a long time."

"Ma ma." Bea clapped and reached for her mother. "Yums Mimi Grapaw yums."

"Did you hear that? That was a full sentence."
Roman smiled at Bea.

Rosemary grinned. She wasn't sure which was more
adorable: Bea's baby-speak or Roman's abundant pride
over his granddaughter's accomplishment.

"You go see your mama." Aunt Mags handed off
Bea.

"Hello, love. Are Mimi and Grampa giving you yums?
They are taking good care of you, aren't they?" Shelby
hugged her daughter. "Thank you for letting me sleep.
Both of you." Shelby smiled at Aunt Mags and her father.

"Our girls need taking care of, don't they, Mags?"
Roman smiled up at his daughter. "That means you,
not just Bea."

Rosemary wasn't the only one who picked up on the
our girls comment. Aunt Mags looked like she'd been
pinched—before she smiled. A lovely smile.

That's a surprise. But Rosemary took a sip of her
coffee and tried not to stare. When her gaze bounced
from Tansy to Astrid, they both had the same wide-
eyed, mile-high eyebrows-of-surprise showing over
the rims of their coffee cups.

Interesting.

"What's on the agenda for today?" Aunt Camellia
had a small notepad and pencil. "By that, I mean who's
going to be here for dinner?" After a head count, Aunt
Camellia made up a grocery list.

"You were saying something about DMs about her
books?" Tansy nudged Dane. "Before you got side-
tracked by food."

After all the back-and-forth, Rosemary had completely forgotten, too.

"Very good food." Dane didn't hesitate to reach for

another muffin. "After Kerrielynn posted that video of the hot guy reading to Nova, our Instagram and Facebook got a ton of messages asking where to buy the book. Assuming everyone that messaged actually bought a copy of the book, you'd be looking at a hefty chunk of change."

Which was another surprise. "Really?"

Dane nodded. "Really."

"I'm sorry, hot guy reading?" Astrid snorted.

"That's what they were calling Everett in the comments." Tansy laughed. "There were a *lot* of comments on that video. Some about Everett but plenty about the book and illustrations. He did a pretty good job of showing it off."

Rosemary didn't see what was funny about the hot guy comment. Everett was very…hot. But then, she loved him, so it made sense that she'd feel that way. The bite of muffin she swallowed stuck in her throat.

Tansy took a sip of Dane's coffee. "Who knew a handsome man reading to a cute kid is marketing gold?"

"Do you want a cup of coffee?" Dane asked her.

"No. I've got yours." Tansy beamed up at him.

"I'm telling you, Rosemary, I know beekeeping is where your heart is, but this could be a really lucrative side hustle for you." Shelby sat at the table with Bea in her lap. "There's no reason you can't make money off of something you love doing—assuming you love doing it?"

"I do." She had already started working on a bee-centered story that introduced colors and another about counting to ten. "I really do."

"We can sell them on the farm and boutique website." Aunt Mags was all about business. "Just think, we'd be selling a book with your name on it, Rosemary. That's quite an accomplishment."

"Wholesome Foods left a comment on the post saying they hoped to be carrying them in stores soon." Tansy fed Dane a bite of muffin. "Who knows, maybe we'll be getting a call from them to talk distribution."

Rosemary was excited—*really* excited. So excited she wanted to call Everett and tell him all about it. That was what best friends did, and heartbreak or not, he was still that to her.

"SHE HATES GARDENING." Everett ran a hand over his face, his phone pressed to his ear.

"I told her that. But with this new medication, she's been more like her old self. Lots of energy and sass. She said she wants to give gardening a try now that she's feeling more like she's sixty than eighty." Jenny laughed.

That put a smile on his face. "I like the sound of that."

"Me, too." Jenny paused. "If you're free to bring her home after it's over? I've got a date, or I'd do it." She paused. "Hold on, she's right here, and she wants to talk to—"

"Everett?" It was Gramma Dot. "You think you can make time in your busy schedule to drive me home?"

"Let me check my calendar." He chuckled, teasing. How often did his grandmother ask him for a thing? Rarely, if ever. That was the reason he'd do it—*not* because Rosebud would be there. "It looks like I can pencil you in."

"Listen to you, all feisty." But there was a smile in her voice. "You might have to help me pack up, too."

"Pack up?" They were talking about gardening club, weren't they? What was there to pack?

"The flier said to bring whatever gardening supplies you have. I figured I'd bring along Albie's old toolbox full of gardening supplies." She sighed. "I think he'd like that."

Everett tilted his chair back and smiled. "I know he would." Other than fishing, Granddad had loved gardening. He said watching the vegetables, plants, and flowers he tended grow big and healthy filled him with a sense of achievement. Gramma Dot hadn't been much of a gardener, but she'd sit on one of the wooden rockers outside and keep Granddad company while he worked. "I'll see you later this evening."

"Don't forget me."

"I won't." He was still chuckling when he hung up.

After the morning he'd had, the phone call lifted his spirits some. Last night, @paint.ballers had struck again, and he'd been on the phone all morning. Mayor Hobart had made sure Everett knew this wasn't acceptable. Willadeene heard not too long after that and had all sorts to say about the city watch's success—or lack thereof.

He wasn't any happier about it than everyone else. It had been a solid week since Willow Creek—long enough for Everett to hope that maybe this whole debacle was over.

The damage done to Glendale's historic bell tower was significant. The limestone tower had been peppered in neon pink and yellow paint. Limestone was porous, old limestone even more so. The cleanup would be even more tedious and complicated than Willow Creek's.

"Not that any of the cleanups have been easy," he muttered.

He frowned when his phone started ringing and Robbie Contreras's number popped up.

"Everett here."

"Everett. You free for lunch?" Robbie wasn't one to mince words. "Got a few things I wanted to run by you."

By now, Everett was getting familiar with this tactic. Whenever Robbie wanted to *run something by him*, it meant he'd later expect Everett to do whatever it was. But Everett was done carrying so much extra weight. That was all going to change—starting today. "I could do lunch, if you're paying."

Robbie chuckled. "Deal. Meet you at Delaney's in ten minutes."

"I'll be there." He disconnected.

"Knock, knock." Libby leaned in. "Hey, boss, I've gotten some phone calls and emails about you and some children's book? Would you know what that's about?"

He nodded. That video had said everything he couldn't—and shouldn't. Every time his gaze had shifted to Rosebud, the look on his face had been pure adoration. The way Dane looked at Tansy or Charlie at Astrid. He'd stared at his own image, calling himself a fool, then spent a good half hour scrolling through the other videos and pictures.

"Want to clue me in?" She stepped into the office and closed the door behind her.

"Kerrielynn Baldwin posted a bunch of stuff this weekend from the beekeeping convention. It's all for some school assignment. One of them has me reading a book to Nova Driver."

"How sweet is that." She smiled. "Look at you, blowing up the internet. Are you trying to get famous or something?"

"No, ma'am." If anything, Kerrielynn's posts had showed all the selfish things he'd done over the weekend. Most of them had to do with Rosebud. He'd showed off a book she'd intended only for her family. He'd encouraged her to do that panel with James Voigt without ensuring it was something she wanted to do. Then there was the whole kissing her and lying to her and ripping his own damn heart out of his chest so she could be happy and there was no risk to their friendship.

"Earth to Everett?" Libby waved her hand in front of his face. "You're beginning to worry me with the way you check out like that."

"I've got a lot on my mind, Libby." Namely, all the ways he'd been a jackass.

She sat on the edge of his desk, crossing her long legs and smoothing her short denim skirt in place. "Is there anything I can do? As your secretary? Or your friend?"

He glanced at his watch. "I've got to meet with the mayor." He pushed his chair back and stood.

"Off to do important things, I'm sure." She slipped off his desk and stepped forward. "Your tie is crooked." She straightened it, smiling up at him. "There." She patted his chest and stepped back. "About these emails and phone calls. Can they buy this book online?"

"No." He tucked his phone into his pocket. "Rosebud—Rosemary wrote it, and as far as I know, she has no plans to sell it."

"Rosemary wrote a book?" Her tone was oddly insulting. "Is there anything she can't do?"

It wasn't the first time he'd sensed Libby's hostility

toward Rosebud. "You two not getting along?" As far as he knew, they had only exchanged a few words.

"We're fine." Libby's smile was forced. "I mean, she's been much nicer to me now. Almost friendly."

He hesitated. There was more going on here, he could feel it. If he didn't have to go meet Robbie, he'd find out what exactly that was. Since he did, it would have to wait. "I'll be back in an hour or so. Feel free to take your lunch."

"Will do, thanks, boss."

Everett headed to Delaney's with a purpose. And while Robbie Contreras wasn't thrilled to learn that Everett wasn't interested in running for mayor, he certainly understood. He was less understanding when Everett pushed back the additional responsibility Robbie tried to give him. It wasn't his job to oversee the city watch program, that was something the mayor or city council should manage. It was a city program, he reminded Robbie, not a county program. By the time they finished their lunch, Robbie's mood had dampened while Everett felt ten times lighter.

Which was a good thing since he had to spend the rest of the afternoon finalizing his next year's budget proposal and get it in for approval before the end of the day.

He turned the budget in before five, then tried to wrap up as many loose ends as he could. When he glanced at his clock, it was six forty-five. The gardening club would be ending soon. He hung his tie and sport coat on the coatrack in the corner and headed outside.

There was a surprisingly brisk, almost cold breeze. The sun was low, leaving the sky streaked with red and pinks and long flat blue-gray clouds. It was one of those rare almost-fall days. He took a deep breath and scanned the crowded courthouse lawn.

He didn't see Rosebud or her dark red hair. But he'd seen enough of her in his dreams. He did spy his grandmother on the edge of a flower bed on the far side of the lawn.

"Heavens to Betsy, Everett. I didn't know there were so many senior citizens interested in gardening in Lewis County." Gramma Dot sat on a folded towel. She wore flowered gardening gloves and a matching apron. "I'm pooped. Give me a hand?"

"I can do that. Have fun?" Everett asked, inspecting the flower bed. "It sure looks pretty."

"Of course it does. Albie would be proud, don't you think?" Gramma Dot took his hands and let him pull her up. "Besides, I wasn't going to let that woman outdo me."

"What woman?" Everett asked, following his grandmother's steely-eyed glare. "Willadeene?" He managed not to groan aloud. After their phone call earlier, he'd reached his Willadeene quota for the day—hell, the week. He loaded up his grandfather's gardening box, took the gloves she handed him, and grabbed the wooden handle. "Is that everything?"

Gramma Dot took a quick look around and nodded. "Looks like it." She hooked her arm through Everett's, her voice lowering. "I was surprised to see her here. She's so spiteful, I can't imagine she could coax any living thing to grow."

Everett was so startled he burst into laughter.

"Hush now, or you'll get her attention." But Gramma Dot was grinning.

"We wouldn't want that." He led her to the edge of

the group gathering around the gazebo in the middle of the lawn, keeping a safe distance from Willadeene—and Rosebud.

From the looks of it, Rosebud had enlisted several members of the Junior Beekeepers: Leif, Kerrielynn, Felix Abraham, Halley, and Benji. And Nicole? He took a deep breath. Nicole and Willadeene in the same place at the same time? That had potential disaster written all over it. Last he'd heard, Nicole and Willadeene weren't seeing eye to eye on much—which meant Willadeene would go out of her way to poke and prod at her daughter. But if that had happened, Gramma Dot would have told him all about it the minute he walked up.

Even after Gramma Dot had shed some light on Willadeene's past, he didn't have much sympathy for the woman. She had a daughter and grandson she could love and support. Instead, she chose to torment her daughter and emotionally blackmail her grandson. He'd never understand. No child should ever question the motivation behind their parents' love or affection. It should be constant and unconditional. If and when he was lucky enough to have children of his own, he'd make sure they knew they could always count on him. Like he'd been able to count on his parents and grandparents.

"You think you'll come back?" he asked.

"I do." Gramma Dot smiled up at him. "Rosemary was tickled to see me, and that just about made my day. She's so kind and patient with everyone. That girl is a gem, I tell you."

She is. His gaze scanned the crowd until he found her. Rosebud. Her dark red hair was twisted up on the back of her head, and there was a smudge of dirt on her cheek. She was flushed and a bit windblown—and more beautiful than ever. He ignored the twist in his chest and took a deep, steadying breath.

Rosebud handed a clipboard to Nicole and climbed the steps of the gazebo. "Thank you all for your hard work tonight." Rosebud smiled at the crowd. "I didn't expect such a big turnout. Next time, I'll make sure we have more plants. Take a look around you at how refreshed and vibrant the lawn looks—all because of your efforts. These fall-blooming plants are great pollinators and pretty to look at." Rosebud paused long enough to point out each flower bed. "Thank you to our awesome Junior Beekeepers for helping out, too."

There was a smattering of applause over this.

"I think Kerrielynn managed to get you all on video, so I'll see if we can arrange a viewing of it once it's finished." Rosebud winked at Kerrielynn. "We're all anxious to see how it turns out." The evening breeze caught a long strand of her hair so that it brushed along her cheek and neck. She reached up, tucking it behind her ear. "Once you make sure you have all your gardening supplies, you're free to go. And thank you again."

"You ready?" he asked his grandmother.

"After I say good night to Rosemary." She tugged him along with her—not that he bothered resisting. "Rosemary, I just wanted to tell you what a delightful evening it was."

"I'm so glad you came, Gramma Dot." Rosebud gave Gramma Dot a big hug. "I promise, next time I'll be a little more organized."

"Sweet girl, I don't see how that's possible." Gramma Dot patted her back, then released her. "You consider tonight a success and give yourself a pat on the back. You've earned it."

"Yes, ma'am." Her smile was shy but delighted.

That smile was too much for him. Everett's lungs emptied, making it hard to breathe.

Those green eyes settled on him now, that smile never wavering. "Everett. I'm glad you're here."

"Oh?" He liked hearing that too much.

"Don't sound so surprised." She shook her head. "I've decided to sell my book—partly because of you." She clasped her hands in front of her. "And write some more."

"Congratulations, Rosebud. That's great news." She looked so damn happy she was all but glowing. "But what does that have to do with me?"

"The video of you reading to Nova? There were so many DMs asking about where to buy the book I thought, why not?" She shrugged. "It could still be an epic failure, who knows." Her gaze searched his as she said, "There were lots of questions about you, too, in case Dane or Tansy hasn't told you."

He rolled his eyes. "You think Dane hasn't told me? He's eating it up."

Rosebud's laugh rang out.

Everett sucked in a deep breath, ignoring the sharp tug in his chest.

"You wrote a book?" Gramma Dot was wide-eyed. "Land sakes, child, you're full of surprises." She smiled, stifling a yawn. "I can't wait to read it. Everett, get me a copy won't you?"

"Can do. I'll buy a copy." Everett nodded. "Make any other big decisions? What about the job? Texas A&M? Still thinking about it?" He braced himself.

"Not really." Rosebud nibbled on the inside of her lip. "I've been busy. With this and the books and Aunt Camellia coming home."

"Makes sense. I'm sure they'll wait for you." He nodded, pondering what that expression meant. After all this time, he still hadn't figured out how to read her.

Gramma Dot looked back and forth between them. "Well, I'm sure you want to head home and have some time with your family. Please give my love to your aunts, Rosemary."

"I will." Rosebud nodded, offering up a little wave. "Good night. Be safe going home." Her gaze lingered on his a second longer.

"Rosebud." He pulled his handkerchief from his pocket. "Hold up." He stepped forward, wiping at the smudge on her cheek. "You got a little dirt right...here." Another swipe, a little harder. "Gone." *Don't do it. Don't do it.* He looked down at her, that vise grip clamping down on the contents of his chest tighter than ever.

She blinked, then pressed a hand to her cheek. "Was it on my cheek the whole time?" She closed her eyes and took a deep breath. "Not exactly the professional look I was going for." She smiled up at him, a pink flush on her cheeks.

He swallowed. "I don't know about the *whole* time." Dirt or no dirt, she'd still taken his breath away. That was what happened with Rosebud—his reaction to her was instinctual. Knowing that, he needed to be smart and keep some distance between them. Or he'd wind up staring at her and making a fool of himself. *Like I'm doing right now.* "I should get Gramma Dot home." He blew out a slow breath. "Night, Rosebud." He'd no doubt he'd see her later, in his dreams.

"You all right, Everett?" Gramma Dot was worried. Everett had never been one for long silences. He was a talker. So much so, she'd need a few hours of quiet after he'd visit. But he hadn't said one word since they'd climbed into his truck.

"I'm fine. I'm good." He glanced at her, his smile pinched. "Long day, is all."

"Mmm-hmm." Dot sighed. "You're too young to be so tired, Everett."

He chuckled. "Maybe I am."

"There's no maybe about it." She paused, mulling over what to say next. If Albie was here, he'd know what to say without actually saying it. He'd been good at that. Talking around something but getting the point across. She'd never mastered the art of subtlety. "What are you going to do about it?"

He chuckled again. "I think I'm going to go fishing."

"That's good." She studied her grandson. "Albie said fishing helped him clear his mind—and got us a tasty dinner."

Everett's smile wavered. "I miss him."

"Oh, darling boy." She drew in a quivering breath. "I do, too. So much."

He reached out and took her hand and gave it a squeeze.

Albie, our boy needs help. And she didn't know what to do to help. The way she saw it, things were pretty cut-and-dried. Everett wanted Rosemary, and Rosemary wanted Everett. But the two of them were dancing around it.

"Did I ever tell you how Granddad and I almost didn't get married?" Gramma Dot glanced at Everett.

Everett turned to stare. "What? No."

"Believe it or not, Granddad didn't want to marry me and have me become a widow or have to care for a broken man. Vietnam was a hard war—so many men came back changed. Though I don't suppose there's such a thing as an easy war?" She shook her head, remembering it like it was yesterday. "I told him he was being ridiculous, but he didn't budge. He said either one of us might find someone else, and neither of us should feel guilty about that." She pressed a hand to her chest. "He took my heart with him, of course. He still has it." She sighed. "I didn't give up on him. I wrote to him, never expecting a letter in response, until I learned he was coming home."

"Because he'd lost his hearing?" Everett turned off the main road.

"Deaf in the left ear and not so great in the right." Dot nodded. "Unless he wore his hearing aid. Then he could hear just fine—unless it was something he didn't want to hear." She grinned. "There were times he'd forget them when I suspect he didn't want to be bothered with other people." That man had been full of mischief. "Anyway, I was waiting for him on his front porch when he got home. He stepped out of the car, took one look at me, and I thought he was going to cry. I knew then he'd done it because he wanted me to be happy—but I don't think he ever understood that I'd only truly be happy with him in my life. I stood up and walked over to him and took his hand and that was that. We held hands every day."

"You did." Everett nodded.

"Later, he admitted he hadn't wanted to go off to war worrying about me, but it hadn't worked, of course." She knew she was carrying on but hoped he'd listen. "I know you're taking after Albie, Everett, by trying to put her happiness first. But for all you know, Rosemary is like me—wishing you'd get some sense knocked into your head, wishing you'd see what was right in front of you, take hold of it, and never let go." She yawned, thankful they were almost home. "I've spoken my piece. What you do with it is up to you."

She squeezed his hand again. *I hope I did all right, Albie. I hope you're smiling down on us both.*

CHAPTER FIFTEEN

"THANK YOU. You guys were such help." Rosemary locked the supply closet in the basement of the city hall.

"No prob." Kerrielynn turned, taking in the dim interior. "Plus, this place is creepy-dark down here."

"Good thing you've got a big strong man to protect you." Leif grabbed her hand.

"My hero," Kerrielynn said softly. "Is there anything else we can help with?"

Rosemary shook her head. "I've got to do a few things in the office before I head home. You two have plans?" She led them back up the stairs to the first floor.

Leif shrugged. "Hang out."

"Well, have fun." Rosemary waved and headed toward Everett's office. After every class, Lorna told her to make a copy of the sign-in sheet, keep the original in her binder, and leave the copy for Everett's secretary to input for tracking purposes. Since she didn't have another class until next week, it made sense to do it before she went home tonight.

She opened the office door and came to a stop.

"Libby." Rosemary hadn't expected anyone to be here this late.

"Rosemary." She didn't look up from her monitor. "What are you doing here?"

"Making a copy." She pointed at the copy machine in the corner.

"Fine." She barely glanced her way.

Rosemary headed to the copy machine, placed the original on the screen, and closed the lid.

Libby's phone rang. "Hey. I'm still here."

Rosemary pressed the button. The machine whirred, but nothing came out.

"It was a horrible weekend." Libby's sigh was long and drawn out. "Everett and I had that fight, and he went off to sulk." She paused. "He's over it now."

Rosemary pressed the button again and waited. No copy. She opened the lid and closed it again, scanning the copy machine's small screen for any messages. Nothing.

"He's hot, then cold." Libby's whisper was clearly audible. "I can't keep up with his mood swings."

Which was nothing like Everett. Nothing at all. Rosemary opened the top of the machine, then closed it. Nothing happened. Who was Libby talking to anyway? Why was she still here—so late? She mashed the button again. Nothing.

"But he is so hot." Libby giggled.

Rosemary didn't want to interrupt, but she did want to get out of here. "Libby." She cleared her throat. "Libby, I'm sorry to interrupt."

Libby's blue eyes were ice-cold. "What, Rosemary?" A pause. "Yes, she's here making a copy."

"I need a hand with the copy machine." She nodded at the machine. "It's not working."

"Hold on." She held up one finger. "I'll call you back, Kate." Then there was a brilliant smile on Libby's face. "Yes. Okay. I'll tell her." She hung up.

Rosemary stared at the phone. That had been Kate? She shoved the long-standing anxiety aside, refusing to let the sisters get the better of her.

"Kate told me to tell you hi and that she hopes to catch up with you soon." Her tight smile was full of menace. "The machine is old. Sometimes you have to flip it on and off for it to work." Libby flipped the switch, then looked at her. "How many?"

"Um…one." She swallowed.

"What's the matter with you?" Libby frowned and pressed the button. "Are you sick? You look pale. And sweaty." She took a step back. "I can't afford to get sick." She handed her the copy, then the original.

"I'm fine." Rosemary took the papers from her.

"You don't look fine." Her blue eyes narrowed. "You look… Something's wrong."

"Tired, I guess." She swallowed, a jagged lump blocking her throat, and held out the copy. "I'm supposed to leave a sign-in sheet for you?"

"I'll take care of it." Libby snatched the paper back. "I'm behind because I've been getting calls all day about your book." She scanned the list and carried it back to her desk. "Everett told me you're not going to sell it. I don't know why you'd put it on social media like that." She peered up at Rosemary, one brow arched high.

"I didn't—"

"Right." Libby rolled her eyes. "Kerrielynn did." She sat back and crossed her arms over her chest. "What are you doing here, Rosemary? Really? Your whole life, you've been bragging, over and over, about how you've got 'important work' to do." She used air quotes around *important work*. "How you couldn't wait to leave Honey. Yet here you are."

"I never said I couldn't wait to leave Honey." She frowned. She'd never wanted to *leave* Honey. She'd thought she had to.

"Whatever. Why are you sticking around?" Libby brushed her hair from her shoulder, her features smoothing. "Is it because Everett has a chance to be happy— and it doesn't center around you? You can't stand that, can you? That he could be happy without you."

She swallowed hard. "Libby... I want Everett to be happy."

"Then leave." She stood. "If you really mean that, you'll go. You come home, and his family and friends are on him to pick you, woo you, *always* you... Even if it's not what he wants. You put a lot of pressure on him, whether you mean to or not." Her blue eyes swept over her face. "Do you know what he wants? I bet you haven't even asked him. And you're supposed to be his best friend."

Yes, she knew what he wanted. To be friends, only. Not that she'd ever tell Libby as much. Where was this hostility coming from? Rosemary paused, scrambling for something coherent to say.

"My whole life, no one has ever measured up to you and your sisters. The Bee Girls. The good girls. The perfect Hill family and their precious bees." She broke off, her voice turning brittle. When she spoke again, she was calm. "Could it be that, outside of Honey, you're not everyone's darling? That you need to make sure you've got an adoring fan club, so that when you leave, you know you'll be missed?" Her tone was deceptively soft as she continued, "You're selfish. Before you go making more decisions that affect the people who love you, you should make sure it's what's right for everyone.

Your sisters and aunts haven't been sitting around pining for the day you'd come home. They've been doing and living. I'm sure you were missed, but they were all fine without you, Rosemary. No, they were all happy. Everett was, too. Think about that."

Rosemary was stunned into silence.

"Now…" Libby shook her head and headed back around her desk. "If you'll excuse me, I have to finish my work. Not important work, like yours, but work nonetheless."

"Libby… I don't know what happened to make you dislike me so much, but…if I did something to you to make you feel lesser or slighted or insignificant, I'm sorry." She took a deep breath. "That's a horrible feeling. I'd never intentionally try to hurt or demean you or anyone."

Libby's hand froze, the phone halfway to her ear. "You couldn't make me feel any of those things." But there wasn't the same bite to her words.

"Then maybe it's time you find someone else to bully? Or better yet, stop. There's no point in holding on to such…such anger all the time. We're not in high school anymore, Libby. You're an adult. You can be happy. I don't know why you're still trying to hurt me, but it won't work now." She kept her voice low and even, refusing to reveal just how hard she was fighting against her anxiety. "I mean it when I say… I wish you well."

For a split second, maybe two, Libby was shocked speechless. "Whatever. Stop wasting my time," she snapped, dialing the phone and turning away from her. "It's me. I told you'd I'd call you back." She glared at Rosemary. "She's gone. We're free to talk."

Rosemary backed out of the room, the office door

closing so loudly it echoed up and down the empty hall-way. She hurried, all but running from the building, down the steps, and to the Honey Hill Farms van parked in the staff parking lot around back. She put the key in the ignition and started the van—but she was shaking too hard to drive. Instead, she gripped the steering wheel and burst into tears.

She'd done it—tried to breech the gap between her and Libby. It hadn't been successful, but at least she could say she tried. Rosemary had grown and changed, but Libby seemed stuck in time—as petty and hateful as ever. Chances were she'd never figure out why Libby hated her, but it didn't matter. Rosemary wasn't going to let any of the nastiness Libby had hurled her way get to her.

Everett wasn't involved with her. He never would be.

She didn't need praise or a fan club or attention—that had never been what drove her. Making a difference did.

And even though Libby would be all too happy for her to leave town, she knew her family and friends wouldn't be.

She wiped at her tears with the back of her hands and took a deep breath. Poppa Tom had once said the Owens girls were hard-hearted because they had to be. But try as she might, she couldn't dig up sympathy for Libby. Kindness was a choice. Libby had never shown her kindness. Instead, she'd continually zeroed in on Rosemary's insecurities and exploited them. Like her shyness. Her "freakish" intellect. And her friendship with Everett.

Jenny and Gramma Dot were right—Libby must want Everett for herself and thought of Rosemary as competition. Considering Everett wanted to keep things status quo between them, Libby had no reason to feel threatened. Not that Everett would date someone like Libby. He wouldn't. Rosemary knew that.

By the time she parked the van behind the honey house, she was calm. Exhausted but calm. She opened the driver's door of the van and slipped out, unsteady on her feet. She leaned against the side and closed her eyes, sucking in deep breaths while trying to hold her tears at bay.

There was a chill in the air, enough to prick up the hair along her arms and the back of her neck. The faint coo of a dove echoed in some far-off pasture. The crickets were warming up for their evening serenade. But it was the faint buzz in the air that chased away the remaining ick from her run-in with Libby.

Honey would always draw bees, and there was always honey in the honey house. Frames heavy with honey, frames waiting to be stored for later use, or the large metal extractors or tools dotted with sticky golden beads of honey the bees were happily collecting. She opened her eyes, letting her vision adjust to the growing dark.

A bee's life was simple. Bees did what needed to be done to take care of one another, to protect their hive, and never give up. *Humans could learn a lot from bees.*

"I'm not going to give up, either," she murmured, walking along the path that led to the house. From now on, she wasn't going to let Libby get into her head. Today, the tide had turned, and there was no going back. And it felt good.

The kitchen was crowded: her sisters and aunts, Shelby and Bea, and Van and Roman.

"Rosemary. There's a plate for you in the microwave." Aunt Camellia was slicing into her triple-layer honey butter cake. "But you can have dessert first, if you like."

"Dessert first?" Tansy looked up from the puzzle covering the kitchen table. "That's not fair." Her eldest sister's gaze met hers. "Rose?"

Astrid's mossy green eyes found her. "Rosemary... what's wrong?"

Her sisters hurried around the table.

"You're as white as a sheet." Aunt Magnolia draped an arm around her shoulders. "You need some tea."

"I'm fine. I'm great, actually." But she couldn't manage a smile. In fact, she was dangerously close to bursting into tears again.

"Roman." Van stood, nodding toward the kitchen door. "You still game for that chess match?"

"Yep." Roman all but ran from the room after Van.

"They don't have to go." Rosemary stared after them. "Really, I-I'm fine..." She took a deep breath. "I told Libby Owens-Baldwin off. Sort of. For me anyway." So the deep guttural sobs ripping from her chest and spilling out of her didn't make any sense. "I don't know why I'm crying."

"Oh, Rose." Tansy pulled a chair close and sat beside her. "I can see how confronting your childhood monsters face-to-face might be a little emotional." She draped an arm along Rosemary's shoulders. "I wish I'd been there to see it. You're such a badass."

"First Dr. Voigt. Now Libby." Astrid rubbed her hands together. "I'm impressed."

"Don't be. I am sobbing in the kitchen." Rosemary wiped away her tears. "It's just..." She broke off and shook her head.

"Don't do that." Astrid's voice was gentle. "Don't shut us out. Together, we can sort this out. Whatever it is."

"I'm feeling insecure." Which was true. And an understatement. "I know everything she said was just to make me do this." She pointed at her face. "And I know she's full of…shit. So why do I let her get to me?"

"Because she's been responsible for years of torment?" Astrid suggested.

"Maybe she said something that hit one of your own fears?" Aunt Camellia's tone was gentle.

"What, exactly, are you feeling insecure about?" Aunt Mags was filling the teakettle with water.

"Life." She took the tissue Shelby handed her, smiling her thanks when Shelby set the whole box in front of her.

"Been there." Shelby sat opposite her. "We are our own worst critic."

Rosemary was pretty sure Libby Owens-Baldwin was right up there, but she only nodded.

"I've always… If I want to stay here, in Honey, is that okay? Because I want to stay here? Not for a little while. I want to *stay* here." She twisted the tissue between her hands. "But…am I letting you down? Or getting in the way? Am I disappointing Poppa Tom?"

That led to a moment of absolute silence.

"Rosemary." Aunt Camellia placed a huge piece of cake on the table in front of her, then ran a hand over Rosemary's hair. "Sweet girl, you could never disappoint Poppa Tom. Never. And why on earth would you think you'd need to ask if it was okay for you to stay here?"

"Of course we want you to stay." Astrid was crying

then. "I'm pregnant, so I can be as emotional as I want, okay?" She took a tissue. "I never wanted you to leave."

Rosemary smiled at her sister.

"But we wanted you to be happy, so what sort of sister would I be if I told you to stay?" Astrid blotted at her tears. "A bad sister, that's what."

"When you love someone, that's what you want, Rose. Right? Even if it sucks." Tansy sniffed and took her hand. "We'll support whatever you want. But if you're asking us what we want then, yeah, what Astrid said. You being gone was…horrible." A tear slipped down her cheek.

Tansy's words bounced around in her head. They'd held their silence so she'd be happy. *Everett.* Could that be what he was doing? Or was she so desperate for him to love her, she wanted that to be the case?

"Rosemary." Even Shelby reached for a tissue now. "For what it's worth, I'd like you to stay, too. I'd like to get to know you. You're all my family—but it's all so new. And wonderful."

"It is, isn't it? We are lucky to be Bee Girls." Rosemary was crying again.

"Always." Tansy rested her head on Rosemary's shoulder.

"I didn't mean to hurt you. Any of you." Rosemary rested her head on Tansy's. "I'm sorry."

"That's enough of that." Aunt Mags placed a cup of tea in front of her. "You will not apologize for doing what you needed to do to figure out what you wanted. That's just life, Rose. That's the way it should be." She smiled. "Selfishly, I'm delighted that you're home to stay. As long as that's what you want."

"This is what I want." Rosemary took another tissue. "It's just, Poppa Tom wanted me to do big things—"

"You have," Aunt Camellia said. "And you will. You'll do big things right here in Honey. Be that discovering the next honey-based vaccine or having a dozen babies or writing a series of bee-centric children's books…"

"Or all of the above," Astrid interjected.

"Or all of the above." Aunt Camellia nodded. "Whatever you decide to do will be big to us, Rose."

"Your confrontation with Libby brought this on?" Aunt Mags sat beside Shelby, her eyes laser-focused.

All eyes swiveled to Rosemary.

"Partly." She swallowed. "Everett." She swallowed again. "I love him." So much. "Even though he doesn't want to be anything more than friends, I do. And if there's even the smallest chance he's doing what you all did, I should tell him how I feel, shouldn't I?"

She hoped so, because tomorrow, bad idea or not, she was going to tell Everett Michael Taggert how she felt.

THIS LATE, the back country roads between his parents' house and his own were normally deserted. There weren't many lights along the winding road—not exactly the sort of drive to make after dark. Even he, who made the trek a dozen times or more a week, didn't relish being out this late. That was why it was a surprise to see an unfamiliar car on the side of the road.

He pulled far off onto the shoulder and parked, rifled through his glove box for a flashlight, and went to check out the situation.

From the looks of it, there were three people inside— triggering all sorts of red flags. He paused and fired off a text to the local state highway patrol before getting out, leaving his headlights on.

"Hello?" he called out. "You need some help?" He spied the blown back passenger tire. "I can give you a hand changing that tire, if you want?"

The passenger door opened, and a teenage boy got out. "Thanks, mister. We've got a friend coming."

"You sure?" Everett pointed the flashlight into the car. Sure enough, two other teens were inside. He didn't like the idea of leaving a bunch of kids out here on their own.

"We're good." The boy shifted from one foot to the next.

Everett glanced down at the boy's feet. Black shoes. Black pants. Black shirt. Black hoodie. Not something most of the kids in these parts wore. Unless it was one of the @paint.ballers. *Dammit.*

"Who else is in there?" he asked, leaning forward and shining the flashlight inside. "Wes? Wes Hobart, is that you?"

"Yeah. We said we got it." Wes glared his way.

"You got a spare in the trunk?" He flashed his light into the back seat. The kid there covered his face.

"I don't know, man," Wes grumbled. "Probably not."

"Let's check." Everett straightened and headed to the trunk. "Open it up." He rapped on the trunk with his knuckles.

"We don't need your help, mister." The first kid was going an alarming shade of red now. "Thanks, though."

"Right." Everett shook his head. "Your parents know you three are out here?"

"You don't know who my parents are." The kid crossed his arms over his chest, looking smug.

"Not yours." Everett pulled out his phone and hit Hobart's number. "But I have Dennis Hobart on speed dial."

Wes scrambled out of the car. "You don't have to call him—"

"Hello?" Dennis Hobart snapped through the phone. "It's awfully late for you to be calling me, Everett."

Everett put the call on speaker mode. "I'm standing here with your son." Everett smiled at the boy. "He's got a flat. You know if he's got a spare in the trunk?"

"What?" Dennis sputtered. "Wes is here... He's up-stairs in his room."

"You sure about that?" Everett watched as Wes Hobart's hands fisted. "Why don't you go check?"

"Wes?" Dennis spat out. "You better answer me, boy."

Wes glared at the phone but kept his mouth shut.

"Answer me, Wes." Dennis Hobart was on the verge of screaming.

"The whole damn county can hear you," Wes muttered. "Calm down, old man."

Everett took a deep breath. "How about you open up the trunk, Wes?"

"How about you mind your own business?" Wes fired back, his chin thrust out defiantly.

"That's fine." He glanced at his phone. "A state patrol officer will be here shortly. I'm sure he'll have no problem opening it."

"You called the cops?" The boy in the back seat of the car slid out the window, his braces flashing in Everett's headlights. "Wes, this is... This..." The kid took off into the trees.

"One of them just took off running, Dennis. Kid with braces." Everett didn't bother running after the

boy. "Interestingly enough, they're all wearing matching outfits. Black shoes, black pants, black hoodies. I
bet, when the trunk gets opened up, we're going to see
some black masks and paintball guns."

"You think? Great work, Detective." Wes leaned
against the car. "You going to make a citizen's arrest?"

Everett didn't answer. There was no need. A black-
and-white state trooper's car passed them by, then
looped back around.

"Police are here, Dennis." Everett figured the least
he could do was keep the man informed.

"What were you thinking, Wes?" For the first time,
there was no bite to Dennis Hobart's words. "You know
what's going to happen now?"

"You're the mayor." Wes snorted. "You're so important you can get me out of this."

The police car pulled up, parked, and two officers
got out.

"No, son, I can't," Dennis mumbled. "I'll meet you
at the county jail." And he hung up.

"Dad?" Wes called out. "Dad?" He pushed off the
car. "What the hell?"

From there, things went pretty quickly. Everett wasn't
surprised to see five paintball guns in the trunk as well
as containers of green, pink, yellow, and orange paintballs. If anything, it was a relief. Maybe not for Dennis Hobart—but for the rest of Lewis County. Once the
boys called the third kid back, they were all loaded into
the police car and headed back into town, with Everett following.

It was a long night. Long and miserable. He'd never
been a fan of Dennis Hobart, but the man's shattered
disappointment affected him nonetheless. It didn't help

that Wes remained defiant and unapologetic through it all.

By the time he got home, he managed a couple of hours of sleep before showering and heading back into town. As tempted as he was to call in to work, he figured he needed to be there to do as much damage control as possible—all things considered. First things first, food.

He walked into Delaney's and sat at a booth, waving at Leif and Kerrielynn, Benji and Halley at the booth across the way. He accepted a cup of coffee with a nod of thanks.

"Everett." Libby stood beside the booth. "I heard you had quite a night last night." She slid into the booth opposite him. "You're a hero."

He sure as hell didn't feel like one. "Word travels fast." He sipped his coffee.

"Um, you know where we live, don't you?" She smiled. "This sort of stuff spreads faster than wildfire."

He shook his head. "I'd appreciate it if you didn't help fan the flames."

"Of course." She cocked her head to one side. "I just wanted to tell you how proud I am of you. You… Well, you're one in a million, Everett. You know that?"

He ran his fingers through his hair. "I might have heard my Gramma Dot say so a time or two."

"Smart woman." Libby leaned forward. "You know, Everett." She cleared her throat. "I've never had to work this hard for attention before."

Everett took a sip of his coffee and frowned. "Come again?"

"You." She sighed. "I've been trying to get you to see me. As Libby. As someone who would like to be more than your secretary." She licked her lower lip. "A lot more."

He set his coffee cup down. "I'm flattered—"

"Don't be flattered. Be adventurous." She reached across the table, running a finger across the back of his hand. "You work too hard, Everett. You deserve to have some fun. That's what I'm offering you. Fun. Lots and lots of it."

He blinked, slowly pulling his hand back. "Libby, I'm not sure where this is coming from, but I'm not interested in you in that way."

"Really?" She was very good at that—looking equal parts seductive and innocent. "Because I'm pretty certain I've caught you checking out the merchandise more than once."

"Sounds like you might need to make an appointment with the eye doctor." He sat back, frowning. "I don't play games. I'm not playing with you."

"Is this because of her?" She sighed, crossing her arms beneath her breasts to give them a boost. As if her skintight brown top didn't already showcase her assets. "Because of Rosemary?"

He stared into his coffee. "Libby, I'm really tired."

"Oh, Everett. When are you going to wake up and realize she'd not interested in you that way? Period. Like zero chance of scoring with Miss Rosemary Goodie-Two-Shoes Hill."

"I'd appreciate it if you'd be more respectful of Rosebud." He pushed his coffee cup away.

"Why? Because you've been in love with her since you were, what, five or something? Because you've put her on some sort of pedestal—as if she wasn't untouchable enough?" She shook her head. "You deserve a real woman, Everett. Someone that sees you and knows what a man wants and needs and who you'd be proud to have on your arm. That's me, Everett. Not *Rosebud*. You're wasting your love on her. It's a little…pathetic."

"Love isn't a choice, Libby." He was all out of patience. "If you think my loving the same girl my whole life is pathetic, fine by me. It's true. I do love Rosebud. I always will. And because I love her, I want what's best for her—even if that isn't me." He shook his head. "Real love takes work and time. It's not about making one another feel good all the time, it's about sticking it out through good and bad times. It's about wanting her happiness over mine. Her well-being above all others—" He broke off and stood, dropping his napkin on the table. "You wouldn't understand it, Libby. And as sad as I am for you, I can't explain it."

"Now you're going to get all sanctimonious on me?" She held her hands up. "Fine. You do you. I still think you're making a mistake."

"I think you're right about that. Since our employment policy states there's no fraternization among coworkers, I think it's best if we find you a different position. It's clear what's happened here would make for a compromised working environment."

"Thanks but no thanks." She stood up, pressing her finger in the middle of his chest. "I quit." She grinned. "You do realize your precious Rosebud works for you now? It's almost like the two of you aren't meant to be together." She spun around and walked out of the diner.

He eyed his coffee and slid back into the booth, fuming, when his phone started ringing.

"Dane?" He hadn't meant to snap. "What's up?"

"Someone woke up on the wrong side of the bed

this morning." Dane chuckled. "Heading into town. Where are you?"

"Delaney's." Everett flipped over the menu. "I'm not much company, but you're welcome to join me."

"On my way." Dane hung up.

Everett glanced across the way at Leif's booth. The boy waved at him, a sympathetic smile on his face. For the first time, Everett looked around the café. It wasn't packed, but there were plenty of prying eyes and ears to relay everything that had just taken place. Lucky for him, he was too tired to worry about that now. Later, when he'd had some sleep, he'd likely regret almost every word that came out of his mouth.

He was through his third cup of coffee when Dane arrived. "What's that look for?"

"You look like hell." Dane slid into the booth, frowning.

"Yeah, well, it's been a hell of a twenty-four hours." He waited for the waitress to fill up Dane's coffee cup. "You hear?"

"That you're a damn hero who brought down the @paint.ballers? I might have heard something about it." Dane grinned. "I bet you're feeling pretty proud of yourself this morning."

Everett frowned. "Not really. They were kids. And Dennis Hobart was devastated." Dane's expression revealed his skepticism. "I'm serious. That man has never been speechless, but he was last night. From the looks of it, all sorts of torn up inside, too."

Dane shrugged, sipping his coffee. "Can't say I'm sad all that's over."

Everett nodded. "What brings you into town?"

"I got an SOS call." Dane pointed at Leif. "He said

you'd landed in the middle of it—again—and might need backup."

"He's a good kid." Everett chuckled. "But you missed a show."

Dane shook his head. "You might remember someone tried to warn you about Libby—"

"You came all this way to say 'I told you so'? Really?" Everett propped himself up with one elbow.

"No." Dane smiled, but there was no denying he was concerned. "I came all this way to sit here in case you, I don't know, wanted to talk."

Everett covered a yawn with his hand. "I've already done too much talking." He didn't know what sort of consequences his too-loud, too-public exchange with Libby would lead to, but there'd be some. Libby was right about talk in small towns; it spread faster than wildfire. He could only hope the story didn't get too twisted along the way. If it did, by the end of the day people might be thinking he was a fool for Libby, not Rosebud. "You said something the other day. I keep thinking about it."

"What's that?" Dane asked, taking a gulp of coffee.

"How big of a jackass I am." Everett laughed as Dane spewed coffee all over the table.

At this point, there wasn't much else he could do except laugh. Yet again, he'd made a fool of himself. While he'd like to think the @paint.ballers resolution might overshadow this morning's standoff with Libby, he wasn't going to hold his breath. All he could do was breathe and laugh and hope the worst was over.

CHAPTER SIXTEEN

ROSEMARY WOKE TO someone jostling her arm. She sat up, a crick in her neck bringing her up short. "Ow," she murmured, pressing a hand to her neck and slowly rolling.

"Sorry to wake you, Rosemary."

She pried her eyes open and blinked. "Kerrielynn? Leif?" She yawned, trying to orient herself as Leif grinned at her. She didn't remember dozing off. But she must have because she was still in the kitchen. The table was covered in last night's creative frenzy. Now, she had an almost finished story for Everett. Almost. "What time is it?" She shifted a page aside, pleased with the images she'd pored over for most of the night. Her gaze shifted to the kitchen clock, then to the two teens. "Isn't it a school day?"

"Yes." Kerrielynn glanced at Leif. "It's eight, and we need to get to school, but I wanted to show you something first." She held out her phone.

"You guys don't want to be late." Rosemary stood and stretched, trying to ease the discomfort in her neck. "You can show me after school. I'll be here."

"I really think you'll want to see this." Kerrielynn held the phone out again. "Now."

Rosemary took the phone, glancing between the two teens. "Is everything okay? You two look awfully serious." Too serious for this time of the morning.

The front door slammed, making Leif and Kerrie-lynn both jump. "Did you hear?" Astrid came hurry-ing into the kitchen. "Did you hear that Everett caught the kids? The @paint.ballers?"

Rosemary set Kerrielynn's phone on the table. "He did?" Of course, he did. "That has to be a huge relief." Good for Everett. She was so proud of him and relieved for him—for all of them.

"Who's yelling?" Tansy came skipping down the stairs and into the kitchen. "Leif? Kerrielynn? Why are you two here? Don't you have class?"

"We do." Kerrielynn nodded. "But we wanted Rose-mary to know—"

"The @paint.ballers have been apprehended," As-trid repeated for Tansy, all smiles. "Thank goodness."

"Really?" Tansy rubbed at her eyes, still puffy with sleep. "That's amazing. I mean, I was certain Honey would be next."

"Me, too," Rosemary nodded. And she dreaded what the vandals would do to her beloved town.

"Who was it?" Tansy asked, turning to Astrid. "Who caught them? Tell me everything."

"Um, Rosemary." Kerrielynn picked up her phone. "I'm really sorry to interrupt, but…"

"Just play it," Leif said, reaching forward to press Play.

Rosemary paused. Libby and Everett. In a booth at Delaney's, from the looks of it.

"When was this?" Astrid whispered, standing close behind Rosemary.

Libby leaned forward, an especially inviting smile on her face. Rosemary couldn't breathe.

"This morning." Leif nodded at the phone.

Rosemary didn't like the way Libby traced the back of Everett's hand. "Why are we watching this?" She shoved the phone back to Kerrielynn. "That seems a little too personal to film, don't you think?" She didn't want to see what happened next. Her imagination was all too happy to fill in the blanks.

"I know." Kerrielynn's cheeks were red. "It's just… Libby was up to something. I could tell."

"Just watch, will you?" Leif's tone was impatient, but he slid his arm around Kerrielynn. "You'll see."

It played in slow motion. Horrible at first, then wonderful. From there, it only got better. Every word. Every action. It was more than Rosemary could have hoped for. By the time Libby stormed out of Delaney's, Rosemary had sunk back into her chair—her legs had gone all wobbly and her chest—her heart—was so full.

"Wow." Astrid sat down beside her. "First he saves Honey, then he tells Libby off…"

He is amazing. She'd always known that.

Tansy spoke with a sort of awe. "Everett Taggert is—"

Mine. This was a new development.

"A badass," Leif finished, smiling. "Now, come on. We're going to be late." He grabbed Kerrielynn's hand.

"Wait." Rosemary hopped up, hugging them both. "I'm sorry if I snapped. I was…scared to see what might happen there." She'd been so certain things would play out differently. But they hadn't. And she couldn't stop smiling. "Thank you. Both of you. I mean it… This means more than you know."

"I *do* know." Kerrielynn grinned. "That's why we came out here." She hugged Rosemary again. "Sending the video to you," she called out as Leif dragged her from the kitchen.

"Holy crap." Tansy sat, her eyes wide and alert now. "That was… That was…"

Everything. Everything Rosemary could ever have hoped for—and then some.

"Romantic." Astrid took Rosemary's hand. "Incredibly romantic."

Everett. He loves me. And he thought she was leaving. Now all she had to do was tell him she loved him, too. It was that easy. "Why am I so nervous?" she whispered, glancing at her sister.

"When you know you have everything you ever wanted, losing it is more terrifying than ever." Astrid patted her hand. "But you don't need to worry about losing Everett, Rose. He has loved you forever."

"And ever." Tansy nodded. "And ever."

Rosemary smiled, her heart thumping along at an abnormally rapid pace. It felt good. No, wonderful. Absolutely blissful. "I've got this last page to finish." She pushed aside the pages until she found the sheet of watercolor paper with the unfinished image. "He's either going to think this is ridiculous—"

"Pretty sure he's going to love it," Tansy interrupted, then said, "And grab you and kiss you."

"I have to agree with Tansy on that front. Charlie said he could tell how Everett felt about you from the minute he saw the way Everett was looking at you. He said Everett loved you—really loved you. My Charlie is quiet, but he's become quite emotionally intuitive."

While her sisters made coffee and chattered on about Everett, Libby, and the whole paintball thing, Rosemary did her best to concentrate. The sooner she was finished, the sooner she could go to him.

It didn't need to be too detailed, it just had to feel

right. She added a few more touches to the two bees. One wore a detailed and intricate crown, the other was heavier and tall, and the effect made her smile. She added six last words and sat back, her fingers shaking.

"Looks like we have a full house." Shelby came in with Bea on her hip.

"Oh, little Bea, we have so much to catch you and your mommy up on." Tansy poured a cup of coffee.

"It has been quite a morning," Astrid gushed. "*And* I'm not nauseous."

"Hold on, everyone else is on the way." Shelby nodded at the kitchen door.

While Rosemary searched for a pen and paper, her aunts, Van, and Roman came into the kitchen. She had no doubt her sisters would tell them everything, so she'd let them. She slammed the drawer and opened another. "Found it," she murmured, the pen flying over the paper. It was short and direct and professional. She skimmed over the words, folded it, and tucked it into an envelope. When she turned, all eyes were on her. "Good morning." She couldn't stop smiling.

"It would appear to be a very good morning." Aunt Mags was reading over the pages on the table. "This is lovely, Rose."

"It certainly is." Aunt Camellia was still reading. "Van, look."

"I see." Van chuckled. "You're going to make Everett the happiest man in Honey today, Rosemary. I'm happy for you both."

Rosemary's throat was too tight to answer, so she nodded.

Roman nodded, clearing his throat. "If this was for me, I'm not sure I'd be able to stay dry-eyed."

"You cry?" Aunt Mags turned, her brows high.

"There's no reason a man can't show his emotions." Roman shrugged, unbothered by her aunt's inspection. In fact, he was grinning at her aunt.

"He cried every time we watched *The Lion King* or *Old Yeller.*" Shelby nodded, bouncing Bea on her hip.

Aunt Mags smiled. "Both tearjerkers."

Rosemary didn't have time to analyze the exchange—not now anyway. She was a woman on a mission. She headed to the table and stacked up the pages. "I should change and get cleaned up." She placed the stack of papers into the paper box. "I'll get changed."

She hadn't thought she'd invited her aunts and sisters and Shelby up to her room, but they all trailed after her. While she showered, they picked out her outfit. When she was out of the shower, they did her hair and fussed over whether or not she needed makeup.

"I love you all very much." She stepped out of their reach. "But I need to go. Now." And with that, they all headed back downstairs.

Roman handed her the paper box, Van the letter, and they all followed her out onto the front porch. She giggled at the sight of them waving her off from the front porch. She turned on the radio, humming along to the music, and tried not to speed as she headed into town.

Main Street seemed especially busy this morning. People were out, sitting on benches, poring over the paper with coffee cups in hand. No doubt reading about the paintball vandals being apprehended. It was such big news, the whole staff of the *Hill Country Gazette* likely came in early to make sure they got the word out first.

She parked the Honey Hill Farms van along the courthouse lawn and climbed out. Cradling the paper box to her chest, she hurried along the path, into the old building, and down the hall to Everett's office. Only then did she pause. She took a deep breath and opened the door.

The waiting room was empty. No Libby. No blue eyes full of resentment. It was a nice change.

She reached Everett's door and knocked.

Nothing. She knocked again but there was no response.

She opened the door and peered inside.

He was leaned back, his head resting on his leather chair with his mouth parted in sleep.

Poor Everett. She slipped inside and closed the door behind her. After the night he'd had, she didn't feel right disturbing him. But leaving wasn't an option, either. So she sat, her phone slipping from the pocket of her green dress and hitting the floor with a solid thunk. She winced, frozen, hoping—

"Rosebud?" Everett's voice was thick.

She glanced up to find him propping himself on one elbow and rubbing his eyes. "I didn't mean to wake you."

"You should have." He shook his head. "I'm at work. I'm pretty sure it's frowned on to sleep on the job."

"I'm pretty sure you've earned a day off." Between the fall of his thick dark hair onto his forehead and the dark stubble lining his jaw, he looked extra manly and gorgeous this morning. *And he loves me.*

His crooked grin was wary. "Guess you heard?"

"Everyone has heard." Rosemary nodded, smiling. "Congratulations."

He ran a hand over his face. "I'd be feeling better about it if those kids' families weren't so torn up. I don't think they had any idea what they were doing—not really? I know they need to be stopped and held accountable, but… I feel like a jerk for being the one to make that happen. They're just kids." He paused. "Well, I'm not so torn up over Wes Hobart. That kid needs a swift kick in the rear." He chuckled, his eyes sweeping over her. "You look all dressed up this morning."

She stood and placed the envelope on the desk in front of him. "First, this."

He pulled the letter from the envelope, unfolded it, and read. The muscle in his jaw tightened as he nodded. When those brown eyes met hers, the pain in his eyes hit her so hard she was frozen in place and not running to him to tell him she was here because she loved him, like she should.

EVERETT STARED AT her until he could force the words out. "I was expecting this." He tapped Rosemary's resignation letter on his desk. He'd been expecting it, but that didn't mean it hurt any less. And, boy, did it hurt. Here he thought he'd been prepared, but he wasn't. The pain rolled over him to lodge in his chest so it could shred what was left of his heart.

"Everett." Rosebud stood. "Hold on. There's something else." She set a paper box on his desk. "I wanted to show you this."

He stared at the box, doing his damndest to hold it together. "A new book?"

"It's a little different from the first." And she sounded excited about it.

"You're going to have to give me a minute." He took a deep breath. "I'm not quite awake." His chuckle was flat—he heard it, and so did she.

"I'll read it to you, if you'd like?" She scooted her chair closer to the desk.

He nodded. If she wanted to read it to him, he'd try to ignore the ache in his chest and do his damndest to listen.

She pulled the box back, opened the box, and pulled out the top page. "Once there was a busy bee who wanted to see the world." She held up the picture.

She looked so excited, he forced himself to concentrate. "Beautiful." He marveled over every vein on the leaf of the strawberry plant, the movement of the bee's wings, and the bold vibrant colors.

"She buzzed all over, hoping she'd find something to fill the hole in her heart. Looking for the place she belonged." She showed him the next picture, the bee— flying from flower to flower to flower. "When she came home to rest, she was tired."

He chuckled at the picture of the bee, resting in a daisy with a sleeping mask over her eyes.

"Her hive greeted her with open arms. Especially her best friend. No matter where the busy bee had flown, he'd supported her dreams." She showed him a picture of the bees having a party, complete with streamers and cake. "They had a party and made her their queen."

"I like the party hats." He smiled. "Nova would approve."

"I thought so, too." Rosebud nodded, her gaze holding his. "Queen Bee realized that when she was with her best friend, the hole in her heart was gone." She cleared her throat. "She realized that all of her buzzing and searching brought her back to where she started. This was where she belonged."

He stared at the picture of the two bees holding hands. Had Rosebud painted baby goats in the distance?

"Queen Bee was content, but to be truly happy, her

best friend needed to become her king. She wanted them to have adventures and their own hive, together. And she hoped he wanted the same." She held up the last page. Two bees in one heart, each wearing a crown, surrounded by flowers and ribbons and fancy curlicues. "Would they live happily ever after?"

"It's cute…" He broke off, more than a little confused. "But even I know there are no king bees." He frowned. If she was planning on writing educational stories, this didn't work.

"I know." She frowned. "This was me, trying to tell you…" She broke off and stood, leaving the pages on his desk. "I wrote this last night. And this morning. I didn't know what you'd think or say… But I'm trying to put myself out there, even if you are still over me." She sighed. "I thought I was being clever or romantic."

Over her? Romantic? What the hell did her book have to do with how he felt about her? And when had his feelings for her become relevant to this conversation? Everett was beyond confused now.

"I'd almost finished the book when Kerrielynn and Leif showed up this morning." Her words were rushed. "Kerrielynn recorded your conversation with Libby. I didn't want to watch, didn't want to pry, but then… I heard you, and I hoped that you meant it when you said you loved me."

Kerrielynn had recorded that? And showed Rosemary? He blinked, processing. But one thing jumped out at him and left him reeling. "You…you hoped that I loved you?" What was going on?

"Everett." She took a deep breath. "I wrote the book… because… Well… It's about me and you." Her words were a whisper. "I'm the queen, and you… I want you to be my king." She ran a hand over her face. "Maybe we should forget about the book. It was a bad idea."

The book was about them? He leaned forward, scanning over the pages once—then again. *To be truly happy, her best friend needed to become her king.* This was about *them*? He stood, moving slowly toward her. This was really happening? He wasn't asleep and dreaming at his desk. "Rosebud?"

"I'm really bad at this." She closed the space between them. "Terrible, apparently."

"What is this, exactly?" Before he let himself feel any hope, he needed to know—without a shadow of a doubt.

"This is me telling you I love you," she whispered. "I love you so much." That wasn't a whisper. It was strong and certain, and her gaze remained locked with his.

She loved him? And even though she'd just said exactly what he'd wanted her to for over a decade, he couldn't process it. "But what about your research? Doing big things? Taking a job that gets you excited? You want those things, I know you do."

"I do. And I can do all of that here. I can guest lecture." Her gaze searched his. "I don't know about you, but *this* is a big thing." She rested a hand against his chest, over his heart, and smiled brightly. "This could be the biggest thing that ever happens to me."

Every word she said mended the pieces of his heart back together. Now, beneath her hand, its rapid beat had no problem telling her what he hadn't. "I need to be sure."

"Of what?" She stepped closer and cradled his face.

"That this is what you want? That you're not sacrificing something important, something that makes you who you are, for me. I couldn't bear that, Rosebud." She had no idea how important this was to him. "I meant it when I said I don't want us doing something you'll regret."

"Everett... First, this is what I want. And I won't sacrifice you—who are something important. The most important thing to me." Her breath was a little unsteady as she went on. "Second, how do I know you won't be the one regretting things? That the reality of being with me will be entirely different than the idea of being with me?" A furrow formed between her brows.

"That could never happen, Rosebud." He took a deep breath, struggling for the words to accurately express what she meant to him. "There are a few things that will never change. I breathe, I sleep, and I love you. It's the way things are."

Rosebud's eyes widened. "Oh, Everett." She shook her head. "I will never regret giving you my heart. Never."

He pulled her gently into his arms. "You love me?" He could stare into her beautiful green eyes all day, every day, and never be bored.

"That's why I resigned. So there are no obstacles." She nodded, a smile on her face. "And I really liked the job, too."

"That's why... We might have to talk to city council about making some policy changes so you can stick around." He laughed then, so damn happy his heart was bursting. "You about gave me a heart attack. I thought you were leaving." His throat went tight.

"And you'd let me go?" She ran her fingers along the side of his face.

He swallowed. "Don't you know? All I want is for you to be happy."

She grabbed his shirtfront. "In time, you'll believe

that *you* make me happy. Everett. *My* Everett. I'll make sure you know that every day from this day forward." She stood on tiptoe. "You are what I want. This is what I want." Her eyes flashed. "Always."

"Good to know." He leaned forward, the sweep of his mouth across hers, featherlight.

Her arms slid around his neck, her fingers raked up and into his hair, but the look on her face was what rattled him most. She did love him. He saw it. Felt it. Knew it. And there was nothing like it.

What he'd intended to be a gentle kiss wound up leaving them breathless and clinging together.

"Maybe I need to take the day off?" His forehead rested against hers.

"Maybe?" She smiled.

"I'm never going to hear the end of this." He shook his head. "Gramma Dot's going to be saying 'I told you so' for the foreseeable future."

"She's a wise woman." Rosebud rested her head against his chest.

"She loves you. My whole family does." He ran his hand up and down her back. He had his Rosebud in his arms, and it was heaven.

"I'm glad. I think having a positive relationship with your in-laws is important." She sighed.

"In-laws?" He chuckled. "Are you going to marry me, Rosebud?"

She looked up at him, her smile more beautiful than ever. "Yes, Everett. I will marry you."

He laughed, then shook his head. "No sense wasting any more time." He brushed a kiss to her forehead.

"Nope." She stared up at him. "I don't want to waste

another minute." Her fingers ran along his jaw. "I love you, Everett."

He'd never get tired of hearing her say that. His heart was so full he couldn't contain the joy inside, so he smiled, so she'd know just how he felt. "Always and forever, Rosebud. Always and forever."

EPILOGUE

"I THOUGHT WE were fishing?" Rosebud's voice was breathy and thick.

"We are." His hand smoothed along her back. "I'm just occupying myself until we get something." He kept dropping kisses along her neck. "This is the best fishing trip ever."

She arched her neck for more kisses, her laugh soft. "If we don't bring home any fish, they'll know what we've been doing." She pushed ever so gently against his chest.

"What?" He stopped kissing her but didn't let her go. "What have we been doing?"

Her cheeks went red.

"Oh, that." He chuckled. "Yeah, I guess we have." He smoothed the hair from her shoulder. "I didn't hear you complaining."

"Nope." She leaned closer to him. "And you never will, either."

The fishline bounced, bringing both of them into a sitting position.

"Was that…" Rosebud whispered, her eyes fixed on the fishing line.

Everett grinned. "Looks like our secret's safe." Five minutes later, they'd caught a large catfish. "As much as I'd like to keep on fishing, I think we'd better head back to the house."

"The baby shower is at four." Rosebud sat on their blanket, her hair mussed and her lips swollen from his kisses. "We've got a little time, don't we?" She looked sexy and feminine, and he wasn't opposed to the idea of lingering a few minutes more.

"We can't." He held his hand out, pulling her to her feet. "The aunts are counting on you to help decorate, and I promised Dane I'd set up the folding tables and get the grill started."

"You're right. But later, maybe we can find some time alone?" Rosebud leaned into his kiss.

"Count on it." He sighed, hating to let her go. "Did Shelby say if the next books would be in before baby Nuc is born?"

"She did." Rosebud got excited whenever they talked about her books. "Three books. Can you believe it? I hope all the Hill babies like them as much as Nova and Bea have."

"They will." He had no doubt. "You'll have time to write a few more before we get started on our own family, I think."

"You think?" Rosebud's laughter rang out. "Let's get through the engagement party and the wedding first, okay?"

His sigh was long-suffering. "I'll try."

"It was your idea to wait until spring, remember?" Rosebud was grinning as she shook out their blanket and draped it over one arm.

"I don't know what I was thinking." He shook his head.

"You didn't want to overshadow Nuc's birth or Christmas because you're amazing and kind and generous and an incredibly good kisser." She pressed a kiss to his cheek. "You wanted it to be our special day. And it will be. Just me and you and the family."

"Only family." He chuckled. "The Hills. The Drivers. The Knudsons. Kerrielynn. Roman. Nicole and Benji. The Taggerts. Am I missing anyone?"

"I don't think so." Rosebud shook her head. "Would you have it any other way?"

"No." He took her hand. "I can't say that I would." His fingers threaded with hers as he took a minute to stare into her eyes. "I'd say things are about as perfect as they can be, Rosebud."

From the sweet smile on her face, he knew she agreed.

* * * * *

HONEY HILL FARMS RECIPES

HONEY SPICE BREAD

⅔ cup packed brown sugar
2 lg eggs, room temperature
⅓ cup 2% milk
½ cup honey
2 cups all-purpose flour
⅓ cup canola oil
1½ tsps baking powder
½ tsp ground cinnamon
½ tsp ground nutmeg
⅛ tsp ground cloves

Glaze:

⅓ cup powdered/confectioners' sugar
2 tsps 2% milk

1. Preheat oven to 325 degrees.

2. In a small saucepan, combine brown sugar and milk. Cook over low heat, stirring until sugar is dissolved. Remove from heat.

3. Whisk flour, baking powder, cinnamon, nutmeg, and cloves in a large bowl.

4. In another bowl, whisk eggs, honey, oil, and brown sugar.

5. Add egg mixture to flour mixture and stir until moistened.

6. Transfer into 8x4-inch loaf pan greased with shortening. Bake 50–60 minutes or until toothpick inserted into center comes out clean. (Can cover top with foil to prevent overbrowning.)

7. Cool in pan for 10 minutes, then remove to wire rack to cool completely.

8. In small bowl, stir glaze ingredients until smooth; drizzle over bread.

HONEY PEANUT BUTTER COOKIES

½ cup shortening
3 cups all-purpose flour
1 cup creamy peanut butter
1 cup sugar
1 cup honey
1½ tsps baking soda
2 lg eggs, room temperature, beaten
1 tsp baking powder
½ tsp salt

1. Preheat oven to 350 degrees.

2. Mix shortening, peanut butter, and honey in bowl.

3. Add eggs, mix well.

4. Stir flour, sugar, baking soda, baking powder, and salt in separate bowl.

5. Add flour mixture to peanut butter mixture—mix well.

6. Roll into 2-inch balls and place on ungreased baking sheet.

7. Flatten with fork dipped in flour, crisscross pattern.

8. Bake for 8–10 minutes and cool on wire rack.

HONEY-LIME ALMOND COOKIES

1 cup butter, softened
1 Tbsp grated lime zest
½ cup sugar
3 Tbsps honey
2 cups all-purpose flour
1 lg egg yolk, room temperature
1 cup finely slivered almonds
1 tsp lime juice
Confectioners'/powdered sugar

1. Cream butter and sugar in large bowl until light and fluffy (5–7 minutes).

2. Beat in honey, egg yolk, lime zest, and lime juice.

3. Gradually beat in flour.

4. Stir in almonds.

5. Divide dough in half, shape into 5-inch-long rolls, wrap, and refrigerate until firm (approx. 1 hour).

6. Preheat oven to 350 degrees.

7. Unwrap dough, cut into ¼-inch-thick slices.

8. Place 1 inch apart on ungreased cookie sheet and bake 10–12 minutes or until edges are light brown.

9. Cool on pans for 2 minutes, transfer to wire racks to fully cool.

10. Dust with powdered sugar.

HONEY ROASTED HEIRLOOM POTATOES

2 lbs. fingerling potatoes, halved lengthwise
2 tsps ground mustard
¼ cup finely chopped onion
1 tsp dried parsley flakes
3 Tbsps olive oil
½ tsp coarsely ground black pepper
2 Tbsps honey
2 garlic cloves, minced
Additional honey, if desired

1. Preheat oven to 375 degrees.

2. Place potatoes in greased 15x10x1-inch baking pan.

3. Combine remaining ingredients in small bowl.

4. Pour mixture over potatoes, toss to coat.

5. Bake uncovered until golden/tender (approx. 35–40 minutes), stirring potatoes once halfway through cooking.

6. If desired, drizzle with additional honey out of the oven.

PEANUT BUTTER PROTEIN BALLS

⅔ cup old-fashioned rolled oats
¼ cup unsweetened, shredded coconut
2 Tbsps mini-chocolate chips
2 Tbsps honey
1 Tbsp chia seeds
1 Tbsp flaxseeds
¼ tsp ground cinnamon
¼ tsp vanilla extract
Pinch of salt
⅓ cup natural peanut butter
2 Tbsps milk

1. Line baking sheet with parchment paper.

2. Combine oats, coconut, chocolate chips, flax, chia, cinnamon, and salt in a large bowl.

3. Stir in honey, peanut butter, vanilla, and 1 Tbsp milk (slightly crumbly—add 1 Tbsp of milk if too dry).

4. Wet hands and roll mixture into small balls.

5. Place balls onto baking sheet and refrigerate for 30 minutes.

HONEY ARNOLD PALMER

Lemonade:

3 cups water, divided
¾ cup granulated sugar
¾ cup lemon juice (freshly squeezed is best)

Tea:

4 cups water
⅓ cup honey
5 black tea bags
Ice
Fresh mint
Lemon wedges

Lemonade:

1. Bring 1 cup water and sugar to boil in small pot over medium heat.

2. Stir until sugar is dissolved. Let boil 2 minutes.

3. Let cool to room temperature.

4. Combine with 2 cups remaining water and lemon juice.

Tea:

1. Bring water to boil in medium pot over medium-high heat.

2. Add honey and stir to dissolve.

3. Turn off heat and add tea bags.

4. Let steep 5 minutes. Let cool to room temperature.

Arnold Palmer:

1. Combine lemonade and tea in large pitcher.

2. Serve in large glasses over ice. Garnish with mint and lemon wedges.

HONEY GARLIC CHICKEN

6 boneless chicken thighs (with skin)
2 tsps garlic powder
Salt and pepper to taste
6 garlic cloves, crushed
⅓ cup honey
¼ cup chicken broth
2 Tbsps white wine vinegar
1 Tbsp soy sauce
Garnish (optional)

1. Season chicken with garlic powder, salt, and pepper—set aside.

2. Heat skillet over medium-high heat and sear chicken thighs on both sides until golden and cooked.

3. Reduce to medium-low heat. Drain excess pan, leaving 2 Tbsps for added flavor.

4. Arrange chicken skinside up.

5. Add garlic around chicken and fry until fragrant (approx. 45 seconds).

6. Add honey, chicken broth, vinegar, and soy sauce.

7. Increase heat to medium-high and cook until sauce reduces and thickens (3–4 minutes).

8. Serve over rice or pasta and garnish with parsley.

SKILLET SALTED HONEY APPLE CRISP

1 stick butter, divided
1 cup old-fashioned rolled oats
¼ cup brown sugar
1 cup chopped pecans
2 Tbsps flour
½ cup sugar
¼ cup honey
1 tsp salt, divided
Zest and juice of one small orange
1 tsp ground cinnamon
½ tsp ground nutmeg
Additional honey for drizzling
4 crisp, tart apples, cored and cut into ½-inch slices
(e.g., Granny Smith apples)

1. Preheat oven to 375 degrees.

2. Cut half butter into small cubes.

3. Mix butter, oats, brown sugar, pecans, and flour
   until crumbly—clumping together in a medium
   bowl. Set aside.

4. Melt remaining half of butter over medium heat
   in oven-safe saucepan or skillet. Add honey, or-

ange juice and zest, sugar, and salt. Cook for 15 minutes until light brown, syrupy. Should be reduced by half.

5. Add cinnamon, nutmeg, and apples. Toss to coat and cook for 6–8 minutes.

6. Turn off heat. Add crumbled pecan mixture to the top of apples.

7. Place in oven and bake 10–12 minutes or until topping browns and apples are bubbling.

8. Serve warm with honey drizzled on top.

HONEY GINGERBREAD COOKIES

1½ cups of honey
¾ cup butter, softened
1 egg
5 cups all-purpose flour
2 tsps baking powder
1 Tbsp ground ginger
1 Tbsp ground cinnamon
1 tsp ground cloves

1. Cream honey and butter in a large bowl until light and fluffy.

2. Beat in egg.

3. Add flour, baking powder, ginger, cinnamon, and cloves. Mix well.

4. Wrap in plastic wrap and refrigerate at least 2 hours.

5. When chilled, divide in half. Return one half to refrigerator.

6. Heat oven to 350 degrees.

7. Dust work surface with flour.

8. Roll dough to ¼-inch thickness.

9. Use desired cookie cutters and move cookies to well-greased baking sheet.

10. Cook 10–12 minutes, then move to wire rack for cooling. Should yield 3 dozen cookies.

HONEY POT CIDER FOR ONE

1¼ cups apple cider
1 Tbsp honey
1 pinch cinnamon
¾ oz applejack brandy
1 stick cinnamon
2 apple slices

1. Combine apple cider, honey, and cinnamon in small saucepan.

2. Stir over medium heat for 5 minutes—until heated.

3. Stir in applejack brandy and pour cider into mug.

4. Cut small hole through apple slices, string with cinnamon stick, and place garnish in cider.

HONEY BACON CHEDDAR SCONES

2 Tbsps honey
4–5 chopped bacon strips
2 cups all-purpose flour
1 Tbsp and 1 tsp baking powder
¼ tsp salt
Pinch of black pepper
1 cup grated cheddar cheese
10 Tbsps cold and diced butter
¾ cup heavy cream, plus more for brushing

1. In medium skillet, cook bacon over medium heat, stirring until crisp—approx. 5 minutes. Remove with slotted spoon and place on paper towels. Set aside.

2. Whisk flour, baking powder, salt, and pepper in large bowl.

3. Using your fingers, add cold butter and rub into flour mixture until it resembles coarse crumbs.

4. Mix honey and heavy cream in small bowl.

5. Create a small well in the center of flour mixture.

Pour cream mixture into well and mix with fork until dough comes together.

6. Work in crisp bacon and cheese.

7. Roll dough into a circle on a floured surface. Circle should be ¾-inch thick. Cover with plastic wrap and refrigerate for 30 minutes.

8. Preheat oven to 400 degrees.

9. Cut the circle into 8 wedges with sharp knife.

10. Transfer wedges to parchment-lined baking sheet. Leave ½ inch between wedges.

11. Brush the top of each wedge with remaining heavy cream.

12. Bake 20–23 minutes or until golden brown.

13. Remove from oven and cool slightly on baking sheet. Serve warm.

BANANA PANCAKE BITES WITH ORANGE HONEY BUTTER

Pancake Bites:

½ cup all-purpose flour
½ cup whole wheat pastry flour
¼ tsp salt
1 tsp baking powder
1 Tbsp orange blossom honey
1 cup low-fat buttermilk
1 banana, mashed
1 lg egg, beaten
2 Tbsps melted butter
1 tsp vanilla

Honey Butter:

4 Tbsps unsalted butter, softened
Zest of 1 orange
2 Tbsps orange blossom honey

1. Preheat oven to 425 degrees.

2. Whisk baking powder, salt, and both flours in large bowl.

3. Add mashed banana, egg, melted butter, buttermilk, honey, and vanilla to the bowl and mix until combined—do not overmix.

4. Spray mini-muffin tray with cooking spray and pour heaping teaspoons into each mini-muffin mold.

5. Bake 8–10 minutes—until puffed and slightly golden.

6. Blend unsalted butter, orange zest, and honey until creamy and well combined. Transfer to serving dish.

7. Remove pancake bites from oven, cool slightly before removing from pan.

8. Serve with honey butter.

Serves 6–36 total bites

BANANA, ALMOND, AND OATS SMOOTHIE

1 cup vanilla yogurt
½ cup old-fashioned rolled oats
¾ cup vanilla soy milk
¼ cup honey
2 bananas, cut in half and frozen
⅓ cup almond butter

1. Combine all ingredients in a blender.

2. Pulse until bananas are broken up, then blend on high until smooth and creamy consistency.

3. Add soy milk if needed to create wanted consistency.

4. Serve immediately.

Can substitute milk, almond milk, or coconut milk.

Yields 2 16-oz smoothies

QUEEN BEE ROYALE FOR ONE

1½-inch piece honeycomb
1 oz honey liqueur
5 oz sparkling wine or champagne

1. Pour honey liqueur into a champagne flute.

2. Add honeycomb and fill with sparkling wine or champagne.

SAVORY TO-GO HONEY MUFFINS

¾ cup low-fat milk
4 Tbsps butter, melted
2 eggs
¼ cup honey
1½ cups all-purpose flour
1 tsp baking powder
½ tsp salt
2 tsps chopped chives
¾ cup shredded Gruyère cheese—
plus ¼ cup for sprinkling on top

1. Preheat oven to 350 degrees.

2. Line 8-muffin pan with liners or nonstick cooking spray.

3. In large mixing bowl, whisk butter, milk, honey, and eggs.

4. Stir in baking powder, flour, salt, cheese, and chives—setting aside ¼ of the Gruyère for topping.

5. Divide into muffin cups evenly, filling ¾ full.

6. Bake 20–25 minutes or until golden on top.

7. Remove from oven and sprinkle Gruyère cheese on tops.

8. Turn on broiler and broil for another 2 minutes (until cheese is melted and lightly browned).

Yields 8 muffins

CARROT CAKE OVERNIGHT OATS

Oats:

1 cup old-fashioned rolled oats
½ cup carrots, finely grated
¼ tsp pumpkin pie spice
1 Tbsp chia seeds
2 Tbsps chopped dates
¾ cup unsweetened soy milk
¼ cup honey
1 tsp vanilla
½ cup plain Greek yogurt

Toppings:

¼ cup Greek yogurt
2 Tbsps chopped pecans
Drizzle of honey

1. Combine all Oats ingredients in medium bowl and cover (excluding toppings).

2. Refrigerate at least 6 hours or overnight.

3. Stir and add toppings to each serving.

4. Enjoy cold, room temperature, or warmed up.

Yields 2 servings